"PACKED WITH [illegible] SUSPENSE AND TRAGEDY, *FLIGHT OF THE INTRUDER* OFFERS PROFOUND AND GRIPPING INSIGHT INTO THE LIVES AND LOVES OF NAVAL CARRIER PILOTS."

—Clive Cussler
author of *Cyclops*

"A SUPERBLY WRITTEN STORY . . . As did Tom Clancy, former Intruder pilot Stephen Coonts laces his story with intricate technical details of modern aerial warfare and authentic dialogue and relationships of pilots at war and at play . . . *FLIGHT OF THE INTRUDER* IS EVERY BIT AS GOOD AS MR. CLANCY'S TWO NOVELS—AND THAT IS STRONG PRAISE INDEED."

—*Washington Times*

"Grafton's humanity separates him from both the image of Rambo and 'war criminal' epithets. His hands shake and he occasionally succumbs to the panic lurking just beneath his 'Cool Hand' façade . . . *FLIGHT OF THE INTRUDER* IS A WINNER."

—*Philadelphia Inquirer*

"First novelist Stephen Coonts makes us care deeply about the fate of Jake Grafton, his decent, sensitive hero . . . The action scenes are vivid and authentic: COONTS MAKES US SEE, SMELL, HEAR, TASTE AND FEEL BATTLE. THE FINAL CHAPTER OF *FLIGHT OF THE INTRUDER* BECOMES ESPECIALLY EXCITING."

—*Cleveland Plain Dealer*

A BOOK-OF-THE-MONTH CLUB ALTERNATE SELECTION

(more . . .)

"Stephen Coonts has brought to naval air warfare the intimacy and quiet thoughtfulness that Stephen Crane gave to *The Red Badge of Courage* . . . *FLIGHT OF THE INTRUDER* is a moving novel of men at war that captures the horrifying sweep of battle and its nerve-shattering emotional effects . . . Coonts also brings a sense of immediacy to the battle scenes, where miles are covered in seconds and reactions must be split-second . . . Here, the reader feels the threat and tension of death, looming below, above and from all sides . . . COONTS CAREFULLY DEVELOPS THE PLOT TO A CLIMAX OF FEAR AS HE SPINS THE TALE INTO ITS FINAL EPISODE IN THE STEAMING JUNGLES OF VIETNAM."

—*San Diego Union*

"When he is flying, Jake's exhilaration is contagious; his instincts meld with the controls of his aircraft, and his life-or-death decisions sharpen his senses . . . A THRILL-A-MINUTE . . . RIDE."

—*The New York Times Book Review*

FLIGHT OF THE INTRUDER IS "SO REALISTIC I FELT I WAS RIGHT THERE IN THE COCKPIT WITH THE PILOT, HEDGE-HOPPING THE JUNGLE TREES AT THE SPEED OF A PISTOL BULLET."

—Robert L. Scott, Jr.
author of *God Is My Co-Pilot*

"A description of the death of a U.S. pilot shot down in Laos is as horrifying as anything in any American war novel. The technical descriptions of electronic warfare, of the wizardry of radar and sensors and missiles are as good as anything in Tom Clancy . . ."

—*Washington Post Book World*

"*FLIGHT OF THE INTRUDER* is to the Vietnam war what *The Bridges of Toko-Ri* was to the Korean war. Stephen Coonts puts his readers into the cockpit of the A-6 and into the heart of the pilot in A VIVID, EXTRAORDINARY STORY OF COURAGE AND DETERMINATION. I COULDN'T PUT THIS BOOK DOWN."

—Frederick Downs, Jr.
author of *The Killing Zone*

"*FLIGHT OF THE INTRUDER* KEPT ME STRAPPED IN THE COCKPIT OF THE AUTHOR'S IMAGINATION . . ."

—*St. Louis Post-Dispatch*

"Stephen Coonts's accounts of the riveting drama of combat flights—taking off at night from the pitching deck of an aircraft carrier—are first-rate, as are the scenes of wisecracking camaraderie aboard ship and on leave ashore. The crisp prose makes the pages whisk by . . . entertaining and often thoughtful reading . . . A COMPELLING TALE OF AERIAL WARFARE."

—*Denver Post*

Books by Stephen Coonts

Final Flight
Flight of the Intruder
The Minotaur

Published by POCKET BOOKS

STEPHEN COONTS

POCKET BOOKS
New York London Toronto Sydney Tokyo Singapore

This book is a work of fiction. Names, characters, places and incidents are either the product of the author's imagination or are used fictitiously. Any resemblance to actual events or locales or persons, living or dead, is entirely coincidental. Nothing is intended or should be interpreted as expressing or representing the view of the U.S. Navy or any other department or agency of any governmental body.

POCKET BOOKS, a division of Simon & Schuster Inc.
1230 Avenue of the Americas, New York, NY 10020

ISBN: 0-671-70960-7

First Pocket Books printing October 1987

15 14 13 12 11 10 9 8 7

Printed in the U.S.A.

To the memory of Eugene Ely, the first person to land an airplane aboard a ship, and all the men and women of U.S. Naval Aviation who died in the service of their country.

The Naval Institute Press is the book-publishing imprint of the U.S. Naval Institute, a private professional society for members of the military services and civilians who share an interest in naval and maritime affairs. Established in 1873 at the Naval Academy in Annapolis where its offices remain today, the Naval Institute has some 90,000 members worldwide.

USNI membership includes a subscription to the influential monthly naval magazine *Proceedings,* substantial discounts on the more than 250 books, art prints, and photographs available from the Press, and access to oral history transcripts and to professional-development seminars conducted around the country.

The Press's publishing program, begun in 1898 with basic guides to naval practices, has broadened its scope in recent years to include books of more general interest. Now, more than forty new titles are published each year that range from how-to books on boating and navigation to battle histories, biographies, ship guides, and occasional fiction.

For a free catalog describing books currently available, or for further information on USNI membership, please write to:

U.S. Naval Institute
Annapolis, Maryland 21402

All the wide sky
Was there to tempt him as he steered toward heaven,
Meanwhile the heat of sun struck at his back
And where his wings were joined, sweet-smelling fluid
Ran hot that once was wax.

—Ovid, *Metamorphoses,*
translated by Horace Gregory

ONE

The starboard bow catapult fired, and the A-6A Intruder accelerated down the flight deck with a roar that engulfed the aircraft carrier and reverberated over the night sea. The plane's wings bit into the air, and the machine began to climb into the blackness. Fifteen seconds later the bomber was swallowed by the low-lying clouds.

In a few minutes the climbing Intruder broke free of the clouds. The pilot, Lieutenant Jake Grafton, abandoned the instrument panel and contemplated the vaulted stars. A pale slice of moon illuminated the cloud layer below. "Look at the stars tonight, Morg."

Lieutenant (junior grade) Morgan McPherson, the bombardier-navigator, sat on the pilot's right, his face pressed against the black hood that shielded the radar screen from extraneous light. He straightened and glanced up at the sky. "Yeah," he said, then readjusted the scope hood and resumed the never-ending chore of optimizing the radar presentation. He examined the North Vietnamese coastline a hundred miles away. "I've got an update. I'm cycling to the coast-in point." He pushed a button on the computer, and the steering bug on the pilot's visual display indicator (VDI) slipped a quarter-inch sideways, giving the pilot steering information to the point on the coast where the Intruder would cross into North Vietnam.

Grafton turned the aircraft a few degrees to follow the steering command. "Did you ever stop to think maybe you're getting too wrapped up in your work?" he said. "That you're in a rut?"

Morgan McPherson pushed himself back from the radar hood and looked at the stars overhead. "They're still there, and we're down here. Let's check the ECM again."

"The problem is that you're just too romantic," Grafton told him and reached for the electronic counter-measures panel. Together they ran the equipment through the built-in tests that verified the ECM was working. Two pairs of eyes observed each indicator light, and two pairs of ears heard each beep. The ECM gear detected enemy radar emissions and identified them for the crew. When the ECM picked up radar signals it had been programmed to recognize as threatening, it would broadcast false images to the enemy operator. Satisfied all was working properly, the airmen adjusted the volume of the ECM audio so that it could be heard in their earphones yet would not drown out the intercom system (ICS), over which they talked to each other, or the radio.

The two men flew on without speaking, each listening to the periodic bass tones of the communist search radars sweeping the night. Each type of radar had its own sound: a low beep was a search radar probing the sky; higher pitched tones were fire-control radars seeking to acquire a target; and a nightmare falsetto was a locked-on missile-control radar guiding its weapon.

Fifty miles from the North Vietnamese coast, Jake Grafton lowered the nose of the Intruder four degrees, and the A-6 began its long descent. When he had the aircraft trimmed, Jake tugged all the slack from the harness straps securing him to his ejection seat, then exhaled and, like a cowboy tightening a saddle girth, pulled the straps as snugly as he could. That done, he asked for the combat checklist.

Leaving nothing to chance or memory, McPherson read each item off his kneeboard card and both men checked the appropriate switch or knob. When they reached the last detail on the checklist, Jake shut off the aircraft's exterior lights and turned the IFF to standby. The IFF, or "parrot," radiated electronic energy that enabled an American radar operator to see the aircraft as a coded blip he could readily identify as friend or foe. Grafton had no desire to appear as a blip, coded or uncoded, on a North Vietnamese radar screen. In fact, he hoped to escape detection by flying so near the ground that the radar return reflected from his plane would merge with the radar energy reflecting off the earth—the "ground return."

The pilot keyed his radio mike. The voice scrambler beeped, then Jake spoke: "Devil Five Oh Five is strangling parrot. Coast-in in three minutes." "Devil" was the A-6 squadron's radio call sign.

"Roger, Five Oh Five," responded the airborne controller circling over the Gulf of Tonkin in an E-2 Hawkeye, a twin engine turboprop with a radar dish mounted on top of the fuselage. The Hawkeye also had launched from the carrier.

The Intruder was going on the hunt. Camouflaged by darkness and hidden by the earth itself from the electronic eyes of the enemy, Jake Grafton would fly as low as his skill and nerves allowed, which was very low indeed.

The pilot cast a last quick look at the distant stars. Flying now at 450 knots, the bird plunged into the clouds. Jake felt the adrenaline begin to pump. He watched the pressure altimeter unwind and shot anxious glances at the radar altimeter, which derived its information from a small radar in the belly of the plane that looked straight down and measured the distance to the ground or sea. He briefly wished that he could turn it off because he knew its emissions could be detected, but he needed this device. The pressure altimeter told him his height above sea level, but tonight he would have to know just how high he was above the earth. As he passed 5000 feet, the radar altimeter began to function and matched the readings of the pressure altimeter perfectly, just as it should over the sea. The pilot breathed deeply and forced himself to relax.

Dropping below 2000 feet, he eased the stick back and slowed the rate of descent. With his left hand he advanced the throttles to a high-cruise power setting. The airspeed stabilized at 420 knots, Grafton's preferred speed for treetop flying. The A-6 handled very well at this speed, even with the drag and weight of a load of bombs. The machine would fly over enemy gunners too fast for them to track it even if they should be so lucky as to make out the dark spot fleeting across the night sky.

Jake Grafton's pulse pounded as he brought the plane down to 400 feet above the water. They were below the clouds now, flying in absolute darkness, not a glimmer of light visible in the emptiness between sea and sky. Only the dimmed lights of the gauges, which were red so as not to impair the night vision of the crew, confirmed that there was a world beyond the cockpit. Jake peered into the blackness, trying to find the telltale ribbon of white sand that marked the Vietnamese coast on even the darkest nights. Not yet, he told himself. He could feel the rivulets of sweat trickle down his face and neck, some running into his eyes. He shook his head violently, not daring to take his stinging eyes from the red gauges on the black panel in front of him for more than a second. The sea was just below, invisible, waiting to swallow the pilot who failed for a few seconds to notice a sink rate.

There, to the left . . . the beach. The pale sand caught his eye. Relax. . . . Relax, and concentrate. The whiteness flashed beneath them.

"Coast-in," Jake told the bombardier.

McPherson used his left hand to activate the stop-clock on the instrument panel and keyed his radio mike with his left foot. "Devil Five Oh Five is feet dry. Devil Five Oh Five, feet dry."

A friendly American voice answered. "Five Oh Five, Black Eagle. Roger feet dry. Good hunting." Then silence. Later, when Devil 505 returned to the coast, they would broadcast their "feet wet" call. Grafton and McPherson knew that now they were on their own, because the Hawkeye's radar could not separate the A-6's image from the earth's return without the aid of the IFF.

Jake saw moonlight reflecting faintly off rice paddies, indicating a break in the overcast ahead. The weather forecasters were right for a change, he thought. Out of the corner of his eye the pilot saw flashes: intermittent flashes in the darkness below.

"Small arms fire, Morg."

"Okay, Jakey baby." The bombardier never looked up from his radar scope. His left hand slewed the computer cross hairs across the scope while his right tuned the radar. "This computer is working great, but it's a little . . ." he muttered over the ICS.

Jake tried to ignore the muzzle flashes. Every kid and rice farmer in North Vietnam had a rifle and apparently spent the nights shooting randomly into the sky at the first rumble of jet engines. They never saw their targets but hoped somewhere in the sky a bullet and an American warplane would meet. Big morale booster, Jake thought. Lets every citizen feel he's personally fighting back. Jake saw the shuttering muzzle flashes of a submachine gun. None of these small arms fired tracer bullets so the little droplets of death were everywhere, and nowhere.

Patches of moonlight revealed breaks in the clouds ahead. The pilot descended to 300 feet and used the moonlight to keep from flying into the ground. He was much more comfortable flying visually rather than on instruments. With an outside reference he could fly instinctively; on instruments he had to work at it.

Off to the right antiaircraft artillery opened fire. The tracers burned through the blackness in slow motion. The warble of a Firecan gun-control radar sounded for a second in his ears, then fell silent.

A row of artillery fire erupted ahead of them. "Christ, Morg," he whispered to the bombardier. He picked a tear in the curtain of tracers, dipped a wing, and angled the jet through. McPherson didn't look up from the scope. "You got the river bend yet?" Jake asked as the flak storm faded behind them.

"Yep. Just got it. Three more minutes on this heading." McPherson reached with his left hand and turned on the master armament switch. He checked the position of every switch on the armament panel one more time. The dozen 500-pound bombs were now ready to be released. "Your pickle is hot," he told the pilot, referring to the red button on the stick grip which the pilot could press to release the weapons.

Again and again fiery streams of antiaircraft shells spewed forth like projectiles from a volcano. The stuff that came in the general direction of Devil 505 seemed to change course and turn behind them, an optical illusion created by the plane's 700-feet-per-second speed. The pilot ignored the guns fired behind or abreast and concentrated on negotiating his way through the strings of tracers that erupted ahead. He no longer even noticed the flashes from rifles and machine guns, the sparks of this inferno.

A voice on the radio: "Devil Five Oh Eight is feet dry, feet dry."

There's Cowboy, Jake thought. Cowboy was Lieutenant Commander Earl Parker, the pilot of the other A-6 bomber launched moments after them. Like Jake and McPherson, Cowboy and his bombardier were now racing across the earth with a load of bombs destined for a target not worth any man's life, or so Jake told himself as he weaved through the tracers, deeper and deeper into North Vietnam.

"Two miles to the turnpoint," the bombardier reminded him.

An insane warble racked their ears. A red light labeled "MISSILE" flashed on the instrument panel two feet from the pilot's face. This time McPherson did look up. The two men scanned the sky. Their best chance to avoid the surface-to-air missile was to acquire it visually, then outmaneuver it.

"There's the SAM! Two o'clock!" Jake fought back the urge to urinate. Both men watched the white rocket exhaust while Grafton squeezed the chaff-release button on the right throttle with his forefinger. Each push released a small plastic container into the slipstream where it disbursed a cloud of metallic fibers—the chaff—that would echo radar energy and form a false target on the enemy operator's radar screen. The pilot carefully nudged the stick forward and dropped to 200 feet above the ground. He jabbed the chaff button four more times in quick succession.

The missile light stopped flashing and the earphones fell silent as death itself.

"I think it's stopped guiding," McPherson said with relief evident in his voice. "Boy, we're having fun now," he added dryly. Grafton said nothing. They were almost scraping the paddies. The bombardier watched the missile streak by several thousand feet overhead at three times the speed of sound, then he turned his attention to the radar. "Come hard left," he told the pilot.

Jake dropped the left wing and eased back slightly on the stick. He let the plane climb to 300 feet. The moonlight bounced off the river below. "See the target yet?"

"Just a second, man." Silence. "Steady up." Jake leveled the wings. "I've got the target. I'm on it. Stepping into attack." The bombardier flipped a switch, and the computer calculated an attack solution. The word "ATTACK" lit up in red on the lower edge of the VDI, and the computer-driven display became more complex. Symbols appeared showing the time remaining until weapons release, the relative position of the target, the drift angle, and the steering to the release point.

Jake jammed the throttles forward to the stops and climbed to 500 feet. The Mark 82 general-purpose bombs had to fall at least 500 feet for the fuses to arm properly; they were equipped with metal vanes that would open when the weapons were released and retard them just long enough to allow the plane to escape the bomb fragments.

The needle on the airspeed indicator quivered at 480 knots. The stick was alive in the pilot's hand. Any small twitch made the machine leap. Jake's attention was divided among the mechanics of instrument flying, the computer-driven steering symbol on the VDI, and the occasional streams of yellow and red tracers. He felt extraordinarily alive, in absolute control. He could see everything at once: every needle, every gauge, every fireball in the night. With his peripheral vision, he even saw McPherson turn on the track radar.

"Ground lock." The bombardier noted the indication on the track radar and reported it to the pilot with an affectation of amazement. The damn track radar often failed. McPherson was glued to the radar screen, his entire world the flickering green light. "Hot damn, we're gonna get 'em."

He feels it too, Jake thought. With the track radar locked on the target the computer was getting the most accurate information possible on azimuth and elevation angle.

On this October night in 1972, Devil 505 closed on the target, a "suspected truck park," jargon for a penciled triangle on a map where the unknown persons who picked the targets thought the North Vietnamese might have some trucks parked under the trees, away from the prying eyes of aerial photography. Trucks or no trucks, the target was only a place in the forest.

The bomb run was all that existed now for Jake Grafton. His life seemed compressed into this moment, without past or future. Everything depended on how well he flew Devil 505 to that precise point in space where the computer would release the bombs to fall upon the target.

The release marker on the VDI marched relentlessly toward the bottom of the display as the plane raced in at 490 knots. At the instant the marker disappeared, the 500-pound bombs were jettisoned from the bomb racks. Both men felt a series of jolts, a physical reminder that they had pulled a trigger. The attack light was extinguished when the last weapon was released, and only then did Grafton bank left and glance outside. Tracers and muzzle flashes etched the night. "Look back," he told the bombardier as he flew the aircraft through the turn.

Morgan McPherson looked over the pilot's left shoulder in the direction of the target, obscured by darkness. He saw the explosions of the bombs—white death flashes—twelve in two-thirds of a second. Jake saw the detonations in his rear-view mirror and rolled out of the turn on an easterly heading. Without the drag of the 500-pounders, the two engines pushed the fleeing warplane even faster through the night, now 500 knots, almost 600 miles per hour.

"Arm up the Rockeyes, Morg."

The bombardier reset the armament switches that enabled the pilot to manually drop the four Rockeye cluster bombs still hanging under the wings. "Your pickle is hot," he told Grafton. He put his face back against the scope hood and examined the terrain ahead.

Grafton kept the engines at full throttle as he scanned the darkness for an antiaircraft artillery piece he could destroy with the waiting Rockeyes. It would have to be fairly close to his track and firing off to one side so that he could approach it safely. He referred to this portion of the mission as "killing rattlesnakes."

Somewhere below, a North Vietnamese peasant heard the swelling whine of jet engines approaching, first faintly, then rapidly increasing in intensity. As the whine quickly rose to a crescendo, he lifted an ancient bolt-action rifle to his shoulder, pointed it at a 45-degree angle into the night above, and pulled the trigger.

The bullet punched a tiny hole in the lower forward corner of the canopy plexiglas on the right side of the plane. It penetrated Morgan McPherson's oxygen mask, deflected off his jawbone, pierced the larynx, nicked a carotid artery, then exited his neck and spent itself against the side of the pilot's ejection seat. Reflexively, Morgan keyed his ICS mike with his right foot, gagged, and grabbed his neck.

Jake Grafton looked at the bombardier. Blood, black in the glow of the red cockpit lights, spurted from between McPherson's fingers.

"Morg?"

McPherson gagged again. His eyes bulged and he stared at the pilot. His eyebrows knitted. He spat up blood. "Jake," he gurgled. He coughed repeatedly with the ICS mike keyed.

Jake tore his eyes from McPherson and thought furiously as he checked the instrument panel. What could have happened? Without noticing he had drawn the stick back and the aircraft was up to 700 feet over the delta tableland and exposed on every enemy radar screen within range. He shoved the stick forward. "Don't try to talk, Morg. I'll get you home." He leveled the plane at 300 feet and was once again hidden amid the ground return.

Jesus! Jesus Christ! Something must have come through the canopy, a piece of flak shrapnel or a random bullet.

A whisper: "Jake . . ." McPherson's hand clutched Jake's arm, then fell away. He raised his hand and again clutched at Jake, this time more weakly. Morgan slumped over, his head resting on the scope hood Blood covered the front of his survival vest. Holding the stick with his left hand, Jake struggled to unfasten McPherson's oxygen mask. Blood spilled from the rubber cup. Black stains covered the sleeve of his flight suit where McPherson's hand had seized him.

A battery of guns opened up ahead with short bursts of orange tracers that floated aloft: 37 millimeter. They were shooting generally off to the right, so Jake Grafton turned the plane slightly to fly directly over the muzzle blasts. He guided the plane into a gentle climb and as the guns disappeared under the nose, he savagely mashed the bomb-release pickle on the stick. Thump, thump, thump, thump; the Rockeyes fell away a third of a second apart.

"Take that, you motherfuckers!" he screamed into his mask, his voice registering hysteria.

He looked again at McPherson, whose arms dangled toward the floor of the cockpit. Blood still throbbed from his throat.

With one hand on the stick, Jake pulled the bombardier upright where the shoulder harness engaged and held him. He searched for the wound with his fingers. He could feel nothing with his flying glove on, so he tore it off with his left hand and probed for the hole with his bare fingers. He couldn't find it.

He glanced back at the instruments. He was rapidly becoming too busy, an error that he knew would be fatal for both himself and McPherson. The plane would not fly itself and certain death was just below. Raise the left wing, bring the nose up, climb back to 500 feet, then attend to the wounded man. He felt again in the slippery, pulsing blood of McPherson's neck. Finding the wound, he clamped down with his fingers, then turned back to flying the plane. Too high. Flak ahead. Trim the plane. He jerked his left hand from the stick to the throttles, which he pushed forward. They were already hard against the stops. He could feel the throbbing of the flow from McPherson's neck noticeably lessening. He felt elated as he wrestled the plane, thinking that the pressure on the wound might be effective, but the euphoria faded quickly. How could he possibly land the plane like this?

His head swiveled to the unconscious man beside him, taking in the slack way his body reacted to each bump and jolt of the racing aircraft. Jake pressed harder on the wound, pressed until his hand ached from the unnatural position and the exertion.

He remembered the hot-mike switch that would allow him to talk to the bombardier without keying the ICS each time. He released the stick momentarily and flipped it on with his left hand. "Hey, Morgan," he urged, "hang in there, shipmate. You're going to make it. I'll get you back. Keep the faith, Morg."

He could feel nothing now, no pulse, no blood pumping against his fingers. Reluctantly, he pulled his hand away and wiped it on his thigh before grasping the stick. He found the radio-transmit button and waited until the scrambler beeped. "Black Eagle, Devil Five Oh Five, over."

"Devil Five Oh Five, this is Black Eagle, go ahead."

"My bombardier has been hit. I'm declaring an emergency. Request you have the ship make a ready deck for recovery on arrival. I repeat, my bombardier has been shot." His voice sounded strong and even, which surprised him as he felt so completely out of control.

"We copy that, Five Oh Five. Will relay." The radio fell silent.

As he waited he talked to McPherson. "Don't you give up on me, you sonuvabitch. You never were a quitter, Morg. Don't give up now."

More flak came up. He pushed at the throttles again, unconsciously trying to go faster. They were already traveling at 505 knots. Perhaps he should dump some fuel. He still had 10,000 pounds remaining. No, even with the fuel gone the old girl would go no faster; she was giving her all now, and he might need the fuel to get to Da Nang if the ship couldn't recover him immediately.

Finally, the white-sand beach flashed beneath. Grafton turned the IFF to Emergency. "Devil Five Oh Five is feet wet." McPherson had not moved.

"Black Eagle copies, Devil Five Oh Five. Wagon Train has been notified of your emergency. Do you have any other problems, any other damage, over?" Wagon Train was the ship's radio call sign.

Jake Grafton scanned the instruments, then stole another look at Morgan McPherson. "Just a BN in terrible shape, Black Eagle."

"Roger that. We have you in radar contact. Your steer to the ship is One Three Zero degrees. Squawk One Six Zero Zero."

"Wilco."

The pilot settled on the recommended course, then flipped on the TACAN, a radio navigation aid that would point to the carrier's beacon. As the needle swung lazily several times he turned the IFF to the requested setting, the "squawk." The TACAN needle stopped swinging, steady on 132 degrees. Jake worked in the correction. He leveled off at 5000 feet and kept the engines at full throttle. The TACAN distance-measuring indicator finally locked in, showing ninety-five miles to the ship.

The overcast hid the moon and stars. Inside the clouds he felt as though he were the only human being alive on earth. He kept glancing at McPherson, whose head rolled back and forth in rhythm to the motion of the plane. He squeezed McPherson's hand tightly, but there was no response. Still he held on, hoping McPherson could feel the presence of a friend. He tried to speak on the ICS but found his voice merely a croak.

The commanding officer of the USS *Shiloh* was on the bridge when news of Devil 505's emergency reached him. Captain Robert Boma had spent twenty-seven years in the navy and wore pilot's wings on his left breast. Tall, lean, and graying, he had learned to live on three hours sleep with occasional catnaps; he was in his elevated easy chair on the bridge every minute that the carrier had aircraft aloft. "How far is it to Da Nang?" he asked the officer-of-the-deck (OOD) as he weighed the options. Da Nang was the nearest friendly airfield ashore.

"Nearly two hundred miles, sir."

"We'll take him aboard." The captain leaned over and flipped a few switches on the intercom. "This is the captain. Clear the landing area. Make a ready deck. We have an emergency inbound."

Within seconds the flight deck became organized bedlam. Arming and fueling activities ceased, and the handlers began respotting aircraft forward on the bow, clear of the landing area on the angled deck. Five minutes after the order was given, the carrier's landing area was empty and the ship had turned into the wind. The duty search-and-rescue helicopter, the Angel, took up a holding pattern off the starboard side. The crash crew, wearing asbestos suits, started the engine of the flight-deck fire truck. A doctor and a team of corpsmen appeared from deep within the ship and huddled beside the island, the ship's superstructure.

Grafton's roommate, Sammy Lundeen, was smoking a cigar in the A-6 squadron's ready room when the news came over the intercom mounted on the wall at the duty officer's desk. The squadron skipper, Commander Frank Camparelli, put down his newspaper as he listened to the squawk box. Lundeen drew his cigar from his mouth and fixed his eyes on the metal intercom.

"Sam, you go up to the LSO's platform and stand by on the radio." Camparelli looked at the duty officer. "Hargis, I'm going to CATCC. Get the executive officer and tell him to come to the ready room and stand by here."

Commander Camparelli strode out of the room, headed for the Carrier Air Traffic Control Center with Sammy Lundeen right behind on his way to the landing signal officer's platform. Lundeen's cigar smoldered on the deck where he had dropped it.

"How badly is the BN hit?" the air operations officer asked the strike controller over a hot-line telephone. In the next compartment the controller, focusing on a small green dot moving slowly toward the center of his radar screen, stepped on his microphone switch.

"Devil Five Oh Five, Wagon Train Strike. State nature and extent of BN injuries, over."

Jake Grafton's voice came over the public-address

system in the control center. "Strike, Five Oh Five, I think my bombardier's been shot in the neck. It's hard to tell. He's unconscious now. I want a Charlie on arrival."

"Devil Five Oh Five, Strike. Your signal is Charlie on arrival." Charlie was the command to land.

"Roger that."

"Five Oh Five, switch to Approach on button three, and squawk One Three Zero Zero, over."

"Switching and squawking."

At the next radar console the approach controller noted the blip on his screen that had blossomed with the new IFF code. When the pilot checked in on the new frequency, the controller gave him landing instructions.

The air ops boss turned to the A-6 skipper who had just entered the compartment. "Frank, looks like your boy must be hit pretty badly. He should be at the ramp in six or seven minutes."

Commander Camparelli nodded and sat down in an empty chair beside the boss's chair. The room they sat in was lit entirely by dim red light. On the opposite wall a plexiglas status board seven feet high and twenty feet long listed every sortie the ship had airborne and all the sorties waiting on deck to be launched. Four enlisted men wearing sound-powered telephone headsets stood behind the transparent board and kept its information current by writing backwards on the board with yellow greasepencils. A black curtain behind them and the red light made the men almost invisible and caused the yellow letters to glow.

Commander Camparelli stared at the board. "505, Grafton, 9.0," it read. Camparelli's thoughts began to drift. Grafton and McPherson. Morgan's married to that dark-haired stewardess with United and has a two-year-old boy. Christ, he thought, I hope I don't have to write and tell her she's a widow.

"What kind of pilot is this Grafton?" the air ops boss asked.

"He's on his first tour, second cruise over here. Steady," said Camparelli. He added, "Good driver," but the ops officer had already turned away, trying to sort out what flights could be launched after Grafton had been recovered.

Frank Camparelli breathed deeply and tried to relax. Twenty years of fast planes, stormy nights, and pitching decks had given him a more than casual acquaintance with violent death. And he had found a way to live with it. Eyes open, half listening to the hushed voices around him, he began to pray.

The wind on the landing signal officer's platform tore at Sammy Lundeen's hair and clothing and roared in his ears as he stood on the lonesome perch jutting out from the port side of the landing area. He saw the Angel, the rescue helicopter, circling at 300 or 400 feet off the starboard side. Looking aft he could see the ship's phosphorescent wake and the running lights of the plane guard destroyer bobbing along a mile astern, waiting to rescue aircrews who ejected on final approach to the ship—if the chopper couldn't find them and if the destroyer crew could. Too many ifs. Small clusters of lights several miles away on either beam revealed the presence of two more destroyers.

"Here's a radio, Lundeen." The landing signal officer on duty tonight, Lieutenant Sonny Bob Battles, handed him a radio transceiver, which looked like a telephone, and then turned to the sound-powered telephone operator, an enlisted airman called a "talker." "Where is he?" Battles asked.

The talker spoke into the large microphone held by a harness on his chest. "Twelve miles out, sir. Level at twelve hundred feet."

"What freq?"

"Button three."

The LSO bent and twirled the radio channelization knob on the large control console mounted level with the deck edge. He and Lundeen held their radio transceivers up to their ears and heard the approach controller talking. "Five Oh Five, hold your gear until eight miles."

"Wilco." Jake sounded tired.

The LSO was an A-7 pilot, but like most aviators who acquire the special designation of landing signal officer, he was qualified to "wave" aboard all the types of aircraft the ship carried. He was prepared to talk a pilot aboard using only his eyes and the experience he had acquired observing more than ten thousand carrier approaches and almost as many simulated approaches at runways ashore. He had various sensors arrayed in a panel at his feet, but he rarely had time to glance at them.

"Who's driving Five Oh Five, Sam?"

"Grafton."

"Flies with McPherson?"

"Yeah."

Sonny Bob nodded. Both men heard Grafton give his gear-down call. The approach controller started Devil 505 descending on the glide slope. "Five Oh Five, call your needles."

"Up and right."

"Concur." A computer aboard ship located the A-6 and provided a glide slope and azimuth display on an instrument in the cockpit. But Jake would have to fly the jet down the glide slope and land it manually, a task that was as nerve-racking and demanding as any aviation had to offer.

On the LSO's platform Battles and Lundeen searched the darkness. The LSO keyed his mike. "Lights."

Jake Grafton had forgotten to turn on the aircraft's

exterior lights when he crossed the Vietnamese coastline on his way out to sea. Now the lights came on, making Devil 505 visible. Lundeen thought that if Jake had forgotten the lights perhaps he had also failed to safe the weapons-release circuits. "Check your master arm switch," he told Jake. He heard two clicks of the mike in reply, a pilot's way of responding when he was too busy to speak.

"Green deck," the telephone operator shouted.

"Roger green deck," Battles replied. The landing area was now clear and the arresting gear set to receive an A-6.

The Intruder moved up and down on the glide slope and shifted left of centerline, to Battles's right. The LSO keyed the mike. "Paddles has you now, Five Oh Five. Watch your lineup."

The A-6 turned toward the centerline, where it should be.

"Just settle down and keep it coming. How do you feel?"

"Okay." The voice was thin. Tired, very tired.

"Easy on the power. Call the ball." The ball call was essential. It told the LSO that the pilot could see the light, the "meatball," presented by the optical landing system that was located on the port side of the landing area. This device used a yellow light arranged between two green reference, or datum, lights to give the pilot a visual indication of his position in relation to the proper glide path. If he kept the ball centered in the datum lights all the way to touchdown, he would catch the third of four arresting-gear wires rigged across the deck.

"Intruder ball, Six Point Oh."

Down in CATCC the invisible men behind the status board erased the last fuel state for Devil 505 and wrote "6.0" beside the pilot's name. Six thousand pounds of fuel remaining. Commander Camparelli and the air ops boss checked the closed-circuit television monitor that gave them a picture from a camera buried under the flight deck and aimed up the glide slope. They waited.

From his perch on the flight deck, beside the landing area, the LSO could see the lights of the approaching plane grow brighter. In CATCC and in every ready room on the ship, all eyes were fixed on the television monitor with its picture of the glide slope and center-line cross hair and, just visible, the lights of the approaching plane.

Lundeen heard the engines. The faint whine grew louder, and he could hear the compressors spooling up and down as the pilot adjusted the throttles to keep the machine on the glide slope.

Battles's voice: "You're starting to go low." The engines wound up slightly. "Little more power." The engines surged. "Too much, you're high." A whine as the power came off, then a swelling of sound as Jake added power to stabilize his descent.

The A-6 approached the end of the ship, its engines howling. Battles was six feet out into the landing area, braced against the thirty-knot wind, concentrating on the rapidly approaching Intruder. He realized the plane was about three feet too high even as he heard the throttles come back and saw the nose of the machine sag slightly. He's going for the deck, the LSO told himself as he screamed into the radio, "Attitude!"

The Intruder flashed by, a gigantic bird feeling for the deck with its tailhook and main landing gear, its wingtip less than fifteen feet from the LSO's head. Battles sensed, rather than saw, Jake pull the stick back in response to his last call. The A-6 slammed into the deck, and the tailhook snagged the number-two arresting cable, whipping it out. As the plane raced up the deck, the engines wound up toward full power with a blast of sound and hot fury that lashed the two unprotected men. Lundeen almost lost his footing, as he had already begun running up the flight deck the instant he saw the hook pick up the arresting wire.

Training and reflex action had caused Jake Grafton to slam the throttles forward and retract the speed brakes the moment the wheels hit the deck in case the hook failed to snag a wire and he ran off the end of the deck, a "bolter." As he felt the arresting gear slow the plane, he slapped the throttles to idle, flipped the external-light master switch off, and raised the flap handle. The A-6 jerked to a halt and rolled backwards. The pilot pushed the button to raise the hook, then applied the brakes. The Intruder stopped with another jolt, this time remaining at rest.

Jake could see people running toward the plane from the island. He chopped the right engine and opened the canopy. A corpsman in a white shirt scrambled up the ladder on the BN's side of the plane and reached for McPherson. He raised the bombardier's head, looked at his neck, then motioned to the overhead floodlight switch on the canopy bow, the steel longitudinal frame that split the top of the canopy plexiglas. Turning it on, the pilot squinted and blinked as naked white light bathed the cockpit.

Rich red blood was everywhere. Blood covered McPherson and coated the panels on his side of the plane. Grafton's right hand was covered with it, as was the stick grip and everything else he had touched. The cockpit was a slaughter house.

More men draped over and on the cockpit. They flipped up the ejection seat safety latches to prevent the seat from firing accidentally, then released the fastenings that held the bombardier to the seat. They lifted his body out of the cockpit and passed him to the waiting hands below.

Fighting for self-control, Jake folded the wings and switched off the electronic gear. He became aware of Sammy standing on the ladder beside him. Lundeen reached into the cockpit and pulled the parking brake handle, then shut down the left engine. Grafton unlatched his oxygen mask and removed his helmet. His eyes were riveted on the stretcher bearing Morgan McPherson to the island superstructure until it disappeared behind a swinging metal door.

Silence descended on the cockpit. The wind down the flight deck dried the sweat coating Jake's hair and face. He began to chill. He looked again at the blood, on his hand, on the stick, blood everywhere under the harsh white light. The clock in the instrument panel was one of the few things not smeared with blood. The pilot looked up into the face of his friend.

"Sammy—" He felt the burning vomit coming up his throat and caught it in his helmet.

TWO

Early the next afternoon Jake Grafton walked aft through the hangar bay, picking his way around the planes and past the sailor-mechanics tending them. RA-5 Vigilante reconnaissance planes, F-4 Phantom fighters, A-7 Corsair and A-6 Intruder attack planes, a couple of helicopters—all were carefully arranged so that every square foot of space was used. Here in the hangar were performed the routine maintenance and emergency repairs that could not be done in the wind and rain of the flight deck. Here also were those planes needing spare parts that would be delivered by ship or resupply plane. The hangar bay, an impressive acre and a half of aircraft, usually held a fascination for Jake, but not today.

When he reached the back of the bay, he walked through a set of open fireproof double doors into the Engine Repair Facility. Young men wearing the enlisteds' usual at-sea attire—bell-bottom jeans and faded denim shirts stained with oil, grease, and hydraulic fluid—attended to a half-dozen jet engines resting on waist-high dollies. Rags dangled from hip pockets, and wrenches and screwdrivers protruded at odd angles.

Back in the States, these men must have been dressed much the same way on those long summer evenings when they tinkered with their Chevys and Fords.

Jake approached the shop chief, a trim middle-aged man. "Chief, do you have an old busted wrench or some scrap metal I could have?"

The chief petty officer took in the officer in khakis. About six feet and 175 pounds, Jake Grafton wore pilot's wings above his left breast pocket and the blue nametag of the A-6 squadron above his right. Clear gray eyes looked out past a nose that was at least one size too large for the face, and his brown hair had begun to recede from his forehead. Under one arm the officer was carrying a wadded-up flight suit.

"Sure, Mister Grafton." The chief rummaged through a metal box beside a desk stacked with forms and publications. He selected two pieces of odd-shaped rusted steel, together weighing five or six pounds, and handed them to the pilot.

"Thanks, Chief."

Jake continued on aft past the shop and stepped through an open hatch onto the fantail of the ship, a giant porch-like structure about fifteen feet above the water with the flight deck as a roof. Ordinarily the engine mechanics used this space to bolt their jet engines to massive stands and test them before reinstalling them in the aircraft, and often the marine detachment aboard used the fantail for small-arms practice, firing at cans or rags tossed into the wake. Today, though, the place was deserted.

Jake unrolled the flight suit, placed the metal in one of the deep chest pockets, then zipped it closed. Dried blood, now a rusty brown, covered the right sleeve and splotched the one-piece suit. He threw the suit over the rail into the wake, a river of foam reaching toward the horizon. The green cloth floated briefly, then settled beneath the roiling surface on its long trip to the sea's floor. The cloth would last a few years before it disintegrated but the steel would take maybe as many as a thousand years before it surrendered completely to the ageless sea. But the sea would win. That he knew.

Even after the cloth had disappeared several hundred yards astern, he remained mesmerized by the water agitated in the wake of the ship's four massive screws. The water came up white with a tinge of green, ceaselessly renewing itself. Except for the steel and the bloody cloth sinking slowly into the depths, not a trace of man's passage would remain after the wake dissipated miles behind the ship.

Maybe I'll end up there, he thought, trapped in a shot-up cockpit or drowned after ejecting from a plane at night. He visualized sharks. Attracted by the smell of blood or the thrashings of a man trying to stay afloat, the gray shapes would come out of the dark and rip a man to pieces. He imagined how it might be when the sharks tore at his flesh. He grimaced and turned away.

Commander Camparelli's stateroom was two decks below the hangar deck, off a quiet passageway. Jake made sure his shirttail was properly tucked in before he knocked and stepped inside.

Camparelli sat in a chair at the desk. Lieutenant Commander Cowboy Parker, the squadron's operations officer, sat on the bunk and the executive officer, Commander Harvey Wilson, had the sofa. The top of a small refrigerator, conveniently close to the desk, made a handy place for Camparelli's file stacks. The only other furniture was a knee-high table in front of the sofa and a dresser-locker recessed into one bulkhead.

As the commanding officer of the A-6 squadron aboard the *Shiloh*, Frank Camparelli was responsible for sixteen aircraft, forty officers, and three hundred sixty enlisted men. Twenty years had gone into earning this assignment, and he regarded it as the high point of his career. He was just getting used to all these men calling him "Skipper." Behind his back they called him the "Old Man." The same name was given to every other commanding officer in the navy, but on occasion, such as this evening, Camparelli felt that he in particular richly deserved it. Short and muscular, he had a habit of running his fingertips lightly over the stubble of his crewcut whenever his mind was fully engaged in solving a problem. Tonight the fingertips were in constant motion.

One of Camparelli's burdens was that he had several bosses. His immediate superior on operational matters was the commander of the air wing. The air wing was composed of the eight squadrons aboard the ship. This officer, a senior commander, was known as the CAG, an acronym from the days when a ship's squadrons were constituted as an air group. On administrative matters, Camparelli answered to a rear admiral back in the States who supervised all the A-6 squadrons assigned to the navy's Pacific Fleet. And because the squadron was embarked in a navy ship, the commanding officer of the ship, Captain Boma, had a rather large say both operationally and administratively. Camparelli had to be an adroit politician to stay afloat in this Byzantine world, complicated by strong personalities and overlapping operational and administrative concerns. The effort challenged his ingenuity and patience, but he felt he usually measured up. Most of the time, in fact, he thrived on it.

"Sit down, Jake." Camparelli waved at the bunk. Grafton sat down beside Cowboy. "We'd like to hear about the flight, again, and ask you a few questions. Cowboy is getting the operational loss report and the X.O. is heading the accident investigation. We've read your combat report." The skipper nodded at the papers on his desk.

Jake repeated the essence of his combat report. The others occasionally tossed in a question, but mostly they listened. Cowboy Parker took notes on a yellow legal pad. As the squadron operations officer, he was responsible for ensuring that the aircraft were operated in accordance with regulations, the "book." He supervised the preparation of the flight schedule and saw to it that every crewman was properly trained. He was teacher, coach, and, when necessary, slave driver. Because he was regularly required to make judgment calls, he was guaranteed a place on the hot seat at the first hint of trouble. In spite of his authority, Parker was popular with the junior officers; they respected his professional abilities and delighted in his willingness to occasionally participate in a sophomoric prank. Tonight, as usual, his angular face revealed nothing of his thoughts.

Harvey Wilson, the executive officer, or X.O., took few notes even though he was the nominal head of the accident investigation team. He had a bulging midriff and little black currant eyes that almost disappeared in his fleshy face. Grafton realized that Wilson would expect the junior people on the accident investigation team to do all the research and write the report, which he would then sign after ordering three or four drafts. He would become the next commanding officer of the squadron after Camparelli left a year from now. Jake expected to leave the squadron before Wilson got his chance to be a leader of men in combat. He had even called his detailer, the officer in Washington who wrote orders, for reassurance.

Frank Camparelli, on the other hand, was as good as they come. He listened to Jake's account of the mission, observing the pilot with clear blue eyes that seemed to notice everything. Finally Camparelli leaned back in his chair and propped his feet on the wastebasket.

"This whole thing sounds like an unavoidable tragedy to me. We'll get the best results with our airplanes if we use them the way they were designed to be used, that is, low-level night attack. We get the most accurate hits at low altitude. The errors of angle in the radar, computer, and inertial result in larger miss distances the farther away from the target we release the weapons, as you gentlemen are well aware. And if we are up high, alone, five to ten thousand feet, the SAMs are going to make our life rough. Above ten thousand feet we don't have enough bombs when you figure the probability of an accurate hit. No," he concluded, "we have to come in low at night. And occasionally a random bullet is going to do some damage, cost us a plane." He glanced at Grafton. "Or a life."

"If they get too good at shooting at low fliers we may have to mix it up, send some guys in high and some in low to keep them guessing," the X.O. offered.

The skipper ignored the comment. Jake wondered how having some planes up high would lessen the threat if the gomers learned to bag the guys down low. It seemed to him that any low flier would have difficulty regardless of how many were at altitude. But he was only a lieutenant.

The skipper spoke to him. "You said in your combat report that the SAM they fired at you leveled off, then ceased guiding and went ballistic when you descended to 200 feet?"

"Yes, sir, that's right."

"Two hundred feet is too damn low," the X.O. grumbled. "You hiccup at that height and you've bought the farm."

"Maybe," the skipper said and turned back to reading the combat report. Jake fought the urge to tell Wilson he wasn't given to hiccups over North Vietnam. He looked at Cowboy, who wore his usual blank expression. If you didn't know better, you'd suspect Cowboy's IQ was no greater than his age. Jake faced the skipper but examined the X.O. out of the corner of his eye. Wilson's reluctance to fly at night was the subject of whispers and sneers among the junior officers. Behind his back he was known as "the Rabbit." McPherson buys the farm, Grafton thought, and assholes like Wilson just keep on ticking. Damn it, Morg, why did it have to be you?

"The thing I'm worried about is this," the skipper said. "Are the North Vietnamese getting enough technical improvements from the Soviets to break us out of ground clutter on their radar? Or putting heat seekers on those SAMs? If they do either, those missiles are going to start coming down on us and we'll be in real trouble."

"Out of altitude and out of luck," Cowboy said without looking up from his pad.

The skipper sucked at his pencil, then directed his attention to Cowboy. "Parker, you tell the ordnance shop to start loading a couple of those infrared flares in the chaff tubes. Maybe the fourth and twelfth tubes. That should give us an IR flare for each of the first two missiles, so if they do put heat seekers on those things, we'll already have them foxed." Cowboy made a note. "And keep Jake off the flight schedule tonight." Cowboy shot a look at Grafton.

"Okay, fellows. That's all. I want to talk to Jake for a moment." The X.O. and Cowboy left. Camparelli waited until the footsteps had faded in the passageway before he spoke. "I think you know how I feel. Losing Morgan is damned tough."

"Yessir, it is."

"I want you to write a letter to Morgan's wife. I'll mail it in a few days with one from me. That'll give her a little time to get over the first shock."

"Sure."

"Anything you want to tell me about that hop that you don't want in the official reports?"

Jake was surprised, and it showed. "No, sir."

"If there is something, you had better let me know. I have to know what the hell is going on in these airplanes. I have sixteen planes and eighteen crews to worry about and I don't like to lose people or machines."

Jake swallowed. "Skipper, that hop was as straightforward as they come. No fuck-ups. The gomers just got lucky."

Camparelli lit a cigarette. His cropped hair showed flecks of gray, and crow's-feet radiated from the corners of his eyes. Like most aviators he had a deeply tanned face, but his arms, routinely encased in a fire-proof flight suit, were white. In the center of his forehead was a prominent scar, a souvenir from his younger days when he had belly-landed an A-1 Skyraider and smashed his head on the gunsight. "No fuck-ups? The doctor tells me you pressed so hard on McPherson's neck you damaged the tissue. And at the same time you were motoring around over the treetops with your left hand trying to stay in the air. Bet that little trip resembled a roller-coaster ride." He blew smoke in Grafton's face. "The only way you could have stopped the bleeding would have been to stuff a finger in the bullet hole and seal off that artery. Then McPherson would have died from brain damage due to oxygen starvation."

Camparelli leaned forward in his chair, put his elbows on his knees, and looked into Grafton's eyes. "I know you didn't know how badly he was hit, but you could have smacked in while you were playing doctor. Then you and McPherson would both have one of those little farms with the stones and flowers. Of course, you wouldn't be there. You two would be splattered across a half mile or so of rice paddies. Your intentions were good, but I'm here to tell you that no matter what the circumstance, sound judgment is the only damn thing on God's green earth that's going to keep you alive long enough to die in bed. And even that may not be enough."

Camparelli drummed on the table with his fingers. His voice dropped. "There is no such thing as luck. If you think you're lucky and that'll carry you through, you're living on borrowed time." He was talking to himself. "The luckiest men I ever met are all dead now. They thought they were surrounded with a golden halo of good fortune, a magic shield that couldn't be pierced." He looked at Grafton. "And they are dead!" He pronounced the last sentence slowly, emphasizing each word.

"I know, sir, you're right, but what bothers me"—Jake's respect for Camparelli warred with his anger over McPherson's death—"is why in hell we keep getting men killed and planes chewed up over garbage targets? A 'suspected truck park,' for God's sake! A good man's life in exchange for some beat-up trucks? If they were there, which is not very damned likely. There's got to be some better targets in gomer country. Why can't we bomb something that makes a difference?"

The Old Man leaned back in his chair. "There's nothing anyone aboard this ship can do about the targets. In this war the politicians and generals do the targeting, based on politieal considerations." He pronounced "political" like a preacher using a cuss word. He waved his hand, dismissing the subject of targets and the men responsible for them. "I don't want you in the air unless you're one hundred percent. I can't spare any more bombardiers and I damn sure don't want to lose an airplane. All you have to worry about is your ass and your bombardier's, but I have eighteen aircrews I'm responsible for. Understand?"

"Yes, sir."

He spoke more briskly. "And I don't want anybody in these airplanes who thinks he's John Wayne on a vengeance mission."

Jake Grafton said nothing.

"Okay, get some sleep. Take tonight off and write that letter. It'll be tough but it'll help get this behind you."

"Yes, sir." He stood hesitantly and watched the skipper pull a can of Coke from his refrigerator. "Thanks, Skipper."

"If you kill yourself, son, I'll piss on your grave."

"I understand."

The commander nodded absently and ripped the pull-top off the can. "Get some sleep, Jake."

As he walked toward his own stateroom, Jake decided that Frank Camparelli was all right. He could tell a man to go to hell and make him happy to be on his way.

Jake and Sammy were drinking. Earlier the squadron flight surgeon had stopped by and delivered two airline bottles of twelve-year-old bourbon. He made a point of delivering medicinal whiskey whenever he heard of a particularly harrowing flight.

"Real sorry about McPherson," he had said, handing over the bottles. Then he had added, "But these things happen."

Grafton had at that instant loathed the man. "Yeah, that's the breaks of naval air."

Jake saw that the sarcasm had registered on the doctor, who was known among the airmen as Mad Jack the Jungle Quack in honor of the tour he had recently completed with the marines in South Vietnam that had left his arms red and inflamed from a tropical skin disease, one that his patients fervently hoped was not contagious.

"No offense. I'm sorry." He gazed distractedly around the little stateroom at the rumpled flight suits hanging from hooks, the flight boots lying in the corner, and the papers strewn about the two desks. In his mid-thirties, with a roll of fat around his middle, the doctor seemed out of place among the pilots.

As he departed Mad Jack had paused. "If you want to talk or visit . . ." Grafton had shown no response.

So now the two pilots had settled down to business. They had finished off the airline bottles, and Jake was working on a bottle of bourbon while Lundeen, who had to fly in eight or ten hours, sipped a can of Coke. Lundeen kept the bottle sequestered in his small desk safe, which the navy provided for the storage of classified documents. Unlike the skipper, they had no refrigerator, so there was no ice. After the first glass Jake had dispensed with the water.

Jake watched his friend tip his can of Coke. Lundeen was almost six feet, four inches tall, near the limit for a pilot, and had a great deal of upper body strength and smooth, quick movements. He had been a tight end in college but was too small for the pros. In the compact stateroom he looked huge. Besides flying, he also acted as the squadron's personnel officer, supervising a chief and five clerks. The only portion of his administrative duties that he did not visibly detest was his work as awards officer. He drafted the citations and recommendations for medals and gave them to the X.O., Harvey Wilson, to approve and forward up the chain of command. Lundeen kept a thesaurus on his desk that he referred to constantly as he drafted the award citations. He would gleefully read his better efforts to Jake as proof positive that the military in general and the navy in particular were "all fucked up."

"How'd you guys do tonight?" Sammy asked, for he knew Morgan had been hit after the bomb run.

"Well, you know how hard it is to tell at night. No secondary explosions. But Morg had a ground lock with the track radar and the system was tight. If we missed, it sure as hell wasn't for lack of trying. Of course, what we hit was probably just a couple acres of forest that some jackass thought we ought to drop a few bombs into."

"The toothpick hypothesis," Sammy said. "After we turn all the big trees into toothpicks, they'll have to surrender."

"Damn, I wish we had some decent targets! There has to be something in North Vietnam that's worth the trip. Morgan gets zapped and we don't have a goddamn thing to show for it, not even a secondary explosion." Jake splashed more bourbon into his glass. "And the skipper says there's nothing we can do about it." He got up and paced the small room. He knew the targets were assigned daily on a master "frag" list. The strike orders were further fragmented into a group of targets for each squadron. This chore was handled by the Strike Ops Department, which matched the targets to the capabilities of the various aircraft and the number of aircraft each squadron had available, and gave each target a mission number. The target lists then went to the schedules officer of each squadron, who, after consulting with the squadron operations officer and perhaps its skipper, assigned a crew to each mission.

The flight schedule was printed and shoved under the door of every crewman at least three, preferably four, hours before the first launch of the day. After consulting the schedule, the A-6 pilots and bombardiers went to the Mission Planning section of the ship's Intelligence Center where coded mission numbers were matched with photographs, map coordinates, and, if available, radar photography of the intended targets. This information was compiled for each mission by the squadron's air intelligence officers, nonfliers who specialized in this field.

Surrounded by all the data they could get, the bombardier-navigators planned the flight, usually with their pilots watching over their shoulders. The BNs would choose a route that would avoid the worst of known enemy defenses, select navigation checkpoints, measure headings and distances, and calculate the flight time for each leg of their route. They would write down information from the charts to feed into the navigation/attack computer. While the pilots cut up large charts and put together a small strip chart of the route which they'd carry in the cockpit, the bombardiers, applying the skill acquired through countless hours of practice, would sketch predictions of what they believed the target would look like on the radar screen, given the planned angle of approach and altitude. Because the aircraft would approach the target at 500 knots, over 800 feet per second, the bombardier would have only a moment to pick it out from among the hundreds of objects that reflected radar energy and cluttered the scope. A mistake here meant that the bombs would strike in the wrong place, and the whole mission would be for nothing.

McPherson had been a wizard with the scope, Jake remembered. He had had an uncanny ability to pick out a building or checkpoint from a confused glob of ground clutter. The problem wasn't the bombing, Jake thought, but the unimportance of the targets assigned.

"Well, at least it won't go on much longer," Sammy said, breaking into his thoughts.

"What do you mean?"

"Haven't you heard? Kissinger just announced 'Peace is at hand.' It was on the closed-circuit television last night. The war's almost over."

Jake felt as though he had been punched in the stomach.

"Oh, shit," Sammy said. "You and Morgan were flying when they announced it. Didn't anybody tell you?"

"No." It was a whisper.

"Christ, man, I'm sorry. I am really sorry."

THREE

Both fire-warning lights glared a brilliant red. The plane was out of control. The hydraulic gauges still showed plenty of pressure. The nose slammed up and down with an evil perversity, and the machine rolled left. He jammed the stick full right, but the left roll continued. He looked at Morgan. His head was gone. Blood spurted in little fountains from the stump of his neck. The canopy glass was gone on the right side, and the wind howled through the cockpit. The stick was firm, yet the plane did not respond. His body slammed back and forth as the G forces and wind tore at him. With the altimeter racing down, he fumbled for the ejection handle between his legs. It wasn't there! His hands went to the primary handle over his head, but it too was gone! He couldn't tear his eyes from the wildly spinning altimeter. Maddened by the roar of the hurricane wind, he screamed.

The scream woke him. The darkness and the panic were real. Unable to orient himself, he fought the sheets. One fist struck the bulkhead, and the pain sobered him. He fumbled for the bunk light switch.

He kicked the sheets aside and put his feet on the

floor. Sweat covered his brow. He lit a cigarette with trembling hands. Three o'clock in the morning. Sammy Lundeen was flying somewhere over North Vietnam. Morgan McPherson was in a body bag in the ship's morgue.

He had drunk too much bourbon. His head throbbed and his hands still shook. He levered himself upright and fumbled for some aspirin in the medicine cabinet. He wet a face towel and lay down again with the cool cloth on his forehead. He left the light on. He needed the light.

He concentrated on the sounds of the ship working in the seaway. Metal rubbing on metal, the great weight of the ship rolling ever so gently back and forth as it met the swells, the rhythm of movement. He could also hear the sounds of men and machinery. From the engineering spaces below his room came the ringing of hammer blows. He silently cursed the fellow with the hammer, some boilertender, no doubt, delicately adjusting a precision instrument.

But his mind kept coming back to the flight, obsessively. That bullet that got Morg could have smacked me instead, he thought. Two inches lower and it would have gone under his chin and got me in the ear. Smack. I wouldn't even have felt it. Just smack: then nothing.

The silent scream started. He felt his guts heave. Stop. Stop! You think about this stuff too much and you'll be cold meat, just like McPherson.

He rolled out of the bunk, grabbed his towel, and went down the passageway to the showers. Water was being conserved because of recurrent problems with the ship's evaporators; a notice posted on the door announced that showers were permitted only from 0600 to 0700 and again from 1800 to 1900. Jake ignored the sign. He tried the shower faucets, found they worked, and stood for ten minutes under the tap. Fuck the navy!

And fuck the asshole who can't keep the goddamn evaporators working!

He dressed in a clean khaki uniform. Before he put on the trousers, he rammed his fist down each pant leg to break up the starch. He went by the ready room, decided he wasn't in the mood for people, and wandered up to the hangar deck. Aircraft 505 was near Elevator Two. Two mechanics, on a work stand alongside the fuselage, were replacing the damaged canopy pane. One of the men, a first class petty officer whom Jake knew by sight, turned toward him.

"Too bad about Mister McPherson."

Yeah, too bad.

"Not another bullet hole in this whole airplane, Mister Grafton. We spent half an hour looking to see if they hit you anywhere else."

The pilot just nodded and went on. He walked out onto a sponson on the port side amidships. The only light came through the open hatch from the hangar bay. Two large capstans stood ready to take the lines when the ship tied up portside to a pier. Jake heaved himself up on one. He could see the lights of a destroyer or frigate several miles away. The wind was heavy with the smell of the sea.

After a half hour or so he went back inside the skin of the ship and climbed the ladders to the O-3 level, the deck above the hangar bay and immediately below the flight deck. Instead of salt air, he smelled paint and the lubricating oil on the hatch hinges. Following a maze of passageways, he located the junior officers' bunkroom where McPherson had lived.

The door was open. Two navy-gray steel footlockers sat on the floor on one side of the eight-man bunkroom. Little Augie Odegard and his bombardier, Joe Canfield, were packing clothes and personal effects into the lockers.

"How's it going?" Jake muttered as he took a seat on the bunk opposite the pilot.

"Packing out Morg's stuff. Rotten job," said Little Augie. "It all has to be packed up so they can ship it home to his wife when we get to the Philippines in three days." This duty always fell to the roommates of the dead or missing, which was why the two men who made up a crew were not allowed to live together in a double stateroom.

Canfield sat at McPherson's desk going through the letters, magazines, and souvenirs that McPherson had accumulated in the last six months. Canfield's nickname was Big Augie because he was two inches taller than his diminutive pilot and the men bore a remarkable resemblance to each other, even though the pilot was white and the bombardier black. "Morg was squeaky clean, Jake. Not even a porn mag or a letter from an old girlfriend. Man, whoever has to clean out my desk is going to get an eyeful reading my stuff." He opened another envelope, verified it contained a letter from Morgan's wife, then replaced the letter in the envelope and added it to a large pile that would eventually go in one of the steel boxes. "Finding out how squared away Morg was is having a beneficial effect on my morals."

"He was a good guy," Jake said.

"Sure going to miss him." Little Augie eyed Jake with a raised eyebrow. "So how're you really doing, shipmate?"

"Doing okay. The skipper gave me the night off, but I'll be on the flight schedule tomorrow."

"Only a few more days before we go to Subic Bay," Big reminded them.

"I'm just going to lay around the pool and drink gin and tonics," Little Augie said.

"This time of year it may rain like hell."

Jake watched the two men work. Little Augie meticulously folded the uniforms, underwear, and civilian clothes before putting them in the boxes. When Morgan McPherson's personal effects were gone and the paperwork done, the men of the squadron would have finished burying him. When would Jake get him buried?

"Do you guys think the war is about over?"

"You mean that Kissinger statement 'Peace is at hand'?" Little Augie scoffed.

"Yeah." Grafton's voice was so soft that Big shot him a hard glance.

"It won't be over until the treaty is signed and the gomers let the POWs come home," Little told him. "It isn't going to happen soon."

"You don't think?"

"Nah, they've been talking for three years. Heck, it took them a year to decide on the shape of the conference table. I figure that at the rate they've been going we'll have a treaty by the turn of the century."

Big said, "Morgan isn't going to be the last guy, Jake. Don't blame yourself. There's a lot of dying left to do."

Jake rose to go.

"Take care," Little told him.

"You aren't flying for at least twenty-four hours. Go get a drink," Big advised.

"I already did that."

"So get another."

Back in his stateroom Jake removed his uniform and pulled down a hinged board, part of a dresser recessed into the bulkhead. When lowered, the board became a desk. Papers and books were stored in the cavity, which also contained the safe for classified material. He reached in and turned on the fluorescent tube that, because of its recessed position, lighted the small work area but left most of the room in darkness. The subdued light gave the room an intimacy that seemed almost impossible on a 95,000-ton warship with a crew of five thousand. Jake turned off all the other lights in the stateroom so he could seek refuge in the secure world of the lamp.

What could he possibly say to Sharon McPherson? Dear Sharon, I'm sorry I got your husband killed. How could he say he was sorry and make it mean anything? Her world gets smashed to bits and he's "sorry."

His hands were still shaking. Adrenaline aftershock, he decided. He picked up a sheet of paper and placed it on top of his splayed fingertips. The paper vibrated. Like everything else in his life, like the targets, like what happened to Morgan, it was beyond his control. He stared into the shadows of the room. He remembered the look on Morgan's face, and the gagging, and the blood. Blood everywhere. The body holds an unbelievable amount of blood. Maybe the people he and McPherson had killed had died like that, bleeding to death. Or maybe they had died instantly from the blast of the bombs. He would never know.

He chewed the pencil, his mind as blank about what he would say to Sharon as the sheet of paper in front of him. What do you say to a widow and mother? Dear Sharon, We just hit a target that wasn't worth a damn. Now your husband's in a body bag in the meat locker. I am sorry as hell he's dead: sorry, oh so sorry, but he is stone cold dead and sorry won't bring him back, and you and I and Morgan's boy have to live with it.

What do you say to the widow of the man who had saved your life?

They had been younger then and the carrier was still in their future. They had finished their training at the replacement squadron on the same day and had walked across the parking lot side by side to the new hangar, to their new squadron, the fleet squadron. Somehow they were assigned to fly together.

Flying without an instructor was still a new experience then. They were just getting to know each other, much like newlyweds on a honeymoon. The honeymoon ended that night.

They had flown south parallel to the coast of Washington twenty miles out to sea as the sunset died on the western horizon. To their right, the day sky slowly surrendered to the night through shades of yellows, oranges, and reds. On their left, layers of heavy stratus reflected the dying glow that was the lingering remnant of the day. Between the layers, blues and purples deepened into black.

They passed the mouth of the Columbia River and continued south for another eighty miles. Jake retarded the throttles and began his descent. At 5000 feet McPherson called the turn and the pilot swung east toward the land, still descending.

They leveled at 1000 feet, and he set the throttles for a 360-knot cruise. They went in under the clouds, the last of the light gone. Jake selected the search-radar terrain clearance mode on the visual display indicator and rotated the offset impact bar to give himself 1000 feet of clearance. The VDI presented a graphic of the terrain ahead generated by the computer from returning radar energy. The information was displayed in a series of cribs, or range bins, to give the presentation a three-dimensional effect, and one of the bins was coded with vertical stripes. The pilot had to vary the altitude of the aircraft to keep the fixed offset impact bar on the coded range bin so that the plane maintained the desired degree of clearance, and no less.

Before they had gone very far inland the aircraft entered the clouds. The rotating anticollision light reflected off the cloud and flashed in the cockpit, creating a distraction, so the pilot turned it off. Morgan McPherson had his head pressed against the radar hood and was probably unaware that they had entered heavy clouds. The squadron operations manual dictated that this particular training route through the coastal mountains not be flown in instrument conditions. Grafton knew this, but tonight he decided to press on. Perhaps it was a matter of conquering fear by facing it.

Within minutes the plane was threading its way up a valley, and Jake was perspiring profusely. He concentrated on the VDI. The display was updated once a second, and he had to instantly judge the rate of change in the rising topography, and any heading correction necessary, then control the plane accordingly. The aircraft responded to stick displacement, but that displacement merely created a rate of change, not the change itself. Selecting the proper rate of change was the art. Sweat trickled down his forehead and stung his eyes.

McPherson, his head against the scope hood, fed Grafton a running commentary. "We're in the valley . . . looks good for five miles ahead, ridges on both sides . . . the valley will bend right . . . we'll be coming right in two miles . . . your altitude looks good . . . begin a right turn . . . harder right . . . looking good . . . steady up. . . ."

And so they sped up the valley. In five minutes they crossed the divide and descended into another valley leading toward the interior plain, the desert. The turns were steep at first, the pilot reluctant to force the nose down, but as the valley widened and straightened he let the machine sink until the impact bar rested on the coded range bin and the radar altimeter read 1000 feet.

"Looks real good . . . ridges moving away from our track . . . hold this heading . . . clearance looks good. . . ."

They turned to a heading that would take them to a lake seventy miles away. Halfway there McPherson pushed back from the scope hood and began tapping the coordinates of their next turnpoint onto the computer keyboard between his knees.

After the fierce concentration of the last fifteen minutes, the pilot unconsciously relaxed, took several deep breaths, and scanned the engine instruments and the fuel gauge as McPherson typed and checked his kneeboard cards. Satisfied that the computer had taken the new information, the bombardier put his head against the scope hood and Jake heard him scream.

"Pull up!"

Now Jake saw the display. They were dead men. The coded range bin was way above the impact bar, up near the top of the display. He slammed the throttles forward and jerked back on the stick. His eyes swung to the radar altimeter. The needle was sinking through 200 feet.

We're dead!

The aural warning sounded. The needle passed 100 feet. He had the stick locked aft.

So this is how it feels to die.

The needle on the radar altimeter fell to 50 feet, hovered there for a second, then began to climb. The pilot's eyes came back to the VDI. Twenty degrees nose up. He kept the stick locked aft. The radar altimeter needle raced clockwise.

He couldn't release the back pressure on the control stick. Forty degrees nose up . . . fifty . . . sixty . . . seventy.

At eighty degrees nose up he felt the stall buffet and then, only then, did he ease the stick to neutral.

Two hundred knots and slowing. They were passing 9000 feet.

He stared at the instruments. He had to do something! They were going almost straight up and running out of airspeed!

"Come on, Jake." Morgan's calm voice.

The pilot rolled the plane ninety degrees and let the

nose drop toward the horizon. Slowly, slowly it came down and the airspeed crept up. When the nose reached the horizon, he rolled wings level.

They were at 13,000 feet. He was shaking uncontrollably. What had he done? He had almost killed them!

Morgan must have sensed how shaken he was. As they droned around on autopilot in a lazy circle with Jake shivering, the bombardier had talked to him. Jake could never remember what Morgan had said. He had just talked to let Jake hear the sound of his voice, calm and soothing; he talked until Jake was over his panic. And when they had landed, McPherson never mentioned the incident to anyone, had never reported the near disaster. He merely shook Jake's hand in the parking lot and gave him a parting smile.

And he had saved both their lives!

Now he was dead. Two years and hundreds of thousands of miles later, he was dead.

Jake began to write. After three drafts he had the semblance of an acceptable letter. It wasn't really acceptable, but it was the best he could manage. Two more drafts in ink gave him a letter he was prepared to sign.

Dear Sharon,

By now you have been notified of Morgan's death in action. He was killed on a night strike on a target in North Vietnam, doing the best he could for his country. That fact will never fill the emptiness that his passing leaves but it will make him shine even brighter in my memory.

I flew with Morgan for over two years. We spent over six hundred hours together in the air. I knew him perhaps as well as any man can know another. We both loved flying and that shared love sealed our friendship.

Since I knew him so well, I am well aware of the depth of his love for you and Bobby and realize the magnitude of the tragedy of his passing. You have my deepest and most sincere sympathy.

Jake

What would she think when she read it? Would she save it and get it out in those moments when the past must be revisited? Ten or twenty years from now, on a cool spring day when she's cleaning the attic, would she find this letter from her lost past? The paper would be faded and yellow then. She would remember how it looked when she received it, the final notice that the dreams of her youth had died far away, in a forsaken land, in a forgotten cause. Perhaps she would show it to her son when he asked about his father.

He stared at himself in the mirror over the sink. Where would he be in twenty years? Dead like McPherson and the nameless men who died under his bombs? Or selling insurance and paying off a mortgage, busy with the day-to-day affairs that fill up life yet somehow leave it empty?

He turned off the light and lay down on his bunk. Tired as he was, sleep would not come. He reviewed that last flight from beginning to end. There must be something he could have done differently. But the bullet had come out of nowhere; he couldn't have avoided it. Now Morgan was dead, and for what? He wanted to get the bastards for that! He remembered the Rockeye attack on the guns. God, that had felt good! He had pickled the four cluster bombs at precisely the right moment. Too bad the A-6 didn't have a gun like the A-7 Corsair had. If only he had a gun! He could just drop the nose, put the pipper in the sight a fraction below the target, pull the trigger, and walk those big slugs right up onto the gomers. As he lay there in his bunk, he could feel the recoil from the hammering weapon. The sensation was so real he panicked and groped for the light.

With the light on there was only the small room. He found Lundeen's bottle and, sitting down in his desk chair, took a pull of the liquor. Camparelli's words came back to him. "I don't want anybody in those planes who thinks he's John Wayne on a vengeance mission." But it was damn hard not to want revenge. An eye for an eye, a tooth for a tooth, a body for a body. . . .

So he's dead and nothing can bring him back. He died bombing a bunch of trees in a shitty little place in a shitty little war that we don't have the guts to try to win, and he would get a flag for his coffin. Jesus, you lose him like that and you want something more than a flag. You can't help wishing that if he had to die that he'd died bombing a target that might have meant something. So you could honestly say, so Sharon could truthfully say, so his son could say with pride in the years to come: He died for. . . . My dad helped win the war by. . . . He died in the name of. . . . What? Nothing. Christ, what you want is for his death to *mean* something. You want a reason.

Maybe you *can* make his death mean something. You could sneak north some dark night and bomb something worth the trip. Really kick the gomers in the nuts

He was up and pacing around the little room. It *is* possible, he told himself. Yes. No one but your bombardier knows where you go after you cross the beach. The Americans can't follow you on radar, and the gomers have no idea where you're supposed to go. So you can go anywhere you please and attack any damn thing.

What crazy thoughts! You pull a stunt like that, Jake, and you'll be court-martialed . . . crucified.

Fuck that. So what? McPherson's dead. I want a

target that will make the gomers bleed. Like they made Morgan bleed. And Sharon. And me. . . .

When he lay down on his bunk again, he left the light on and concentrated on the creaks and groans of the ship as its steel beams and plates moved to meet the stresses of the swells.

He lay a long time listening to the sounds of the ship.

FOUR

It was a rotten night in the tropics. The rain had resumed just after sunset. On the bridge of the *Shiloh* the officer of the deck made a note of the time for the log. After a few minutes the OOD ordered the bridge's windshield wipers turned on, and he searched the blackness for the lights of the destroyer that should be out ahead of the carrier. She had been visible only a moment ago. He checked the radar screen. Still just where she should be, five thousand yards ahead. "Let me know if the *Fannon* gets out of position," he said to the junior officer of the watch, then called down to the Combat Information Center and repeated the order to the watch officer who sat surrounded by surface- and air-search radar consoles. Even the air on the bridge was laden with moisture. The one hundred percent humidity prevented sweat from evaporating, so damp hair, shirts, and underwear gave each man his own particular odor.

The OOD walked over to the port wing of the bridge and looked at the rain-whipped flight deck below. The airplanes were huddled together in the blurred red light. Their upthrust wings reminded him of arms raised in supplication. The tropical rain was good for the planes; it would wash off some of the grime and salt spray. The sound of the rain pounding on the bridge's steel and the rhythmic swish-swish of the wipers made the watch officer feel alone in the night.

This line period would be over in two days time. Then the ship would leave Yankee Station for the pleasures of Subic Bay, a thirty-six-hour trip across the South China Sea. On that cheerful morning, the jungle-covered mountains that encircled the U.S. Navy's home in the South Pacific would rise from the sea and break the monotonous horizon. Five glorious and mostly carefree days and nights of maximum liberty awaited most of the men. For some, of course, there would still be long hours of hard work, but even they could look forward to evenings on the beach.

U.S. Naval Station Subic Bay and the adjoining U.S. Naval Air Station Cubi Point, the Philippines, were not places normally advertised on travel posters, but dry land is dry land. Well, it was dry land until a tropical storm opened heaven's gates, but then a sailor could always rationalize that mud is preferable to saltwater.

When sailors on liberty grew tired of drinking in the bars, or playing golf in the blazing sun, or strolling through the navy exchanges, they could then amble across the bridge that spans the Perfume River, really a drainage canal, and sample the exotic delights of Olongapo City. Some 150,000 people struggled to stay alive in this crowded town of half-dirt–half-paved streets.

Most of the people of Po City made a living, of sorts, chasing the Yankee dollars brought across the bridge by thirsty, sex-starved American servicemen momentarily free of Mother, God, and the U.S. Navy. A kaleidoscope of sensual delights, the city offered cheap booze and horse-piss beer and legions of little brown girls with only wisps of pubic hair who would perform almost any sex act imaginable for the right price. And to the never-ending delight of the horny Americans, the right price was always ridiculously low.

Tonight, two days out of port, the doctors and corpsmen in the hospital spaces were buying five-buck squares in the clap pool: nearest square to the exact number of VD cases diagnosed in the next line period would take the pot. Up in the captain's office a yeoman was putting the finishing touches on a report of a drug-overdose death from the ship's last port visit. In the galleys the night shift, busy baking the fifteen hundred loaves of bread and the five thousand doughnuts the crew would consume the following day, was calculating the number of loaves and doughnuts between them and Subic Bay. From the keel to the signal-bridge, every man aboard was looking forward to nights ashore as the ship lay tied to the NAS Cubi Point carrier pier.

Beneath the flight deck in the cubicle that housed the Strike Operations office, the men charged with directing the ship's combat sorties sat over coffee and cigarettes, considering a map of the war zone spread on the table before them. On top of the map lay the latest weather forecast, which was consulted again and again. The Gulf of Tonkin, where the ship was located, and North Vietnam were blanketed by rain clouds that also covered Hainan Island and most of northern South Vietnam. The men decided, after a few questions to the weather forecasters, on a new air plan for the twelve hours beginning at midnight, and the plan was quickly written, printed, and distributed throughout the ship.

The ship would sail south. Beginning at midnight, the A-6s would be launched at the preassigned targets in the North. Their electronic eyes could penetrate the clouds and rain and darkness. The Phantoms would still provide fighter cover for the task force, and the early-warning planes, the E-2s, would fly above the weather and ensure that the sky and sea remained free of unfriendly ships and planes. At dawn everything that could fly and carry bombs would head south to work with Air Force Forward Air Controllers (FACs). "Hate to let the boys up North have a day off, but don't see any other way," the strike ops boss said to his staff.

In response to the new air plan, the ship's navigator plotted a new course to first-launch position and handed it to the OOD. The watch officer notified the carrier's escorting ships of the new course and necessary maneuvers and checked their positions in relation to the carrier before he ordered the course change. He watched the helmsman spin the wheel to bring the ship about, then glued his head to the radar repeater to ensure that none of the screening ships attempted a turn across the behemoth's bow. The huge ship heeled only two or three degrees in a long, slow turn. Rainwater sluiced off the flight deck into the scuppers, then fell the sixty feet to the sea.

Someone was shaking him. He was coming up from a long way under and someone was shaking his arm. "Rise and shine, Jake. Time to go fly." Lundeen shook him one more time to make sure he was awake.

From his bunk, Jake watched his tall roommate lather up his face. Every muscle in Jake's body was relaxed. "How long did I sleep?"

"At least fourteen hours. You were really zonked." Lundeen hummed as he shaved. "We have a brief in five minutes for the first launch at midnight," he said. "You have a tanker."

"Weather?"

"Heavy sea running. Raining enough to float the Ark. Another great navy day." Lundeen continued humming.

Jake looked at his watch, 10:25. Reluctantly, he kicked away the sheet and sat up. He was covered with a fine layer of perspiration. He stretched and yawned.

"Your humming is really inspirational. What's that tune?"

"I don't know. I make it up as I go along."

Jake pulled on his new olive-drab flight suit, a one-piece fire-resistant coverall. As he laced up his steel-toed flight boots, he asked, "Sammy, if you could bomb any target in North Vietnam, what would you bomb?"

"Why are you asking?"

"What's the most important asset they have?"

"Ho Chi Minh's grave."

"Be serious."

"I am serious. They don't have anything worth a piddle. If they did, we'd have bombed it."

"Bullshit. You know that isn't true."

Sammy rinsed his razor and wiped his face. "It'd be in Hanoi. If they have anything valuable, it's in Hanoi where it can be defended. And about all the navy ever bombed there were the bridges and the rail yard. Maybe a power plant or two."

Both men opened their desk safes, drew out their revolvers, and dropped them in a chest pocket. The baggy one-piece suits sagged. They locked the safes, turned off the lights, and locked the stateroom door behind them. "But you can't just go bomb something on your own, Jake, and you know it," Sammy said as they walked toward the ready room.

"Yeah."

"Don't get any big ideas."

"Sure, Sam. You know me."

Jake stopped at the main wardroom pantry adjacent to their ready room. He filled a mug with coffee and scrounged a slab of roast beef from the steward, a leftover from the evening meal which he had slept through. He even cadged a bread roll, tore it in half, and put it around the beef.

Inside the ready room the brief was in progress.

Grafton settled into one of the large padded chairs beside Razor Durfee, his BN for the flight. Razor was taking notes from the brief being broadcast over the closed-circuit television, which was mounted high in one corner. The same show was playing in all eight of the ship's ready rooms. One of the A-6 squadron's air intelligence officers, Abe Steiger, was giving the brief to the air wing for the first launch. Jake ate his sandwich while Razor took notes.

"Real tough about Morgan," Durfee whispered, his eyes on the television. Jake grunted and kept eating. Yeah, it was tough. And Morgan had despised Durfee. As he thought about it, he concluded he didn't think much of the man, either. He watched the bombardier take notes. Razor's hairline was in full retreat and, as if in compensation, he sported a luxuriant mustache that he stroked compulsively.

Sammy Lundeen and Marty Greve would fly one strike while Cowboy Parker and Miles Rockwell flew the other. Little Augie and Big Augie had the standby tanker; they would man up but launch only if Grafton's plane had a mechanical problem. All the men in the room had settled into the high-backed padded chairs, and most had their feet propped up on the arms of the chairs in front of them. A more casual-looking crowd would be difficult to find. From hard experience they all knew that forced relaxation was the best way to control the rising agitation of stomach and nerves as launch time neared. Perceptible nervousness being contagious, enforced cool was the unwritten law.

When Abe Steiger finished listing the targets on the television, the camera panned to Clouds, the duty weatherman. Everyone's eyes zeroed in on the charts at the end of Clouds's pointer. "Not a good evening, gentlemen. Overcast and raining throughout the Gulf of Tonkin, Hainan Island, and most of North Vietnam. This layer extends inland to the backbone range of mountains that divides Vietnam from Laos and Cambodia. Tops should be about eighteen thousand feet, winds out of the northeast at twelve to fifteen knots on the surface. Currently seas are running six to eight feet out of the southeast. We'll have the Winds Aloft Chart in a moment. Forecast is for freshening winds and seas and continued rain and clouds for at least the next twelve hours. To the south, however, from a point about fifty miles south of Da Nang, the clouds begin to break up. Later today when the sun rises, the folks down there should have a reasonably nice day with scattered clouds and scattered showers." Charts of the winds and temperatures aloft appeared on the screen, and Clouds went over them.

Jake closed his eyes for a moment. He could feel the movement of the ship in the seaway. Back on the fantail, five hundred fifty feet behind the ship's center of gravity, the movement would be pronounced. It was going to be a bad night to get aboard.

"And now back to Mister Steiger, who has an entry in the 'Name the Dirty Baby' contest." Steiger reappeared on the screen, all ears and glasses and teeth. He held up a six-inch doll, an obscenely voluptuous female. The camera panned to the figure that Steiger held with a fingertip on each side of the waist.

"This entry comes from Ready Three," Steiger said as the camera lingered on the Dirty Baby. "Looks like Sonny Bob Battles sent this in. 'Puss-less Peggy, the Olongapo Pussycat.'" Somewhere in the studio one person clapped, then the screen went blank.

"That Steiger has the filthiest mind on this whole ship," Razor announced to no one in particular. It was common knowledge that Steiger rarely received entries to his contest but made up most of them himself.

"No, he doesn't," Jake replied. "He's just trying to stay sane." He knew time hung heavy for Steiger any day he didn't receive a letter from his wife, which was most days. That was one college romance the war was going to break up sooner or later.

"He's not having much luck at it," Razor said. "By the way, you look terrible. Are you feeling okay?" he asked as he stroked his lip hair and regarded Grafton obliquely, perhaps checking, Jake thought, for telltale traces of impending nervous collapse.

"Fit as a goddamn fiddle," the pilot replied disgustedly and left his seat to check his mailbox, a small shelf with his name on it among the many similar shelves in a converted bookcase under the television. There was a letter from his parents and one from Linda, his girl. He tried to remember when she had last written; in the past three months her literary output had dropped dramatically. He tucked her letter into the cigarette pocket on the left sleeve of his flight suit, having decided to save the letter and read it in the air. On a tanker flight, staying awake was sometimes the challenge of the evening.

One of the chiefs from Maintenance Control brought in the maintenance logs on the assigned planes and left them on the desk in the rear of the ready room. Jake picked out his book. He read each discrepancy, or "gripe," that had been written for the last ten flights. Serious problems that affected the safety of the plane were "down gripes" and had to be repaired before the machine could be flown again. Less serious problems, or "up gripes," would be repaired as the opportunity presented itself. A plane with many minor problems could be a real headache. Since the squadron had only six tankers and each of the serviceable ones flew at least three times a day, there was always a thick stack of up gripes. He looked them over carefully, signed for the plane, and placed the metal-bound volume back in the stack.

After replenishing his coffee cup, Jake settled into a chair in a quiet corner and read his parents' letter. In the front of the room the two strike crews carefully went over their planned missions and emergency procedures.

One by one the airmen drifted out, stopping at the head, then going on to the locker room where each man stored his flight gear: G-suit, torso harness, survival vest with attached inflatable life preserver, and flying bag for helmet, oxygen mask, kneeboard, and Southeast Asia aeronautical pubs. Many pilots and BNs wore pistol holsters also.

When Jake reached the locker room most of the other crewmen were there. He opened his locker and took out the G-suit. It was covered with dried blood, as was the survival vest. He had forgotten about the blood.

He stared. The stains were dark brown, rusty, not at all like the rich, red, coppery-smelling fluid that flowed from Morgan McPherson's neck. He dropped the gear and walked to the head where he vomited the coffee and beef he had just eaten.

When his stomach was under control, he returned to the locker room. Sammy Lundeen was scraping the G-suit with his survival knife. "You can turn this stuff in after this hop and get some new gear from the parachute rigger," he said.

Razor saw Jake's ashen face. "Are you ready to fly?" he asked, his tone indicating his doubts.

"Yeah," said the pilot, taking the G-suit from Lundeen and zipping it around his legs.

"You may think you are, but it'll be my ass in that plane, too, you know."

"Listen, shithead," Lundeen snarled. "If you don't have the guts to fly tonight, why don't you just say so?"

At this, Cowboy came around the end of the aisle and watched Jake pull on his torso harness, a body suit without arms or legs to which the parachute fittings and lap fittings attached. He caught Jake's eye. "Are you ready to fly?" Jake nodded. "Then you fly," Cowboy pronounced with an edge of finality and turned away.

"Just like that?" Razor Durfee asked Cowboy's back as he jerked at one end of his mustache. "Just like that you want me to risk my life with Cool Hand?" He switched to the other tip of his lip muff. "Maybe he ought to go see Mad Jack."

Cowboy paused and regarded the bombardier coldly. "He flies and so do you, Durfee. Now shut up and get dressed."

"You aren't the skipper. This is my ass we're talking about! What gives you the right to tell me I have to fly with him?" Cowboy ignored him and walked back to his locker.

Big Augie chuckled. "Because you're a junior grade lieutenant and he's a lieutenant commander, Razor. And he's the Ops O. Or didn't they cover these fine points of military etiquette at Canoe U?"

"If you're referring to the Naval Academy, you ROTC puke—" Razor was pointing with his finger.

"Look, guys," Little interjected, "Razor's showing us how many flowers to send to his folks if he buys the farm tonight."

Big chimed in. "If your dick were as sharp as your tongue, Razor, you'd have to get a serial number tattooed on it and keep it in your safe."

Cowboy's Texas drawl silenced them. "Cut the crap, gentlemen, and get yourselves up to the flight deck. Now!"

Razor slammed his locker and spun the combination lock. He paused at the door. "If I have to go for a swim tonight, Parker, I'm gonna personally jam one of these size-twelve boots up your ass clear to my knee. And I don't give a flying fuck if you make admiral in the meantime." He gave the Augies the finger, then slammed the door behind him.

"That would cure your hemorrhoids, Cowboy," Big Augie snickered.

"Then Cowboy will be a perfect asshole," Little told his BN.

"Ah, the camaraderie of fighting men. Warms the spirit."

The Augies closed their lockers and followed Razor toward the flight deck, still exchanging quips. On his way out Parker winked at Jake and gave him a thumbs up. Jake weaved his pistol belt through the holes in his torso harness to prevent it from coming off in an ejection, then he donned his survival vest. This bulky garment contained fifteen pounds of survival gear and an inflatable life vest. He carefully checked the lanyards on the CO_2 cartridges.

Lundeen took his time dressing, and when he and Jake were the only ones still in the room he paused beside the pilot, his helmet bag in his hand. "You be careful out there tonight, okay? Don't let bastards like Razor grind you down." He slugged Jake on the arm and smiled. "Just be careful and keep the faith."

"Sure, Sammy. Sure."

Jake Grafton stepped out of the island onto the flight deck. Red light illuminated the planes and the swarms of men working in the rain. The wind drove the rain at an angle and whipped the red safety flags hanging from the bomb racks.

He found his airplane, 522, sitting just two feet short of the port bow catapult shuttle. He would only have to ease the plane forward the short distance and the shuttle would engage the tow bar on the aircraft's nose-wheel assembly. Razor was already in the cockpit. Jake did a walk-around preflight check with his flashlight set for white light because in red light any red hydraulic fluid leaking from the plane would be almost invisible. He paid careful attention to the refueling package on the underside of the fuselage, about fifteen feet forward of the tail. This feature distinguished the KA-6D tanker from the bomber version of the A-6. The tanker was a fuselage designed to carry fuel aloft and lacked the two radars, computer, and inertial navigation system of the bomber. In place of bomb racks, the external store stations each carried a 2000-pound drop tank, five of them in all, which gave the plane, with its internal tanks, a total fuel capacity of 26,000 pounds, or 13 tons. It was a load.

Satisfied, Jake mounted the ladder on the left side of the cockpit and checked the ejection seat. When he had all five safety pins removed and stored, he sat down. The plane captain, a nineteen-year-old from Oklahoma known as Maggot, stood at the top of the ladder and leaned in to help Jake strap himself to the seat.

If anyone asked, Maggot would tell him he owned this aircraft. He was responsible for its pre- and post-flight servicing, its routine inspections, and its movement from place to place aboard the ship. Devil 522 was his baby, and as a morale booster the squadron had painted his rank—airman—and name in black letters on the fuselage: AN D.E. Shutts, PC.

"Great night to be out aviating, Mister Grafton."

"If I were a flying fish, Maggot, I'd probably agree with you."

"Looking forward to getting into port?"

"Sure, how about you?"

"Yep. Can't stand working outside in all this rain. I've beat off so many times in the shower, every time it rains I get a hard on."

The pilot grinned. "Just don't fall down and break something. By the way, heard anything about your dad?"

Maggot's father had suffered a heart attack recently and no word had come through from the family asking for the son to return home on emergency leave. "Not yet, sir. I'm going to call 'em when we get to Cubi if I ain't heard nothing by then."

"Talk to Mister Lundeen in Personnel and he'll get it fixed up so you can use a government line. Won't cost you any money."

"Okay, Mister Grafton. I'll do that." Maggot was finished now, yet he lingered on the ladder. "All us plane captains were real sorry about what happened to Mister McPherson. He was an all right guy and a good officer."

Jake looked at the sailor. Wet with rain, the earnest young face glistened in the red light. He had never ridden the catapult or seen the flak and the missiles, but he respected the men who had. Did they deserve that respect? Well, at least McPherson had. "We're all going to miss him," the pilot replied.

"You gents have a good flight and catch a three wire." Maggot descended to the deck and pressed the external canopy-close button to keep the rain off the crew. Razor sat with his head back against the headrest and his eyes closed, apparently working on recovering his temper.

Jake held his helmet in his lap and looked past the edge of the flight deck into the black nothingness beyond. He hated night catapult shots. So much could happen on the way down the cat, all of it bad. Any problem would demand the pilot's instant attention even as he was recovering from the acceleration of the shot and trying to coax the plane to fly in the night air, sixty feet above the sea. He went over some of the more likely emergencies and what he would do if one occurred. He moved his left hand from the throttles to the gear handle. If an engine quits or a fire light flashes, gear up. His fingers climbed to the emergency jettison button. Push that and hold for one second. All five drop tanks will then be jettisoned. Ten thousand pounds lighter, maybe the plane will still fly on one engine. His eyes flicked to the standby gyro. Keep eight degrees nose-up no matter what. Much less and we go into the water; much more and we'll stall and go into the drink anyway. He checked the gauges: airspeed, pressure altimeter, angle-of-attack, radar altimeter, the gyro. These instruments had the information that would keep them alive. And if one of the instruments failed, he had to immediately notice that its information did not jibe with the other gauges and disregard the culprit.

He felt his stomach knot up, and automatically he reached between his legs and checked the position of the alternate firing handle for the ejection seat. There might not be time to reach the primary handle over his head.

Every moment that passed was only preparation for the coming instant when he would be catapulted out over the dark ocean just fifteen knots above stall speed in a machine near maximum gross weight—in a machine that was merely a cunning collection of complex equipment that failed too often. His life depended on the correctness of his every thought, on his touch with the stick, on the quickness of his reflexes, on the knowledge and skill he possessed. The penalty for failure would be swift and sure. And the man beside him would also pay.

What if we lose the generators? He reached back to his left to check the position of the ram-air turbine handle. A tug on this handle would cause the wind-driven emergency generator to pop out of the wing and power the flight instruments and critical cockpit lights. Closing his eyes, he began touching and identifying every switch, knob, and handle around him. He knew this cockpit better than he knew his car: he knew it better than he knew anything else in the world.

He looked down the catapult, as he had countless

times before. Beyond the deck was the end of the world. He was marooned on an island of red light adrift in a black universe. Only the here and now, this place and this time, existed.

The rain drummed on the canopy. The men on the flight deck stood motionless, waiting for the "start engines" signal. They waited like horses in the rain, resigned to their misery. The ship began its turn into the wind and the sailors leaned into the quickening breeze. The height of the plane above the deck and the buoyancy of the high pressure tires magnified the effect of the shift of the deck. The pilot could feel the motion as the ship shouldered the swells aside.

He glanced again at Razor. The BN had not changed his position, but his face appeared relaxed. Had he fully recovered from his locker room doubts, or was he just working overtime on his prelaunch cool?

He wouldn't be so damn complacent if he knew how my stomach felt, the pilot reflected. How do these BNs do it? How did Morgan do it? The BNs sit there and ride these pigs to hell and back with almost no control over their fate. Day in and day out they climb into that right-hand seat.

The men who rode the right-side seats, who mastered the complex equipment and conquered the natural reactions of their stomachs, were professionals with great pride in their abilities. Like most of the pilots who respected the naval flight officers they flew with, Jake paid them tribute by bowing to the unexplainable. He never once thought to ask a BN why he continued to do his job. To do so would mean asking the same question of himself. So he regarded the bombardiers' motivations as mysterious, as inexplicable as love, faith, or loyalty.

The deck loudspeakers blared. The time had come. Grafton and Durfee put on their helmets. The plane captain twirled his fingers for the starting sequence.

When both engines were at idle and all the aircraft's systems were functioning properly, Jake and Razor turned on their red, L-shaped flashlights. Jake clipped his to the front of his survival vest. He tapped the standby gyro and Razor nodded. The bombardier would hold his flashlight in his hand and keep it focused on the standby gyro for the critical seconds after launch. This way, if both generators failed, the pilot could still see the attitude reference. The gyro, only three inches in diameter, would provide vital information without electrical power for at least thirty seconds. That would be more than enough. They would be either safe or dead long before it spun down. Jake spread and locked the wings and lowered the flaps.

Now the taxi director gave Jake the signal to come forward. He released the parking brake and eased the laden plane to the waiting shuttle. He felt a jolt as the metal pieces mated. The pilot jammed the throttles forward to the stops and cycled the controls as he watched the stabilator—the horizontal tail—and flaperons move in his mirrors. He put the heel of his left hand behind the throttles and curled his fingers around the catapult grip. This would prevent an inadvertent throttle retardation during the catapult stroke. One more look at the gauges and another wiggle for the stick. Engine temperatures normal, controls free and easy: all was as it should be.

At full power the machine quivered like a hound on a leash. His heart pounded, and he could feel his temples throb.

"You ready?" he asked Razor.

"I was born ready. Let 'er rip."

Jake placed his head back in the headrest and used his left thumb to flip the exterior-light master switch on the catapult grip. He saw in his rear-view mirror that the light on top of the tail had come on.

The catapult officer saluted and swung his yellow wand in a long arc until it touched the deck, then brought it up to the horizontal where it froze, pointing down the catapult track.

Soon . . . any second . . . it's coming—

The catapult fired.

FIVE

The altimeter recorded their upward progress. 10,000, 11,000, 12,000 . . . They were still in clouds.

"Looks like the weather guys were wrong about the tops of this stuff," Razor remarked. He fished a packet of chewing gum from his left sleeve pocket and held it out. "Want one?" Apparently the scene in the locker room was history.

"Yeah, open it for me."

They climbed in a constant turn that kept the plane on a circle with a five-mile radius. The center of the circle was the carrier.

"Wonder how high this stuff goes?" Razor said.

"To the moon, probably. Maybe even halfway to Mars."

Jake leveled the Intruder at 20,000 feet, still circling the carrier. "Better give 'em the word," he told the bombardier.

Razor held his oxygen mask to his face. "Tanker Control, Devil Five Two Two."

"Go ahead, Five Two Two."

"We're in the clag at base plus twelve." On unscrambled radio transmissions the true altitude was the sum of the reported altitude plus the never-mentioned base number, tonight a positive eight. "It's solid all the way up. Do you want us to find the tops, over?"

The radio was silent for several seconds. Then the reply came back: "Go on up to base plus twenty-two."

"Wilco." Jake pushed the throttles forward and eased the stick back. The altimeter began to climb. Razor chomped on his gum. "Gonna be a bad night at Black Rock for the fighter pukes if they need gas down below," he observed over the ICS. Tanking was a precision maneuver that required good visibility, especially at night. The aircraft needing fuel was vectored to the vicinity of the tanker, but the pilot of the thirsty plane had to acquire the tanker visually and execute a rendezvous, a join up into close formation. Once the two aircraft were flying side-by-side they could fly into a cloud, but they could not safely join up in one. Tonight the sky seemed to consist of nothing but clouds. But at 27,000 feet, the men saw the glow of the moon. At 28,000 they bounded out of the clouds. Jake climbed another 500 feet above the ragged tops before leveling off. The pale moonlight made the cloudscape look like heaps of cotton.

"Tanker Control, Five Two Two. Tops are at base plus twenty."

"Roger. Two customers are on their way up. Request you give them three each."

Jake clicked the mike twice in reply, then let the plane drift on up to 30,000 feet where he leveled at 250 knots and engaged the autopilot. It held the bird nicely in a twelve-degree left turn. In a few moments he saw the first Phantom emerge from the clouds, a winking red anticollision light beaconing through the darkness. The fighter pilot was on an opposite course but soon saw him and turned hard to intercept. Jake turned on the fuel-transfer panel and set the fuel counter for three thousand pounds. He streamed the drogue, a basket twenty-six inches in diameter that resembled a badminton shuttlecock, on the end of a fifty-foot hose. The unit was ready to transfer fuel when the hose was fully extended. After a ton and a half of jet fuel had been pumped, the transfer would automatically cease.

The lead fighter closed smartly on a forty-five-degree bearing; the second F-4 was several miles away on the same rendezvous course. Both fighters flew inside Jake's circle to close the distance. "Here they come," Jake said.

In less than a minute the first Phantom joined on the tanker's left wing. As Jake watched, the refueling probe emerged from the right side of the plane beneath the canopy and locked out at a forty-five-degree angle. Jake made a circular motion with his red flashlight and received in reply two flashes from the fighter's rear cockpit. Then the fighter slid back and disappeared astern. Jake disengaged the autopilot—it had a tendency to porpoise the plane when the receiving aircraft pushed in the drogue—and devoted his attention to maintaining a smooth, steady course on the great circle.

The fighter pilot managed to fly his probe into the drogue on his first attempt. When he pushed the drogue six feet toward the tanker, the green light on the refueling panel in the A-6 illuminated, and the counter began to meter the fuel in hundred-pound increments. Jake noticed the second fighter slide in alongside his left wing, its grinning shark's mouth and yellow eye just visible in the sweep of the tanker's anticollision light. The bombardier reported to the ship that the tanker was "sweet," that is, it could transfer fuel, so the spare tanker on deck would not be needed. When the first plane had finished, Razor reset the counter and Grafton flashed his light. The second Phantom moved in behind the Intruder as the first one took up a cruise position on the right wing. This pilot made two attempts before he captured the drogue. The maneuver required a delicate, sure touch with the stick and throttles, especially if the planes were bouncing in turbulence. One frustrated fighter jockey had been heard to lament, "It's like trying to stick a banana up a wildcat's ass."

When it had taken on its allotted fuel, the second plane crossed to the lead fighter's right wing. Razor visually checked both planes to make sure they weren't behind the tanker in the unlikely event that the drogue and hose separated during retraction. When the panel indicator showed that the drogue was stowed, the bombardier glanced again at the lead Phantom. A confirming red light flashed from the fighter's rear cockpit.

The two hunters turned away and took up a course to their assigned station one hundred fifty miles to the northwest of the ship. They constituted the Barrier Combat Air Patrol, the BARCAP, charged with intercepting and shooting down any unidentified aircraft coming out of North Vietnam.

Razor watched them disappear into the moonlit sky. He keyed his radio mike and told the ship that tanking was completed.

The ship replied, "Roger, request you fly a forty-mile arc around the ship and see how extensive this cloud cover is."

Jake leveled the wings and descended until he was just above the clouds. Although he had slowed to maximum endurance airspeed, 220 knots, they still had the illusion of great speed as the cloud tops raced beneath. Occasionally they collided with a silver ridge, bored through, and popped out the other side. Because of the glass-smooth flying at this altitude, five and a half miles above the ocean, the men felt as though their machine were at rest in space while the earth whirled beneath them.

After they had circled the ship at forty miles, they

reported that the clouds were unbroken and returned to the five-mile circle. The great tedium began. With the machine on autopilot, there was little for the crew to do except monitor the fuel and engine instruments and check the night sky for other aircraft. Convinced all was well, Jake removed his gloves and wedged them into the narrow crevice between the left side of the instrument panel and the windscreen. Then he drew his girl's letter from his sleeve pocket. He read it in the tiny circle of red light from the pencil spotlight mounted on the overhead canopy bow.

With every line he felt a growing despondency. On the first page she recalled the good times they had shared. On the second, she told him she was marrying another man. The third and final page contained her list of all the reasons their relationship would not have worked. He read the letter again slowly, replaced it in its envelope, and returned the envelope to his sleeve pocket.

After his first cruise, when the squadron had flown in from the ship to Whidbey Island, she had come to meet him. She had watched while he climbed from the cockpit and walked across the ramp to her, waiting until he had reached her before opening her arms to welcome him. The other women had run toward their men. He should have had an inkling then.

Their last time together, that Sunday in San Francisco, they had walked from Fisherman's Wharf to the Corinthian columns at the Palace of Fine Arts. They had ridden the cable cars, listened to the folk singers, and watched the soaring birds as the sun fired the pastel city. She had said, "You don't belong in the navy. My God, Jake, you pull off the road to look at a rainbow. Why would you want to be part of that system?

"And so many navy fliers we've known have died in

crashes. I always wonder, after I've seen or talked to you, whether I'll ever see you alive again." Why hadn't he known then?

The radio squawked. Tanker Control directed them to proceed northwest to tank the BARCAP again. The fighters had enough fuel to stay airborne until recovery time, but it was prudent to have more than enough in case the enemy attacked the task force. This time the tanker rendezvoused on the fighters. When each fighter had received another twenty-five hundred pounds, the tanker returned at 220 knots to the five-mile orbit.

They tuned the second radio, a luxury the tanker had that the bombers did not possess, to the Strike frequency and finally heard Cowboy Parker, then Sammy Lundeen, call feet wet. The challenge of night landings aboard the carrier lay before them all.

The minutes went by slowly. Grafton had to work to stay awake in spite of his recent fourteen-hour sleep. After a check of the altitude in the cockpit, he took off his mask and helmet and placed them in his lap. The noise level was loud but not intolerable. He extracted a plastic baby bottle from a pocket of his survival vest and poured some water down the back of his neck. That helped wake him up. He took a swig of the warm water, which tasted of plastic. He poured some in his hair and rubbed it on his face. Then he poured more on his hair and rubbed his head vigorously. He felt it trickle down his forehead and nose, and one little rivulet scooted down the back of his neck. He capped the bottle, put it away, then replaced his helmet and oxygen mask.

"Five Two Two, are you up?" It was Lundeen's voice.

"Affirm," he replied over the radio.

"Go Tactical," was the reply.

Jake rotated the radio-channel selector knob to the

squadron's assigned frequency, waited five seconds, then said, "Devil's up."

"Where are you, Jake?"

"Overhead at base plus twenty-two."

"I'll be there to see you in a bit."

Click, click.

"Let's go secure."

Razor keyed the ICS as Jake turned on the scrambler. "What do you think?"

Grafton shrugged. He had no idea why Sammy wanted to rendezvous over the ship. Maybe he needed fuel. Maybe he had a problem with his airplane. Maybe he just wanted to grin and wave and fly along together under the moon and stars because Jake was his friend and Sammy was like that. They would soon know.

The pilot checked the amount of fuel left in each drop and internal tank. He did this by depressing a button for the appropriate tank and getting a reading on the fuel gauge. Normally the gauge gave only a total figure, but like every other electrical or mechanical device, the totalizer could fail. The careful man who hoped to eventually die in bed always checked. The arithmetic of fuel calculation was unforgiving of error: there were no negative numbers. They had transferred eleven thousand pounds, had used two thousand in their launch and climbout, and were now consuming a mere four thousand pounds per hour at maximum endurance airspeed. After an hour and a half of flight, Jake reckoned, they should have seven thousand pounds remaining. The gauge totals came to seventy-two hundred pounds. Close enough. All the drop tanks were empty, as were the wing tanks. The two fuselage tanks held the remaining fuel. With twenty or thirty minutes to go until he crossed the ramp of the carrier, he should recover with about five thousand pounds. He leaned back in the seat.

"How far to Da Nang?" he asked Razor. That would

be the nearest friendly airfield ashore if he couldn't get aboard the ship for any reason.

The bombardier consulted his briefing notes. "One fifty," he told the pilot.

"Better verify that with the ship." Razor asked the question of the controller at the radar screen in Strike Ops, deep inside the big ship 30,000 feet below. After a pause, the controller informed them the distance was one hundred forty miles and gave them the heading. Both men jotted it down on their kneeboards.

Sammy should be coming in from the northwest. Jake began to search that quadrant for the telltale flashing-red anticollision light. In less than a minute it caught his eye. He watched the light grow brighter as the Intruder came on and waited for it to change course to rendezvous, which would mean that the bomber crew had seen them. When no such change occurred after fifteen seconds, he keyed the radio. "I'm at your ten o'clock, Sam." Now the other plane began to turn.

Lundeen joined up on Grafton's left wing. "Look me over, Jake," he said. "I've got the lead." With the lead change, Grafton now had the responsibility of maintaining the separation between the two aircraft.

Grafton clicked his mike and retarded the throttles. He slid aft and down so that the other Intruder filled the windscreen. "Hit them with your white flashlight," he instructed Razor. McPherson would not have needed prompting.

The beam played over the pale gray skin of the bomber. The bomb racks were empty; the copper arming wires glistened in the weak beam. Each mechanical bomb fuse had a wind-driven propeller vane on the nose that the arming wire held immobile while the weapon waited on the rack. As the bomb fell away, the wire was extracted. The wind spun the vane for a preset number of seconds, and the weapon was thus armed a safe distance from the aircraft. An absence of arming wires on a bomber returning from a mission meant that all the bombs it had dropped had been duds; the wires had prevented the propeller vanes from spinning and arming the bombs.

Razor shone the flashlight over the right wing, then began to work aft toward the tail. Behind the wing root, on the right side of the fuselage in front of the horizontal stabilizer, they saw the holes. Many tiny jagged holes.

"Work the light aft," Jake said. More holes splattered the right side of the vertical tail and horizontal stabilizer. Jake eased the tanker in until less than ten feet separated him from the bomber's tail. He could feel the wash of the other plane forcing his left wing down, and he compensated with right stick.

"Sammy, you have a hundred or so little holes on the right side, aft of the wings, on the fuselage and the tail. Looks like flak bursts."

"Check the pitot tube."

Jake's eyes flicked to the top of the bomber's tail. The tube that measured the bird's speed through the atmosphere was gone. He told Lundeen.

"I thought so," Lundeen sighed. "The airspeed indicator reads one hundred ten knots. Better check the other side, too."

Jake slid across and Razor moved the light along the tail and forward up the fuselage. They found one medium-sized hole in the port flap.

"Now take a squint at the gear doors," Lundeen directed.

Jake slipped forward until they were immediately beneath the bomber. The doors were stained with grease and yellow preservative but appeared intact. If they weren't, the tires within would probably be flat. Razor informed the bomber crew that they could find no other damage.

"We have no airspeed indicator, the computer's

frozen solid as an ice cube, the radar altimeter's kaput, the TACAN is intermittent, and our ICS is screwed up. ADF isn't working, either. Let me drop the hook and let's see if it comes down." It did and Grafton told him so. "Maybe we had better go down on your wing," Sammy said.

"Okay," Jake said. He slid out to the left and pulled abreast the bomber. "I've got the lead now. Let's go to Approach and you tell them your story."

"Uh, while we're doing that how about giving me a sip? I could use a grand."

Jake checked the fuel indicator again. He wasn't going to have any reserve as it was, and he had already informed Tanker Control he had no more gas to give. But Sammy wouldn't ask if he didn't need it. He flipped the power switch on the tanker package and streamed the drogue.

"You're cutting it pretty goddamned fine," Razor complained.

"I'll get just as wet as you if we punch out," the pilot said. "That could be us over there."

Razor voiced no more objections.

After an extensive conversation with Approach, the two Intruders were issued Marshall instructions. "Your Marshall one six zero degrees at two four. Pushover at zero one four eight. Five Two Two will drop Five Oh Six on the ball, be vectored downwind, and trap on the next pass."

Razor repeated the controller's instructions, received an acknowledgment, then looked at Grafton. "Nine thousand feet at twenty-four miles."

"I agree."

Marshall points were holding fixes whereby aircraft were stacked to await recovery at night or in weather too bad for a visual approach. The lowest altitude that could be assigned was five thousand feet at a distance of twenty miles from the ship. Each subsequent aircraft would receive a fix a thousand feet higher and a mile farther away. So the fixes were defined as five thousand feet and twenty miles, six thousand and twenty-one, seven thousand and twenty-two, and so on. The altitude was omitted from the radio call because it is always fifteen less than the mileage assigned. When the pushover time, or moment of descent, arrived, the pilots were expected to have their planes exactly at the Marshall fix inbound to the ship.

Pushover times were assigned at one-minute intervals, and because approaches were flown at 250 knots until the landing gear was extended at twelve miles, the planes would be strung out one minute apart on their approach to the ship. Such was the theory at any rate, thought Jake, and it worked out in practice most of the time, except for nights such as this when the weather was so crummy.

He listened as the other aircraft checked into Marshall. They were all assigned lower altitudes and earlier approach times. On this recovery, there would be only six aircraft: the two Phantoms that had been the BARCAP, the two A-6 bombers, the EA-6B Prowler electronic warfare aircraft, and Jake's KA-6D tanker. An E-2 Hawkeye early-warning turboprop was also airborne, but since it had such a low rate of fuel consumption it would remain aloft for its usual four hours and land on the second recovery. On this recovery Jake's tanker would be the last plane to come aboard. If Lundeen crashed on deck or couldn't be towed out of the landing area, then only the tanker would be stranded aloft low on fuel. This couldn't be helped because someone had to lead Sammy down.

When Lundeen had his fuel, Jake lowered the nose of the tanker, let the airspeed increase to 250 knots, then retarded the throttles. "Turn your mirror a little." Razor obligingly tweaked the rear-view mirror on the canopy rail above his right leg. Jake could now see his wingman with only a glance at the mirror. He reached for the light panel and secured his anticollision light, which would reflect off the clouds and disorient Lundeen.

They skimmed a hummock, then left the moon and stars and entered a dark world. At first Lundeen maintained about twenty feet between his cockpit and Jake's right wingtip. But as they descended through the sodden clouds, the rainwater streaked in horizontal lines across his canopy, distorting the fading lights of the tanker. So Sammy moved closer until less than ten feet separated his plexiglas from the tanker's wingtip. Sammy began to perspire. He knew that if he made one error—a little more or less adjustment to the stick or throttles than necessary—he would slide away and lose the tanker in the blackness, or the planes would drift together, wings would tear off, and the machines would cartwheel into the ocean.

Marty Greve informed Lundeen, "The TACAN's dead." Because the ICS was malfunctioning, the bombardier had to shout over the cockpit noise. Without TACAN, the radio navigation aid, finding the carrier would be possible only with the bomber's radar. Of course, Lundeen could receive radar vectors from the ship as long as the radio functioned, but without accurate airspeed information he was getting too close to disaster for comfort. Once the gear came down, the angle-of-attack indicator would become accurate enough to use. He had to stay with Grafton so that no matter what else went wrong electrically he could locate the ship.

As long as he had Grafton . . . "How much gas, Marty?" Sammy asked, keeping his eyes fixed on the tanker.

"Three thousand," came the shouted reply. It would be tight.

Jake leveled at 9000 feet and flew toward the fix. As

he crossed it, Razor reported to the ship, "Five Two Two in Marshall at time three nine. State four point eight."

Marty Greve made his report. "Five Oh Six in Marshall at time three nine. State two point nine."

Jake couldn't resist rubbing it in. "Hear that?" he asked Razor. "If we hadn't given them that gas those bastards would be sucking their seat cushions up their asses right now."

In the bomber Marty Greve leaned toward his pilot and remarked, as casually as he could at the top of his lungs, "We should have gotten some more fuel from Jake."

"There are other guys up here who may need a drop, too." Lundeen's voice broke up several times on the intermittent ICS, so just to be sure Greve understood, he added, "We can make it with what we have."

Greve merely waggled his eyebrows. He had learned long ago that a king-sized ego was as necessary to a good pilot as his flight suit. Pilots owned the space they occupied. Lundeen thought he could fly his machine through the eye of a needle and was willing to bet his life on it. The navy took them from all walks of life and winnowed out anyone who showed signs of self-doubt —in other words, anyone who carried the usual baggage of humility that weighed down most of the human race—and retained only those with balls the size of grapefruit and a brain the size of a pea, or so Marty liked to announce after a couple of drinks at the officers' club. Still, he reflected, Lundeen had a remarkable ability to look disaster in the face, flip it a bird, and go merrily on his way.

Tonight the bombardier's eyes kept swiveling back to the fuel gauge. Greve had not been able to find the target on the first bomb run. Lundeen had insisted on flying a racetrack pattern and making a second attempt. Lundeen was driving, so that is what they did. But as they turned onto the final bearing for the second try, they had run right into a flak trap. Lundeen had cussed and yelled and threatened the bombardier's life if he didn't break the target out of the clutter this time. He did. After the drop, Lundeen had turned hard and gone back to drop the Rockeyes on the concentration of antiaircraft weapons, and the plane had been peppered again. The Rockeyes were cluster bombs: each 500-pound cannister contained almost two hundred fifty bomblets that spread out to form an oval three hundred feet long by two hundred feet wide. Each bomblet contained enough wallop to disable a tank.

They had used too much fuel, stayed too long at full throttle. Lundeen had intentionally not told the ship about the little drink they needed from the tanker so that they would never have to explain that Marty couldn't find the target on the first pass. The pilot would never tell, would pound him on the back and roar to the world that Marty Greve was the best goddamn "beenie" who ever strapped an A-6 to his ass. But right now, Greve thought, he would admit to any sin short of sodomy if that would squeeze another grand or two of gas into the tanks.

Even as he worried, the refueling drogue on the tanker streamed again. Greve pointed out the waiting hose to Lundeen, who was not too proud to accept a gift and maneuvered aft for a plug. When the green light went out on the tanker package, their fuel state was almost thirty-eight hundred pounds.

"Jake's a helluva guy," Greve said.

The Approach controller announced a time check and Razor and Greve set their clocks precisely at the mark. Jake crossed the fix inbound at 0144 and settled into a lazy turn with ninety degrees of heading change each minute.

On the right wing, Lundeen moved up and aft until he was looking at the red kneeboard light on the canopy rail near Razor's right knee. When the clamshell speed brakes, or "boards," began to open on the wingtip, they would block the kneeboard light from his view. If Lundeen missed the opening, or "cracking," of the boards he would not be able to slow his craft to the same degree as the lead aircraft, even with his throttles at idle. From Lundeen's point of view, it would appear as if he were sliding forward in relation to the leader.

At thirty seconds to pushover, Greve warned him and he intensified his concentration. "Any time," the bombardier hollered just as the red light in the tanker's cockpit disappeared. Lundeen squeezed out his speed brakes and jockeyed the throttles. Jake had cracked his boards, waited a half-second for Lundeen to react, then brought them on out to the full open position. That was the way it should be done but too many pilots forgot.

"Five Two Two leaving Marshall on time with Five Oh Six in tow. State three point eight."

"Five Oh Six leaving Marshall with three point six," Greve chimed in. Jake had kept just enough fuel for an extra circuit around the pattern, which he knew he would have to fly after he dropped the bomber on the glide slope.

Approach acknowledged and directed a frequency change. Both bombardiers changed the radio channel, then checked in.

At 5000 feet Jake slowed his descent and changed course to intercept the final bearing inbound to the carrier. They were still in the goo. At 4000 Lundeen sneaked a glance at the radar altimeter, which he saw was not functioning. The black boxes containing the electronics for the instrument were in the rear fuselage, presumably damaged by flak.

At 2000 Jake reduced his rate of descent still further and retracted the speed brakes. Sammy stayed right with him. With the throttles back they descended to 1200 feet and leveled there, still in the clouds, closing on the ship at 250 knots as they bounced in the rough air. They were twelve miles from the ship when the first F-4 missed all four of the arresting gear wires and caromed back into the air. "Bolter, bolter, bolter," the LSO shouted over the radio.

"Boards," Jake directed over the radio, and brought out the speed brakes. "Gear," he added, and dropped the landing gear and flaps.

Lundeen stayed right with him through the transition to landing configuration. "Just like the Blue Angels," he told Marty with a hint of pride in his voice, which did not escape the bombardier. A successful pilot—who would be any pilot still alive—found satisfaction in the smallest things: a good rendezvous, a well-flown instrument approach, a smooth configuration change while flying on instruments. Flight instructors nurtured this tendency from the first day the fledgling pilot crawled into the cockpit by criticizing and advising on every detail of the flyer's art. Marty Greve had once witnessed a ten-minute conversation on the best technique of bringing a taxiing aircraft smoothly to a stop.

The turbulence was not doing Lundeen's equilibrium any good at all. He no longer knew if his wings were level or whether he was in a turn or dive. The only points of reference were the tanker's wing and ghostly fuselage. More rain than ever streamed along his canopy.

The tanker crew tuned the backup radio to the LSO's second frequency in time to hear Cowboy Parker trap aboard. Alternate landing frequencies were assigned to minimize the danger that the landing signal officer's comments to the pilot on final approach would be misconstrued by the pilot immediately behind to be for him. Jake heard the second F-4 bolter and be given a downwind heading. Every plane that boltered was vectored downwind and turned into the landing pattern again with at least a five-mile straightaway on final approach. On a bad night with, say, twenty planes trying to get aboard, the bolter pattern could become jammed, the frequencies would be crammed with instructions, and the LSO would have to fight to edge in a word of advice to the pilots on the ball. Fortunately only a few planes were recovering tonight. Now Jake heard the EA-6B successfully trap.

Jake slowed to 116 knots. The angle-of-attack needle and the indexer—a stoplight arrangement on the left windscreen rail he could see as he looked toward the landing area—showed he was fast. He elected to stay fast, to counteract sudden drops in airspeed caused by turbulence, until he was on the glide slope.

They were still in thick clouds. "Five Two Two, you are approaching glide path. Begin descent." Jake brought the power back and saw the rate-of-descent needle sag. "Five Two Two, you are up and on the glide path." Jake clicked the mike. "Five Two Two, call your needles."

Jake glanced at the automatic carrier landing system, or ACLS, which provided a glide slope and azimuth display from information data-linked with a computer aboard the ship. "Needles right and centered," he responded, which meant the instrument cross hairs showed he was slightly left of centerline but on the glide path.

"Disregard your needles. You are slightly high and right. Come left and increase your rate of descent." Apparently the two planes in formation were deceiving the shipboard computer. Jake concentrated on the instruments, scanning the heading, the rate of descent, the indexer. His eyes roved constantly over the panel. They swept every instrument, taking in the information that constantly had to be correlated with the reality of descending on a 3.5-degree glide slope in a sensitive machine in unstable air. Now he took off some power and trimmed the nose up a click to get to 112 knots and the on-speed indication on the indexer. Then he checked the pressure altimeter and matched it with the radar altimeter. "You are on glide path and on centerline. Come right two." Grafton obeyed.

The LSO spoke to the Phantom ahead. "Deck heaving, keep it coming . . . a little power . . . not too much! . . . bolter, bolter, bolter!"

"Five Two Two is on glide path, slightly left of centerline." Jake dipped the right wing to correct. He was passing 500 feet. How low does this stuff go? "Five Two Two, on glide path, on centerline."

They broke out of the clouds at 300 feet. "Ball," Razor told him.

"Five Two Two, three-quarters of a mile. Five Oh Six, call the ball."

Marty Greve keyed his mike. "Five Oh Six, Intruder ball, three point three." Sammy Lundeen kept his eyes on the tanker until he saw Grafton retract his speed brakes, add power, and break away to the left. He heard his roommate tell Approach, "Five Two Two breaking away," and heard the instruction in reply for Grafton to climb to 1200 feet and turn downwind.

Lundeen looked forward. There was the ship. He saw the ball on the left side of the landing area, the white centerline lights, and the red drop lights. These drop lights traveled down the back of the ship to the water and provided a three-dimensional reference. Instead of a windshield wiper, the A-6 used bleed air from the engines to clear rainwater from the windshield, and Greve already had it on. The indexer showed the plane was on-speed, and the ball told Lundeen he was slightly low. He made the correction.

"I've got vertigo," he told Marty. He involuntarily took his eyes from the ball and glanced at the visual display indicator to reassure himself that the wings were level. He felt as though he were in a left turn and had to resist the urge to lower the right wing to correct.

His eyes told him he was wings level, so his instincts were lying.

"Wings level," Greve shouted. Lundeen tore his eyes back to the ball and the landing area. The ball was seesawing between the reference lights, revealing the ship's up and down motion in the sea. He fought the nausea that came with spatial disorientation and the impulse to correct to every twitch of the glide slope indicator light, the "ball." Out of instinct he nudged the throttles forward slightly.

"Too much power," the LSO advised.

"Wings level," Marty reassured him again. Lundeen jammed on the power as they sank in the turbulence created by the ship's island, then jerked it off as they reached smoother air.

Then he crossed the ramp. Miraculously, the ball was dropping, which meant the deck was coming up to meet the descending plane. The wheels smashed into the steel, the nose pitched forward, and Sammy Lundeen thrust the throttles to the firewall and automatically thumbed the speed brakes closed. He felt the welcome jolt as the aircraft began a rapid deceleration. He jerked the throttles back to idle, and the muscles in his body began to relax. "Hot damn," he told Marty. All carrier landings were no more than controlled crashes.

On the downwind leg Jake Grafton knew Lundeen had trapped because there had been no bolter call. His attention turned to the Phantom wingman whose fuel state was becoming critical. The wingman had boltered twice, while the lead trapped on his second attempt. Built for supersonic flight, the fighters had flight characteristics that were a result of design compromises. Their approach speeds were thirty knots faster than the A-6's, and they were harder to handle at landing speeds. At low altitudes with their gear down their engines drank fuel at a gluttonous rate.

As Jake turned to the final bearing the lone F-4 still

in the air, Stagecoach 203, called the ball with four thousand pounds. "Why don't they send him to Da Nang or up to tank?" Razor asked on the ICS.

"I dunno," Grafton replied as he dropped the gear and flaps for his approach. "They know what they're doing." Maybe, he added to himself.

As he slowed to an on-speed indication on the indexer he heard the tanker that had just launched check in on one of the landing frequencies. "He must have problems," Jake said to Razor.

Now there were no "sweet" tankers—tankers capable of transferring fuel—in the air. Undoubtedly, Jake thought, the ship would soon shoot the manned spare sitting on deck. If they waited much longer the lone fighter still trying to get aboard would not have enough fuel to reach an altitude at which he could rendezvous with the tanker. The fighter pilot on the ball surely knew that, too, and that knowledge would not help his concentration.

"Bolter, bolter, bolter!" the LSO shouted over the air. The frustration could be heard in his voice. "Two Oh Three, you are overcorrecting. You are trying to chase the ball. Just average it out and be smooth." "Be smooth" was the universal admonishment for every piloting sin. Play the stick and throttles like Paganini, as if he could have fiddled in a jolting jet beating through turbulent air with rain soaking up all the light.

"Five Two Two, you are approaching glide path, begin your descent. . . . Five Two Two, up and on the glide path. . . . Five Two Two, call your needles."

"Up and right."

"Concur. Fly the needles."

Jake Grafton concentrated on the ACLS gauge, which meant he looked at it about half the time and scanned the altimeter, angle-of-attack, rate of descent, and gyro the other half. Flying the needles was much easier than flying the ball since the carrier's computer stabilized the electronic glide slope regardless of the ship's motion in the heavy swells. The optical landing system was stabilized in pitch and roll, that is, in the horizontal plane, but it could not compensate for instability in the vertical plane, the up-and-down motion of the ship known as heave.

As he descended he heard the pilot of the Phantom inquire about tanking or diverting to Da Nang, the nearest jet base ashore. "Da Nang is closed temporarily due to a rocket attack and the tanker is dry. We'll get some gas in the air shortly."

"Shortly may be just a little too late," was the acid reply.

The tanker broke out of the clouds at 280 feet. Instantly Jake made the transition from instrument flight to visual flight, scanning the angle-of-attack, the ball, and the lineup while Razor made the ball report. Razor had the bleed air blasting the rain from the windscreen. As Jake approached the ship he began to see the light—the ball—cycle up and down between the green reference lights. He went from high to low to high again without any movement of the stick or throttles. He tried to ensure the high cycles were no farther away from the correct, centered ball, than the low cycles. Each cycle took about eight seconds as the plane closed on the ship.

Then they were there. The drop lights swept under the nose and the ball began to rise, indicating the plane had flattened its approach angle or the deck was descending. Jake pulled off a handful of power, moved the stick forward a smidgen, then pulled it aft as he shoved the power back on. This maneuver violated every rule in the book—it was called "diving for the deck"—but it was a sure way to get aboard when you had to. The main wheels struck the deck with a tremendous thud and the nose wheel fell the three feet to the rigid steel as the main gear oleos compressed.

The engines were winding toward full power when the deceleration threw both men forward against their unyielding shoulder harnesses.

"Shit hot," Razor said. "God, I hate this fucking business."

The taxi director led the plane to the front of the island. When it was parked, one of the squadron maintenance chiefs lowered the pilot's ladder, opened the canopy, and clambered up. Jake tilted the left side of his helmet away from his ear so he could hear the chief. "We're going to fill your internal tanks and shoot you again," the chief shouted over the whine of the idling engines. "The spare tanker went down. This is our last good machine." "Down" meant that the aircraft had mechanical problems that had to be corrected before it could fly again. Even as the chief spoke the purple-shirted men in the Fuels Division dragged a hose to the tanker and attached it. Jake depressurized the tanks and gave the men a thumbs up.

"We're going again," the pilot told Razor on the ICS "The spare crapped out."

"Lucky us. How come we gotta go again? How come they don't have another crew out here? Get the chief over here. Tell him to get the spare tanker crew to come hotseat this thing. Cowboy's got it in for me because I gassed him in the locker room."

"He just landed, Razor. Can it, willya?"

"When the weather gets cruddy I get stuck going up and down like a goddamn yo-yo. It happens every time. Doesn't anyone else want a little of this fun?" Jake ignored the bombardier, who continued to fume on the ICS.

The refueling took five minutes. During that time the sour tanker trapped, but Stagecoach 203 boltered again in a shower of sparks as the hook point scraped the steel of the deck.

Perhaps the air boss would order the barricade

rigged. That giant net of nylon webbing, raised on stanchions just forward of the last arresting gear wire, could stop an aircraft on deck with only minor damage to the plane. But the pilot had to get his machine down on deck before he went into the barricade or there would be a catastrophe. Perhaps the air boss was weighing the pros and cons with the air operations officer. Jake glanced up at the air boss's throne in the glassed-in compartment high on the island known as Pri-Fly. He was glad he didn't have to make that decision.

"Too bad the barricade stanchions are out of whack," Razor commented.

Jake felt embarrassed. That information must have been in the brief, and he had missed it. Damn! He wasn't functioning as he should tonight. And he had given Sammy that gas without telling the ship. Razor had been right—he shouldn't have flown tonight.

When the fueling was complete and the canopy once more closed, the tanker was directed forward to the foul line at the right edge of the landing area. They would have to be launched from one of the waist catapults as both bow catapults were stacked with parked aircraft. Stagecoach 203 came out of the rain and mist one more time, but this time the fighter pilot knew his approach was hopeless and rotated to climb away before the wheels even touched the deck. The taxi directors motioned Grafton forward to the number-three catapult on the waist as the cat crew piled up from the catwalks, removed the protector plate from the shuttle, and retracted it for the shot. The pilot spread the plane's wings, dropped the flaps, cycled the controls, and slipped into the shuttle. Twenty seconds later the tanker was airborne and climbing.

Jake got on the radio. "Two Oh Three, what is your state?"

"Fifteen hundred pounds," was the answer.

"Okay, listen up. You don't have the gas to get on top, so I'll rendezvous with you if you bolter on this next pass. Stay at about 250 feet, underneath the clag, pull up your gear and flaps and I'll join on you. Where are you now?"

The F-4 pilot gave him his position—downwind at 1200 feet—seven miles out. Jake leveled the tanker at 1500 feet and turned to the downwind heading, which was the exact opposite of the ship's course.

The air ops officer got on the air. "Two Oh Three, if you bolter this next pass and you can't hook up with the tanker, I want you to climb to five thousand feet straight ahead and jettison the airplane. The Angel will pull you two guys out of the drink. Understand?"

"Two Oh Three, wilco." As if they had a choice.

"And don't either one of you fly into the water."

Jake didn't even bother clicking his mike. Neither man wanted to commit suicide. Of course, if they weren't real goddamn careful, they'd be just as dead. More to the point, if the two men in the Phantom had to eject into this sea, they ran a good risk of getting tangled in their chutes and drowning before the helicopter moved in.

Jake planned his approach. He had already screwed up twice tonight, not counting his dive for the deck. Please God, don't let me get zapped passing gas! He concentrated on the problem before him. The Phantom would slow when it dropped its gear and flaps, and the tanker would close the distance. They would have to be beneath the clouds then, about 250 feet over the water. Jake would not have time to constantly check the altimeter. "When we get below three hundred feet I want you to call the altitude every five seconds," he told Razor. The bombardier would have to watch the altimeter very carefully. Any unnoticed sink rate would lead to watery oblivion in a matter of seconds.

"If you kill me, Grafton," Razor told him, "I'll kick

your ass in hell for the next ten thousand years." When the pilot did not respond, Razor added, "Why in the fuck didn't I have the good sense to join the goddamn army?"

Jake Grafton extended his pattern downwind as the Phantom turned crosswind to intercept the final bearing inbound. When he was sure he had enough separation, Jake also turned crosswind and let the plane begin a gentle descent toward the water. He was at 500 feet when he turned to the final bearing and began to close on the ship. Two Oh Three was at two miles on the glide path.

Come on, you son of a bitch, get aboard this time!

But Jake knew it was a forlorn hope. The fighter pilot had lost confidence, much like a football team that is twenty points behind. He needed something to restore his faith in himself. Maybe a full bag of gas would calm him down. Jake descended through 300 feet, still in the clouds. At 250 feet he was in and out of clouds but he leveled there, afraid to go lower.

The airspeed read 275 knots, the distance on the TACAN five miles. The F-4 was at a mile now, calling the ball. This should work out.

He was listening to the LSO between Razor's altitude calls when a cluster of lights loomed ahead in the darkness.

Holy—!

"Pull up!" Razor screamed.

Jake jerked the stick aft and slammed the throttles forward as confusion and adrenaline flooded him. His eyes darted to the distance indicator on the TACAN as the Gs slammed him down into the seat and the nose came up. It couldn't be the carrier!

Oh, God! It was the plane guard destroyer.

He pulled the throttles back and shoved the stick forward. The two men floated in their seats as the plane nosed over. They were at 1000 feet and two miles from the ship. They had to get down under fast. Jake let the nose go to ten degrees down, then put two Gs on to pull out at 250 feet.

"Bolter, bolter, bolter!"

After a last check to ensure he was level, Jake looked ahead through the rain. The adrenaline kept pumping. He could see nothing and terror welled up. He fought it back.

"Get ready to put the hose out," he told the bombardier between altitude calls.

At last he saw the carrier, a mass of dim red light in the rain. He added power. The fighter was somewhere up ahead at 250 knots. Grafton squeezed on more power. The airspeed increased. They went by the ship at 350 knots, 250 feet. "Stagecoach Two Oh Three, call your posit."

"Two miles straight ahead, four hundred pounds." The fighter's fuel was almost down to the accuracy margin of the fuel gauge; it could flame out at any second.

"Speed?"

"Two fifty." Jake saw him now. Elation replaced the fear that had gripped him seconds before. He levered back the throttles and cracked the speed brakes a trifle.

"We'll tank at three hundred," he announced. In seconds they were together. Jake passed the fighter on its left wing, stabilizing at the chosen airspeed as the F-4 pilot increased power—perhaps for the last time if he didn't get fuel—trailed in behind the tanker, and guided the refueling probe home in one smooth, sexual motion. Grafton raised the nose when he saw the transfer light come on and began to climb. "You're getting fuel," he said over the air.

Apparently the Phantom's crew didn't trust themselves to speak, because the reply was several mike clicks.

"How much does Stagecoach Two Oh Three get?" Razor asked the ship.

"Give him five grand and if he doesn't get aboard on the next pass, he can divert to Da Nang. The field is open now. You copy, Two Oh Three?"

"Roger. Copy one more approach."

As they reached 1200 feet Jake turned downwind and led the fighter back for another approach. The fighter pilot keyed his mike when the Phantom finished tanking: "Thanks for saving our assets, you guys." He dropped his gear and flaps and receded in the tanker's rear-view mirror. Good luck, thought Grafton as the lights of the fighter faded.

Confidence is so slippery: one either has it at a given instant or one does not. Now the fighter pilot, whose name Jake did not know, had it—that will-o'-the-wisp that had eluded his grasp so many times—now he had it, for he successfully trapped aboard on his next approach.

"Now let us get down again," Razor muttered almost in prayer after the Phantom had trapped.

"Five Two Two, you are at seven miles on final approach. Slow to landing speed. Say your state."

"Three thousand pounds." Jake slapped the gear and flap handles down and lowered the arresting hook.

"Three down and locked, flaps in takeoff, slats out, boards out, hook down," Jake told Razor, who then read the rest of the landing checklist as the pilot slowed to the on-speed indication on the angle-of-attack indexer and stabilized there.

"Five Two Two, you are approaching glide path." Jake retarded the power and clicked the nose trim forward.

"Five Two Two, you are below glide path." Damn! He had taken off too much power too soon. He added some and checked the vertical speed needle as he tried to flatten his descent and intercept the glide slope. The plane was bouncing in the turbulence and the needles flopped maddeningly.

"Slightly below glide path. Call your needles."

"Low and right."

"Disregard. You are below glide path, on centerline."

He was fighting the controls. He knew it, yet there was nothing he could do. Finesse seemed impossible. No adjustment of power or stick brought exactly the right response from the machine; it was either too much or too little.

"You are below glide path, three-quarters of a mile, call the ball."

Razor made the call. "Five Two Two, Intruder ball, two point eight."

"You are low." That was the LSO.

Jake clicked his mike and added power. Too much.

"You are high and fast."

Jake could see that. Frustrated, he pulled off a wad of power and clicked the nose up, trying to descend and slow down all at the same time. It was working. The ball was sinking. He added power to catch it. Not enough. The ball sank below the green datum lights that marked the glide path, and turned from yellow to red. Can't stay down here; the ramp's down here, and tearing metal, black sea, and watery death. He crammed on the power and tweaked back the nose.

He crossed the ramp with the ball climbing and reduced the power. Too late! The ball squirted off the top of the mirror just as the wheels collided with the deck. He rammed the throttles to the stops and thumbed in the boards.

"Bolter, bolter, bolter!"

The deceleration didn't come. The engines were still winding up when the speeding aircraft ran off the deck into the night air sixty feet above the water. He rotated to ten degrees nose up and eyed the altimeter as it began to register the climb.

He caught himself lingering upon individual instruments, taking precious seconds to decipher the bits of information. His scan was breaking down.

Come on, Jake, he told himself. Keep those eyes moving. One more time! One more good approach!

Razor toggled the bleed air switch as they sank beneath the clouds on their next approach, but nothing happened. Rain drops which were swept away at 300 knots ran up the windscreen in vertical streaks at 120, creating a prismatic miasma of double images.

"Gimme air," Jake demanded of Razor.

"It's not working. Your wings are level."

The yellow ball and green datum lights were merely smears on the windscreen. Jake fought back panic and tried to respond to the half-heard comments from the LSO. The desire to trap was now an obsession. He was fast—the LSO and the angle-of-attack indexer agreed—but in this living nightmare he couldn't reduce the power. He fought the stick with a death grip. The red splotches that were the drop lights swept under the nose and he leaned sideways to view the ball through the plexiglas quarterpanel. The ball was a little high and sinking! He felt the wheels smash home and the nose drop down. He held his breath as he jammed the throttles forward and waited for the deceleration, then exhaled convulsively when it came. Oh, that welcome thrill as the arresting gear machinery below deck soaked up the millions of foot-pounds of kinetic energy! He felt the little wiggle the plane gave as it quivered on the arresting hook like a snagged bass. Then it came to a complete stop and began to roll backwards.

Later Jake relived the entire sequence in the darkness of his stateroom. He examined his confidence and attempted to glue the missing pieces back together. He told himself no one would ever notice the damage.

When Jake Grafton and Razor Durfee got off the escalator on the second deck, the pilot went into the head. He relieved himself, then sat on the toilet and lit a cigarette. The place reeked of stale urine and disinfectant, but the cigarette tasted good after hours without one. Jake rested his elbows on his knees and cupped his chin in his hands as fatigue permeated him.

His flight boots were almost worn out. One sole had an inch-long split along the side. The leather was cracking. Not once in five years had he polished the boots.

Most of the blood stains were gone from the G-suit and survival vest, rubbed off as he sat and walked and moved around. The fire-retardant nomex outer layer of the G-suit was oily and dirty and torn in places, but the worst of the brown stains had faded to mere discolorations, difficult to see. Grief is like that, he thought. It fades in the course of living.

He closed his eyes and savored the darkness. At length he opened them and stared at his hands. They quivered, and he could not still the tremors.

The door opened and Sammy Lundeen stepped inside. He slouched against the door.

"That was a helluva chance you took to tank that guy, Cool Hand."

"Yeah." Jake stared at the faded brown stains, all that was left of Morgan McPherson. "Is the skipper pissed off?"

"No. He's smoking his cigar, as usual. That fighter crew's in the ready room telling everybody what a hero you are. They keep saying something about you saving their butts, but all fighter pukes are crazy and they'll say anything."

Jake took a deep drag on his cigarette. "Boy, we're having fun now," he said, thinking of Morgan. "What happened on your hop, anyway?"

"We flew right into a flak trap and almost got our asses shot off. Still haven't figured out why they didn't get us. Then we had to run the target without the computer."

"Any luck?"

"Who knows? No secondary explosions. We probably missed that truck park by a mile or two. Some commie's probably complaining right now to some half-wit reporter that the American warmongers just bombed another church."

"A truck park?"

"A suspected truck park."

"Is that worth dying for?"

"There isn't anything in Indochina worth dying for, man, and that's a fact. But tonight those gomers shot like we were trying to bomb Ho Chi Minh's tomb. I'll bet the Kremlin doesn't have that many guns around it. We were real goddamned lucky." He shook his head. "Real lucky. Got three secondaries when I dropped the Rocks on the flak trap, though." Lundeen showed his teeth. "That made it worth the trip."

Jake shifted enough to drop the cigarette butt into the bowl. "How come the spare tanker didn't get airborne?"

"Haven't you heard? A plane captain got sucked down an intake."

"Good God! What a way to buy it."

"He didn't buy it, amazingly enough. The chief saw him approach the intake, figured he was going to go and made a diving grab. He caught the guy's legs just as he went in. The plane captain went down the intake headlong to his knees. He's shook up plenty, though. Lost his helmet and goggles and flashlight into the engine. There's $150,000 of the taxpayers' money down the crapper."

"Who was the poor sucker?"

"Maggot. He's down in sick bay."

"Maggot! Poor guy!" Jake stood up, helmet bag in hand. "Think I'll stop down and say hi."

"When you finish there, you'd better take off that flight gear and go to the ready room. That fighter pilot is dying to kiss you and introduce you to his virgin sister."

Jake found Maggot in one of the wards in the sick bay suite. Mad Jack was standing beside him.

"He's still in shock," the doctor said. "He's a little deaf, too, but he'll get his hearing back in a few days. Don't stay too long." Glancing at the stains and ground-in dirt on the pilot's flight gear, he added, "And don't touch anything down here, either."

Jake dropped his helmet bag beside the bed and sank into the only chair. Maggot's face was almost as white as the bedsheets. The pilot leaned forward and spoke loudly. "You'll do anything to get out of a little work, won't you?" The corners of the boy's mouth twitched. "I hear you about went to see The Man."

Maggot nodded nervously and licked his lips. "It just sucked me up like I was a leaf or something, Mister Grafton. I was walking and then I was going down that intake headfirst. I thought I was a goner."

"From what I hear you almost were."

The boy's eyes were wet. "Damn, Mister Grafton, I was scared. It was dark and the noise was unbelievable and I couldn't see anything and I could feel myself being pulled toward that compressor. I knew those blades were there, turning, ready to chop me into hamburger, *but I couldn't see them.*" He gazed at the wall a moment and blinked back the tears. "I think I peed my pants. Don't tell anyone."

"I won't tell. But I know what you mean about being scared. McPherson and I have been scared so many times I lost count." Jake put his lips near Maggot's ear and spoke in a stage whisper. "Any man who hasn't had the pee scared out of him just hasn't done anything yet." The trick was not to show the fear, to bury it deep. He rose to go. "Just don't swab out any more intakes, okay?" The reply was a wan smile.

The ready room was crowded when Jake opened the door. Lundeen was right. The crew of Stagecoach 203 was more than grateful. The pilot pounded Jake on the back and pumped his hand repeatedly. He had a dark, well-groomed mustache against which his teeth looked porcelain white when he grinned. "Just shit hot, Grafton! Just shit hot! I owe you a fifth of your favorite and you'll collect it this time in port, believe you me."

This was getting out of hand. "It was nothing you wouldn't have done if our positions had been reversed."

The fighter pilot, whose name tag proclaimed he was Fighting Joe Brett, released his grip on Jake's hand. "I'd like to think that, Grafton. But I mean it about the bottle."

A dozen loud conversations were going at once, while up in the front of the room the skipper and Cowboy were conferring in low voices. These laugh-and-scratch sessions were a necessary part of getting back to earth. Just then the LSO in his white pullover shirt strode into the group. In his hand was the little green book where he recorded in cryptic shorthand the details of every pilot's approach to the ship.

"Grafton, you set something of a record tonight, two no-grade passes and one cut pass. That last landing was the worst I've seen in many a moon."

The men fell silent. Half of them were looking at the LSO and half were gazing at Jake, startled. A cut grade meant the pass was dangerous, almost an accident. No-grade was just above a cut.

The LSO continued. "Now you know as well as I do that with a pitching deck you have to be extra careful. You did a little dive for the deck on your first trap, overcontrolled on your bolter pass, but then on that last approach you really went for it. You could've easily torn the wheels off that plane or smashed it on the ramp. Some fine navy night you're going to cram those main struts right up through the wings."

Durfee wasn't taking this lying down. "Hey, asshole, you heard me tell you the bleed air wasn't working. Jake couldn't see shit out the windscreen."

The LSO turned to him. "Did it ever occur to you two geniuses to take a waveoff and check the circuit breaker on the downwind leg? Did you check the circuit breaker?" he demanded of Razor.

Razor's face turned red, and he leaned toward the LSO. "Did you hit the goddamn waveoff lights, butt-face?"

The LSO ignored the bombardier and focused on the pilot. "You ever come aboard like that again and I'll see to it you never land another plane on this boat." He turned and walked toward the front of the room.

Jake felt like a nude in church. He shrugged and looked at the embarrassed men around him. "Hell, I was desperate."

Joe Brett grasped Jake's hand again, and the skipper's voice boomed out, "Jake, you go get some sleep. We have a brief in four hours." Without another word the pilot turned and headed for his stateroom.

But Commander Camparelli was not finished yet. He motioned with his finger at the LSO, who obediently came over and stood in front of the skipper's chair. "Listen, mister," said Camparelli. "You know your job and you call 'em like you see 'em. But if you ever again read out one of my pilots like you just did, I'll have your ass on a plate. Do you understand me?"

"Yessir, but—"

"I decide who flies and who doesn't in this squadron, not you. All I expect from you is your opinion."

"Yes, sir."

"Now get out of here. I'm tired of looking at you." The LSO marched out the door. The skipper looked around the room at the hushed crowd. He settled on the mustachioed fighter pilot and smiled at him. "Have you got a sister?" he asked.

SIX

The two Intruders were alone in the crystal-blue morning. Several miles below, ragged clouds partially obscured the South Vietnamese countryside. Overhead, the morning sun blazed with full tropical fury, warming the airmen's necks and causing bodies encased in olive drab nomex to perspire agreeably.

Jake Grafton was relaxed. He kept his position about 300 feet aft and to the right of the skipper's plane without conscious effort. Each plane carried sixteen Mark 82 500-pound bombs beneath its wings, plus the usual 2000-pound fuel tank hung on the centerline—or belly—station. The dark green bombs appeared almost black in the brilliant sunshine, in sharp contrast to the off-white airplanes that looked clean and polished.

Both Jake Grafton and Marty Greve, the bombardier for this flight, spent much time looking outside the aircraft. On most flights they were too busy to sightsee, and over the ocean there was little to observe except clouds.

The radar controller in some anonymous hut near Da Nang directed the two warplanes south. On the left the South China Sea reflected the sunlight through the tears in the cloud blanket, while to the right they could see swatches of solid green jungle. As the earth slipped beneath them, the open spaces between clouds grew larger. The controller passed the flight to a forward air controller, a FAC, who would be flying a light plane with the call sign "Covey" somewhere up ahead. Greve toggled the radio to the assigned frequency, and Grafton keyed the mike twice to let the skipper know he was with him on the new frequency.

"Covey Two Two, this is Devil Five Oh One."

"Five Oh One, Covey Two Two. Go ahead with your lineup and ordnance, please."

"Devil Five Oh One is a flight of two Alpha Sixes, side numbers Five Oh One and Five Oh Five. Five Oh One has the lead. Each aircraft has sixteen Mark Eighty-Twos, over."

"Copy your lineup, Devil. Say your position."

"We're about five minutes north of your location."

"Roger. Here's the situation. We have troops in contact, maybe two companies of Victor Charlie dug in along a tree line. We're going to let you try and blow them out of there. The tree line runs north and south. About three hundred meters to the east we have friendlies. Your run-in will be from north to south or vice versa, as you prefer. Best bail-out is to the east, out to sea. No reported flak in the area. Do you copy, over?"

"Roger. Copy all."

"How many runs can you give me?"

"Two each." The skipper never took unnecessary chances; two runs were the most he would ever make. He felt that if you couldn't hit the target in two attempts, you were just hanging out your ass to no avail.

Marty leaned over and set up the ordnance panel to release eight bombs. Grafton consulted a card on his kneeboard and made the necessary adjustment on the bombsight mounted on top of the instrument panel in front of him. To see straight ahead he had to look through the glass of the bombsight. The pilot raised his seat slightly so his right eye aligned perfectly with the yellow cross hairs in the sighting glass. He double-checked the switches on the armament panel. Except for the master arm switch, which would put electrical power to the panel and weapons circuits, all was ready.

The skipper led Jake down from 22,000 feet in a gentle, descending turn. Only a few low clouds dotted the scene below. Inland from the white-sand beach, a road ran parallel to the coast. From three miles up, the airmen saw the stream that meandered toward the sea and the bridge that crossed it, and the rice paddies that lay near the road and stretched as far south as the eye could see.

"The point of interest today, gents," the FAC said, "is the rice paddy on the western side of the road, south of the stream." A single line of trees edged the western side of this paddy. Behind the trees was low vegetation spotted with pools of stagnant water. From this height the landscape looked like a meadow, but it was probably swamp and tall grass. The V.C. had a backdoor if they wanted to use it.

"Okay, Devils, the Charleys are in that tree line south of the stream. I want the lead plane to start at the stream and march his bombs along that tree line. Number Two, you pick up where lead left off and march yours on down the tree line. Plaster the whole line. Got it?"

The skipper rogered and continued to descend. By now, the Intruders were down to 15,000 feet and inscribing a circle counterclockwise around the target. Grafton knew the men on the ground could hear and make out the white specks in the blue sky. The Viet Cong, or maybe North Vietnamese regulars, were probably trying to dig into the earth and pull the holes in after them. The ARVN commander was undoubtedly watching the warplanes circling like hawks and grinning to himself. Viet Cong, you will die cheap.

Jake pulled back the throttles and dropped farther and farther behind the flight leader. He wanted to see where Camparelli's bombs fell before he rolled in for his dive.

"Devils, do you have Covey in sight?"

Both the A-6 pilots craned to find the little spotter plane. They saw it circling to the east, over the beach. As they watched, it turned and fired a smoke rocket into the tree line. Jake watched the smoke intently. It seemed to be drifting slowly toward the northwest. Maybe ten knots of wind. He would need to allow for the wind as he aimed.

"That's the target, guys."

Both attack pilots acknowledged.

"Okay, Devils, you are cleared in with Covey in sight. Call in hot and off safe." The hot and safe calls referred to the position of the master armament switch. With the friendlies so close, an inadvertent weapons release for any reason could be disastrous.

The skipper angled in toward the target. Now the sun flashed on Camparelli's wings and he was in his dive. "Lead's in hot."

Jake watched the accelerating airplane streak toward the earth. He saw the vapor condensation pour off the wingtips as Camparelli laid on the Gs to pull out of the dive. Yet nothing happened along the tree line.

"Lead's off safe but we didn't get a release," Camparelli reported. A malfunction somewhere in the weapons-release system had kept the bombs firmly attached to the bomb racks.

Jake trimmed the plane for 500 knots. After a last glance at the altimeter, he locked his gaze on the trees and came in toward the line at an angle, trying to find that precise spot in space where he could roll and end up in a forty-degree dive on the proper run-in bearing, with his nose just short of the target.

When it felt right, he keyed the mike. "Two's in hot." He rolled the plane over on its back and pulled the nose down to the tree line as Marty flipped the master arm switch to the armed position.

He rolled upright and adjusted the throttles. The airspeed increased dramatically, and he monitored the indicator and the altimeter without conscious thought; he felt intensely alive. The yellow cross hairs on the bombsight glass were tracking just to the left of the trees. He made a small right turn to allow for the crosswind, then leveled the wings again. Marty was on the ICS: "Ten thousand . . . nine thousand. You are shallow. Eight thousand, thirty-eight degrees. . . ." Jake eased in a correction for the shallow dive, and as the airspeed approached the 500-knot trim setting, he felt the pressure on the stick neutralize.

Now! He mashed the stick pickle with his thumb. The plane shuddered as the bombs were kicked free. When the tremors stopped, he hauled back on the stick and the G forces drove the men down into their seats.

As the nose climbed above the horizon Jake searched the blue for the white speck that would be the lead Intruder. The bombardier lifted his left arm against the Gs and pulled the master arm switch down, then keyed his mike. "Two's off safe."

"Nice hit, Devil Two. Right on the money."

Jake glanced back. The trees were enveloped in black smoke roiling aloft in the clear air. He dropped the left wing and soared up and around for another run.

He was back at 15,000 feet when he saw the skipper's plane racing earthward, then pulling off. "No soap today, Covey. They won't come off."

It was Jake's turn again. Trim set, he rolled. Again Marty caught the master arm and called the altitudes. This time Jake was right on forty degrees. The tree line grew larger and larger in the sight and he began to distinguish individual trees. At 6000 feet he pickled. On the pullout, he checked the altimeter. It stopped unwinding at 3700 feet and began to register their progress upward as the nose of the aircraft pointed ever higher.

Jake saw the skipper's plane ahead and kept the throttles full forward to catch him. As the two planes headed northward, the FAC came back on the air: "Devil Two, I give you one hundred percent on target. Nice job. Devil One, sorry you couldn't get your rocks off."

"Yeah, we'll have to do it again sometime."

"Have a safe flight home. Toodle-loo from Covey Two Two."

He held the photo under the desk lamp. It shook slightly in his hands so he tightened his grip. He and Linda and Morgan and Sharon sat on the hood of his Olds 442 with the Olympic Mountains in the background. They had taken a day trip to Hurricane Ridge. When was it? Oh yes, that day in August 1971, after their first cruise. The faces in the picture were all young, all smiling. A long time ago.

He laid the picture on the desk and stared into the shadows of the stateroom. He took a sheet of letter paper from a box in a drawer and played with his pen. He doodled awhile. He opened her letter to him and read it through several times. He examined the way the point of the pen slid in and out when he pressed the button on the top. He took the pen apart and looked at the spring and the refill and the little plastic cam. One by one, he dropped the parts into the wastebasket. The paper he wadded into a ball. He tore Linda's letter into tiny pieces and dribbled them slowly into the wastebasket.

At least Sharon had had the courage to try. He put

the photo back in his safe and slammed it shut. Where did Lundeen keep his whiskey?

The following day Jake again flew toward South Vietnam but this time he was the flight leader. Big Augie Canfield sat beside him in the right-hand seat. His wingman was Corey Ford, a quiet aeronautical engineer from MIT who wanted to become a test pilot because it was a first step to becoming an astronaut. Ford's bombardier was Bob Walkwitz, who had a very different personality from that of his pilot. Whereas Ford never spoke without weighing his words, Walkwitz was the master of the flip comment. He was noisy and irreverent, a man who lived for the moment. Because of his raging thirst for female companionship, which alcohol aggravated, Walkwitz was known to his comrades as the Boxman.

This morning the two machines flew south as the controllers on the ground called each other in a vain search for a target. Ordnance in the air was a valuable asset that had to be used before the aircraft ran low on fuel. "Anything in your sector?" "I have two fast movers who need a target." "Any activity over your way?"

Fifty miles north of Saigon, the controller turned the flight northwest toward the central highlands. "Hope this isn't a wild goose chase," Big Augie muttered, glancing at the fuel gauge.

The rice paddies of the coastal plain gave way to meandering ridges and valleys covered with jungle. Gashes of red earth from old bomb craters appeared occasionally, but this rugged terrain had not suffered the scars of war like the areas around Hue and the Demilitarized Zone far to the north for the simple reason that here the Viet Cong reigned supreme.

A low haze lay upon the ridges, but the sky was a temple of the sun. The nomex-clad airmen perspired freely. Big Augie vainly thumbed the air-conditioning switch, already on its coldest setting.

The controller ordered a frequency shift, and Jake checked in with a FAC, call sign "Nail Two Four." The A-6 crewmen listened as the FAC briefed them and a flight of A-7s. "I was flying up this road and saw a squad of about nine guys in black pajamas strolling along. They dived into the bush on the south side of the road as soon as they saw me. All were carrying small arms. We're going to see if we can get 'em."

"Any friendlies about?" asked one of the Corsair pilots.

"Nearest friendlies are ten miles away."

When the Intruders arrived at the scene, they began orbiting to the left at 18,000 feet. Jake saw the pair of A-7s several thousand feet below on the opposite side of the circle. Far below, silhouetted against the tree-tops, the spotter plane weaved along. When the reconnaissance was completed, the spotter plane fired a smoke rocket.

"The smoke is the farthest west I want you to go. I'd like you to work your bombs east, just a pair at a time, along the southern edge of the road. You're cleared in hot with Nail in sight. Call rolling in and off safe."

The lead A-7 peeled away from his wingman and pointed his nose at the earth. Seconds later, the shock waves from the concussions of each pair of bombs spread through the foliage in concentric circles. Two by two, the explosions marched along the edge of the road for three hundred yards. Black smoke boiled up. Chatter on the radio was limited to the required calls: "Lead's in." "Off safe." "Two's in." "Off safe."

Anxious eyes scanned the jungle and the air around each diving plane for muzzle blasts and flak bursts. The planes were most vulnerable when diving, as they were then committed to a descending, predictable straight path The eyes searched in vain. Perhaps some of the nine enemy soldiers were shooting with their assault rifles, but if so they were wasting their ammunition. The jets never descended below the maximum effective altitude of a rifle bullet, which was 3500 feet.

When each Corsair had dropped its ten bombs, the leader had a request: "We have some twenty millimeter to expend, Nail. Permission to make some high-angle strafing runs."

"Hose down the area south of the bomb impact zone."

This time each Corsair emitted a stream of white smoke as it dived, just a trace really, for several seconds before the machine began its pullout. The twenty-millimeter cannons threw a hundred shells a second at the jungle.

Jake Grafton watched in silence.

What must it be like down there? To be huddled on the ground near one of those trees, perhaps digging frantically in a pathetic attempt to create shelter against random death from the sky? The pilot worked his fingertips up under his visor and swabbed the perspiration from his eyes.

When the Corsairs had joined up and disappeared to the northeast, the Intruders began their runs. Each Intruder carried sixteen 500-pounders, which also dropped in pairs. The impact area was widened and deepened south of the road. The weapons were randomly spaced. The bombs exploded in white flashes that were immediately engulfed in black smoke. As the fury subsided, the breeze caught the smoke and wafted it away gently.

Jake kept the Nail FAC and Corey Ford in sight and concentrated on the image of the yellow dot in the bombsight as it walked across the jungle below. Big Augie called the altitudes in a monotonous chant as they dived, but he didn't mention the dive angle. They were bombing the hell out of an area containing nine tiny men; precision really didn't matter.

As the A-6s made their final runs, the FAC briefed a flight of arriving A-7s. Grafton pulled out of his last run into a gentle circling climb so Ford could join with him. The pilot scanned the scene below one last time as his wingman worked the inside of the turn and closed the distance. The lush jungle was now pocked with red scars where the bombs had torn and slashed. The earth itself seemed to bleed. Dirty-gray puffs of smoke drifted off in a string toward the northwest.

When Ford was on his right wing Jake turned to the northeast, toward the sea and the waiting ship. He checked the clock on the instrument panel. He would have to hurry to make the recovery. He pushed the throttles forward and slipped the stick back and let the power of the engines carry them upward into the blue emptiness.

Cumulus clouds, all at the same height, floated over the sea. Jake descended until he was skimming the tops, then eased lower and began to thread his way through the silvery mounds. For the first time that day Jake Grafton consciously took note of the sun, which bathed the cockpits and the cloud tops in a tawny glow. He could feel the tension ebbing; a sense of well-being suffused him. This was the last flight of the line period. He glanced in the mirror at Ford and found satisfaction in the precision with which his wingman maintained his place as they weaved downward.

Jake selected a cloud ahead and flew straight toward it. Just short, he lifted the nose and began a slow roll. His eyes caught Ford's in the mirror, and he saw the wingman hold his position throughout the roll. Jake dropped through a gap between the clouds and descended toward the sea in a series of hard turns, necessary only because he whimsically chose to avoid the cloud pillars.

Now they were underneath. Just as the white cloud tops were at a uniform altitude, so were the grayish-blue bases. Here was a darker world, where the pillars cast shadows on an otherwise brilliant sea. From this vantage Jake sensed he had entered a temple without walls, a shrine composed only of shadow and light. The men could never describe, even to one another, the feeling that flying gave them: a sense of perfection that only God—or maybe just bad luck—could take away.

They saw the ship when they were twelve miles out. Grafton led his wingman in a wide turn that brought them up the ship's wake at 3000 feet. Then he slid into a counterclockwise orbit on the *Shiloh*'s port side that brought him over the ship on each circuit. After he had completed one turn around the circle, the ship began a 180-degree turn into the wind. The ship's wake had been a mere feather. Now the mighty screws churned the sea to accelerate the 95,000-ton airfield to 22 knots, which, combined with the 8-knot trade wind, would give the *Shiloh* 30 knots of wind across her deck.

Jake could monitor the progress of the planes on deck, their wings still folded, as they moved toward the catapults. He saw the machines on the catapults spread their wings and saw the first two planes, an A-6 tanker on a bow catapult and an F-4 Phantom on one of the waist cats, simultaneously begin their journeys into the sky. At this altitude and distance an observer had no sense of the speed and violence involved in launching. The birds moved slowly toward the deck edge, left it behind, then skimmed across the surface of the sea like low-flying gulls.

He searched the sky and found the other machines, small and difficult to see, that were moving in similar circles but not at his altitude. Below on the flight deck the landing area was emptying as the catapults threw the planes aloft. He located the Phantoms that were lowest in the holding pattern. They were descending, as were the A-7 Corsairs below him. Jake let the nose drift down and followed them.

The flight of four Phantoms in fingertip formation swung wide and gave themselves a two-mile straight-away as they flew up the ship's wake at 800 feet. The fighter on the leader's left wing slid down and under the remainder of the formation and took the number-four position in a right echelon. Over the ship the leader peeled away from the formation and made a hard turn to the downwind leg as he slowed to landing speed. This maneuver was known as the "break." Each of the other planes peeled off at eight-second intervals. As he came abeam of the ship's fantail, the fighter lead began his turn onto final approach. Had he judged it correctly? Would the ship have a ready deck when he rolled out of the turn onto the ball? Not a word had yet come over the radio: daylight recoveries in good weather were "zip-lip." As Jake watched, the familiar Phantom shape flew up the wake and stopped on the deck. The second fighter was turning final. The A-7s, all four in echelon, were approaching the ship for their break.

Jake swung wider and led Ford down. He was absorbed in watching the planes ahead and judging the intervals. A plane should cross the ramp every thirty seconds; any more seconds would be time wasted, fewer seconds would mean a wave-off because the previous plane had not yet cleared the landing area. How well you flew around the ship, where everybody could watch you, formed the keystone of a carrier-pilot's reputation.

The two Intruders flew up the wake at 800 feet with their hooks down. Corey Ford was welded onto Grafton's right wing. Jake was watching the last A-7 on the downwind leg. Not yet . . . almost. . . . "Now!" In the right seat, Big Augie splayed the fingers of one hand open in Ford's direction, the "kiss-off." Jake slammed the stick over and rolled into a sixty-degree bank as he chopped the throttles to idle and extended the speed brakes. Four Gs. The altimeter needle was glued to 600 feet. Slowing through 250 knots, he tapped the gear and flap handles down and relaxed the Gs. He let the plane slow to landing speed as the gear and flaps extended.

On the downwind leg, Jake and Big Augie chanted the liturgy of the landing checklist. The interval between them and the A-7 ahead looked good. On speed, 118 knots. The indexer on the glare shield matched the airspeed indicator. Jake's eyes took it all in. He turned off the abeam position . . . still on speed . . turning . . descending nicely . . . ninety-degrees off final . altitude okay. Crossing the wake he saw the ball on final and centered ball . . . watch that line-up . . coming down . . . looking good . . . on speed with the ball centered . . . crossing the ramp . smash! They were thrown forward against their harness straps. Jake opened the canopy as they taxied, and the salty seawind swept through the cockpit.

SEVEN

Grafton slept until almost five P.M., when Lundeen shook him awake. "Time to go eat or you'll be awful hungry tonight, pal."

"What's for dinner?"

"Curry."

"Forget it. I'll eat popcorn at the movie. Go 'way and let me sleep."

"If you don't get up now, you'll never sleep tonight."

"Are we headed for the Philippines?"

"Yep. Headed for five glorious days and lusty nights in the sweetest spot this side of Tijuana."

Jake turned on the bunk light and sat up in bed. "I've made a big decision, Sammy. I'm going to quit the navy."

"What're you going to do when you're out?" Lundeen asked.

"Just what every other history major does when he hits the big, wide world: sell used cars or insurance."

"Life's a bitch and then you die," Lundeen pronounced in his best man-of-the-world voice. "You need to turn your mind to something important, like getting laid this time in port."

"Sure. All I need's a good dose of the clap." Jake

picked up his soap, shampoo, and towel and headed for the shower.

Son of a bitch, Jake muttered to himself as the water massaged his body. Flying's like a goddamn drug. I've centered my life around it, and when the euphoria is gone, reality is completely grim. Here I stand, feet firmly planted on the shower floor, and the only truth is that Morgan is dead and the targets are crap. Maybe some Soviet spy leaves a list of useless places on a Pentagon desk every night and the military puts it on the wires the next day. It's a wonder we haven't been ordered to attack the Haiphong garbage dump.

Someone pounded on the side of the shower stall. "Take a navy shower in there, fella."

Jake turned off the water and lathered himself all over. He turned the shower on again and rinsed. He was drying himself when Cowboy Parker strolled in, clad only in a towel.

"Jake, if that fighter pilot lets you pay for a single drink while we're in port, he doesn't have a hair on his ass."

"Old bald ass. He said he'd buy me a bottle."

"One lousy bottle. Does he think attack pilots live on milk?" Cowboy stepped into a shower stall and turned on the water. "One lousy bottle," he shouted. "Fighter pukes are such tightwads. Imagine him thinking his ass is only worth one bottle of cheap whiskey? By God, he should be buying bottles for the entire squadron."

Cowboy kept talking and the water kept running. As Jake went by, he pounded on the side of the stall. "Save some water for everyone else, Cowboy."

"Water? Why, you young twerp! I was taking navy showers when you were still in junior high school. Hell, when I was a kid down in Texas, every morning I used to take a cake of soap and go out and roll in the grass while the dew was still on. That's a Texas shower." The water continued to run. "I didn't even see rain until I was ten years old. I thought a creek was nothing but a dry ditch where rattlesnakes lived." He continued the monologue. Jake paused at a washbasin, then turned the cold water tap wide open. A scream and a cloud of steam emanated from the stall. Jake scooted out the door as a bar of soap flew through the air in his direction.

Lundeen was sitting at his desk when Jake returned to their stateroom. "I just singed Cowboy's backside in the shower."

"He'll get you for that. Sometime when you least expect it." Sammy continued to flip through a magazine.

"Got any idea who I'll get as a BN?"

"Nope. Don't think any of the crews in the squadron want to shift around. Cowboy and the Skipper will make that decision. Maybe you'll get this new bombardier who's going to meet us in Cubi. I saw the message about him just an hour ago."

"What's it say? Anything about his experience?"

"Uh-uh. Actually there are two bombardiers and a pilot. The pilot and one bombardier are coming from VA-128, and one BN is coming from VA-42." Attack Squadron 128 was the A-6 replacement squadron based at NAS Whidbey Island with the responsibility of training all the A-6 crewmen bound for squadrons attached to Pacific Fleet carriers. Attack Squadron 42 performed the same function on the East Coast.

"I hope I don't get a nugget." A nugget was a new man on his first tour of duty.

"How come?"

Jake hung his towel behind the door and sat on his bunk. "Because I need a BN who's got it all in one sock."

"These BNs are all good. They're pros."

"I want a guy who really wants to fight."

Sammy tossed the magazine on the desk and laced

his fingers together behind his head as he gazed at Jake speculatively. "Don't do anything crazy, Jake. Don't even think about it. You're the guy who figures every damn angle before the chips are down."

"I'm tired of bombing trees, Sammy."

"If you let the war get personal, you'll get dead real quick. What you really need is to get drunk and laid this time in port. I thought I did, but nowhere near as badly as you."

"Yeah."

"It ebbs and flows, shipmate. A hot woman and a cold beer will put all this in proper perspective."

After dinner that evening, the skipper called an all-officers meeting in the ready room. The room soon overflowed with the squadron's forty officers. Several men sat on the duty officer's desk, and three latecomers squeezed in at the rear of the room. Commander Camparelli, standing by the podium, asked Cowboy if everyone was present.

"No, sir. Big Augie is up checking out the evening movie." Big had been appointed movie officer after Camparelli had been required to visit with the captain of the *Shiloh* concerning that young gentleman's regrettable lack of decorum in the Alameda officers' club the night before the ship had sailed. The movie officer was required to sign out a movie every day after flight quarters and to operate the projector in the ready room. Big was now a fair hand at changing reels and held what was widely believed to be the ship's record, a mere thirty-two seconds.

"Well, we can't wait on him," the skipper said. "Tomorrow at 1000 on the flight deck there will be a memorial service for McPherson. The uniform for officers will be tropical white long." He paused, as if searching for something he should add. When the silence had gone on too long, he continued. "Enlisted evaluations E-1 through E-3 are due by the end of this month. You people will have them completed and turned in to your department heads by the time we get to Cubi Point. You guys are getting sloppy. This paperwork has to be done regardless of flying or fucking or anything else. No evals, no liberty.

"On another subject, we're going to put a couple planes on the beach this in-port period. We're getting a new pilot and one or two new BNs, so we'll do some field qualifications to get the pilot up to speed on landings. Lundeen and Greve, Grafton and Mad Jack will take the planes to Cubi. The quack has been working pretty hard, so we'll give him a ride. Launch at 0700 day after tomorrow."

A wistful sigh drifted through the room. A few extra hours on the beach were always welcome. "The ship will pull in about 1000. The gangway should go over about 1030 or so." Cheers greeted this announcement. The ship had been at sea for fifty-two days.

"You fellows in the back lock the doors." The crowd murmured. Whatever was coming was going to be good.

"What I am about to say is not to go beyond this room. If my wife writes and tells me the Officers' Wives Club is discussing this, I will hang the sonuvabitch who wrote it home. None of the ladies in the 'Waste a Day Club' has any business hearing what I'm about to say." Camparelli paused for effect. Silence was total.

"I spent a half hour with the other squadron skippers up on the bridge this afternoon. It seems we have a phantom shitter on board."

Most men hooted at this announcement, but a few simply looked bewildered.

Camparelli surveyed the room. "I see an explanation is required for the innocents among us. The phantom is a phenomenon that has plagued navy ships from time to time. It's been years since I heard about one, but apparently we have a phantom aboard this ship." Various people exchanged grins and nudges. "Recently members of the ship's engineering and air departments found human feces in spaces that had been unoccupied for several hours. Then the phantom started getting cute. He would put little notes in the ship's suggestion boxes to the effect, 'Tonight I am going to shit in number-four catapult room,' and sign it 'The Phantom.' Sure enough, the next morning there was that little brown pile."

The room rocked with laughter. Audacity toward authority always made a good joke. As the noise diminished Cowboy wanted to know, "What's feces?" More roars.

"It's that stuff you're full of," came an answer from across the room.

When the laughter subsided, the Old Man continued. "Anyway, yesterday afternoon another note was found in the suggestion box saying the Phantom would strike last night on the quarterdeck. The captain secured access and stationed marine sentries outside with orders to admit no one." The commander paused and looked about him. Not a whisper could be heard. The Old Man's eyes twinkled. "This morning they found a pile on the quarterdeck."

Men laughed so hard their eyes watered. They pounded each other on the back and stomped their feet.

All this was too much for Sammy Lundeen. He got up from his seat and tiptoed up the aisle, turning his head this way and that and peering about. The laughter subsided and all eyes were locked upon him. A few giggles rolled around. When Sammy got to the front of the room, he cast a few more surreptitious glances, then unfastened his trousers, pulled them down, and squatted. The guys in the back row stood on their chairs, craning to see better.

The skipper spoke. "Sam, if you shit on my ready room deck—" The rest of his remark was lost in a hurricane of noise. Sammy was trying to keep a straight face but was having trouble. He stood and pulled up his trousers, took a last careful look around, then quickly tiptoed back to his seat. The storm of applause and laughter shook the walls.

"Okay. Enough. X.O., have you got that folder?"

"Uh, yessir, but, uh . . . do you really think . . . ?"

The Old Man held out his hand and Harvey Wilson reluctantly passed him a manila folder, then retired with a serious look to his chair. Camparelli put the folder on the podium and flipped through it, examining every document.

"Parker, front and center." Cowboy got slowly to his feet and proceeded to the front. There wasn't enough room for him to stand in front of the podium facing the skipper, so he stood beside it facing the audience.

The skipper held a sheet of paper in his hand and read it to himself. Finally he turned and looked at the operations officer. "It says here that on the 6th of October you were found by several officers whose reputations are spotless . . . well, their reputations are fairly good . . . average maybe . . . heck, these guys drink, smoke, and cheat at cards. Anyway, they found you wandering stark raving naked through the passageways." Giggles broke out again. "What do you have to say for yourself, Mister Parker?"

"Well, Skipper, I was in the shower and somebody stole my towel."

"Mister Parker." The skipper's voice dripped contempt. "Let's not blame your perversions on a fellow officer. You were observed to be almost a hundred feet away from your stateroom, naked as a Sunday chicken, knocking on every door."

"Uh, someone locked the door to my stateroom, sir. I think I was the victim of a conspiracy." Cowboy glowered at the crowd. The audience hooted. "The party or parties unknown who plotted this foul deed were trying to besmirch my reputation, sir. As unbelievable as that sounds, it's true."

The skipper grinned at the crowd. "We have a medal for you, Mister Parker, for exhibiting perversity in the face of adversity." From an envelope he took a long ribbon and placed it around Cowboy's neck. Dangling from the ribbon was a stateroom key. "Wear this if you wear nothing else, my boy." With a wave of his arm he sent Parker toward his seat.

When things gradually quieted down, the men in the rear of the room became aware of pounding on the door. They opened it and Big Augie walked in bearing reels of film. "What the hell's going on in here? I could hear the uproar a hundred feet down the passageway."

Everyone tried to answer. Camparelli yelled over the hubbub, "What's the show tonight, Big?"

The noise died down. "Uh, Skipper, it's called *Two Lane Blacktop.*"

"Never heard of it," said Frank Camparelli, who never missed a chance to rag the movie officer.

Cowboy spoke up. "I've seen it, Skipper. It's not too bad."

The commander regarded Cowboy with narrowed eyes. "Any skin?"

"Some."

"On a scale of one to ten, how would you rate it?"

Cowboy gazed at the ceiling and scratched his chin. Finally, he looked at the skipper. "About a twelve."

"Asssss!" someone hissed enthusiastically.

"Roll it, Movie Officer," the Old Man directed as he plopped into his chair.

* * *

After the movie, Jake went to the squadron personnel office, a ten-by-twelve-foot cubbyhole against the outside skin of the ship. He signed out the service records of the two enlisted men in his division who needed evaluations done. He set off for the airframes shop located one deck above the hangar deck, on the opposite side of the ship.

Chief Eugene Styert was there, as he was every waking moment except when he was eating, which he did four times a day. "Evening, Mister Grafton."

"Hey, Chief." Jake accepted the indicated chair. Chief Styert had a padded chair with arms, and, except for the desk, there was no other furniture in the compartment. Jake looked the place over. Tools hung everywhere and spare parts jammed a set of shelves opposite the desk. The floor was filthy with grease and hydraulic fluid tracked in from the hangar deck. "How's everything going?"

Chief Styert placed his hands on his ample belly and leaned back in the chair. He had worked with and for junior officers most of his twenty-five years in the navy and knew the routine. He supervised a crew responsible for solving fuselage and structural problems on all of the squadron aircraft, ensured all work was accomplished in accordance with technical directives, and kept his little band firmly on the job. Chief Styert was the navy as far as his men were concerned. He was the man to whom they introduced their parents on those rare occasions back in the States when the folks from home visited the ship.

Like every chief, he reported to a junior officer, a young college grad who might or might not make the navy a career. Chief Styert believed that the young officer was there to learn and not to make his job more difficult. He knew the officer's visits in the shop were good for the men's morale, but the less he saw of the young gentleman, the better. Except when he needed an officer to go to bat for the men, of course, and Grafton never hesitated to do that.

"Everything's fine," the chief replied. "Going to clean this place up in the morning, before the men put on their whites for that memorial service." The chief added quickly, "Real sorry about Mister McPherson. Pretty tough, going like that."

Jake nodded. He took out his cigarettes, offering one to the chief. After they lit up, Jake gestured to the files in his lap. "Eval time on the nonrated. Jones and Hardesty. Have you done a rough of their evals?"

The chief rummaged through a drawer and passed two sheets of notebook paper to Grafton, who scanned them. English composition was not one of the chief's most shining accomplishments. When Jake had finished reading, they discussed the marks each man should get. Both understood the officer would polish the evaluations and put in the numerical grade for the five specified categories, but the numbers on the paper would reflect the chief's recommendations. If the men ever thought that Chief Styert did not have a firm grip over their destinies, his ability to rule his little fiefdom would be impaired.

When they had finished with the evals and the officer had tucked the notes into the service records, the chief showed him a request chit. Hardesty wanted four days leave in the Philippines. On the chit was the scrawl: "Visit my wife."

Jake eyed the chief. "I thought he was single?"

Styert shrugged. "Guess he isn't anymore."

"When did you learn about this?"

"About thirty minutes ago when Hardesty gave me that thing."

"Well, do you want me to approve this?"

The chief squirmed. "Shit, if he's really married we could catch hell if we don't. Get a letter from his mother or some congressman." From his tone Jake gathered that the chief thought mothers and congressmen were liabilities for sailors, much like an appendix that might go bad at an inopportune time.

"Do you need him for work this time in port?"

Styert shook his head. "I'll call the berthing compartment and have him come down here." He dialed the number.

While they waited, Jake asked, "You think this marriage is for real, Chief? Do you think Hardesty has thought this through?"

"I doubt it. Thinking has always been one of Hardesty's weak areas. He's got a picture of her. She's a looker. He probably met her in some bar or whorehouse. Probably the first piece of ass he's ever had."

When Hardesty came in he stood in front of the desk but certainly not at attention. Jake fought the temptation to stand. He looked the man over before he spoke. The chit was on the edge of the desk beside him. Hardesty was nineteen years old, had been in the navy ten months, had an eleventh-grade education and a bad case of acne, and shaved probably once a week.

"What is this about you being married? I thought you were single."

"I didn't tell nobody about it until I put this chit in. See, I want to take her and go see some of her relatives in Manila."

"When did you get married?"

"Last time in port. About two months ago." Hardesty looked at his shoes. Jake was reminded of those times when as a boy he had been called on to explain his conduct to his father.

"Did you know there is a requirement to get permission from the navy before you marry a foreign national?"

"No sir." Hardesty didn't look up.

"How old is your wife?"

"She's sixteen." Eyes still on the deck.

Jake sighed. "Did you report this to Personnel?"

"No."

"Why not?"

"Well, I ain't got a copy of the marriage license yet. You can't get anything quick in the Philippines." Except the clap, Jake thought. "And I knew that Personnel would make me come back when I got it, so I ain't bothered to go see them yet."

"Why didn't your wife send you a copy?"

"She knew I'd be coming back in a few months, and I could just get it then."

"What if you had been killed while we were at sea? Your wife wouldn't have gotten a penny of your GI insurance. There's no official document in American hands that proves you're married to anybody. I assume you also haven't told Disbursing?"

"No, I haven't told anyone."

Chief Styert interrupted. "No, *Sir,* when you talk to an officer, Hardesty."

The boy raised his eyes. "Sure, Chief."

Jake continued. "Federal law requires that personnel E-4 and below send an allotment to any dependents they have. Did you know that?"

"Yessir. I'm going to get all that straightened out as soon as I can."

"Have you told your folks about your marriage?"

"Yessir."

"What did they say?"

"Well, Pop has been dead for a while now and Mom ain't written back yet." He regarded his shoelaces again.

"Do you love her?" As soon as the words were out Grafton regretted them.

"Oh yes, sir." Hardesty's eyes glowed. "Here's her picture." He pulled a wallet-sized photo from his shirt pocket. She had the long black hair typical of Filipino women, the usual small nose, and the slightly Oriental eyes. She looked regal.

The officer passed the photo back to Hardesty and glanced at the chief, who had his eyes resolutely fixed on the far wall. Love? Jake could almost hear the story being told in the chiefs' mess: "And then he asked, 'Do you love her?' " Slightly embarrassed, the pilot returned to the issue at hand.

"I'll sign this chit, Hardesty, but let me tell it to you straight. By marrying without permission you violated a general regulation. The Skipper may decide to take disciplinary action against you."

"Sir, I didn't know nothing about any regulation." The sailor set his jaw and focused on Jake's nametag.

"You're responsible for knowing the regulations, though, and if you disobey them you're subject to discipline. But that's neither here nor there. I expect to see a certified copy of the marriage license when we pull out of port or you're going to be in hot water for failing to support your lawful dependents. You realize that you are legally and morally obligated to support this woman now that you've married her?"

"Yessir. I understand that. I'll get a copy of the license." The lieutenant signed the chit and told Hardesty to take it down to Personnel. Hardesty thanked him and left.

Grafton stood up to leave. "If he thinks he can marry one of these women and get laid every night in port," he told the chief, "then wave a permanent good-bye when we go back to the States, he has another think coming."

The chief shrugged. "He's just a kid," he said.

"What a mess." The officer went up to the ready room to tell the skipper.

"What do you want to do, Jake?" Camparelli asked.

"Captain's Mast?" Routine discipline problems were handled by the commanding officer in periodic formal hearings, which had been known as "Captain's Mast" since the days when the captain dispensed justice before the main mast on a sailing ship.

"No, sir. I'd just as soon forget the discipline end of it, give him his leave, and ensure he does right by her."

"Okay. Hope it all works out. By the way, pull up a chair, Jake." The pilot complied. "I hope you understand about the shenanigans in the ready room this evening?"

"Yessir."

"It was no disrespect for Morgan. But we have to keep morale up or this outfit can't fight." The skipper eyed him. "You do understand?"

"I understand, sir."

"I doubt if most civilians would. But this was Morgan's profession. We have to keep going regardless of who gets bagged. In fact, losing people makes it all the more essential that we let off some steam." He shifted his weight in the chair. "You see, the aircrews are the weapons, not the planes."

Jake nodded.

"Okay. Just wanted to be sure you understood."

Back in his stateroom Jake worked on the evaluations. When he had them finished it was almost 0100. He went up to the forward wardroom on the O-3 level, right under the flight deck, for a hamburger. Abe Steiger was sitting by himself. "Hey, Jake. Drop anchor." The air intelligence officer had a book opened beside his plate.

"Hi, Spy. How's it going?" The pilot slid into a chair. As he bit into his burger he looked at the book.

"Jake, we got a bomb-damage assessment on that hop you flew yesterday down south with the Skipper." Abe grinned.

"Yeah?" Jake lifted the book and read the title. *The Rise and Fall of the Third Reich.* He had read it in college.

"Yep. Let me tell you, you did one hell of a job on those gomers, baby. You got confirmed forty-seven killed in action."

Jake put down the book. "Forty-seven?" he whispered.

"Yep. Forty-seven KIA." Abe grinned again. "You really plastered them. That's our best single-mission damage assessment this cruise. Probably a Navy Commendation Medal in there for you, Jake. Maybe even an Air Medal."

"Why, you greasy little. . . ." Steiger wore a frozen grin. Jake felt his stomach churn. "You shit! What in hell did you tell me something like that for? You think I need to know that?" He was shouting. "Do you know their names? Tell me that! I'll bet you have their names!"

"Well, I just thought you'd want to know—"

"Why the fuck would I want to know? Now I'm the poor shit who has to live with it. Me. Grafton. You asshole!"

"I didn't mean—"

"And a fucking medal! You think I give a shit about a fucking medal? What the hell kind of guy do you think I am? Do you think I'm some idiot glory hound?" He was spraying saliva. He wiped his mouth with the back of his hand.

"Hey Jake, I—"

"A fucking medal to wear on my uniform so every time I put it on I'll remember I killed forty-seven men. Yeah, I need that, you stupid bastard. I need a medal like that. Now why don't you get the hell out of here and run down and write the report up. Go tell Lundeen. He writes up shit like that for Wilson. Go tell him!" He lunged across the table trying to get his hands on Steiger, who jumped up and back so quickly his chair fell over. "Get outta here, Steiger! Go tell him!"

The intelligence officer strode out quickly. Jake glared at the audience he had attracted. They turned their faces, and Jake sat down, breathing hard, and stared at his coffee cup. What does Steiger know about flying? What does Steiger know about killing? Jesus Christ!

EIGHT

In their white uniforms, the men in ranks were incandescent in the morning sunlight. A modest breeze ruffled the flags and pennants flying from the mast on the ship's island. Jake Grafton sat behind the podium in the chairs reserved for the officers of the A-6 squadron. He kept his gaze on the ever-changing points of light on the swells of the South China Sea.

How did they know there were forty-seven men? Why not forty-six, or forty-eight? What did they count to get forty-seven? Noses, tongues, penises? What could be left after four tons of high explosive and shrapnel had ripped and pulverized human bodies and had welded together flesh and earth?

When he had been in flight training, Jake had been assigned to an accident-investigation team. Walking in rows through a pasture in Mississippi, they had searched for the pieces of a training plane that had slammed into the ground at more than 400 knots. The engines had dug long furrows, but the rest of the machine had disintegrated and scattered parts over a third of a mile. He had found a little patch of skin, a piece about the size of a quarter, which he had carefully placed in a transparent bag. It had been just a little piece of a man, from somewhere on his body—no telling where—lying there in the grass. A crash would be a good way to die. The two guys in that training plane were gone in less time than it takes for a single sensation to register on the brain. Maybe dying under the bombs had been fast like that. Morgan hadn't been that lucky.

When they came off target, he had made that turn for the coast. Morgan had reset the armament panel and was working on the computer. If only—

"Time to go, Jake." Sammy was standing beside him. Everyone was leaving.

Morgan hadn't been lucky at all.

That evening Harvey Wilson called Jake to his stateroom and handed the pilot the evaluations on Jones and Hardesty. "These aren't good enough, Grafton. You must've spent four years trying to pass freshman English. I want them redone before you fly off the ship in the morning."

"Yessir."

"You just don't know how to do paperwork, Grafton. You should talk to your roommate Lundeen. The awards stuff he writes is outstanding. Have him give you some tips." Wilson leaned back in his chair. He had a stateroom to himself but a smaller one than the skipper's. Jake stood by the desk.

Wilson tapped his pencil on the desk. "I was down in CATCC the other night when you 'saved' that F-4." He let the statement hang in the air. After a moment he stopped playing with the pencil and scrutinized the lieutenant. "That little trick of giving Lundeen gas might have backfired on you."

"Yessir."

"These people think you're some kind of hero,

Grafton, but I know different. You bend the rules, and one of these days it's going to blow up in your face. You're a fucking hot dog."

Jake just looked at the man. The Rabbit had a way of jutting out his jaw when he was on the offensive. He was living proof of the imperfections in the navy promotion system. Next would come the threat.

"You'd better shape up." Surely he could do better than that. "Another stunt like that and you'll be flying one of these things"—he waved the pencil—"full time. Now go work on those evals."

"Yessir." Out in the passageway, Jake added, "Yessir, yessir, three bags full."

Grafton regarded the doctor with an irrepressible smile. The medical man looked slightly ridiculous with his girth encased in forty pounds of flight gear. He looked, Jake thought, like a giant pear or even—and Jake smiled more broadly—an egg with legs. "Okay, Jack, you've flown in these pigs before?" Mad Jack nodded affirmatively. A sheen of perspiration was visible on his forehead, and the pilot decided his passenger looked paler than usual.

"Have you ever had a cat shot? No? Well, you're in for the thrill of the month. This will be about the most exciting thing you've ever done with your clothes on. Just keep your hands in your lap, don't touch a single switch, knob, or anything at all, and do like I tell you." Mad Jack bobbed his head. "The only time you'll have to do anything is if I tell you to eject. The command will be 'Eject, Eject, Eject.' Three times."

"And if I say 'Huh?' I'll be talking to myself."

"If you say anything after I give you that command you will be all alone on your first, and probably last, solo in an A-6. And, of course, if I get too busy or forget to tell you and you see me eject, then you'd better hurry right along." More head bobs, nervous ones, Jake observed with a trace of satisfaction.

"Now, I want to go over how the ejection seat works with you." Jake took the doctor to the blackboard, drew a rough sketch of the seat, and explained the ejection sequence. Jake knew the doctor had heard it all before, but both he and Mad Jack had been around navy airplanes long enough to know the value of, and not be bored by, repeated instruction.

Grafton went over the intercom system. "Your ICS mike switch is the toe pedal by your right foot. Just stay silent if you hear me talking on the radio. I'll have my switches set up so that I can hear any radio transmission coming in even if you're talking. Feel free to ask questions, talk, tell jokes, lie, whatever. I want you to enjoy the hop." Jake smiled. He really meant it.

As they left the ready room, Jake put the evals he had polished in Wilson's mailbox. The sonuvabitch could read them when he got out of bed.

Lundeen's plane was ahead and to the left of Jake's as, ten minutes after launching, they approached the coast of Luzon. Low green mountains rose out of the cobalt sea, and early-morning shadows played across the white-sand beach.

The two planes dropped to 200 feet and turned northward, about five hundred yards out to sea, parallel to the surf. Occasionally they saw a fishing boat, but mostly the airmen looked at an empty sea separated from unbroken tropical forest by a filament of beach that ran from horizon to horizon. Here and there a fisherman's shack broke the lonely sweep of beach.

Jake Grafton felt refreshed. It was good to be flying again with nothing to worry about, to be sightseeing and sporting along. The cockpit was as comfortable as a living-room armchair.

"How about that cat shot, huh?" Jake asked. The

doctor, who was still on hot mike, was breathing hard. "Next time be sure to give a war whoop as you go down the cat. That seems to magnify the sensation."

The doctor chuckled, and his breathing slowed toward normal.

Up ahead, Lundeen dipped lower and lower. A lone hut was visible far ahead. The warplanes dropped to about 50 feet. Crossing the surf, they thundered down the sand toward the structure. They passed over the shack at 300 knots. As they pulled up into a steep climb, Lundeen shouted "Yahoo" over the radio and did a victory roll. Jake came alongside Sammy's right wing. Lundeen waved and Marty Greve flashed him the finger in salute.

They turned east, inland, and threaded their way up a valley at 500 feet. Jake dropped astern, assuming the tailchase position, about one hundred fifty feet aft and just above the leader. After a few sharp turns, they crossed the ridgeline, shooting through a narrow gap where the clouds almost rubbed the mountain rock. The uplands fell away quickly to forests and occasional fields. Every so often, a winding road or village punctuated the landscape.

Sammy's voice boomed in Jake's ears. "Let's go up and tangle." Without waiting for a reply, he angled up and came on with the power. Soon they were climbing through a great hall of clouds illuminated by sunlight. Riding their winged steeds, they soared effortlessly through Valhalla toward the open sky.

They passed the cloud tops at 12,000 feet. A few thunderheads were building and would reach great heights by early afternoon, but now there was plenty of room to play. Leveling at 23,000 feet, Lundeen waved and turned thirty degrees to the left. Grafton returned the wave and veered thirty degrees right. Jake concentrated on Lundeen's rapidly receding plane. How quickly the vastness of the sky swallows up the tiny machines that bear men aloft. "Better tighten your harness and lock the shoulder restraint," he advised the doctor, who did as suggested.

"Damn pilots," was the radio comment Grafton and the doctor heard from Marty Greve.

"Turning in," Jake broadcast.

"Turning in, Mother," he heard his roommate chuckle. "I'm going to wax your ass."

The aircraft approached each other head on. Jake had the throttles wide open and his ship accelerated nicely. This was the fair way to start a dogfight, a head-on pass so that neither pilot had the advantage. Jake glanced about. The sky was empty. Jake's eyes flicked over the gauges, and he noted automatically the information displayed there. The oncoming jet grew larger.

"Loser buys."

They came together at a combined speed of well over a thousand miles per hour. Lundeen went past Jake's left side, his wingtip a scant fifty feet away. Grafton yanked the stick back and to the left.

The G forces tore at his body but he scarcely noticed. He was craning his head over his left shoulder, trying to see which way Lundeen had turned. For several seconds he couldn't locate his opponent. He rolled the ship into ninety degrees of bank and pulled harder on the stick. "Six Gs," Mad Jack groaned. At least he knew where the G-meter was.

Then Jake saw the other Intruder. Lundeen and he were canopy to canopy on the opposite sides of an invisible circle, headed in opposite directions. His eyes fixed on his opponent, Jake decreased the angle of the plane's bank and kept the Gs on. The nose of his machine came up, and his airspeed was converted into altitude. As the plane slowed it needed less room to turn, so now Jake increased the angle of bank and the nose tracked around. In seconds he was only ninety degrees off Lundeen's heading but several thousand feet above him in a lopsided loop, one hundred thirty-five degrees of bank, and coming in on his opponent's stern quarter.

Lundeen was having none of it. He sheered away from Grafton and dived.

Jake relaxed the stick and did a slow roll into a wings-level dive. Only 300 knots. Lundeen had more airspeed and drew steadily away going downward. Both machines accelerated, but Sammy's lead was almost three miles; he was far below and still diving. Then Jake saw the nose of Lundeen's ship come up. He's doing an Immelmann turn, thought Jake, a half loop with a half roll on top. He shallowed his dive, and the two planes flashed past head-on again, Grafton right side up and Lundeen upside down at the top of the loop, flying a little over 200 knots.

Jake pulled the stick back hard. This time he kept his eye on the instruments and applied a steady four-G pull until the nose was pointed up, away from the earth, like a missile.

The airspeed bled off quickly. The lowest reading on the indicator was 50 knots and here was where the needle came to rest. The jet hung motionless in the sky at 30,000 feet, its nose aimed up and the exhaust pipes aimed down at the rain forest. The thrust of the engines held it poised for several heartbeats as the men in the cockpit floated weightlessly. The pilot released the stick and cuffed the doctor lightly on the arm. "Great fun, huh?"

The sensation became one of falling as the bird began a tail slide toward the earth. Then the machine lurched and tumbled over backwards. The weight of the nose and the streamlined shape took effect, and within seconds the gyrations ceased and they were plummeting earthward, gravity and engine thrust acting together to wind the airspeed-indicator needle around the dial at a dizzying rate.

Jake was busy again. He chopped the engines to idle and opened the wingtip speed brakes while searching for Lundeen.

"Do you see him?" he asked his passenger anxiously. They scanned the sky.

"I see you." It was Lundeen.

Jake swallowed hard and brought his gaze up. There was the bastard, level and coming in head on. As fast as thought itself he rotated the plane, retracted the speed brakes, added power, and began a pull to go under Lundeen and force the opponent into an overshoot.

It was good to feel the plane respond to the slightest pressure on the controls, good to see the earth and sky tumble and change positions, good to fly free. Occasional scans of the fuel gauge and engine instruments were the only concessions to the machine. The pilots worked their sticks and rudders instinctively, as training and experience had taught them to do. Each focused entirely on the location of the other aircraft and tried to anticipate his opponent's next maneuver. It was as if men and machines were fused: the fuel was blood, the engines muscle, the wings and speed and soaring flight their spirit. This was flying as the ancients had dreamed of it, when they watched the birds swoop and dart.

The doctor rode in silence, enduring a ride worse than that of any roller coaster. This was a job for a younger man with a cast-iron stomach. Mad Jack managed to remove his oxygen mask, but the little bag he had thoughtfully placed in the lower leg pocket of his G-suit was beyond reach. He ripped off his left glove and vomited into it.

The plane was no longer maneuvering; it was glued to one-G flight as firmly as if it had been welded to a pedestal in a museum display. Mad Jack looked left and met the smiling eyes of Jake Grafton. The pilot winked at him as he told Sammy Lundeen to join up.

Once on the ground at Cubi Point Naval Air Station, the planes taxied to the parking mat near the carrier pier. A sailor guided them into their parking places, and another man chocked the wheels.

With the canopy open and the engines sighing into silence, Grafton removed his helmet and let the afternoon breeze cool his soaking-wet hair. The doctor did the same. Jake ran his hand over his hair and used a finger to squeegee the perspiration from his eyebrows. "What do you think, Jack? Is it worth the final crash?"

Before Mad Jack could answer, they were interrupted.

"Hi, Jake." A khaki-clad figure tossed a can of beer up to the cockpit. The pilot fielded it and handed it to Mad Jack, then caught the next one tossed. The beer was ice cold, an elixir as it raced down Jake's dry throat. The doctor sipped his.

"Welcome to Cubi again, Jake," the beach detachment officer shouted.

"Thanks." The pilot saw Lundeen walking toward him with his helmet bag in hand. "Sam, I want that beer you owe me."

"You can have anything they got, Jake. You're buying."

"Ha! I whipped you so bad I thought you were an F-4 pilot there for a minute."

Lundeen gestured at the heavens. "Have you no honor? God is watching you, Grafton, to see if you will pay a debt of honor, a wager fairly made and fairly lost. There are two gates up there, you know; one for winners and one for welshers. You'll be going in that back gate while I'm around front with Saint Pete listing my virtues."

"And that," called Marty Greve, "will be a damn short list."

By the time the carrier rounded the headland and entered the channel, all four men were sitting in the officers' club drinking beer. The view from the club, which sat high on a hill overlooking Subic Bay and Olongapo City, was breathtaking. Each man had time to drink another beer before the great ship drifted to a stop a hundred yards from the pier and four tugboats nestled against her.

"Let's go up to the BOQ. We'll take some rooms before the guys on the boat get here," Marty suggested, "and maybe work in a dip in the pool."

"Well, fellows," Mad Jack told the airmen as they stood up, "I'm on duty today so I have to go back aboard." He stuck out his hand to Jake. "Thanks for the flight." The doctor smiled. "I won't forget that ride for a while. Maybe you're right. Living fast might be worth the final crash. Maybe that's the secret you fliers know."

Grafton grinned and shook the offered hand. "See you later, Jack."

NINE

The Filipino steward at the BOQ regarded the three airmen with suspicion. "When your ship come in?" he demanded. The BOQ was not to be used by officers whose ships were in port.

"It's classified," Lundeen said with a straight face. "Don't you know there's a war on?" He signed for his room.

The steward folded his arms across his chest. He had no doubt dealt with many navy flight crews, most of whom were inclined to ignore everybody's rules except their own. "You must check out of your room when your ship come in. We have very few rooms."

"You can bank on it," Lundeen told him, then picked up his gear and led the group down the hall. "It's a good thing we got here before the *Shiloh* crowd swarms around the pool. Then he would have known a boat was in." They agreed to meet in fifteen minutes at the pool.

After showering, Jake ran into his buddies in the hall and they trooped to the pool behind the sprawling, U-shaped building. "Six gin-and-tonics for my friends and me," Jake shouted to the bar girl, then plunged into the water. Sammy and Marty were right behind.

By the time the first group of officers from the ship arrived at the poolside bar, the gin, the cool water, and the hot sun had worked together to soothe the three men.

"How's the water, fellas?" Little Augie asked.

"All used up. Too bad you missed it."

Little dropped his kit bag and set his drink on the table. "Like hell I did," he said and dived in, clothes and all.

"Brilliant," said Marty when Little surfaced. "What're you going to use for dry clothes?"

Little hoisted himself out of the water and took off his shoes to drain. "They're in the bag. I plan ahead." He laughed and lifted his drink.

The Boxman, Bob Walkwitz, walked over carrying a tall glass filled with a rum concoction. He pulled up a chair.

"Going across the bridge tonight, Box?" Sammy inquired.

The Boxman took a drink and flexed his shoulders. "Maybe."

"'Maybe' my ass. It'd take wild horses to hold you back."

"Can I help it if I like women?" Box demanded. "What's wrong with you guys, anyway? Ya queer?" He sipped on his drink and leered at the waitress. "Already I'm in love."

"I thought you were in love with her the first time we pulled into Cubi. Didn't she give you something to remember her by?"

Boxman stared at the swaying figure of the retreating girl. "Naw. It wasn't her. Couldn't be." He shook his head. "Naw. They all remember me."

"Did I hear that right?" Sammy wiggled a finger in his ear.

"Talk about confidence!" Jake said, slightly awed. "What've you got that we don't have?"

"Ask Mad Jack the next time you see him," Box said smugly. "He's seen it so often I use him for a reference."

For a while they were free of the navy and the flight schedule, and a good belly laugh made the world a comfortable place once again.

When Lundeen and Grafton arrived at the Cubi Point Officers' Club that evening, they found Cowboy and a group of friends sitting near the back of the dining room drinking whiskey, chewing steak, and shooting the breeze. Cowboy expounded on the scandal of the hour, the Phantom.

"God help that poor idiot when they catch him. He'll get the first keelhauling in a hundred years. That's after they boil him in oil but before they string him up to the yardarm."

Jake and Sammy gave the waiters their orders and settled back to listen to Cowboy. "They're going about catching him all wrong, I reckon. They'll no doubt stake out likely compartments and have a huge investigation."

"Well, how should they do it then?"

"All it takes to catch this guy is a keen sense of smell and a little knowledge of your fellow man." Cowboy cut a piece of steak and chewed slowly. "Now the fellow we seek is an individualist, a rugged individualist as the cliché goes. He does his own thing without much thought as to what the rest of the world thinks. He has a good sense of humor and likes to see other people laugh with him."

"That ought to narrow it down to half the officers in the air wing," Sammy said.

"Oh, but there's more. Our boy likes taking chances. He gets a thrill out of running a risk."

"That eliminates a whole bunch of guys I know, Cowboy," Little Augie snickered.

Cowboy ignored the sarcasm and the pun. "Sure a lot of guys get a charge out of danger. Almost everyone does if the danger isn't too great. But the Phantom's a different breed. He loves danger no matter how great. He seeks it out, relishes it. He doesn't need the applause of the crowd, the medals, or the photos in the newspaper. He's addicted."

Jake shook his head. "We're all addicted to danger. We wouldn't keep climbing into those airplanes if we didn't find it exciting."

"Grafton, let's take you as an example. You enjoy flying but you don't take unnecessary chances, and you rarely do things for the pure hell of it. With you there usually has to be a reason." Cowboy jabbed his fork in Lundeen's direction. "Our Phantom is a man who just doesn't give a damn, like Lundeen here. If Sammy Lundeen doesn't find some danger or excitement in what he has to do, then he either doesn't do it or he manufactures some."

"Crap! From an amateur headshrinker," Sammy protested. "I'm a good officer and you know it. I grind out the routine stuff with the best of 'em. Come down to the personnel office sometime and you'll see the service records are in top-notch shape. Everyone gets his paper shuffled in my shop. Why, you could be the Phantom yourself."

Cowboy grinned. "That thought has not yet occurred to the heavies." He glanced around to see who might be listening. "I wonder what will happen if it does?"

The conversation moved on to the one subject that always proved irresistible—flying. They talked flying at every opportunity. A great deal of knowledge was exchanged in these bull sessions. The underlying theme of all of these stories was how to stay alive when everything goes awry. Because it was considered gauche to tell a story which demonstrated one's aerial virtuosity, the narrator survived despite his own ineptness, ignorance, and stupidity when the world turned to shit and the arresting gear cable broke, or the catapult fired with not enough steam to get him to flying speed, or the tie-down chains snapped and he slid over the side into the hungry sea. But some stories were about the time the world turned to shit and a buddy made a mistake and did not live to tell about it. Then the dead man's sins were mercilessly dissected.

After dinner Jake and Sammy went to the bar, ordered refills, and strolled over to watch the singer. She sang American pop songs without an accent, and she had an excellent voice.

Lundeen's eyes roved around. "I wonder where that cute waitress is tonight."

"I've been wondering, too. Guess she has the night off."

"Well, I think I'll go for a little taxi ride and see my schoolteacher friend." He polished off his drink.

"What do you see in that woman, anyway? She must be pushing forty."

"She's here and so am I. See you later."

Jake wandered down to where the Boxman, Razor Durfee, Big Augie, and a man Jake didn't recognize were huddled around a table crowned with empty beer cans. "Pull alongside and drop anchor, shipmate," roared the Boxman. "Jake, I want you to meet Ferdinand Magellan." Walkwitz put his arm around the stranger beside him. The man had a wholesome look, and his horn-rimmed glasses gave him an intellectual air. "Here in the flesh, the greatest BN who ever slipped the surly bonds and fondled God's face."

"Jake Grafton." He shook the new man's hand.

"Fred Mogollon."

"Like I said, Ferdinand Magellan," hooted the Boxman. "He's one of our new guys. Checked in this evening when the ship tied up. Doesn't know horseshit from peanut butter."

"Where're you from, Fred?" asked Jake as he dragged a chair around.

"St. Louis. Well, the suburbs of St. Louis."

Jake said, "I guess the Boxman and these other guys are getting you checked out on the liberty around here."

"Sort of. I've been here two days waiting for the ship and did some looking around."

"Don't worry, Jake," said the Boxman. "We're going to take care of young Ferdinand. We're going to see that this impressionable innocent gets indoctrinated in the best A-6 tradition, 'in the highest traditions of the naval service,' if I may steal a phrase. In fact, we're about ready to head across the bridge." He waved at the waitress. "One last round, dearest."

Big Augie turned to Jake. "Ferdinand is curious about what it's like to fly in combat, and what type of a fellow his new pilot might be. He's a bit worried he might end up with you."

"No, I'm not." Ferdinand spoke up quickly, obviously wishing he had never brought up the subject.

Jake grinned. "You'll just have to find the answers to those questions for yourself."

"Don't lie to the kid, Jake. Tell it like it is."

"I'll lay it on the line for you," volunteered Durfee. "If you make it through the first flight without crapping in your drawers, you're going to do okay."

"Amen."

"Of course, you probably won't make it through with clean underwear, but there's always hope."

"Let's hit the beach," said the Boxman, standing up. "Let's cross the bridge."

"Finish your beer," he was told.

"Forget the beer. I'm ready. Let's cross the bridge."

"Who's going to take care of the Boxman?" Jake wanted to know. Someone usually had to stick with him to get him back to the ship if his enthusiasms clouded his judgment, as occasionally happened.

"That's gonna be Ferdinand's chore tonight."

"Nobody has to take care of me. I can watch out for myself." Box picked up his beer can and drained it. "You coming, Jake?"

"I thought I'd hang around here for a bit."

"Better come, Jake. There's bound to be one honey in Po City that you can fall in love with."

"Well . . ." Jake was not ready for the fleshpots but Ferdinand looked like a lamb going to slaughter. "Okay, I'll go for a while."

"You're a real guy, Cool Hand."

"Thanks, Box. I needed that."

The five of them commandeered a taxi in front of the club. As they crammed into the Japanese-built car, the Boxman gave the driver his orders: "Main gate and don't spare either of the horses." The little machine lurched off, emitting a cloud of blue exhaust.

The walk across the bridge connecting the naval base and Olongapo City always sobered Jake. Children sat in boats amid the filth of the canal and called for sailors to throw them coins. Jake looked over the rail. The stench from one of the world's largest open sewers knocked him back. "Hey Joe. Throw me a quarter." A boy about ten stood precariously in the bow of a boat holding a fishnet in his hands. A girl, probably his sister, sat amidships with oars, sculling occasionally to hold the craft in place. Jake shook his head.

"Throw me a dime, Joe. Come on, Joe. Just a lousy dime."

"Sorry, kid." Near the boat a bloated pig floated in the brown, scummy water.

"You cheap bastard, Joe. Throw me a nickel and show me you not cheap bastard." Jake found a quarter and tossed it toward the boy, who fielded it expertly in his net. "Thanks, Joe. Hope you don't catch the clap." The kid's white teeth flashed in his brown face.

"I hope you get rich, kid, and become president of a bank."

The Boxman grabbed his arm. "Ain't you ever seen Shit Crick before?"

"Yeah, but—"

"The American Club is where it's at. And where it's at is where we want to be." The five men picked their way along the street, avoiding the clusters of sailors and the Hey-Joe kids begging money or selling glass necklaces. They dodged mud and water thrown up by passing jeepneys, ancient Willys jeeps with canvas tops. Filipino soldiers wearing cartridge belts and carrying shotguns or submachine guns sauntered along the street. In the doorway of every bar, a bouncer, armed extravagantly, stood sentinel.

"You sort of expect to see Pancho Villa come riding down the street," Jake said. Po City never failed to disturb him deeply. He went on, "It would be a great place for a TV evangelist; 'read your Bible, folks, or you'll end up here.' A credit could run at the end of the program: 'Filmed on location in hell.'"

"If they ever give the world an enema, this is where they'll stick the tube," Box observed. "Come on, let's go in here. I know some of the girls." He dived into a dark doorway under a broken neon sign that proclaimed, "Amer can C ub."

One of the girls greeted the Boxman with glee. "Ah, Box, you're back," she squealed and threw her arms around his neck.

"This here is Suzy. She's my *bonita señorita*. Come on, honey, let's find a table for me and my friends."

"You want some girls, too?" she asked.

"No," said Jake and Ferdinand in unison.

"Of course, a lady for everybody, Suzy baby," shouted the Boxman.

They were soon seated around a large table, five men and five women. Suzy, the one the others obviously looked up to, didn't look eighteen. A waitress placed a bottle of San Miguel beer in front of each man and glasses of brown liquid in front of the girls.

"What your name?" asked the small brown girl on Jake's right.

"Jake," he said, looking straight ahead.

"Hake?"

"No. Jake. With a J."

"Oh . . . Hake. I'm Teresa. You like me, Hake?"

He looked down at her. "You're very pretty."

She nuzzled up to him, rubbing her breast against his arm. "I like you, too, Hake."

The other tables were filled up with American men and Filipino girls. All the bartenders were Filipino men, and the only other Filipino male in the house wore a .45 automatic on his right hip and cradled a short-barreled pump shotgun in his arm. He leaned against the bar near the rear of the room, watching the door. God only knew what disaster he was there to prevent, Jake thought. If he started blasting away with that shotgun, he'd take down half the people in the bar. Jake watched the man, who had a wisp of a mustache and seemed about seventeen, and tried to recall if he had ever heard of a shootout in one of these dives. If you were a Hey-Joe watch thief with a hot sister and survived long enough, this was the job you could aspire to.

Teresa tried valiantly to turn him on. "What do you do on your ship, Hake?" She wrapped her hands around Jake's and smiled. With her head tilted up, she looked genuinely curious.

"I shovel coal for the furnaces."

"Oh," she gushed, "such a hot job. But if you American, you must be rich. Why would rich man shovel coal?"

"How old are you, Teresa?"

"I eighteen." She glanced at Suzy, who was busy laughing at the Boxman's jokes. Jake decided she was fourteen or fifteen. He gulped his San Miguel and let the strangeness of the place flow over him. Teresa apparently decided that the conversation was too much work and she began giggling and whispering with the girl beside her.

About the time they had finished their third beer, Boxman got the urge to move on. "Hey Jake, let's buy our gals out of here. I know a little place called Pauline's that's worth the trip."

Grafton was not enthusiastic. "What could possibly be over there that isn't over here?" Jake had seen all he cared to of the local nightlife and was ready to settle in and get seriously soused.

"Come on, Jake. Trust me. This place'll knock your socks off."

The pilot shrugged. Ferdinand Magellan seized the opportunity to bow out and Big Augie and Razor followed his lead. Boxman gave up trying to persuade them. "Let's go, Jake," he said and got to his feet.

American currency slipped to the club's proprietor convinced him he could spare his B-girls for several hours. Soon Jake, Box, Suzy, and Teresa were bumping along in the back of a jeepney.

Pauline's Place looked like every other dive in Po City, except that in front of the joint was a pond that contained a half dozen or so small alligators, or perhaps crocodiles. On the sidewalk vendors sold chicks and ducklings to drunk Americans to feed to the reptiles in the pond.

As Box and Jake and the two women approached the club, they saw a young American in blue jeans and a tank top, with an earring dangling from one ear, lean over the waist-high rail with a duckling in his hand. "Here, boys. Come and get it." He tossed the small bird into the pond. The duckling fluttered its wings, quacked several times, and paddled through the scum toward the edge. From beneath the water came a slimy snout. Two small white feathers remained floating on the water when the turbulence subsided.

"Duck soup!" shouted the sailor. "How about that? Just slurp and smack and it's all over. Gimme another one of them ducks. No, let's try a chicken this time. We know they like ducks. Let's see if they go for chicken à la feathers." He and his buddies laughed uproariously. "We'll perform a scientific experiment. I wonder if it's the wings flopping that attracts them crocs."

"Let's go in before I puke," Grafton said.

They found a table in a corner. Even before a waitress came up, two hostesses approached and looked daggers at Suzy and Teresa, both of whom glared back. The Boxman laughed and motioned to the new hostesses to join them. The women refused his invitation, though, as a group of marines arrived.

Suzy and Teresa ordered the usual brown fluid, while Box ordered a San Miguel and Jake bourbon. The pilot swigged down a mouthful and promptly choked.

"Box, I'm ready to go back across the bridge. I've definitely had all the fun I can stand tonight." He poured his drink on the floor.

Just then the earring man and his friends trooped in and arranged themselves at the bar. They shouted for beer and were soon surrounded by ladies of the house.

Earring was having a great time. He giggled and drank and slid his hand inside the pants of the girl beside him. She whispered to him and stared at the mirror behind the bar. Earring dug his hand deeper and said something to the man beside him. The two howled with laughter. The girl's face was expressionless.

Jake looked at the Boxman. "Am I the only sane man here, or the only crazy one?"

"He's an asshole all right. It must be something in

the water." Box shrugged. "Maybe it's the beer." He picked up his bottle and eyed it. "I don't feel an attack coming on yet, but I probably just haven't had enough."

"Why's he wearing that earring?"

"It's the fucking rage back in the States. Shows he's tuned in and turned on. Bet he doesn't wear that damned junk on the ship."

"Stick with me, Box." The pilot stood up.

"We go again?" Teresa asked. Apparently she and Suzy were their permanent friends, at least for the evening.

"What're you going to do?" Box wanted to know.

"You with me or not?"

Box drained his San Miguel and stood up. "Lead on, Cool Hand." He tossed a handful of pesos on the table.

Jake strolled over to the bar, patted Earring on the back, and flashed his friendliest smile. "Shipmate, bring your girl and come on outside. We're going to feed the 'gators." Earring looked blank. The pilot addressed the crowd. "Hey, everybody, let's go outside and feed the alligators."

Box chimed in on cue. "Bring the girls and come on outside." Ten or twelve men started for the door. Grafton steered Earring along and stayed with him. "Do those alligators like chickens and ducks?"

"You bet, man. One gobble. And a hell of a lot of squawking."

Outside Earring bought a chick and tossed it into the pond. It disappeared in an explosion of water and feathers. Earring cheered wildly. He reached into his wallet, extracted some pesos, and bought two more birds.

As the sailor stepped up to the rail again, Jake nodded to Box, who assumed a position on the other side of Earring. "Give us room," Jake commanded.

The boy leaned over the rail to toss in a bird. Simultaneously Jake and Box reached down and each grabbed an ankle. They lifted smartly and Earring went over the rail headfirst. He screamed, a high-pitched wail that cut out abruptly when his head hit water.

Jake kept a firm grip on Earring's right ankle, but the Boxman let go and threw up his hands with a whoop. The shock of absorbing the man's weight jerked Jake forward into the rail and his hands slipped. He barely managed to hang on. He tried to shout but for a moment was not able to find his voice. Then it came out. "You dumb shit! Get him out of there."

The Boxman's jaw tightened. Galvanized, he reached over the rail and got a double handful of trousers. Both men strained, but the weight was too much.

Jake Grafton saw Ferdinand Magellan in the crowd, gawking with his mouth open. "Help us, for God's sake!" The three of them managed to pull Earring's head out of the water. Other men grabbed hold.

They hauled him up, choking and sobbing and trying to scream, and flopped him out in the dirt. Bits of slime clung to his hair and paper-white face. He sobbed and looked about wildly. Grafton was shaking and leaned on the rail for support.

The Boxman bent over and looked Earring in the eye. "How'd you like it, asshole?"

The boy now looked pathetic to Jake, who turned away into the crowd. The pilot saw a haymaker coming just in time to duck, and the blow glanced off his ear. He swung back with all he had and felt teeth give as the guy went down.

Whistles sounded.

"Shore patrol!"

Jake ran. He bumped into several people but he made it through the scattering crowd and raced down the sidewalk. A block later, he was finding his running rhythm when he saw Suzy gesticulating at him. "Up here."

He blasted through the doorway and up a narrow flight of stairs. Suzy and the Boxman were right behind him. On a second-floor landing, lit only by a naked light bulb, Suzy unlocked a door and the three of them tumbled into a dark room. The light coming in from the street was sufficient to reveal the jumbled outlines of furniture, apparently stuffed in wall to wall.

Breathing hard, they crowded against the window and stared down the street toward Pauline's. The sidewalk and street were empty except for Earring lying in the dirt and the white-uniformed shore patrolmen. Ducklings and baby chicks wandered about, unsure what to do with their freedom after the hasty departure of their captors. Two shore patrolmen lifted Earring to his feet and escorted him away.

"I'll bet that teaches the sonuvabitch a lesson," the Boxman swore.

"We shouldn't have done it." The excitement and adrenaline were wearing off.

"Serves him right."

"He shit in his pants. I noticed it when we pulled him up. We scared him that bad."

"Maybe he'll tell them we saved his ass after he fell in."

"Maybe the sun won't rise tomorrow."

Suzy was grinning from ear to ear. "You teach him big lesson. Not swim alone."

They roared. "That guy should thank us. We gave him the thrill of his life," Box said, laughing.

"I'll bet all he could think of was those greedy ol' 'gators," Jake gasped.

The mirth finally subsided. Grafton's ear throbbed. "Why'd you let go of his leg?"

"Hell, I dunno." The Boxman scratched his head. "I

guess I just sort of forgot about the alligators. It seemed like the thing to do at the time. Just exactly why did we throw him in, anyway?"

"Because he's an asshole."

Suzy hugged Boxman and gave him a dazzling grin. "You wouldn't throw me in?"

"Oh no! Just sailors."

"You like me?"

Box put his arms around her and kissed her on the lips. "I think I like you with a little more salt." She laughed again and placed his left hand on her modest breast. "Yum yum," the bombardier told her.

Jake felt his way back through the dark room to the door. When he opened it the light from the single bulb on the stair landing fell on an old lady sitting in an armchair in the corner. She had silver hair and a wrinkled face and was very small. He could hear Suzy giggling. The old lady gave him a toothless grin. He closed the door softly as he went out. Down on the street the shore patrol was still standing outside Pauline's, so he waited until their backs were turned, then stepped out on the sidewalk and walked away in the opposite direction.

TEN

The sunbeam crept across the bed and woke Jake Grafton. He turned his head to escape it, but the beam continued its march and burned the sleep from him. Somewhere outside a bird was squawking.

Uncomfortable, he sat up against the headboard. His tongue was like a dust rag. The left side of his head was sore, probably from that punch he had almost stopped with his nose. I'll never smoke another cigarette if I live to be a hundred, he swore to himself, or take another drink. The pain seemed to lessen if he remained absolutely motionless with his eyes closed. He had begun to doze again when the door to the room opened.

"How's the hangover?" asked Sammy. He pulled some aspirin from his toilet kit and placed them in Jake's hand. "Take these. They'll help some."

Jake pried open one eye, regarded the white tablets, and weighed their possible benefits against the effort required to transport himself to the water faucet in the bathroom. Finally he heaved himself up, made the trip, and returned to the bed. Lundeen had flopped down on his bed in the shade.

"What time is it?" Jake asked.

"Time for you and me to go to Hong Kong."

Jake glared at his friend.

"That's right. You heard me. Hong Kong. You and me. I've already been down to the ship and seen the Old Man and filled out our leave forms." Lundeen bounded off the bed and flourished two pieces of paper. "We're off to Hong Kong for four days."

"Can't you see I'm dying of an alcohol overdose? I'm half-dead now. You can't be serious. Why do you want to go to Hong Kong, anyway? I don't have the money to go flying all over the Orient. Nor do I have the desire. Let me die quietly, okay?"

"Goddamn you, Grafton," Lundeen shouted. "Get your butt out of that bed and let's go to Hong Kong."

"Okay, okay. Don't yell, my head's about to split." Jake exhaled slowly. "You sure you really want to go?"

"Yeah, I really want to go, you old maid. Now let's get the show on the road."

Jake stood up. "My stomach thinks my throat's been cut."

"You can eat on the plane."

"You're brimming with sympathy today. *You* can eat on the damn plane. I'm eating at the club in twenty minutes."

Fifteen minutes later they were on their way to the club carrying all their flight gear—to be sent to the ship—and their overnight bags. Halfway there Jake dropped his bags on the sidewalk and puked in the grass.

"You're not going to put food in that stomach, are you?"

"Soup. Got to get something in or I'll be sick all day."

"Next time don't drink so much."

"You oughtta be a priest."

"They don't get enough ass," Lundeen replied and marched off down the sidewalk.

Once inside the cool darkness of the club, Jake began to feel better. The waitress came for their order, and Lundeen ordered first. "Eggs Benedict, side order of ham, and a half bottle of champagne."

Jake's stomach fluttered. He put on his sunglasses and ordered tomato soup, milk, and plain toast. After the waitress left, he rested his chin on his hands and stared out the window at the harbor. He tried to recall the events of the previous evening but it was all a jumble.

Sammy remarked, "I heard all about your little adventure in Po City last night. You might be interested in knowing that that's one reason you and I are blowing this dump for a few days. Sooner or later someone's going to shoot off his mouth. It won't hurt an iota to let that storm blow over while you're in Hong Kong. When the ship pulls out of port and they need guys to fill the flight schedule, the powers that be will view that little episode in a more forgiving light."

Grafton shrugged. "How're we getting there?"

"All arranged. Met a guy last night who's stationed here and belongs to the flying club. About noon he's flying a Cessna over to Manila where we'll catch a plane. That's how I knew we could pull this off. He'll take us if we pay for the plane."

"And how much is that?"

"Ten bucks each."

"What're we waiting for?"

Once they had cleared customs in Hong Kong at Kai Tak Airport and exchanged some money, Lundeen and Grafton hailed a taxi and set off for the Peninsula Hotel, a huge old luxury hotel on the Kowloon waterfront overlooking the harbor. Hong Kong Island was visible across the water, about a mile away. "Why do you want to stay here?" Jake asked.

"Robert L. Scott strafed this hotel in a P-40 during World War II. The Japs were using it as quarters for their high command."

"Who's Robert L. Scott?"

"The guy who wrote *God Is My Co-pilot.*"

"And I thought you just liked the view."

Lundeen had insisted on a room facing the water. A chandelier hung from the high ceiling, and there were two large Victorian beds. The enormous, ornate furniture matched the scale of the room. Once the bellhop had been tipped and left, Jake opened the window. A sea breeze filled the room.

"Do me a favor, Sam."

"Maybe."

"Don't mention bombing or the squadron or the war for the next four days. It's shit. It's all shit and I've had a fucking bellyful."

"That'll be easy," Sammy said. It was not long before they went down to the lobby and headed for the bar.

The next morning Jake stood beside his bed, feeling slightly woozy. He looked at his trembling hands. The screams that had awakened him were still in his ears. He shuffled over to the upholstered chair next to the window and slumped down in the soft cushions.

Pieces of his dream receded beyond the reach of his consciousness as if sinking to the depths of the sea. He did recall that he had been alone in an Intruder and had dived at a target that glittered in the night—a target so significant that by bombing it, he, Jake Grafton, could end the war. What *was* the target? How could he pull off the attack without a bombardier? He remembered that after pickling his bombs he had felt no Gs tugging at him as he tried to pull up. Instead the Intruder vibrated, then shook wildly, and began to disintegrate amidst a howling wind that was suddenly overridden by the piercing cries of hundreds in mortal agony.

Jake sighed. So, he had screwed it up. He had tried to bomb a target that was, for once, truly important—and he had clean missed it. Apparently. Was he supposed to think his bombs had instead destroyed a hospital teeming with people? He decided that he wouldn't let the dream lay a guilt trip on him. To hell with it.

He stood up and stretched. He looked at Lundeen, who was sleeping on his back with his mouth wide open, breathing noisily. Jake smiled. Hey, shipmate, he said to himself, you know what I ought to do? For you and Morgan and every other guy who's hanging his ass out for nothing? I ought to find a fat target way up north and bomb the living shit out of it. One good target. For all of us.

He walked into the bathroom, chuckling at his bravado. But what the hell, he thought. I might actually do it.

He didn't bother to shave. He found his running shoes, shorts, and T-shirt buried deep in his clothes bag. He dressed in the weak light coming through the window.

He started running as soon as he reached the bottom of the hotel's back-door steps. It took only a few minutes for him to realize how out of shape he was. His breathing was labored, without rhythm, and his legs felt wooden. It was not a good day for running; the air was chilly and the fine drizzle would soon soak his clothes. He would take a long hot bath when he got back to the hotel.

On the narrow streets Jake had to dodge and weave to avoid obstacles: bicycles, an occasional automobile, pedestrians who looked at him with curiosity, chattering black-haired, shiny-faced children who mostly ignored him, and shopkeepers raising their brightly colored awnings and arranging wares that spilled onto the streets. Jake was surprised there was so much activity shortly after eight in the morning.

He was glad to reach Nathan Road, a four-lane boulevard where the sidewalks were wider. He passed stores selling electronic equipment, cameras, watches, imported perfumes, and clothing; revving buses and honking taxis passed him by. The red-and-white double-decker buses reminded him of London, but the many large unlit neon signs—SONY, WINSTON FILTER CIGARETTES, COCA-COLA—reminded him of Times Square.

After he had run about a mile and a half, a splash of vivid red caught his eye. As he jogged closer he saw a red sweater, worn by a young woman in a straw hat and jeans. She was sitting on a small metal stool beneath a low awning at the entrance to an alley that ran between two apartment buildings. In her lap was a sketch pad, which he glanced at as he ran behind her. He saw the vague outlines of buildings and the beginnings of some human figures.

He decided that he'd run for ten more minutes, five minutes in the same direction and then he'd circle back and hope to find the woman again. His breathing was rhythmic now, and he ran more on his toes. This would make his calves ache tomorrow. Twenty minutes or so would be a good run. Enough for one day.

When he returned she was still there, sketching under the awning. A crowd of children, ranging in age perhaps from five to eight, played in the alley and on the sidewalk, oblivious to the drizzle. The drawing had progressed markedly. The buildings and storefronts had taken shape and she was working on the children, who seemed to present a challenge because she erased some legs.

Jake stood a moment behind her, then he moved up to her left.

"You're doing a nice job," he said.

"Thanks," she said with an American accent. She looked quickly at Jake, who noticed that her eyes were very dark and that she appeared to be in her mid-twenties. "But I'm afraid it's really not very good." She brushed away the eraser crumbs with the edge of her hand.

"It's tough when your models won't sit still."

She was working on the children again and didn't respond right away. "I'm not sure that it would make any difference if they were still as statues," she said, not looking up. "I've always had trouble with legs—bare human legs, that is. Children always give me fits, damn their pudgy little knees."

Jake chuckled. "I have a solution. I'll go down the street and buy long pants for all these kids."

"Including the girls?"

"Sure," said Jake. "I'll explain that they're required to wear trousers in the service of creating great art."

She gave a short laugh. "I'm sure they'll be persuaded by that argument."

"They will be when I give each one a dollar."

She turned her head and looked at him. "Bribery is very effective in Hong Kong," she said with a quick smile. Her white teeth contrasted with her tanned face and her complexion was clear except for a small dark-brown mole on her left temple. She wore no make-up that Jake could detect.

"I don't know much about Hong Kong," he said, wishing that he had shaved.

She didn't take up his remark but held a pencil to her lips and studied her sketch. Waiting for a reply, Jake examined the children in the drawing—they floated above the sidewalk, unconcerned that they had no legs. Finally Jake said, "Ever try taking photographs?"

"No," she said, not looking up.

"I meant that you could take pictures of the kids and work on your sketch at home. You could even trace the legs to get the hang of it." Jake moved closer to her and squatted down with his forearms on his knees. "Hey, I don't know anything about art. Paintings, drawings, what do I know about it? If I made a dumb suggestion just—"

"Do you always run around in the rain in your shorts?" she said, regarding him with raised eyebrows. "Maybe you should go down the street and buy long pants." There was a hint of a smile. "I'll give you a dollar if you do."

Jake grinned. "American dollar or Hong Kong? While I'm at it, I'll buy you a camera."

"Touché," she said. She swiveled on her stool to face him, and smoothed her jeans as if she were wearing a skirt. "You're in the service, aren't you," she said, stating it as a fact.

Jake was surprised. "How'd you know?"

"Your haircut. It's easy to spot a military man. But your T-shirt threw me off. Are you really a member of the Jersey City Athletic Club?"

"No, I stole this T-shirt from a guy named Cowboy Parker. He stole it from a guy named Little Augie. It's only mine until someone steals it from me."

" 'Cowboy,' 'Little Augie'—which service are we talking about?"

"Navy. I'm a pilot."

"A carrier pilot? Do you fly over Vietnam?"

"Unfortunately."

"Why unfortunately?"

"It's a lousy business."

"Then why do you do it?"

Jake looked down. "You wear the uniform, you take the pay, you fly where they tell you."

"That's not very illuminating," she said. "So you're here on leave. How long will you be in Hong Kong?"

"Just a few days. I have to leave Monday morning." With a groan, Jake stood up slowly. "I'm a little stiff."

"You must be chilled to the bone," she said. "Better get something hot in you."

"Aren't you chilly too?"

"As a matter of fact, yes. I think I've had enough of sitting *and* this weather." She turned from Jake and gathered her pencils and sketchbook into a large floppy leather bag. From a side pocket she yanked out a bundled-up khaki raincoat.

Jake put his hands under his armpits for warmth. "What would you say to getting something hot to drink? Coffee, tea, or whatever. I think we both need it."

"I think you need it more than I do," she said, grinning. She bent over her stool. "Sorry. I have a date to go shopping this morning with a friend." She pushed a catch on the stool, and the seat flipped vertical. "I'm meeting her at ten." Gathering the legs together, she fitted the stool into her bag.

"Amazing," Jake said. "That's some gadget. Any chance we can get together later? For lunch or dinner? I'd like to get to know you better."

She stood facing him now, with her arms crossed in front of her. "Well, you're off to a rocky start, I'm afraid. It seems that I've been asking most of the questions. I know something about you, but you don't know anything about me."

"You didn't ask my name," he said.

"Got me there. What is it?"

"Jake. Jake Grafton."

"Hello, Jake." She began unfolding her raincoat. "It was nice talking to you."

Without forethought he put his hand lightly on her left shoulder. Her shoulder fit in the palm of his hand; he felt the smallness of her bones and the warmth of her body through the sweater. She took a step away from him.

Jake said, "Hey, that was a bum rap you laid on me. I guess I'm not the kind of guy who naturally asks a lot of questions." She started putting on her raincoat. He didn't want her to leave. "I really would like to know you better. It would help if I knew your name."

She took a deep breath. "Callie."

"Callie?"

"Yes. That's right."

"Last name?"

"McKenzie." Jake nodded his head in acknowledgment. "Well," she said, "don't you think Callie is an unusual name?"

"I've never heard it before."

"Don't you want to know how I got it?"

"I'll bite. How'd you get it?"

"I'm glad you asked something," said Callie. "When I was little, my brother, who was just a tot, had trouble saying my name, which is Carolyn. So Theron—my brother—called me Callie. It was easier for him to say."

Jake smiled. "Theron?"

"Yes, Theron," she said. "By the way, let me tell you the fascinating story behind my brother's name."

"Uh oh."

"When my brother was a little boy his younger sister—when she was just a tot—had trouble saying his given name, which was—uh—Aloysius. So . . ." She began laughing. Jake joined her. They stood facing each other as pedestrians moved around them.

"Really," said Jake, "how'd your brother get that name? How do you spell it?"

Callie spelled it out for him. "My father got it out of a book he was reading when my mother was pregnant. I think that he . . . Jake! You're shivering." She touched his chest, near his heart. "No wonder, your shirt is soaked. You'd better get back where you can put on dry clothes. Where're you staying?"

"The Peninsula Hotel."

"Oh, the Peninsula. It's a wonderful hotel. Absolutely first class. Do you like it?"

"Yeah, but it's expensive. I guess you get what you pay for."

"You do at the Peninsula. I had a room there for a few days when I first came to Hong Kong, before I moved into an apartment. I enjoyed it so much that I was reluctant to leave. But I got a nice place only a couple of minutes from where I work." Callie lifted her straw hat and brushed her hair back with her hand. Her hair was curly and reached to her shoulders; it was dark brown, but her eyes were darker and shone like black marbles.

"Well," she said, "don't you want to know where I work?"

Jake smirked. "Sure. Of course I do. I've been wondering about that."

"Since you asked, I work at the American consulate."

"What do you do there?"

"I do a variety of things. But mostly I examine the cases of mainland Chinese refugees who want to obtain visas to the U.S."

"Do you like the work?"

"It's okay. The State Department requires a lot of paperwork for these visas, and sometimes I feel as if we're papering over the human misery of the Chinese refugees. These people have risked everything to escape to Hong Kong."

"Paper shufflers! Well, they're everywhere. They're the ones who'll really inherit the earth."

"Too true. Listen, Jake. I really do have to go. And you need to get back to the Peninsula." She picked up her bag and put her arm through the straps.

"Callie, could we get together for lunch?" She shook her head. "How about dinner?"

"Thanks, but I'm afraid I can't make dinner."

"Why don't we take a walk this afternoon, maybe see some sights?"

"It doesn't look like a good day for it." She sighed. "Tell you what. I could meet you for tea."

"For tea?"

"Haven't you ever met anyone for tea before?"

"Nope, but I'm game. Where do we meet?"

"At your hotel. In the lobby. They do a lovely tea there. Four-thirty?"

"Four-thirty would be fine," said Jake. "I'll be there."

She walked away briskly, into the drizzle. When she was half a block away she stopped and turned. He was still watching her. "Don't just stand there!" she shouted. "Go get some dry clothes on."

Jake waved. "See you at the Peninsula!"

He walked away in the opposite direction. After a few minutes he broke into a trot, and he didn't really mind that he was cold and creaky.

"At least you could've asked her if she had a girlfriend," Sammy called from the bathroom where he was shaving.

Jake stood by the window watching the rain and the low gray clouds scudding across the harbor. The water was so calm and dark it appeared oily, and the clearly defined wakes left by sampans, barges, and ferries were like ripples made by toy boats on a pond. After he returned to the hotel, he had spent a long time luxuriously soaking in the tub. Now his calves were beginning to tighten up. "I wish this rain would stop."

"If it had been me, I would've asked if there was a spare girl stashed somewhere for you. The world is full of lonely women pining for a chance to meet some swell guy with a wad of bucks. Here I am, eligible, handsome, modestly well-heeled, and you didn't even give one of those languishing females a chance. Now I ask you, is that friendship?"

Jake turned his head toward the bathroom. "Hey, I was lucky to get a date."

"A date? You call meeting a girl for *tea* a date?"

"It was the best I could do."

"Did you ask if she had a friend? Huh? Bet you didn't even fucking try."

"It wouldn't have worked, Sammy."

Sammy came out of the bathroom in his skivvies. "Okay, Grafton, I'm beginning to get the picture. You just don't want me around mucking up things between you and your tea-and-crumpets girl."

"Nah, that's not it. Like I said—"

"Just forget it." Sammy dismissed Jake with a wave of his hand. "I can find a date for myself. I don't need your help with my romances. I'm just pointing out this little blot on our friendship." He wore a hurt expression. "But I'll never forget this, Grafton. Never. I may even tell Parker that you're the guy who stole his towel and locked him out of his room."

"But you did that!"

"Yeah, but when roommates get on the outs they start telling lies, and who knows where it'll stop."

"Better not," Jake said, "or I might have to tell 'em you're the Phantom."

Lundeen shot him a hard glance, and went over and sat on his bed. He looked at Jake and grinned. "That just happens to be true."

"What?"

"Yeah. I'm the Phantom," he said, laughing. "You never suspected, did you?"

"Are you crazy? They're looking for some pervert to ship to a mental institution. If they catch you, you'll go back to the States in a straitjacket. My God. . . . You're kidding me, right?" He carefully examined Lundeen's face. "You're pulling my leg again."

"Nope. It's the truth. I am the Caped Crusader. No, that's Batman and I don't have a cape, although I could use Cowboy's towel." He stood on the bed and struck a pose. "I am the Winged Wraith, the Ghost of Bureaucratic Stupidity." He sat down heavily. "No, I gotta think of something else."

"You've flipped out, you stupid jock. Why in the name of God did you do an insane thing like that?"

"Why did you throw that guy in the alligator pond? Because you were fed up with senseless blockheads like him! Well, I'm a little fed up, too. 'Lieutenant Peckerhead skillfully and courageously avoided heavy, accurate enemy opposition and pressed home a devastating attack on the Bang Whang Tree Farm. His courage and tenacity reflected great credit, blah, blah, blah, and were in the highest traditions of the naval service.'" His voice rose to a shout. "I've had it up to here with that kind of crap."

He stared at Grafton. "So I got to thinking about all this shit and decided to take a shit. And I got a big laugh out of it and I felt a lot better about the whole thing and I wrote another half dozen recommendations for medals and sent them to Rabbit Wilson and the jerk loved them and I didn't puke."

Jake turned toward the window. Through the mist he

could barely make out the batwing of a junk. He watched a merchant ship with sampans and barges clustered around it, unloading goods. "Everybody's a fucking hero," he said.

"That's the crazy part of the whole thing," Sammy said. "All those guys are heroes. They're out there risking their asses on every damned flight. They dodge the flak and SAMs, they press the targets, they put the bombs right on the money. Flight pay sure doesn't cover it. They deserve the medals." He stood up and kicked the footboard of the bed. "For what? Tell me for what! I sure as hell would like to know."

"I wish I knew . . ." Jake turned to face Sammy. "You ready for lunch?"

Sammy didn't answer right away. "Yeah. I guess so."

They were alone in the elevator. "I didn't do that last job," said Sammy. "I retired before the skipper of the ship got really pissed. Somebody else did that last one."

"I hope you stay retired."

"Yeah, I think I'm gonna. I like to fly too much." The elevator doors opened at the lobby level but Sammy didn't move. "Maybe there's a reason for it all—some kind of reason that makes sense—and I'm just not smart enough to figure it out."

"I hope so," Jake said, thinking of the flak, the missiles, and of Morgan. "I really hope so."

They walked into the lobby. "I wish you had asked her if she had a girlfriend."

"Next time."

Jake munched on a cookie that was too dry and sweet for his taste. He was thirsty but the Darjeeling tea was still too hot to drink. He wanted a beer. His eyes wandered to the ivory-colored pillar behind her. It was as thick as four men and mounted on a marble base and gilded at the top. The high ceilings were gilded as well.

"I can see you don't want to talk about it," said Callie. Her chair faced the same direction as his and they had to turn awkwardly to speak. The tea and cookies—"biscuits" the Chinese waiter had called them —were on a low table between their chairs. "Tell me about the flying part. You really like that part of it, don't you?" She sipped her tea, waiting for him to answer. Without her hat her face was rounder, softer; she seemed younger. Her hair, which she had neatly brushed out, was less curly.

The many voices in the spacious lobby reverberated, and Jake had to speak uncomfortably loud to be heard. "Sure, I like the flying." Why had she brought up the goddamn war? "I used to think that I was the luckiest guy in the world—to be paid by the navy to do something I'd be happy to do for free."

"You don't feel that way any more?"

"Sometimes I do. Sometimes." Jake sipped the tea. It needed sugar. He put down the cup knowing he would not pick it up again.

"Tell me more, Jake. What sort of feeling do you have when you're flying? Do you feel exhilaration? Is it like the feeling I get when I ride a roller coaster?"

"Sometimes it's like a roller coaster. But that's not the true feeling of it." As Jake sought the words, Callie's eyes peered at him above her teacup. "Well," said Jake. "It's like when you were a kid and you pretended you were sick so you could stay home from school. The rest of the world is working, at school, in factories, in offices. But there you are, sitting in your cockpit, feeling like you're getting away with something, flying smoothly along enjoying the sky and the clouds and looking down at the earth. You are free and unfettered and feel privileged you can fly." Jake paused. "But on the ground a pilot is like a man waiting for a train. He's restless, anxious to get away. A pilot just bides his time until his plane can take him away again, into the air. He feels like a visitor when he's on the ground."

Callie put down her cup. "I like the way you put that."

Jake had felt his voice growing hoarse as he talked. "I'm awfully thirsty. Why don't we move to the bar?"

They could sit facing each other now, and the chairs were more comfortable than those in the lobby. Callie had ordered a gin and tonic, and Jake was halfway through a bottle of San Miguel beer. There were only a few people in the bar, and the piano was unmanned.

"I'm not sure you enjoyed the tea," Callie said.

Jake smiled. "I guess I felt out of place. They don't have many teas where I come from."

"Where are you from?"

"A small town in Virginia, called Ridgeville. It's in southwestern Virginia, not too far from the North Carolina border. Not a hell of a lot happens there." Jake took a swig of beer. "Where're you from, Callie?"

"Chicago. Hyde Park. The neighborhood around the University of Chicago. My father teaches in the business school, and my mother's in the foreign language department."

"Did you go there?"

"Most certainly. It was preordained. I did both my undergraduate and graduate work there—in foreign languages, of course."

"A real family affair," said Jake.

"That was the problem. Both Mom and Dad assumed that I would pursue an academic career. They were pretty upset when I took the foreign service exam, and more upset when I passed it. They pleaded with me to go on for a doctorate, but—as the saying goes—I wanted to see the world."

"And you wanted to be your own person."

"That was a good part of it, sure."

"You must speak Chinese, then," said Jake.

"Uh-huh. I speak Mandarin mostly, and I'm studying Cantonese here."

"I'm impressed."

"Chinese—spoken Chinese, that is—isn't as difficult to learn as many people think. The grammar is easy. Reading it, though, is quite a challenge."

"Can you read it?"

"Only a little. It takes years to develop competency Basically it's sheer memorization."

Jake looked at Callie's glass. "Guess you're not ready for a refill."

"Go ahead. Please don't wait for me."

Jake merely looked up and a young Chinese waiter came immediately to their table. He pointed to the empty beer bottle. "Just mine."

"I'd like to know about your hometown," said Callie. "What do people do there?"

"They farm mostly, grow a lot of vegetables. Those who don't farm sell stuff to those who do."

"Tell me something that captures the flavor of the place."

Jake thought a moment, then said, "The last time I was home on leave, the big news in Ridgeville, VA, was that the movie projector in the Plaza had been broken for two months. The guy who owns the Plaza, who'd been promising everybody for months that he'd buy a new projector, finally admitted that maybe a new projector was too expensive—and the Plaza's the only theatre in town."

"What a tragedy!" said Callie with a laugh.

"Yep. And the other big news was that Sam Chaplain's sixteen-year-old daughter—Sam runs the Ford dealership—had gotten pregnant."

"No!"

"For the second time."

"Really?" said Callie, breaking up. "I bet I know when it happened."

Jake grinned. "You do?"

"Uh-huh. It happened one night soon after the projector broke down at the Plaza."

Jake laughed. "You got it! And you know what? There were about fifteen other women in town who all just happened to be about two months pregnant."

"I think we should drink to the Plaza." Callie lifted her glass. "May it quickly get a new projector."

Their glasses clinked.

"But be honest, Jake. Do you like Ridgeville?"

"Actually I do. I grew up there, went to high school there. I liked working on Dad's farm, and I like the hunting and fishing, which I did a lot of. Maybe everybody knows too much about everybody else, and you have the feeling of living in a goldfish bowl, but the people are friendly and ready to help you if you've got a problem. Sure, we've got our bad apples, but most people are okay. I've got a few friends there who I've known all my life and I feel they'll be my friends, and I'll be theirs, until I die."

She asked about his friends and he told her about the impromptu beer and skinny-dipping party at Caldwell Lake following a church-sponsored picnic; he told her about the time he lost his brakes in his '57 Chevy on Hodam Mountain when he and his buddies were returning from a hunting trip and how he wiped out a historic marker; and he told her some other stories that made her laugh. She laughed easily. When she asked again about his flying he told her how he had learned to fly, not in the navy, but in a Cessna 140 at a grass strip on the edge of town. He'd taken his first lesson at fifteen and had gotten his private pilot's license on his seventeenth birthday, the first day that he could legally take his flight exam. The next day his father agreed to go flying with him, to be Jake's first passenger.

"Were you nervous?"

"I was excited, confident. Eager to show off."

"What about your dad?"

"Well, he was pretty nervous at first. Kept asking me about the instruments and controls and whether I'd checked everything. But after a while he realized I knew what I was doing, and he enjoyed the rest of the flight."

"Was he proud of you?"

"I guess he was. I know *I* was."

"That's quite an accomplishment, getting your pilot's license on your seventeenth birthday."

"It's not unusual, others have done it."

"I think you're just being modest."

Jake gestured to the waiter for another round of drinks. He noticed the bar was busier, and he heard crisply enunciated British voices.

"I'm going to be in great shape for tonight," said Callie. Jake looked at her quizzically. "A CODEL—a congressional delegation—arrived yesterday. The CG —sorry, the consul general—is having a reception for them tonight at his place. I don't think he'd appreciate it if I passed out on the carpet."

"Do you want to go?" said Jake. He had a sinking feeling.

"I'm not terribly excited about going."

"Why don't you bag it, then?'

"I should be there. It's part of my job."

"How's that?"

"One of my collateral duties is that I'm the CODEL control officer and—"

"Why aren't you out controlling them now?"

"They wanted to go shopping, so I have some time off. Theoretically, they're here to look at what differences Nixon's trip has made in Chinese attitudes toward America. We always have a difficult time figuring out how to handle CODELs."

"Handle 'em roughly. Without mercy. Just the way the voters handle them." He enjoyed her laughter. "Maybe take them on sightseeing tours."

"You're right. I'm sure we'll roll out the red carpet, but that red carpet is going to lead straight out of the consulate."

"Smart. Keep 'em busy and out of your hair. Probably all they want is to shop anyway."

"That's part of it, no doubt. But there's political hay to be made, too. If relations with China open up, they'll want to take some of the credit."

The bastards, Jake thought, staring into his glass. They go on junkets while good men die going after targets that aren't worth a pint of piss.

Callie said, "A penny for your thoughts?"

Jake looked up and met her eyes. "A plugged nickel would be more appropriate."

"Is something wrong?"

He didn't want to get into it. "No," he said finally. "What about your other work at the consulate? Your work involving visas? How do you like it?"

"There's a lot of paperwork, a lot of drudgery. But there're things about it I like, too. I work in the nonimmigrant visa office and enjoy talking to the young people who want to study in the U.S. Often these people are recent refugees from Red China who unfortunately cannot prove that they'll return to Hong Kong when they finish their education. And that's a requirement for a student visa. These refugees give a picture of the mainland you can't get elsewhere. Some of the stories they tell about how they escaped are awesome."

Callie had been holding her drink in her hands. Now she put it down and leaned toward Jake. "Let me tell you about a boy I interviewed last week. A nice-looking boy, named Wang Chiang. Eighteen years old, small for his age but strong. He escaped six weeks ago by swimming across Deep Bay to the New Territories. He and his—"

"How far did he have to swim?"

"About seven miles."

Jake whistled. "That took a lot of stamina. And guts."

"A *lot* of guts," said Callie. "Chiang, which is his given name, and his older brother—by a year, I think—hid in the hills of China for days, waiting for the conditions to be right to swim the bay. They wanted a dark night so they couldn't be easily spotted and not much wind so they wouldn't have to fight the waves. On a night when the weather was overcast and drizzly—like today, I imagine—they slipped into the bay. They didn't take the shortest route, about three miles, because it's heavily patrolled. Partway across, Chiang's brother began to tire, then he got severe cramps—"

"Oh, no."

"Yes. Chiang told his brother to float, to rest, hoping that the cramps would go away. But the cramps stayed bad. The brother swallowed water and coughed a lot. Chiang tried to hold him up, but eventually they both went under. Chiang couldn't see anything—the water was black—and his lungs were about to burst. His brother was clutching at him. He had to fight loose of his grasp."

"Jesus!" said Jake. "I don't know how he managed to swim the rest of the way after that." Jake could envision the terror in the darkness as the boy fought the panicky clutches of his drowning brother. He remembered that Morgan had also clutched at his arm. "At least Chiang's brother knew what he died for."

"I guess he did know. Mainly he wanted a better way of life. And the family had prepared both the boys. Their father had told each son to go on if the other ran into serious trouble. Chiang's family was very practical. They knew the risks. At least they didn't encounter any sharks." She leaned across and touched the back of his hand. "Are you okay?"

Jake took a deep breath. "Oh, yeah. But Chiang didn't really follow his father's instructions—which I can understand. I'm not sure I would've either. Although I see that it would be much harder now on Chiang if his father hadn't given him those instructions. Does the family know what happened?"

"Uh-huh, they know. There are ways of communicating across the border."

He looked around the bar, at the tables, the British gentlemen in expensive suits tossing back their pints, the Chinese bartender washing glasses, the mirror reflecting and enlarging the room. He thought of struggling to stay afloat at night in a running sea, waiting for the sharks. "Can you get Chiang to the States?"

"I'll do my best, Jake." She sipped the last of her drink and sighed. "Well, I've enjoyed talking to you."

"You have to go?" Jake said.

"Alas, I need to get home and change for the shindig tonight."

"I'd like to see you home."

"Thanks, but there's no need to go through all that. It'd mean two ferry rides for you."

"No problem. Riding boats is one of the things they pay me for."

"No, it's really too much trouble."

"I want to see you again."

Callie looked down at the table. "I have a clear day tomorrow."

"So do I."

She raised her eyes. "Why don't you walk with me to the Star Ferry? We can talk on the way."

* * *

The rain had stopped. Callie and Jake passed by Rolls and Mercedes sedans parked in the curved driveway of the hotel. Although the harbor was only a short distance away, Jake could not see it, so thick was the fog.

Callie ran her hand through her hair. "Ugh! This weather. And I won't have much time to do anything with my hair."

As they crossed the street three teenaged boys came toward them. Their black hair was slicked down and they wore open-collared, long-sleeved shirts in bright, solid colors. They talked loudly and one tried to bump into Callie, who adroitly sidestepped him. "Teddy boys," she said to Jake. "Hong Kong's version of juvenile delinquents."

They edged onto the sidewalk, which was packed with people. Callie and Jake, joining the crowd, had to slow their pace. High-pitched, sing-song voices beat against his ears. Jake felt clammy, and his stomach tightened. "So many people," he said. "There are five thousand men on my ship and it's never this crowded. How do you stand it?"

Callie laughed. "Did I say I could stand it? It's like living in a closet with five million people. Stay with me; it's not much farther." Passers-by jostled him, sometimes roughly.

There were fewer people as they neared the terminal landing, but directly ahead was a dense crowd that Jake assumed was waiting to board the ferry. He caught glimpses of the harbor. Callie stopped. "Look," she said. "See that building? That's the Ocean Terminal where the passenger liners dock and disgorge crazed shoppers." Jake said nothing and they went on.

She told him as they walked about the excellent shops, the many fine things for sale in Hong Kong, and the restaurants—Maxine's Boulevard was her favorite.

She talked about the Star House Arcade, next door to the terminal, where there were other interesting places to shop, including a store devoted entirely to Seiko watches. If he wanted a good watch, that was the place to buy it. She chattered on, and Jake thought she sounded like a tour guide.

"Callie," he said, interrupting her. "Cool it. I'm not some idiot congressman." Callie stopped and looked up at him, astonishment spreading across her face. He put his hands on her shoulders. "I didn't come to Hong Kong to shop. I came to get away from the goddamn war. Now all I want is to be with you." He cupped her head in his hands; his palms pressed lightly against her ears, his fingers entwined in her springy hair. He brought his lips to hers. So soft, he thought. So gentle. He felt her arms encircle his waist; he put his arms around her, drawing her closer. She smelled fresh and springlike—of lilacs. She broke off the kiss and said, "That was a surprise."

Because of the crowd it took five minutes for Jake and Callie to get near a turnstile for the ferry. They decided on their plans for the next day while two ferries filled up and left. Jake escorted her to the turnstile and she went through. Turning back toward him, she called out, "See you tomorrow!" When she smiled broadly and waved, a pleasant warmth suffused him, like the first swallow of a mellow scotch. He watched the green and white ferry slide into the fog.

By the time Jake got back to the hotel it was dark. His stomach felt queasy again. He was glad to enter the lobby and leave the hordes and the humidity behind. When he got to his room he was disappointed that Sammy wasn't there, but not surprised. He had wanted to tell him about Callie.

After a long shower he changed into fresh clothes. Feeling better, he went down to the Swiss restaurant in the hotel, the Chesa, and had a steak and a beer. It settled his stomach. He returned to his room and, lighting up his second cigarette of the day with hands that shook slightly, watched television before going to bed.

At first he thought about Callie, replaying as best he could what they had said to each other and what they had done. Then he recalled those crowds of Asian faces, those voices. They had pressed their flesh against his. Their babble had assaulted his ears. It was as though they wanted him to know they were real.

What you try to do, Jake thought, is to keep it fuzzy in your mind that you kill real people. You pickle the bombs and you don't see them fall and you don't hear the explosions. You see only silent puffs of smoke sometimes and how could they kill anyone? It's not real. You begin to think that maybe Orientals don't breathe, don't eat, don't shit, can't feel pain, don't cry out. You begin to think they're not real. You try to keep it fuzzy in your brain where the truth of it all resides because you know that you don't want to kill—God, you don't want to kill. But yet you do kill, maybe as many as fifty at a time. You have bombs and there are no fair fights and you know it's wrong. You live with shame. It would be different if you knew that if you didn't kill a man he would kill you, like gunfighters facing off or fighter aircraft dueling in the sky. Sometimes you get to attack those who try to kill you with flak and missiles and if you kill them you can handle it. But you have bombs. Mostly you kill those who aren't trying to kill you. It's the children you've maybe killed that give you the worst dreams of all because you can see what your bombs do to their small bodies and you can hear their screams. But you don't really know if you've killed children—maybe you haven't. You can tell yourself you haven't unless you learn that you've screwed up and your bombs have hit a hospital or a school. So you try hard to keep your mind fuzzy about all this, about the truth, about what the truth might be. And you want to rip the balls off any grinning bastard who tells you how many, precisely, you've killed.

ELEVEN

Sammy threw open the curtain and dazzling sunlight burst into the room.

"C'mon, Grafton. Get your arse moving. It's gonna be a great day."

Yawning, Jake said, "Arse?"

"I've been hanging around with the Brits. Smashing guys."

"What time is it?" Grafton noticed that Lundeen's bed had not been slept in.

"Almost ten. Let's go, matey. Up an' at 'em, shit and shave."

"What's the rush?" Jake groaned. "Where were you last night, anyway?"

"These Brits I met—Royal Navy types—fixed me up with an Aussie lassie, an airline stew who immediately recognized my sterling qualities. Couldn't bear to spend the night without me." Sammy rolled his eyes appreciatively. "Cool Hand, this is your lucky day. She's got a friend. A sex-starved female just dying to meet you."

Jake rose and went into the bathroom, and Sammy came over and stood near the door. "Hey, Grafton. Has it been so long you've forgotten what sex is? I said

I got you fixed up. Had to lie a little, of course. Told her you had hundreds of females fighting each other for your bod. But what the hell, a friend's a friend, right?"

"Right," said Jake. He came out of the bathroom. "I really appreciate this, but there's a glitch. I—"

"A glitch? What're you talking about?"

"Remember that woman I told you about yesterday? The one who—"

"What?" said Sammy, incredulously. "You mean Miss Tea and Crumpets? You can't be serious. I've got you fixed up with a *real* woman, also an Aussie. As good as I am, I couldn't possibly handle them both."

"Sure," said Jake. "But I've got a commit—"

"Now look, Jake." Sammy spoke very slowly and deliberately, as though he were speaking to a small child. "Let me make this very clear. You can get *laid* today. By this voluptuous hunk of very tall blonde woman. This woman will overstress your main spar, laddy. You know what I'm talking about. L-A-I-D."

"Yeah," said Jake. "But listen a goddamn minute to what—"

"Okay," said Sammy with finality. "I got the picture." Walking toward the door, he said, "Well, I was gonna go to breakfast with you, but I can see you're off your rocker today and I'm starving, so I'm not gonna wait." Sammy opened the door, then turned toward Jake. "Tell me this. Did you get into her crumpets? Huh? Huh?"

"Go to hell."

"Ha! I knew it! I rest my case." He slammed the door.

Deciding he'd shower later, Jake shaved hurriedly. He caught Sammy at breakfast. The residue of fried eggs was on his plate. Jake ordered coffee, tomato juice, and toast with orange marmalade.

"You should've checked first," said Jake. "I told you about her yesterday."

"And just how could I do that? Anyway, how can I take seriously a broad who says she wants to meet you for tea? *Tea.*"

"I take her seriously. She's all right."

"Yeah, yeah."

"I'd like you to meet her," said Jake.

"Don't see how I could fit that in. I've got a lot of things to do today. Arrangements would have to be rearranged, you know?"

"Yeah, I know. I sure do appreciate what you did. But I want you to meet her. Like to know what you think."

Sammy took two sips of coffee before answering. "Well, as I said, I'll be pretty busy today. But I'll give consideration to it."

When Callie called from the lobby, Jake told her that he wanted her to meet a friend of his. In the hallway Sammy said, "What the hell are crumpets, anyway?"

"Beats me."

As they waited at the elevator, Jake said, "Be nice, okay?"

"Grafton, if my little deal with the Aussie sisters falls apart because I can't come up with another guy, your ass is grass."

They walked into the lobby, which was brighter than Jake had ever seen it. "Is that her," Sammy said, "standing by the pillar?"

"Yep," said Jake, returning Callie's wave. "That's her."

Callie was wearing dark slacks and an unbuttoned white sweater over a yellow blouse. She carried a small shoulder bag.

"Not bad," Sammy said. "Not bad at all."

Jake wanted to hug Callie, but instead he introduced her to Sammy, who stood with his feet together and made a little bow. Callie smiled and said, "Jake told me you're his roomie. Are you a pilot, too?"

"Yes, ma'am," said Sammy. "I'm crazy, too."

Callie laughed. "I didn't know you had to be crazy to fly."

"You gotta be nuts to fly and nuts to be in the navy," Sammy said solemnly. "So we've got a double whammy. Only insane people could live for months cooped up on a ship like a bunch of monks."

"How long have you two been inflicting craziness on each other?"

The men exchanged glances. "We've known each other a couple years, I guess," Jake said.

"Yeah," said Sammy. "And we've been living together for about a year, so I know all Jake's faults. I can make up a list when we get back to our floating monastery and send it to you. That much paper will have to go freight-rate, though."

Callie looked at Jake with raised eyebrows. Then she turned back to Sammy. "Not meaning to change the subject, but are you enjoying Hong Kong?"

"Definitely," said Sammy. "I'm having a blast."

Jake said, "Callie's going to show me the *real* Hong Kong. She's going to keep me out of the tourist traps."

"With one exception," said Callie. "We're going to the Peak. That's one tourist attraction nobody should miss."

"I know," said Sammy. "I was there last night."

"Last night?" said Callie. "You couldn't have seen a thing!"

"My friend and I didn't mind."

"Well," said Jake. "I can see that months of contemplation and prayer have done you no good at all."

"You and your friend should go back," said Callie. "To check out the view."

"I'll seriously consider your advice," said Sammy. "Well, I must leave you young people." He leaned down and spoke softly in Callie's ear. "Jake's list of faults isn't so long. In fact, you're lucky. He's really a great guy."

"What do you think of Sammy?" said Jake as he and Callie stepped out into the bright day.

"He's funny," she said. "Only a little crazy. I like him."

The sky was blue and cloudless, and the air was comfortably dry. It was breezy. Jake took Callie's hand and they walked up Nathan Road. "Most of these stores are open, on a Sunday?" he said.

"They do a booming business. Tourists like to shop here."

Callie led him down a narrow side street where vendors hawked fresh vegetables and plump fruits, the many colors, shapes, and textures overbrimming the large wicker baskets. "What are these?" asked Jake, picking up a small fuzzy object.

"Kiwi fruits. Those are mangoes. They're sweet and delicious."

The air was heavy with the smell of produce and the street was thronged with shoppers, many carrying bulging plastic bags. Jake yanked Callie out of the path of a wobbling bicycle ridden by a boy of seven or eight. "Bet he doesn't have a driver's license," said Callie.

"He's probably late for a date with his girlfriend."

They passed a flower shop. The window bloomed with multicolored plastic flowers. An old woman with missing teeth darted up from the doorway and grabbed Jake's sleeve. "Flowers for the lady? Flowers for the lady?"

Jake smiled at Callie. "If she has some real ones, would you like some flowers?"

"Thanks, but I don't know where I'd put them."

The woman kept up her chant and tugged harder at Jake's sleeve. "No flowers," he said. "The lady doesn't want flowers. No, thank you." The old woman beamed and pulled all the harder at Jake. "No, no. No flowers! No!"

Callie laughed. "She knows a soft touch when she sees one." She then spoke to the woman in Cantonese. Her voice sounded to Jake like the other nasal, singsong voices he'd been hearing. He was startled. For a moment he felt as if Callie were an imposter: a Chinese woman wearing the skin of an American. The old woman immediately dropped Jake's arm. But when she turned to Callie, her eyes were twinkling and she launched into a stream of comment, from which Jake and Callie fled down the street.

After a while, having walked street after street, Jake decided that just about anything a person might want could be bought in Kowloon. But he didn't want any of it—no jade, no sequined sweaters, no watches, no sculptured ivory sampans or concentric balls, no gold trinkets, no enameled rings, no silks, no toys. Although he had gotten hungry, he didn't want to try the duck a vendor was roasting over a charcoal fire, and he didn't want to taste the golden egg yolks that had been salted and dried in the sun. In fact, he temporarily lost his appetite after seeing a butcher shop where chickens dangled by cords and cows' heads lay in pools of blood. And he didn't want his fortune told—that least of all.

Callie tried to talk him into having a suit and some shirts made. "You're missing a terrific opportunity."

"That's all right. I don't wear civilian clothes very often. Are you ready to go to Victoria Peak?"

"Are you tired?"

"Maybe," he said. "All these people, everybody pushing you to buy something."

Callie put her hand behind his head and massaged his neck. Then she kissed him. "I bet you're hungry."

She led him down an alley that was only as wide as a sidewalk. It was lined with racks of cassette tapes and books, some of which were in English.

"These books and tapes aren't for sale," Callie said. "They're part of a lending library."

Farther down the alley Callie stopped. "This is it," she said, and opened the door to a very small room. Jake stepped inside and looked around. There were only three tables, which were covered with newspaper, and in the back of the room a middle-aged man and woman were busy cooking. A young Chinese couple were seated at a table. Callie led Jake to a table by the window, away from the other couple. As they sat down a fly landed on Jake's forehead. He swept it away. "Trust me," said Callie. "It's a lot better than it looks."

The blue walls were faded and a single wooden fan squeaked overhead. The woman came up to them, wiping her hands on her apron. She smiled widely when she recognized Callie. Callie said to Jake, "I'll order us some dumplings. I think you'll like them better fried. Would you like a beer?"

"I sure would. I might not have anything else."

"Ching-ni gei-woman er-shih-ssu-ge chao-tzu, liang-ping pi-jyou," said Callie. Jake was startled again by her verbal metamorphosis. "You're really good," said Jake when the woman had gone away.

Callie grinned. "How would you know?"

"If we get dumplings and beer, I'll know you're good. If we get fried snakes or toasted rabbit ears, I'll know you blew it."

Callie threw back her head and laughed.

The woman brought a mound of dumplings on a single plate, which they shared. Jake gingerly picked one up. "Pretty tasty," he said with his mouth full. He reached for another.

"I told you they'd be good."

After the dumplings were gone, Jake thought about ordering another beer.

"Are you rejuvenated?" Callie asked.

"Like an actress with a facelift. I'm ready for anything."

"Good. Let's go to the Peak, then. It's a wonderful day for it."

As they headed for the Star Ferry, Callie took him down side streets they had not been on before. Jake stopped to look at a man, sitting on a stool, who was writing while a gray-haired woman standing next to him spoke. The black Chinese characters seemed to flow from his pen. "He's a calligrapher," explained Callie. "He's writing a letter for the woman because she doesn't know how to write. She'll pay him for it."

"What's the letter about?"

"Wait just a minute." Callie eavesdropped. After a moment she said, "My goodness, Jake! Her granddaughter has had twins! There's great rejoicing over this event, which portends many good things for the family. But I don't know who she's writing to."

"That's great news," Jake said. "Congratulations," he said to the woman, who looked up at him. Jake raised two fingers in a peace or victory sign. The great-grandmother smiled back and bowed her head in acknowledgment. When they started to walk away, the woman called out something to them. Jake asked, "What did she say to us?"

"Hmm. I'm not sure I should tell you."

"Come on. What'd she say?"

"All right, I'll tell you. She said that she hopes we're similarly blessed."

"That's a nice thought."

The second-class seats on the Star Ferry had thin wooden slats that made Jake fidget. Yesterday the water had been dark, but today it was blue-green and it sparkled. Jake enjoyed the breeze, although it sometimes carried a smell of fish. He marveled at how the slow-moving junks and other small craft managed to avoid colliding with the ferry. Callie sat next to him by the open side of the ferry, and her yellow dropped earrings danced. When Jake put his arm around her, she put her hand on his leg.

As it neared the pier, the ferry vibrated from its backing engines. Callie said, "Let's take a cab. Unless you want to hike uphill."

"I left my mountain-climbing shoes at home."

They waited at the Peak Tram station on Garden Road, passing up opportunities to board until Callie could be sure of getting seats at the rear of the tram on the right side, where the view would be best.

Pulled on rails by a thick steel cable, the rumbling, packed train rose steeply toward the Peak, and the city fell away behind. The L-shaped Hong Kong Hilton and other high rises seemed to be shrinking. Across the street from the tram station was the American consulate, an attractive, balconied building that Callie pointed out to Jake after they had left the cab. She had also pointed out Estoril Courts, her apartment house, a tan concrete building two blocks from the consulate. Most of Callie's neighbors had put out flowers and plants on their balconies; Callie had told him that from her balcony you could see the harbor, but new construction was blocking the view.

The tram stopped a third time, with a gentle rocking back and forth. Jake said, "How many more stops before we get to the top?"

"Who cares? It's such a beautiful day!"

The tram rose even more sharply and Jake felt that he was more lying on his back than sitting down. He said to Callie, "If this tram moved eighty times faster, you'd have an idea of what it's like to zoom-climb in an A-6."

"Sounds like great fun," she said. "Will you take me flying someday?"

Jake looked at her closely. Putting his arm around her shoulder, he said, "You can count on it."

At the Peak, hawkers selling photographic transparencies and other souvenirs aggressively worked the crowds spilling out of the tram station. Callie took Jake's hand and led him across the street where there was an outdoor restaurant.

Jake stopped. "I hope you're not going to suggest we have tea again."

"Not at this tourist trap. But what would be wrong with having tea?"

"Sammy gave me a lot of flak about meeting you for tea. He calls you my tea-and-crumpets girl."

She laughed. "I've been called worse. Well, you can tell Sammy that I think he's a nice guy but a bit presumptuous."

"Presumptuous?"

"Don't you think so? Calling me 'your girl'?"

"Well, I don't know," said Jake with a grin. "Sammy's not a guy who jumps to conclusions."

Reflecting, Callie pursed her lips. "I'm nobody's 'girl,' actually. But I suppose that I could be somebody's. . . ." She gave a laugh. "No! That wasn't coming out the way I intended it to." Callie paused, and said, "Maybe I should try saying it in Chinese."

"No, don't do that," he laughed. "Then I'd never understand you. Look, let's try this. Why don't we see what we can do to not make a liar out of Sammy. Hell, we've got to protect his honor."

Callie shook her head slowly. "Jake Grafton, you're a tricky SOB. But all right. I'm willing to explore, for today anyway, how we can preserve Sammy's honor."

"Time's awastin'," Jake said. He put his hands around her arms and gave her a brief kiss. Then he drew her close to him, and watched her dark eyes slowly close; he felt her relax in his arms. He kissed her again, and this time her body pressed against his. Their tongues touched once, surprising him, and something electric jumped in his body. He didn't want to stop, but she eased them apart. Jake became aware that he was breathing heavily, and he noticed Callie was too.

Running her hand through her hair, Callie said, "We've got to stop doing this in public."

"I don't think the public gives a damn. But I'm easy. I'll do it wherever you want."

"Come on, smart ass," she said, taking his hand. "Let's see what we came here to see."

They stood together near a rusty coin-operated telescope, to which a young Chinese man wearing aviator-type sunglasses held up his gesticulating, noisy, chubby-legged son. Jake was watching them when Callie spoke. "It's so clear I can't believe it. This is really unusual. The pollution is getting so bad that very often you can't see much."

"The visibility is terrific. It'd be a great day for flying." He looked at the harbor, and at the disorderly congestion of sailing craft and motorboats. Only the Star ferries seemed to have destinations. He counted three of them moving between Hong Kong Island and Kowloon.

"See that mountain in the distance, Jake? That's

Castle Peak. Behind it a few miles is Deep Bay, where Wang Chiang's brother drowned."

"I see it."

"On the other side of the bay is mainland China."

Jake gazed at the massive blue-gray mountains. They made the green Virginia mountains he knew so well seem like mere hills. Rugged country if you were shot down, he reflected. 'Yeah," he said at last. "They're impressive."

"Sometimes I come here alone," Callie told him. "I usually walk along the road to the other side of the Peak to get away from the crowds. It's a good place to sort things out. To try and figure out what you believe in."

"Have you figured anything out yet?" asked Jake, still looking at the mountains.

Callie considered the question. "Nothing earthshaking. I've always believed in God. But I decided that organized religion doesn't do much for me. I guess I don't want anything intruding between me and God." She smiled. "Like Moses, I prefer direct contact."

Jake grinned. "But Moses had a mountain. Have you ever brought stone tablets up here and looked around for bushes on fire?"

"No," she laughed. "I'm still looking for the right mountain." She canted her head. "Maybe I should place an ad in the newspapers."

"Let's see. You could say: Wanted, one mountain. Must be able to withstand huge bolts of lightning, hurricane-force winds—and a voice a thousand times louder than thunder."

Callie picked it up. "Will pay generous price for the right mountain, plus a bonus if equipped with stone tablets. Call Sundays. No agents, please."

They laughed together.

Callie's eyes were still wet when she asked, "What do you believe in?"

"These days I'm not sure. But I do believe this. I believe in Jake Grafton. I believe if he's tough enough, alert enough, and good enough, he can keep himself in one piece. Maybe."

Callie furrowed her brow. "That sounds pretty macho to me. Chest-thumping stuff."

"I didn't mean it that way."

"You're talking about surviving. I can understand that. But you must have some beliefs about other things."

"What difference does it make what I believe in if I don't survive? I've *got* to believe in myself. If I don't have confidence in myself, I'm dead. If you're short on confidence and you fly off carriers, you're going to be history pretty quick."

"Haven't you ever lost your confidence?"

"There've been times when it got mighty shaky, but I don't think I've ever lost it. In Intruders, the planes I fly, you get a lot of moral support from the guy sitting next to you in the cockpit, the bombardier."

"This flying you do sounds tough. I guess you can't afford to make mistakes."

"Every pilot makes mistakes. In fact, there's no such thing as a perfect flight. You make a lot of mistakes. Some you correct, and some you can't. You just can't make the mistake that will kill you. That's where the confidence comes in. You have to *know* you'll never make that fatal slip."

They came down from the Peak on a tram that was not full. The late-afternoon breeze was cool and Callie huddled next to him. They had hardly spoken since boarding the tram.

"A plugged nickel for your thoughts?" said Callie.

"They're worth more than that. I was thinking about you."

"I'm flattered."

"I have to leave tomorrow morning."

"I know. I've been thinking about it too."

"I sure as hell don't want to leave you. I wish I had more time here."

"I wish you had a lot more time here. But let's not get gloomy. The night is young, and I'm so hungry I could eat half a horse."

"Half a horse?"

"I've never been hungry enough to eat a *whole* horse."

With a laugh, Jake said, "I'm hungry enough to eat a team. But what I could really go for instead is a good steak."

They took a cab to Jimmy's Kitchen, a Western-style restaurant that Callie said was a favorite with the consulate crowd. They were shown to a table in the corner of the dark, wood-paneled restaurant by a waiter with bushy eyebrows. Jake was amazed at his resemblance to Chou En-Lai, whose picture he had seen in newsmagazines.

"I thought you only drank beer," said Callie, dipping a shrimp into cocktail sauce.

"I like scotch, too." Jake took another swig. He buttered a roll and ate it in three bites. When the waiter brought their salads, Jake ordered another scotch on the rocks.

Callie sipped her gin and tonic. Then she said casually, "I'm still not sure what you believe in besides Jake Grafton."

Jake watched the candlelight flickering in her eyes. When he answered he said, "There's something else I believe in. I believe in keeping the faith with the guys I fly with. You try not to let each other down."

"Does everybody keep the faith, the men you fly with?"

"Yeah, for the most part." Jake put down his drink

and examined it. Then he spoke without looking up. "It has to be that way. Especially with your bombardier." Jake raised his head. "You have to depend on him and he has to depend on you. If either of you seriously screws up, you can both die. There has to be the feeling between you of great trust. But it's not anything you talk about. If it's there, you know it. If it's not, you know that, too." Then he spoke with mock seriousness, emphasizing each word with a jab of his finger. "Never fly with a man you don't trust."

"I don't go anywhere with a man I don't trust," Callie countered. She took a bite of salad and chewed meditatively. "So, not everybody keeps the faith."

"Some do a better job of it than others."

"I know you do a good job of it. I can tell."

Jake took a deep breath and exhaled slowly. "I'd like to think so. But sometimes I'm not sure."

"What do you mean?" she asked with surprise in her voice.

He hadn't planned to tell her about Morgan. When he started out he wondered why he was telling her. But in the end he told her everything about his last flight with Morgan, including what the cockpit looked like when it was over. The dreams, though, he didn't tell her about.

"Surely you don't blame yourself?" Callie said. "It doesn't make sense to do that."

"I don't know. Maybe it doesn't make sense. But I feel some responsibility. Like Chiang does for his brother."

"You did what you could do," said Callie. "You can't do more than that. You kept the faith."

Chou En-Lai's double was supervising the flaming production of two chateaubriands when Callie returned from the restroom. A waiter Jake had not seen before whisked away the glass in which he had been rattling his ice. Callie put her bag on the corner of the table. "I hope you're still plenty hungry. They look huge."

"I could scarf them both."

"You just keep your mitts off mine, Jake. I'm starving."

The waiter put a glass of red wine in front of Callie. Looking at Jake's fresh scotch, she said, "Another one?"

Jake shrugged. "I didn't order it."

"Oh."

With a smile and a flourish, the waiter presented her with a chateaubriand that sizzled in its plate. Callie thanked him in Cantonese. She waited until Jake had been served before cutting her meat.

Callie said, "Fantastic."

His mouth full, Jake nodded enthusiastically. They said little until the steaks were nearly gone.

"You picked a great place," he said.

"I've been thinking," said Callie. "Thinking about you.'

"Not much profit in that."

"I think you're a good man, Jake." She reached across the table and put her hand on his. "I'm glad you told me about Morgan. I'm glad you felt comfortable enough with me to do that."

"It's not a nice story." Jake shoved two french fries around his plate with his fork. "I just wish I was sure what Morgan died for."

Removing her hand, Callie said, "You don't think we ought to be in Vietnam?"

"That's not what I mean," said Jake. "I mean that I worry that Morgan died for nothing because the bastards in Washington won't let us win the war. They're afraid to do the things we need to do to win. We could win the war, you know, if they'd let us."

"Then maybe we shouldn't be in Vietnam at all."

Jake tossed off the last of his scotch. He was uneasy. "It was probably a mistake that we got involved in the first place. Hindsight and all. Especially when you consider that there's hardly any support for the war at home. But that's water over the dam. The fact is, we *are* there, and I don't think we can just cut and run."

"Are you saying that we should stay there only to save face?"

"No, I'm not saying that, that we should stay for that reason only. Look at it this way. What kind of credibility would the U.S. have, what kind of respect would we have, if we ran from a fight for freedom? Leader of the free world? We'd make a mockery of that." Jake paused and traced a circle with his fingertip on the white linen tablecloth. "And there are other reasons."

"I'd like to hear one that makes sense."

Jake felt his face flush. He tried to speak calmly. "Okay. I'll give you one real good reason. Right now there're over a thousand guys in prison camps in Vietnam—nobody knows for sure how many. Those men are being starved, tortured, humiliated. Our POWs are going through hell while long-haired creeps in the States are burning their draft cards or hiding in graduate schools and trying to convince themselves the war is immoral because they know, deep down, that they don't have the guts to fight." Jake coughed, and went on in a lower voice. "We *have* to get our POWs out. If we don't they'll rot to death in the prison camps. We've either got to win the war or put enough pressure on the commies to make them return the POWs and account for our MIAs. We've got to keep faith with those guys."

"I understand what you're saying, Jake. I'd like very much to see those men released, too. But hundreds of people are dying in the war every day. Think of the many thousands of lives that would be saved if we could end the war now."

"End the war now? Cut and run? If we abandon the POWs, if we break faith with them, where will we get men to fight the next war?" He picked up his glass and looked into it "All we have is each other."

He put the glass down and met her eyes. "Let's be realistic, Callie. For you, the war might as well be on the far side of the moon."

"Well it isn't," Callie said softly. "There's something I've been wanting to tell you. Theron, my brother, was—"

"Your brother? Yeah, your brother thinks the war is wrong, immoral. Right?"

"Yes, as a matter of fact. But what I was—"

"Did God whisper in your brother's ear about the joys of living in Canada? Freedom comes a little cheaper there these days. Is he happy, listening to his stereo and smoking pot and feeling very moral? Or is he at Berkeley? Protesting the war between fixes and—"

Callie stood up and grabbed her purse. She leaned over the table and spoke deliberately. "I was about to tell you—before I was interrupted—that my brother lost both his legs in Vietnam. He wants desperately to believe that the war is morally right. But he can't. And it's eating him up."

Callie turned to leave just as the waiter arrived with two cups of coffee. Jake said, "You're not going to leave? Just like that?"

"Oh yes I am. Just-like-that."

Jake stood up. "I didn't know, I . . ."

"You can be very cruel, Jake Grafton." She put out her hand to stop him. "I'd like to leave alone."

The waiter stood holding his tray. He wore a puzzled expression. Callie walked around him and out of the restaurant.

Jake sat down and lifted his coffee, which sloshed out of the cup. For a long time he stared at the full cup on the other side of the table. Then he paid the bill and left.

It was dark outside. He took a cab to the consulate, where he looked across the street and saw a crowd at the tramway station. He looked up to the right and saw the outline of Victoria Peak, dotted with lights. Remembering where Callie's apartment building was in relation to the consulate, he walked up Garden Road. His emotions swirled like autumn leaves caught in a windstorm.

He found the building, finally, and explored the empty hallways, looking at nametags on each door. The sound of his footsteps echoed down the uncarpeted halls. He climbed to the third floor. On a tattered buff-colored tag below the peephole of the door was her hand-lettered name: "C. McKenzie." He knocked, and she opened the door. She was wearing a pale yellow silk robe. Her eyes were puffy.

Jake spoke. "I'm very sorry about Theron. And I'm sorry about what I said."

He watched Callie's tight-lipped expression soften. "Thanks," she said. "Now I know the way I felt was right."

She drew him inside and closed the door.

TWELVE

They were having a riot at the Cubi Point Officers' Club. At least that's what it looked like to Jake and Sammy when they opened the door. A wave of noise immediately broke over them. The rock 'n' roll band made up only part of the assault. Much of the din came from men's voices raised in singing and shouting as the aircrews indulged in one last glorious binge. The ship was scheduled to sail at eight the next morning.

One of the squadron's pilots, Snake Jones, was drinking near the door. "How was Hong Kong, guys?"

"Great," Lundeen replied. "I'm going to live there during my next incarnation."

"You'll have to speak up. I can't hear a goddamn word."

Lundeen hollered, "Great."

"Too bad you had to come back," Snake said. "By the way, you'll have to fetch your own drinks. The waitresses were grossed out over an hour ago."

"What happened?"

"Some A-7 jockey stood on the table and took off all his clothes. Then he passed out. His buddies carried him down to the Tailhook Room. He's laid out down there on the bar."

The two newcomers shouldered through the crush around the bar. "Happy Hour prices, boys," the bartender said and collected a dime from each of them.

"What luck!" Lundeen said to Jake. "You can get skunk-drunk for four bits."

Jake clinked his beer glass against Sammy's and drank deeply. He replaced his glass on the bar and, while waiting for a refill, peered around the smoke-filled room. At the far wall the fighter crews were carolling obscene songs and throwing their empty glasses into the fireplace. Fighting valiantly to hold his own in the decibel ratings, the lead singer was belting out a tune from a platform in the middle of the vast room. Between the band and the bar, dice players were running Klondike games at four tables.

The roommates made their way to the tables. Jake estimated that only a hundred dollars or so was in play at each table, but the night was young. He knew that when the evening had worn on and empty glasses had accumulated, as much as six or seven hundred would be riding on a single roll, and that just before the club closed—when checks were suddenly acceptable—some men would lose a month's pay. The same sports sat at the tables night after night, but the high rollers showed up only the night before the ship sailed. Then the real money was on the line.

Cowboy Parker presided over one table, fronted by a hefty pile of twenties. He nodded at Jake and Sammy, said something Jake couldn't catch above the uproar, then refocused his attention on the game. Jake recalled that Cowboy once told him he had furnished a house from his winnings on his first WestPac cruise.

They spotted Razor Durfee and Abe Steiger with several other men at a table away from the band, below the bar, and cut a path through the human thicket to join them.

"Meet your new bombardier, Jake," Razor said. The

uniformed man beside Razor stood up and stuck out his hand. He was a couple of inches taller than Jake, with wide shoulders and sunbleached hair. Cold, penetrating blue eyes looked out from a suntanned face. Under his wings he wore three rows of ribbons. The upper left one was the Distinguished Flying Cross with two gold stars.

"Virgil Cole." Jake's right hand was gripped in a firm handshake. Sammy shook hands, too, then drifted off. Jake sat down to get acquainted. Cole settled back, apparently content to let Razor do the talking.

Throughout the recitation of his resume, Cole only sipped his beer. "And after two combat cruises, he was an instructor bombardier at VA-42. Now he's joined our posse," Razor concluded.

"He's been in the navy eight years," Steiger pitched in.

Razor leaned over to Jake and whispered in his ear. "Cole ain't a big talker." Grafton had formed that impression already. "And he ain't a big smiler, either."

Jake directed several questions at Cole, asking him where he had grown up and where he had attended college. In reply Jake received, "Winslow, Arizona," and "Phoenix."

Jake lapsed into silence while the hubbub swirled around him. As Razor introduced Cole to various people, Jake observed him carefully.

The hard blue eyes searched each new face. The corners of his mouth remained turned up in a smile of sorts, but the smile never developed. Only the eyes moved in the mask that was Cole's face. He projected an aura of amused superiority.

The new man's reluctance to engage in conversation soon caused the talk to turn in other directions. No one mentioned the alligator pond incident so Jake assumed with relief that it had blown over, as Lundeen had predicted. The group discussed the two other new members of the squadron, a pilot and a bombardier, both just graduated from VA-128. The two had been flying every day and were now ready, Jake overheard, to requalify with six day and three night traps tomorrow when the ship was at sea. The pilot had carrier qualified in A-6s just a month before, but as Jake knew, he would have to do it again on the *Shiloh* to satisfy Camparelli and the CAG.

Lundeen had returned to the fold in time to ask, "Where are these guys?" Told they were in the Tailhook Bar, he motioned to Jake, who stood up.

"Come on, Cole," Jake said. "Let's go downstairs." The bombardier followed the two pilots down the hall to the side door. As they crossed the lawn toward a low cinderblock structure, the annex of the club, Jake asked Cole what he liked to be called.

"Virgil's fine. Or Cole. Doesn't matter." It was the most he had said since Jake met him.

The Tailhook Bar had originally been the basement for a larger building that had either never been built or had been torn down. But that was some time before the memory of the men who congregated there now, and none of them bothered to ask. It was in the Tailhook Bar that the serious rowdies and drinkers hung out. Patrons could buy a hot sandwich from a short-order grill and all the liquor they wanted for a dime a drink during Happy Hour, and a quarter thereafter. No women were allowed.

The place was packed when Jake, Sammy, and Cole entered. Every man there looked as though he had forsaken sobriety hours ago. Sea stories—anecdotes on nautical or aviation themes with presumably some basis in fact—were being recounted in loud voices to listeners less than a foot away. Sure enough, as Snake had told them, a naked, unconscious man lay face down on the bar. Between the cheeks of his buttocks someone had placed a maraschino cherry.

"How come he's on his stomach?" Grafton asked.

"Christ, Jake." Little Augie came up. "Where've you been all your life? Everyone knows you always put a drunk face down so he won't drown if he pukes. Weren't you ever in the Boy Scouts?"

"Makes sense," Jake replied and took a glass from Little Augie, who had two, and gulped down half its contents. Then he handed it back.

"That was my specimen for Mad Jack, Grafton. If you want any more, just let me know."

"Thanks."

Lundeen leaned across the nude and yanked the bartender's sleeve. "Scotch on the rocks . . ." He glanced at Grafton and Cole. "Three of them."

As they worked on their drinks, they watched the activity that centered around a mock cockpit set on rails near the back wall. This contraption was infamously known as "the beast." Propelled forward on the rails by a compressed-air charge, the cockpit ran level for about twenty feet, then down a slight decline, through a set of open French doors, and out to a stagnant pond. The only way to avoid being doused in the water as the cockpit slid to a halt was to adroitly manipulate the one control in the cockpit, a lever that activated a spring-loaded tailhook that could snag a restraining wire rigged across the tracks just before the decline. To catch the wire required split-second timing. Tonight the machine was getting a workout as man after man splashed into the water to the roars of "bolter, bolter, bolter" from the revelers.

Ferdinand Magellan and a man Jake didn't recognize walked over and introduced themselves. The stranger was indeed the new pilot. He looked barely twenty and exuded an innocence that promised to make him the butt of much crude humor.

As they chatted, Jake noticed Cowboy standing beside the group. "Tired of the game?" he asked.

Parker shook his head in disgust. "Too early. Chintzy bastards won't bet enough yet. I'll go back later. I see you met Virgil." Jake nodded. What could one say about this guy?

"How was Hong Kong?" Cowboy asked.

"Okay," said Jake.

"Get laid?" Cowboy demanded.

"Yeah," Lundeen leered as Jake flushed. Jake saw Cole glance from one man to the other. Those eyes were a goddamn X-ray machine, Grafton thought.

Everyone else was watching the most recent rider of the beast being assisted from the device, dripping wet.

"We've got a man for the beast," Cowboy announced in stentorian tones. The crowd parted like the waters of the Red Sea, and Parker grabbed Jake's shoulders and thrust him forward. Jake yelled, "Find someone else. Get this lunatic off me! I don't want to ride the damned thing."

He felt more hands seize him. He was lifted roughly off the floor and carried toward the scum-coated beast. Accepting his fate, Jake allowed himself to be placed in the cockpit and strapped in.

Lundeen and Cowboy fiddled with the control panel. "How do you turn the damn air on, anyway?" Sammy muttered. Perhaps because someone turned a knob the wrong way, a valve blew and compressed air shot the control handle across the room, shattering a mirror behind the bar. Two men barely ducked the projectile and the bartender, with his back turned, jumped when the glass exploded. The crowd considered all this hilarious.

"You idiots," bellowed a burly fellow with a handlebar mustache. "Get outta the way, Lundeen, before you kill somebody. You too, Tex." Amid another outburst of laughter, Cowboy and Lundeen were shoved aside and replaced by more experienced hands.

Someone passed Jake a drink while he waited for the

handle to be reinstalled and a new air bottle hooked up. He was beginning to enjoy this. He leaned back, fished out a cigarette, and propped one foot on the side of the cockpit. "Anytime you fellows get a handle on the situation—" Then he saw Cole, apparently cold and aloof, taking it all in, those blue eyes fixed upon him. He wondered how in God's name was he going to fly with this man every day? He recoiled at the idea of so many hours of enforced togetherness. At that moment, Cole winked at him.

Jake grinned and handed his glass to the nearest spectator. "Are you guys going to take all night?" he asked of the repair party behind him. "We have bandits inbound at ten knots and they're going to blast in through the French doors if you fellows don't shake a leg."

"Who's gonna launch this guy?" Handlebar shouted.

"I am, by God," boomed a voice from the deep South. Bosun Marion Muldowski stepped up. He stood six feet two and transported a substantial pot belly. He had rather narrow shoulders from which massive arms sprouted. Bosun Muldowski was a warrant officer and had worked his way up from the enlisted ranks, "up the hawse pipe," as the expression ran. He had been the catapult maintenance officer on the *Shiloh* for as long as Grafton had been aboard and regularly took a turn launching aircraft. His commanding presence inspired awe in the officers and instant obedience from the sailors, who regarded him with a mixture of respect and fear. Even the air boss, a commander who headed the department that included all the flight-deck divisions, had been known to slip and call Muldowski "Sir."

Every eye in the room was on the southern Pole as he surveyed Jake Grafton and the beast. "You ready in there, shipmate?" he bellowed.

Jake took his foot down and tightened the shoulder straps. "Let's do it, Bosun."

Muldowski drained his beer, crushed the can with his fist, then tossed it outdoors into the pond. He unbuttoned and removed his shirt. On his T-shirt was emblazoned a legend in flaming red: "World's Finest Cat Officer." Snickers rippled through the crowd.

The big man glowered at several people who had had the temerity to snicker. Silence reigned. "I've pissed more saltwater than you puppies ever sailed over." His face was grim. "You back there," he said to Handlebar. "Are you ready yet?"

Handlebar flung both hands above his head and held them there, the standard signal to the cat officer that the cat was ready to fire. "Satisfactory," the bosun pronounced. "Anytime you care to go we will oblige you," he told Jake. The pilot sat at attention with his hand on the hook lever, watching the bosun from the corner of his eye. "Well?" demanded Muldowski.

"Well?" repeated Jake.

"I don't hear your engine running and I don't see a salute," Muldowski said as though he were talking to a seventeen-year-old boot recruit from Iowa.

Taking the cue, everyone in the place, Jake included, began to roar like a jet engine. The thunder from threescore voices filled the room and rolled through the open doors, across the pond, and out into the night. Jake saluted and immediately put his hand back on the hook mechanism. He took a deep breath and chomped down on his cigarette. He tried to watch both the bosun and the safety wire at the same time. The bosun's right hand twirled above his head, then he lunged to his right and his hand came down in a wide arc to touch the floor, the classic launch signal. Grafton tried to look back for the target wire, but it was too late.

Down the track he hurtled. He jerked on the handle but the beast continued to accelerate. He flashed down the incline. Water cascaded over him as the beast slid to a stop.

Jake puffed on his soggy cigarette. He looked back into the barroom. Some of the shouting, laughing men pointed at him with one hand and pounded the bosun on the back with the other.

When the car had been cranked back into battery, the bosun inquired in his flight-deck voice, "How was your flight?"

"Smoother than silk, but the landing was a little rough. Maybe we'd better try it again."

Lundeen leaned in with some whispered advice. "This time watch the wire, not the bosun."

With another mighty warwhoop Grafton swept down the track. And into the pond. As they hauled him back, he announced to the crowd, "That was practice. This time I mean it."

When the hook arrested the beast on the third flight, he almost hit his head on the panel. Applause rattled the windows as a laughing Sammy Lundeen helped him out of the cockpit. Someone thrust another drink at him.

"Which of you shit-hot flyboys is next?" the bosun boomed.

Jake yelled, "Sammy Lundeen."

"Hell, no," said Lundeen without conviction. Eager hands propelled him into the slimy seat. "Now watch the greatest pilot who ever lived catch the wire on the very first try," Sammy chortled. "I was born in a cockpit. I could fly before I could walk."

"Bet that made nursing a lot more fun," someone hooted. "Did you just hover there, like a humming-bird?"

"Watch and weep, swine."

"Have you any money, my boy?" the bosun inquired.

"Fifty bucks, infidel dog, ye of little faith, follower of the false prophet—"

"I'll take ten." "Me, too," was the chorus.

"Thanks, guys," Lundeen announced triumphantly after he grabbed the wire. "It's always a pleasure spending your money." Pocketing his winnings, he and Grafton retreated to the bar where Cole was waiting, the corners of his mouth curving upward a fraction of an inch. The three of them watched Cowboy and five others wrestle the bosun toward the machine.

Jake surveyed the naked drunk on the bar and decided that modesty should be given at least a token nod. He took off his wet socks and put them on the feet of the unconscious Corsair pilot. This accomplished, he turned to Lundeen. "Thanks for taking me to Hong Kong. That was one hell of a good time."

"No sweat."

"Damn, I sure feel good. It's been one fine in-port period. No lie, Sam, I really feel great."

"You're drunk, Jake. You always feel great when you're drunk."

Grafton acknowledged to himself the truth of the statement. He was getting loaded again, and that always felt good.

"Well," said a voice behind them, "this one certainly seems quiet enough." A navy captain in short-sleeve whites observed the nude on the bar. Above his left shirt-pocket, the captain wore four rows of ribbons topped with gold pilot's wings. The uppermost left ribbon was the Silver Star. His close-cropped black hair was shot through with gray, and his cap, with scrambled eggs on the visor, perched precariously on the back of his head. "Is he alive?" the captain asked Sammy in a conversational tone.

"Yessir. Last time we checked, he was."

The captain turned to the small civilian who stood behind him. "I thought you said this man was completely naked?"

"I did and he is. He stood on a table upstairs and

stripped down and greatly embarrassed our female staff."

"He has socks on now. He's partially dressed," the captain observed.

"Sir, we can't keep our employees if this kind of behavior goes on. And who's going to pay for all the breakage upstairs? And this mirror?" The club manager gestured toward the glass fragments behind the bar.

"I'm sure you'll have no trouble getting or keeping help. I have over a hundred applications on file for every civilian job on this base, including yours. And I'm sure these officers are willing to stand good for the breakage. Just send me a tally for everything you want replaced and I'll see that it's paid."

"But—"

"Go on upstairs and manage this place. Send me that list tomorrow." The captain smiled at Grafton and Lundeen. "And how is the evening going?"

"Just fine, sir. But if I may make a suggestion? You'd better remove your cap before someone demands that you buy a round."

The captain put a hand to his cap, then withdrew it. "That *is* the custom, isn't it? Barkeep!" The captain raised his voice. "There is a man in the house with his cover on. Drinks for everyone!" More than sixty men surged toward the bar.

Armed with a drink, the captain scanned the crowd and spotted Bosun Muldowski. "Ski! I thought you retired off my ship four, five years ago?"

"Aye, Captain Harrington, I shore did. But I got tired a sittin' on my ass and listening to the ol' lady, and with the war on and all. . . . Well, here I am!"

The captain surveyed the bosun's wet clothes. "I see you also undertook to give these young gentlemen some lessons."

The bosun looked down at his wet T-shirt in disgust. "That's about the size of it."

The atmosphere in the bar had mellowed. Muldowski fell into a talkative mood, so the men plied him with beer and listened to his stories. He solved all the navy's problems, told Congress where to go, cussed out everyone on earth not wearing navy blue, and gave the men a well-received assessment of most civilians: "Lower than whale shit at the bottom of the sea."

At about two in the morning, four or five guys from one of the A-7 outfits came in and collected their naked shipmate. He was snoring happily before they cranked him up, but once aroused demanded another drink. They gave him ice water, and he gurgled back to life.

Jake walked outside and sat down in the grass some fifty feet away from the building. He could see the *Shiloh,* illuminated with floodlights, lying at the carrier pier. Even from a mile and a half away, she looked gigantic. Beyond her the black water of the bay extended to the high hills on the western shore, while off to the south lay the entrance to the bay. The breeze blowing in off the sea, laden with the wild smell of salt, felt good. He stretched out on the grass and looked up at the stars.

In two days he would be flying again. More worthless targets with lots of flak and no results. He remembered the suspected truck park he and Morgan had bombed—when was it? A week, ten days ago? All that flak. Although it seemed long ago, he would never forget how the cockpit looked after they opened the canopy. All that blood.

He ran his hands through the grass and felt the damp earth. Then he sat up. Wondering about Callie and the future, he looked at the enormous bulk of the carrier and at the dark sea just beyond the entrance to the bay.

THIRTEEN

The *Shiloh* was under way at 0800 the next morning as the sun crept over the scalloped rim of the mountains bordering the bay. The tugs helped her from the pier and then, under her own power, she turned and made for the channel to the sea. Two destroyers steamed ahead and four astern. Once into the open ocean the escorts fanned out, taking up their stations around the giant flattop. The task group soon turned to a westerly heading and stood away from the land. Within three hours the highest peaks in the Luzon shore range had sunk into the ocean. Once again the horizon was empty. Small puffy clouds drifted along on the trade wind.

At noon the ship swung into the southwesterly trades and slowed until the relative wind down the angled deck was thirty knots. Then she began to recover aircraft that had been flying from Cubi Point while she had been in port. F-4s, A-7s, an E-2, and an EA-6B Prowler came aboard in order. Only one of the two Intruders that had been ashore appeared over the ship. When word reached the ready room, a hurried conference was held and it was decided that a repair crew would be transported back to Cubi on the daily cargo plane.

"Looks like Corey Ford and the Boxman will enjoy an extra night on the beach," Parker remarked.

"Hope it doesn't kill the boy," said the Old Man, thinking of Box.

Jake Grafton watched the Devils' pilot, New Guy, from the air boss's vantage point in Pri-Fly. This enclosed space, high in the island, protruded out over the flight deck and offered an unimpeded view of the flight deck and of the aircraft in the air near the ship.

After six landings aboard the carrier in daylight, each pilot new to the ship would make three night traps that evening. After this final exam there would be no graduation or diploma. The air wing LSO would debrief each man individually, and unless a negative comment was made to the operations officer of the squadron to which the man belonged, the new pilot's name would appear on the flight schedule. Without fanfare or celebration, the young aviator was now a carrier pilot. He would stand his watches and fly the scheduled missions and, if he were skillful enough and lucky enough, he would live through his tour of duty.

Jake enjoyed his Pri-Fly stints. Throughout a cruise, each of a squadron's junior officers had to take his turn in Pri-Fly, observing not only the new pilots but the experienced ones as well. In the profession of flying, a man was good enough or he wasn't any good at all, and that fact was written in blood. In the crowd of young officers who gathered behind the chairs of the boss and assistant boss, the action was fast and the comments swift. It reminded Grafton of the grandstand crowd at a horserace. All that was needed, Jake thought, was some enterprising soul to offer bets on which wire the next plane would snag. The air boss kept up a running commentary on the performance of the fledglings for the benefit of the squadron observers, and Jake wrote copious notes in his squadron's log book.

Jake watched the new Intruder driver, who caught the target third wire three out of six times with no bolters. He flew the pattern at the proper distance and kept the right interval between himself and other aircraft, although twice the air boss complained that he was late turning from the downwind leg crosswind toward the ship's wake. Grafton scribbled down the remark.

When all the aircraft were back aboard, the Pri-Fly observers and the recently landed crews made their way to their ready rooms for a debriefing and a written examination. The textbook was *NATOPS—Naval Aviation Training and Operating Procedures*—which came in a separate volume for each type of aircraft. Jake and Sammy regularly drilled each other on the Intruder's hydraulics, electronics, engines, crew safety and comfort systems, and performance under any possible flight condition. They also practiced using the complex graphs from which fuel consumption, airspeed, maximum G loads, and similar information could be extracted. *NATOPS* quizzes were heavy on emergency procedures, although any fact from the book was fair game. A classified exam, based on the secret supplement to the *NATOPS* manual, was given less frequently than the emergency and operating procedure quizzes.

"What if I don't pass?" Little asked loudly.

"If you don't pass, you don't fly," Big Augie answered from across the room.

"But what if I don't want to fly?" Little quavered.

"Then we'll think of something else," four voices sang in unison.

Later that night, Jake looked up Chief Styert to discuss Hardesty and his marriage certificate. "So where is our newlywed?" Jake asked. Chief Styert sent for Hardesty.

While they waited, Jake filled the chief in on some of the administrative items that were discussed at the all-officers meeting. "The Skipper says we're going to be doing a lot of high-priority night work, as well as daytime Alpha strikes. We'll be pushing it this time out, but on our next in-port period we may go to Singapore."

"The men would rather go back to Subic Bay," the chief said. The liquor and women were cheaper and the raunchy night life more to their tastes. Jake sighed. Join the navy and see Po City.

"Yeah, I know that and so does the Captain, but there'll be another carrier in port then, so we'll have to suck it up and go to Singapore." The chief looked glum. Maybe he had a girlfriend in Po City, too.

Hardesty arrived, looking pale. "How did your leave go?" Jake asked.

"Okay." The boy had not shaved in several days and a dozen or so scraggly whiskers had sprouted like weeds amid the pimples on his chin.

"Did you make it down to Manila?"

"Hmm," replied the boy, averting his eyes toward the deck.

"The Chief tells me you went down to Personnel this morning and filled out the paperwork on your wife." Hardesty merely nodded. This was like pulling teeth, Jake thought. "Got a copy of the marriage certificate with you?"

Hardesty drew some papers from his shirt. He shuffled through them, selected a large parchment document, and handed it to Jake without looking at him.

The officer unfolded it. It was the original and in Spanish. Hardesty's name was there. John Thomas Hardesty and Consuelo Maria Garcia Lopez de Hernandez. Lots of official signatures, a couple of wax seals, and a date. Jake glanced at the calendar over the chief's desk, then back to the document.

"This date is just two days ago," he said.

"Yessir."

"You were married only two days ago?"

"Yeah."

"After I told you less than a week ago that you needed official permission from the navy to marry a Philippine national, you went out and did it anyway?" Anger crept into Jake's voice. "You stood there a week ago and lied to me, one lie after another. You lied to me and you lied to the Chief." The boy glanced up, ready to reply, but Jake cut him off. "You violated a general regulation. You signed a false official document when you requested leave." The volume went up. "Goddamn, Hardesty! You think this is a Boy Scout camp? What the hell else are you going to lie about? Are you going to come in here and tell the Chief you've fixed a plane when you haven't? How in the name of God can we trust you?" Jake lapsed into silence and sank back into the chair. The chief cleared his throat. "If you want to toss your oar in, Chief, go right ahead."

As Styert tongue-lashed the boy, Jake pondered the problem. The kid had wanted to marry, decided not to wait for Uncle Sam's official blessing, and lied to get the time off. Is it really any of the navy's business when or whom a sailor marries? So he had said "fuck the navy." So what?

"You're a real fucking dummy," the chief told the boy. "You could've gotten leave if you'd just said you wanted some time off. Didn't you know that?" Hardesty shook his head. "If your goddamn brains were dynamite, you couldn't blow your nose. Why in hell didn't you come to me and talk it over? What do you think your chief is for, anyway? Do you think I'm some kind of freak that just hatched out as a chief? I was a sailor before you were born. I was getting laid in

Olongapo when you were in diapers. Son, you really piss me off."

"Go on up to the berthing compartment, Hardesty," said Jake.

When Hardesty had disappeared, the officer and the chief talked about what he had done. "Looks like one for mast, Chief." Styert agreed. "And you sit that boy down and make damn sure he and the rest of the men know enough to come to you with problems."

"Yessir," said the chief, who seemed to realize that he had just been reprimanded.

Jake found the maintenance officer, Lieutenant Commander Joe Wagner, in his stateroom immersed in the paperwork necessary to keep sixteen state-of-the-art aircraft repaired. After Grafton explained the problem, Wagner rummaged through a drawer and gave Jake a blank report chit. "I think you should talk this over with the Skipper before you fill out the report. It's a little unusual, I know, but this sounds like one of those tar babies that could stir the interest of some congressman. Might as well let Camparelli have his say before we make it official."

Commander Camparelli, clad only in his underwear, sat at his stateroom desk. "Hello, Grafton. Pull up a chair." The skipper slipped his glasses down his nose and peered over the rims. "What's on your mind?"

Jake told him about Hardesty and showed him the parchment. "I ought to write him up for lying to me and the Chief," he concluded. "But Joe Wagner suggested checking with you first before this becomes official."

"Lot of merit in that," the commander said as he studied the marriage license. "There're a lot of things I'd just as soon not know about officially. Like that little fracas in front of Pauline's that I heard about unofficially. Seems one sailor from the deck department somehow took a plunge in the alligator pond and some other fellows were injured—just scratched up really—in the scuffle that followed." His eyes locked on Grafton's. "One man lost a couple teeth."

"Too bad," Jake said.

"You know anything about that incident—unofficially, of course?"

"A little." The skipper waited. "Well, I sort of helped toss the guy into the pond. We were just trying to dip his hair in the water, but he was a little too heavy for us." He paused. The skipper remained silent. Jake felt ashamed of himself for minimizing his part. "Actually the whole thing was my idea. We wanted to give the kid a good scare, but I didn't intend for him to go swimming. And I took a swing at another fellow after he swung at me. I had a good crack at his mouth and may have knocked out some teeth."

"Who helped you?"

"I'd rather not say."

"That's what the Boxman said, too."

Camparelli took off his glasses and chewed on one of the plastic earpieces. "Captain Boma's a bit peeved about this incident. He mentioned that the shore patrol officer complained. It's the opinion of Captain Boma and the shore patrol officer that fights off base are liable to be handled with more force than necessary by the local authorities, who, as you know, are now Philippine Army. Those macho muchachos would like nothing better than an excuse to use their grease guns. Then we'd have a few corpses on our hands and maybe an international incident."

Camparelli replaced his glasses on the lower part of his nose.

"So Captain Boma asked me to investigate—unofficially. I'm glad you decided to come in for a chat."

"Oh."

"I think you'd better stay aboard the ship next time

in port. That's unofficial. No messy paperwork. The term is 'in hack.' "

He could do it officially, too, Jake knew, with a discipline report that would torpedo any chance the pilot might ever have of being promoted. "Yessir."

"Back to the original subject, which is our love-starved sailor. Your gripe is that he lied to you in order to get leave, rather than that he married in violation of a general reg." The skipper leaned back in his chair and crossed his bare legs. To Jake he looked much like a chairman of the board solving a million-dollar problem, except that he wore only skivvies. "How many leave chits have you seen with the reason for the request stated?"

Jake thought. There was not even such a section on the form. He pointed out to Camparelli that Hardesty had inked in his reason in the margin.

"Precisely. And if you ask a sailor where he's going or why, you can bet he probably lies about half the time. A sailor figures that it's none of the officer's business. I'm pleased to hear you aren't too enthused about the violation of this general regulation. The navy's requirement for permission before you commit holy matrimony with a foreign national is a chicken reg, in my opinion, and probably unconstitutional. God only knows what the Supreme Court would do with that one. In any event, I tolerate a lot of high jinks around here. You're a case in point. So long as the bombs keep falling on target and the planes keep coming back, I'll stay off people's backs. Hardesty's bitten off a big chunk and about all we can do is watch. If he fails to support her, or abandons her, or any of that stuff, then we'll do what we can under the regulations. Nothing else."

"I want to put in a special evaluation on Hardesty."

"That's fair. He doesn't seem smart enough to

become a petty officer anytime soon. And don't think Hardesty's off the hook. Chief Styert will make his life miserable for a while. He'll probably do a better job of it than you or I could."

Jake felt worn out. "Anything else, Skipper?"

"No." Frank Camparelli sipped a glass of Coke with ice in it.

Jake stood and reached for the door. "Don't feel too bad about being restricted to the ship," the commander said. "Any junior officer who isn't in hack at least once a cruise is not drawing any water."

"Yessir." Jake opened the door.

"Oh, and by the way, tell your roommate that if I hear of him shitting anywhere but in a head, he'll eat the damn stuff off the deck."

Jake's mouth dropped open.

"That's all, Jake. Good night." The Old Man chuckled.

Jake started through the door, then paused for another look at the commander, who took a long pull from his drink. "Don't slam the door on your way out," Camparelli said smugly.

"Sit down, Sam." They were in their stateroom.

"Huh?"

"Sit down. I have something to tell you." Sammy complied, his eyes on Jake's face.

"The Skipper knows you're the Phantom."

"What?" Sammy searched Jake's face. "Are you sure?"

"For a fact. He knows."

"Good God!" Sammy jumped up. "Damn. Who told him?"

"I think I did."

"Gimme a break—Come on—"

"I think he took a shot in the dark and hit the

bull's-eye." Jake repeated the conversation to Sammy. "Man, I've never been so surprised—and it showed. When he saw my face, he knew he'd hit the mark."

"That old fox. That's it? Nothing else?"

"No. That was the whole conversation on that topic. He fired that salvo as I was going out the door."

Sammy threw himself on Jake's bunk. "I'll be damned," he howled. "Who'd have guessed it?"

"Camparelli seems to have done just that. Maybe Cowboy suggested you to him."

Sammy thought a moment. "No way, man. Not Cowboy. No, I think you're absolutely right. The Skipper guessed." He laughed.

"Don't get too tickled, asshole. I'm in hack."

"What for?"

"Throwing that guy to the alligators."

"Tough. But don't sweat it. Any junior officer—"

"I know, I know. '—Drawing any water.' But I'm not taking your turn as duty officer next time in port, so don't even ask. Jesus, I hope I don't have to make any more of those little trips down to his room."

Sammy lay back and mused, "Where can the Phantom strike next?"

Jake strolled over to the door. "If I were you, shipmate, I'd be a little concerned. Already the Phantom has imitators. Now that Camparelli knows, it may get a little warm for the Winged Wraith if his helpers take it upon themselves to add to his fame and legend."

Jake stepped out, leaving Sammy to his thoughts. He wandered along the passageway, his hands deep in his pockets. Stuck aboard the ship the next time in port! It would be three months before he could see Callie again. Camparelli got a pound of flesh, Jake thought glumly, even though he didn't know it.

Somewhere a compressor was pounding, and Jake could hear the muffled whine of a power drill, perhaps from the hangar deck above his head. Five thousand men, every one of them leading his own life with his own cares and worries and problems. And every one of them thinking the world revolves around him.

As he walked through the enlisted men's mess deck he heard music. He followed the sound. The music throbbed, a driving beat that bounced off the steel bulkheads and echoed down the passageways. He found the musicians on a ladder turnaround, similar to a stairwell landing.

Four black sailors in T-shirts whanged away on electric guitars while one beat a set of drums. The singer, who had a microphone, moved aside without missing a note to let the pilot pass. Jake climbed up to the next deck and went down the passageway a frame or two until the volume did not assault him. He leaned against the bulkhead and closed his eyes.

The music was Motown, the big city sound, the pulsating beat of Detroit. It was the sound he remembered from the radio of his '57 Chevy as he blasted along on summer evenings with the smell of mown hay and plowed earth in the air. The music made him long for home.

On the O-3 level Jake went outboard until he reached a light-trap, a series of turns in the passageway that prevented light within the ship from escaping. He felt his way through and found himself on a ladder leading up four steps to the catwalk that lined the flight deck. Because the shape of the hull funneled air upward, a chilly, spray-laden wind rushed up through the catwalk. The flight deck was at chest height. Above Jake's head, the tails of aircraft were just visible in the dim glow of the masthead lights. The aircraft were parked in rows, wheel to wheel with wings folded. Each plane was backed up with its main mounts against the steel curb around the deck; fifteen feet of its fuselage and tail protruded over the ocean.

Jake walked forward on the catwalk until he stood at the very bow of the ship. Here the wind came head on. By leaning out over the railing he could see the white curl as the bow cut the black water. He rested his arms on the railing.

He thought of Callie. He tried to recall her face, her voice, her warmth, but it was difficult in the overpowering presence of the night sea. Was it love he felt for her?

Get a grip on yourself, Grafton. Reality is another long line period. More worthless targets, more flak, more SAMs. More bombs to drop. Only now McPherson's dead. Dead for a few acres of splintered trees.

And what had Morgan believed in? They had never discussed the war, except professionally. War is night cat shots and going in low and fast and hard. And death.

McPherson. Dead.

"You should have talked to me, Morg. You should have talked to me." The sea wind swallowed his words. He was talking to the infinite night that Morgan McPherson was now a part of. "How come we never talked? You should have told me. . . ."

What would Morgan say to me? I flew with you, Jake, and I lived as you lived and I felt what you felt and I was ready to die when you died. But I died alone. Yet I died swinging, laying the bombs in with a good radar and a good computer.

McPherson would tell him to keep swinging. Keep riding the cat and laying them in. Keep swinging—

At a good target. Swing at something that will make a difference. Swing at something that will make them bleed. Swing with a blade in your hand.

But what can you attack with weapons designed to destroy industrial targets when the enemy has a nonindustrialized, agrarian economy?

Bridges, railroads, and power plants had all been

hammered. There were no oil refineries; fuel was stored in fifty-five-gallon drums, and storage areas were hit wherever they were identified. The one steel mill had been flattened. The Haiphong shipyards had been reduced to servicing only fishing boats. Munitions storage sites? When they could be found by photoreconnaissance, they were pounded. Big factories for making chemicals, cars, guns, glass, cans, television sets, radios, airplanes, dishes, furniture? Not in North Vietnam. Cottage industries, little shops, did all the manufacturing. There weren't even any food processing centers, just outdoor markets so typical of Asia, where rice and seaweed and rotting fish were sold from flimsy stalls. The dams and dikes were vulnerable, but the politicians refused to target them. So what was left? Nothing. Except the people. Their only real resource was people.

Maybe that was the answer. Maybe the Vietnamese communists couldn't afford to lose their leadership. What the hell! He could at least look into it. First, he would need a map of Hanoi that showed the streets and major buildings.

Abe Steiger was in the Mission Planning spaces. "Don't you ever sleep?" the pilot asked.

"Could ask you the same question," Steiger said as he placed his index finger on the bridge of his glasses and pushed them back.

Jake shrugged. "It's been a busy day." He glanced around, hoping to see a map of Hanoi on the bulkhead. He walked over to a chart index of Indochina. "Do you have any large-scale charts of Hanoi? Something that shows the streets?" Steiger consulted the index, then searched through the drawers. "It's no big deal," Grafton added. But he knew Steiger would be curious. "I've been wondering what Hanoi really looks like."

"I know what you mean," Steiger said as he took a

chart from a chest with deep, thin drawers and laid it on one of the tables. "I've taken out this one from time to time for the same reason."

The chart showed the main streets and major buildings and the bridges across the Red River. That was about all. A bombardier would have a hell of a time constructing a radar prediction from this. "Got anything more detailed?"

"Naw, this is about it. We're not *National Geographic*, you know."

"Where's the Hanoi Hilton?"

Steiger's finger went directly to the spot where the POWs were kept. "This old prison here."

Jake lit a cigarette and leaned over the chart. The French, who had been in Indochina for almost a hundred years before being evicted, would have located the important buildings on traffic circles and avenues.

"Got any pictures?"

"Some," Abe said. "Just a minute." The intelligence officer went next door to where reconnaissance photos were developed, studied, and cataloged. About three minutes later he returned with a pile in each hand. "We have a few, but they aren't too recent."

Grafton flipped through the photos. Vertical and side-view shots were mixed together. He glanced at the captions of each, hoping that he would find one marked "Capitol" or "Communist Party Headquarters." He did find two photographs that showed prominent buildings, and one of the structures had a flag in front of it. But that could be the post office. He continued slowly through the stacks, careful not to show too much interest in any one picture.

Jake had not yet apologized to Abe for the wardroom scene, although he intended to at some point. He and Steiger were now alone together for the first time since the incident. Jake sensed a coolness between them, but he avoided the subject and limited himself to occasional remarks about the pictures.

For the most part, the city consisted of endless blocks of three- or four-story apartments—the pictures showed laundry in seemingly every window—and drab, squat little factories with smoke stacks. No hotels for tourists here, and no big public monuments like those in most national capitals. Even Karl Marx, Jake thought, would be appalled at this dreary, cheerless workers' paradise. He found a picture of the remnants of the Paul Doumer bridge and studied it closely. Men had died and airplanes had fallen putting an end to that bridge.

Jake spread out the photos and scrutinized them one by one. If you could pick any target in the country, he asked himself, what would you bomb? Well, it would have to be here, inside the capital. If they have anything worth a damn, it must be here, in these pictures. But what?

"Got any infrared photos back there?"

Steiger looked doubtful. "I'll see." As soon as he had disappeared, Jake slipped half a dozen of the most interesting prints into his shirt. He was trying to pinpoint the major buildings on the chart when Steiger returned with three eight-by-tens taken from directly above the city.

These pictures could be mistaken for time-exposures of the city at night, but the light came from heat sources, not street lamps. The paved streets that had absorbed the sun's energy showed as faint ribbons. Some of the brighter hot spots were probably factories. The pinpricks of light might be kitchen chimneys. What else can I learn from looking at these pictures? Jake wondered. Would hot or cold air flow out of public buildings? Wouldn't it depend on the time of day? A magnifying glass might help. He realized he did not know enough to interpret the pictures, so he finally handed them back. "Mind if I borrow this?" he asked as he rolled the chart into a tube.

Down in their room, Sammy was asleep. Jake sat quietly on his bottom bunk and examined the stolen photos again before locking them in his desk safe.

A significant target—perhaps Communist Party headquarters? If he could drop two or three thousand-pounders into it, what a message that would deliver to the Hanoi leadership! The Communists would assume that the American government had ordered the bombing. Perhaps that would drive them to end the war.

He watched his cigarette tip glow in the dark as he considered the implications of such a raid. It was tempting. This would not be a "suspected truck park" or another raid on a bombed-out rail yard. No, this would be a real target, something worth the trip, a hit that might have a positive effect on the outcome of the war. Communists have a sure feel for gun-barrel politics, Jake told himself. They'd get the message. Of course, they'll throw everything they own into the air to defend Hanoi, and we'll have to get through it.

Morgan would have agreed readily to go after party headquarters, Jake decided, but would Cole? If Cole were a competent bombardier and a fighter, as Jake suspected, perhaps he could be approached. The next few days would tell the tale.

Jake stubbed out the butt and undressed in the dark. It would be so great to smash them!

FOURTEEN

Their torsos glistened with sweat in the early afternoon sun. Stripped to the waist, wearing bell-bottom navy-issue jeans, the ordnancemen worked in teams hoisting the bombs from dollies to the aircraft's bomb racks, almost six feet in the air. Every time they lifted, their muscles stood out. Two different crews worked on the Intruders today. On the "up" shout of the crewleader, eight sailors grunted together and the thousand-pound bomb went up to the rack. They held it there with muscle power alone while the crewleader closed the mechanical latches that mated the weapon to the aircraft, then inserted red-flagged safety pins. When three of the big green sausages hung from each rack, one man went from bomb to bomb screwing in the mechanical nose fuses and installing arming wires. The ordnancemen reminded Jake Grafton of a high school football team, all youth and muscle, all wide shoulders and corrugated stomachs, all cheerful camaraderie.

Several of the men always seemed to find time to chalk a personal message to the North Vietnamese on a bomb or two. Everyone had done that the first month of the cruise, but now the novelty had worn off for most. Their fathers had loaded bombs this way and had written similar messages to the Japanese. One scrawl caught the pilot's eye: "If you can read this you are one lucky gomer."

Jake checked each weapon to see that it was properly installed, then examined the settings on the nose fuses. Each bomb was set to arm after 6.5 seconds of freefall. Today Jake's Intruder carried a dozen 1000-pounders and a 2000-pound belly tank, over twice the payload of a B-17 on its way to Berlin.

"Go get 'em, Mister Grafton," the crewleader told him as he led his gang off to the next plane. Jake went on with his preflight inspection. The sun felt pleasantly warm on his shoulders, and perspiration moistened his T-shirt as he checked tires, brakes, and door latches. Pausing, he closed his eyes and faced the sun, which he could see through his eyelids. The breeze ruffled his hair. He opened his eyes and looked at the towering cumulus in the bright blue sky. Soon. . . .

By the time Jake swung into the cockpit, Virgil Cole was already strapped in and checking his charts and information cards. Maggot, the plane captain, followed Jake up the ladder and leaned in to help him with the harness buckles. "How's your Dad, Maggot?" Jake asked.

"Doing okay now, Mister Grafton. I called back to Texas like you said. I think he's going to be all right. Hey, where're you guys flying to today?"

The pilot reached into the ankle pocket of his G-suit and pulled out his map. Spreading it out, he stabbed with his finger. "Right there."

The plane captain saw green and brown relief for delta and mountains, blue lines for rivers, and dots and circles for cities and hamlets with strange, exotic names. "What's there?"

"A power plant." One that Jake knew had been bombed at least three times in the last six months.

The plane captain asked, "Where's Hanoi?"

Jake opened the chart another fold. "Right here. And we're down here on Yankee Station." He moved his finger to the Gulf of Tonkin.

The enlisted man grinned. "Glad I ain't going with you," he said and disappeared down the ladder.

As usual, the pilot went through the prestart checklist from memory, visually and physically checking the position of every switch and knob within his reach. Jake wiggled into his seat. Aah! he thought. My favorite chair. He closed his eyes and checked the switches again, his fingers closing confidently on each one.

He compared his watch with the five-day clock on the panel. He had three minutes before the air boss would order the engines started. Down on the deck the plane captain and ordnancemen, Jake noticed, now all wore shirts and helmets and, in case the exhaust of a jet engine blew them into the sea below, inflatable life vests. The pilot leaned back and watched the sunlight and shadows weave through the puffs of clouds. "Sure is a great day to be going flying," he told Virgil Cole, who looked up from his computer.

"Yep."

The pilot put on his helmet and waited for the plane captain's start signal. In less than ten minutes they were taxiing toward the number-three cat on the waist, or middle, of the flight deck. Planes launched here went off the angled deck instead of the bow.

As they waited for their turn to launch, Jake watched Warrant Officer Muldowski, who was launching on the waist cats today. The bosun swaggered about the deck like a pirate captain, his belly out and his shoulders back, keeping one eye on Pri-Fly and the light signals mounted there. Once the launch began he was a very busy man, checking the wind speed and setting the steam pressure for each aircraft while monitoring the hook-up of the plane on the other waist cat. He launched each plane individually, first signaling the pilot to wind the aircraft up to full power while he inspected it, then taking the salute and giving the launch signal, a fencer's lunge into the face of the thirty-knot wind. He held the pose, arm outstretched, as the wing of the accelerating machine swept over his head. The wind and hot exhaust blast swirled around him like a gale against a great rock.

The warplanes queued up behind each cat with their wings still folded. A large hinged flap known as the jet blast deflector, or JBD, located behind each cat directed the exhaust gases of the launching bird up and away from the flight deck. These deflectors were lowered after each launch to allow the next bird in line to taxi onto the cat. A group of maintenancemen swarmed over the plane waiting behind the JBD, performing the final safety inspections. A team of ordnancemen removed the safety pins from the weapons racks. Each man was intent on his job, yet vigilant to avoid being run over by a wheel, sucked up an intake, or rolled down the deck like a bowling ball by the blast furnace exhausts. The deck was so crowded that men transiting the taxiway crawled under a moving machine behind the main mounts and in front of the exhaust pipes.

Jake felt the engines spooling up and saw the catapult officer twirling his fingers in the "full power" signal, the crewmen scurrying from under his machine, and the bow of the ship slowly rising and falling to the rhythm of the sea. He anticipated the tremendous thrill when the cat would accelerate his plane to flying speed in two and a half seconds.

Jake howled in exultation as the Intruder swept down the catapult into the clean salt air, a banshee wail on the ICS that caused Virgil Cole to examine him with a critical eye when they were airborne. Jake made a slight turn to the left to clear the bow, then nursed the laden bomber up to 500 feet where it wallowed slightly as the flaps and slats retracted.

He kept the Intruder at 500 feet—as specified by the visual flight rules (VFR) departure procedure—until the TACAN indicated seven miles from the ship; then he soared left and threaded his way upward.

When they topped the clouds at 10,000 feet, Jake saw two KA-6D tankers and their retinue of Phantoms about five miles away to his rear. The tankers were in a constant angle-of-bank turn with the fighters lined up alongside as they waited their turn at the refueling hoses.

Leveling off at 13,000 feet, Jake searched the horizon for A-6s. His eye caught two of them, at least twelve miles away. The pilot steepened his turn and, holding the plane level, crossed above the ship toward them. After he had rendezvoused on the skipper's right wing, Jake glanced back across the holding circle. The last plane of the Intruder foursome was only a mile away and closing. That was New Guy, who would be his wingman on this mission.

Jake settled into the mechanics of formation flying. From now until they pushed over for the dive at the power plant, he would stay glued to the skipper's wing and New Guy would stay glued to him. If the formation broke apart, Little Augie, now on Camparelli's left wing, would stay with the leader while Grafton and his wingman would form a pair. That way, if someone got bagged there would at least be witnesses. The skipper led his A-6 division up a thousand feet and slid in beside the division, consisting of five A-7s, that would lead the strike. As briefed, the Intruders took a position about two hundred feet aft and two hundred feet to the right of the lead division. Another division of A-7s stationed itself in the same position on the left side. All the bombers were aboard.

The radio encoder beeped and Jake heard the commander of the air wing, the CAG: "Devil Five Two Three, Hawk One. How much longer on the tanking?"

"About three more minutes."

"Okay, I'm going to swing across the ship, then head out on course. The fighters can catch up if they aren't finished by then." The CAG had a reputation as a man who never waited for things to happen, which was one reason he had the job he did.

The formation steadied out in a gentle climb on course for North Vietnam. In a few minutes two Phantoms loaded with Rockeyes joined the formation from below. Each took up station on the side of the lead division. These were the flak suppressors and would dive first, aiming their ordnance at the guns and missile sites that ringed the power plant. If all went as planned, the three divisions of bombers would be in their dives when the Rockeyes exploded on the enemy guns. The key was split-second timing.

The formation leveled off at 22,000 feet. The cumulus clouds below looked to Jake like the full sails of clipper ships. Brilliant sunshine filled each cockpit and made the off-white and pale gray planes look dazzling white against the deep blue of the sky. To the east the horizon was a straight line dividing heaven and earth, but ahead to the northwest the earth and sky blended together in a grayish-white haze. Clouds over the target. Grafton sighed.

"Hawk One, Stagecoach Two Oh One. We'll be on station in about two minutes."

"Roger that." Stagecoach 201 was the leader of a section of Phantoms that patrolled twenty to thirty miles ahead of the formation to intercept any enemy fighters. A mile above the bombers, another section of Stagecoach F-4s weaved back and forth, ready to take on any MiGs that eluded the forward section. A pair of fighters from another squadron were also stationed a mile away on each side of the formation.

The CAG checked in with the E-2 Hawkeye and the EA-6B Prowler. These aircraft would remain over the ocean. The Prowler carried a sophisticated package of electronic equipment for jamming the enemy's radar frequencies.

This large strike of bombers, flak suppressors, fighter escorts, and support aircraft, known as an Alpha Strike, was designed to place the maximum amount of ordnance on a heavily defended target in less than sixty seconds, saturating the defenses and minimizing the enemy's ability to concentrate antiaircraft fire on any particular aircraft. Thorough planning and careful coordination among all elements of the group were essential. Good visibility in the target area was also a necessity. Grafton imagined the CAG was probably cursing to himself right now as he looked at the clouds ahead.

Jake found he could stay in position with just a sixteenth-of-an-inch movement of the throttles. He glanced over to Little Augie's bird, flying on Camparelli's left wing. Big waggled a greeting with his index finger, which brought a smile to Jake's face. When the Augies are goofing off, all's right with the world.

The radio beeped, and a voice spoke in a disgusted tone: "Hawk One, Mustang One Oh Four. I just had a partial hydraulic failure." Jake's eye went to the Phantom hanging a hundred feet to the right of the lead division. As he watched, the nearest A-7 in the lead division snuggled up to the Phantom.

"Mustang, you have hydraulic fluid coming out of your belly." The fluid was colored red to make it readily visible.

"Mustang, Hawk One. Go on home."

"Roger that." The stream of black smoke from the exhausts decreased to a trickle and the plane sank out of formation. Several thousand feet below, it began a gentle turn and rapidly fell behind as the formation flew on into the afternoon.

Overhead, a layer of cumulostratus and high cirrus

obscured the sky. Below, the cumulus clouds became thicker until only occasional patches of the sea could be glimpsed. The water lost its blue radiancy and looked dark, almost black. Within minutes the jets were flying in a clear lane with solid clouds above and below. The sun was gone, taking with it heat and light and leaving only a gray sameness. This was the backdrop for which the navy gray-and-white paint scheme was intended.

"Stagecoach Lead, Hawk One. How's the weather look up there?"

"Overcast and undercast. A few holes over the beach. We might be able to bomb."

"Roger."

Jake tightened his chest harness. The CAG was going on regardless. "How's the system?" the pilot asked his new bombardier.

"Radar seems okay, but the computer's a little squirrelly. I'm having trouble controlling the cursors at times. . . ." Cole ran out of steam.

"Optimist," Jake said. When Cole didn't reply, he continued, "Get set for a system delivery. I have a gut feeling we ain't gonna be able to see this damn place."

"I have the target." Cole tuned the radar. "Well, they weren't lying. It's still there. Feet dry in about four minutes."

They became aware of the bass beep of a search radar, an enemy radar, and apparently everyone else heard the faint tone at about the same time because the formation tightened up. The beep sounded again every fifteen seconds or so, the operator merely sweeping the sky, but the volume increased as they closed the enemy coast.

"Black Eagle, Black Eagle, Hawk is feet dry." Jake started the stop clock. The hands began to sweep, counting the seconds, one by one.

Now the entire formation began a gradual descent. The needle of the vertical speed indicator showed that they were dropping 1500 feet per minute, then 2000. The airspeed increased. The search radar tones came more frequently, about every four or five seconds. The operator had narrowed his sweep to a sector scan.

"Mustang One Oh Seven, you stay with us." The CAG spoke casually, as if he were ordering popcorn at the wardroom movie.

"Okay." Another emotionless voice, but the lone flak suppressor pilot must have felt a twinge of relief. Instead of zooming out ahead of the formation and making a solo dive on a heavily defended target, he would now go in with the rest of the bombers. The flak would still be there but at least Mustang 107 wouldn't be hanging it all out by himself.

But perhaps it was all academic. As the formation slid through 18,000 feet the clouds below took on a solid look. Was there a hole? Could they bomb at all?

"Twelve miles to push over," Cole informed him.

Three hundred forty knots indicated. Jake reached over and flipped on the master arm switch. One push on the bomb-release pickle and six tons of high explosive would be on their way.

"SAM, SAM, SAM." "Three o'clock." "Two of them." "Three." "Look out, Pete."

The radio was full of chatter, most of it impossible to comprehend over the wailing of the missile warning. The skipper turned right and Grafton hung on his wing. Jake's ears were assailed by the high-pitched SAM warning. The red missile light next to the bombsight was flashing. The strobe on the warning-direction indicator pointed behind the right wing, back toward Haiphong.

"See them?" he asked Cole.

"No." Cole was looking over his right shoulder. New Guy was still with them but several plane lengths back so Jake had room to maneuver.

"Keep turning, Pete." The radio again. Who the hell

was Pete? Everything was happening so fast. "Watch out!" "Damn!"

From the corner of his eye, Jake glimpsed a missile streaking upward and away from him.

"More SAMs. From the left."

The skipper reversed his turn so he could turn into the threat. The A-6 on his left wing was gone. Jake slipped down and inside the skipper's radius of turn so he could stay with him.

Where were the missiles? The warning light on the panel was still flashing and the warble whanged away. Jake chanced a quick glance downward. Nothing. Only clouds. What a mess! His peripheral vision picked up dark gray puff balls of exploding flak, probably fired blindly through the clouds.

Too many people were talking too fast on the radio. From out of nowhere a lone A-7 flashed in front of Camparelli going from right to left. The strike had fallen apart.

"You got the target?" Jake asked Virgil Cole.

"Steering's good." The pilot's eyes went to the visual display indicator. Steering was pegged right so he rolled hard right, away from the skipper, and dropped the nose.

"Attack when you can," Jake shouted above the radio and ECM noise. He needed computer steering to the weapons-release point, the attack phase, not to the target. Obediently, Cole pushed the button and the attack light came on under the VDI. Grafton checked outside for other planes and glimpsed a string of bombs disappearing into the cloud deck. Someone had dumped his load so he could maneuver better, and five would get you ten that the weapons went armed. God only knew where they'd hit.

When the VDI steering symbol was centered Jake leveled his wings. The Intruder was in a twenty-degree dive. The clouds enveloped them as they rocketed down.

The steering symbol swung hard left and Grafton slammed the stick over to follow.

Cole reported, "Ignore steering. Cursors are running. We're out of attack."

Shit! A computer or inertial problem. Over 500 knots. Get out of the goo and try again. He leveled the wings and pulled the nose up.

"And New Guy's lost us."

They exploded out of the clouds at 13,000 feet, climbing steeply. The pilot continued upward until the bomber threatened to run out of airspeed, then he flattened the angle but continued to climb. Below airplanes flashed by and every now and then a SAM popped out of the clouds. Two hundred fifty knots and climbing.

"What the hell are you doing up here this slow?" Cole demanded. "We're gonna be assholed by a SAM!"

"I'm looking for a hole. We came to bomb. Now get the goddamn system running again or we'll be up here all fucking day."

The higher he went, the better his view of the cloud deck below. Then he saw it: a hole in the clouds, a narrow jagged tear. He swung toward it, trying to see how far down it reached.

"The guys on the ground'll be shooting up that hole, hoping some damn fool'll fly down it," Cole said.

At the bottom of the hole was dark green earth. And a river. And a railroad track. And a power plant.

The bomber shuddered on the edge of a stall. Jake inverted the plane, and the earth and the power plant beside the river were above his head. The nose came down and the power plant was dead ahead, straight down.

The Intruder leapt forward under the combined pull of gravity and two engines at full power. The controls regained their sensitivity as the volume of air over the wings increased. The target was in his bombsight and growing as they hurtled down. Flak puffs mingled with the gray cloud that lined the tunnel. Cole called the altitude. Something on the ground twinkled like diamonds—muzzle flashes.

At 9000, Jake kicked the bombs loose and pulled out of the tunnel and into the clouds. Four Gs. He didn't feel the effect of the Gs.

Five thousand feet in the clouds. They were coming out of the dive, 540 knots. He felt the buffet through the seat as they pushed at the sonic shock wave that prevented any increase in airspeed. He relaxed the Gs and let the plane continue down as his instinct and the howling missile warning urged him to get free of the clouds so that he could see again.

Jake leveled at 2000 feet in rain and foggy gray tendrils that reached down toward the water-covered paddies. The missile warnings had ceased and the excited voices of other pilots filled his ears. He started a shallow turn to the southeast and looked around for other airplanes. He was alone.

Below he saw muzzle flashes and people running along the paddy dikes, but the sea was ahead and they were going home.

"Goddamn," he shouted at Virgil Cole. "We made it." He pounded Cole on the arm with his right hand and pumped the stick back and forth with his left. Heavy-caliber guns flashed, probably out of the Haiphong area, but he rolled and jinked the airplane with the ease of a horse switching its tail. They were invulnerable.

Safely out to sea, Jake and Cole released one side of their oxygen masks and let them dangle from their helmets. Grafton grinned at Cole and the bombardier did his miserable best to grin back. "Call Red Crown," Jake suggested, "and tell them to expect a low pass." The bombardier dialed the radio and made the call.

The pilot retarded the throttles and deployed the speed brakes when the radar picket destroyer appeared on the sea ahead. As they slowed through 250 knots, he dropped the gear and flaps. He stabilized at 150 and let the machine drop toward the water. The destroyer was rolling and heaving in the heavy sea, taking spray over the bow. He went down the starboard side at 50 feet as Cole waved to the T-shirted sailors looking out of the open hatches.

He cleaned up the plane—raised the gear and flaps—and climbed. Above the clouds they found the sun.

Jake Grafton took a long last drag on his cigarette and used the stub to light a new one from a crumpled pack in his G-suit pocket. He leaned back in his chair, adjusted his torso harness straps so they did not impinge upon his testicles, and listened to the men gathered in the Intelligence Debriefing room.

"What a zoo." The CAG was lighting a cigar. "That strike just went ape shit when those SAMs came squirting out."

An A-7 pilot looked up from the debriefing sheet he was filling out. "The weather was so lousy we wouldn't have had any way to bomb accurately even if the gooks hadn't fired a round."

The CAG shook his head. He looked tired. He would have to talk to the admiral in a few minutes. "We're gonna have to get our shit in one sock or we'll never make the target, good weather or not. All those bombs . . . all that gas and sweat. Wasted. And one plane stuck on the hangar deck for three or four weeks with battle damage." He looked over at the intelligence officers in their pressed khaki uniforms. "Did anyone hit the goddamn target?"

Abe Steiger answered. "Yessir. Grafton, over there, dropped visually and one of the other A-6s made a system drop."

The CAG swiveled around to Jake. "Hit anything?"

"Don't know, sir. I didn't have a chance to look back. I was hauling it out of there." The cloud on the pullout had made sightseeing impossible.

The CAG turned to the senior intelligence officer, a lieutenant commander. "I want to see those Vigilante pictures as soon as they're developed. I'll be on the flag bridge. Call me." The RA-5C Vigilante photoreconnaissance plane had flown over the target at low altitude minutes after the scheduled drop time.

The head spy nodded and the CAG walked out puffing on his cigar, not caring a damn who saw him smoking in the passageways.

Grafton and Cole picked up their helmet bags. In the passageway they met New Guy on his way to debrief. New Guy said he had lost Grafton in the pullout from the aborted system run and had attempted a system delivery himself, only to be thwarted by radar failure. Jake murmured sympathetically. New Guy didn't seem much the worse for wear after his first combat mission. "In the future, really try and stay with the leader," Jake advised. "A wingman has to stick like stink on shit." Jake knew that New Guy's self-image as a professional, as a member of the club, required that he win the ungrudging esteem of the more experienced men. He patted New on the back. "Ya' did good," Jake said. A smile of thanks creased the cherubic face.

In the locker room, as they stowed their flight gear, Cole said, "I guess you're stuck with me."

"What d'ya mean?"

"If you'd turned out to be a candy-ass, I was gonna ask for a new pilot. But you'll do."

* * *

"They want you up in the CAG office, Grafton. Some reporter wants to interview you." Boxman was the duty officer, and he delivered the message with a sneer. "Your hometown paper sent the guy. You're going to be on the front page of the county bugle, right between the 4-H news and a picture of a lady who's a hundred and two."

"Box, you're an asshole. Didn't your mother ever tell you?"

"Seriously, some reporter wants to interview you. Now, Jake!"

Grafton walked toward the Air Wing office with mixed emotions, a tiny pitter-patter of elation that he might get his name in newspapers and a large dose of caution as he contemplated the ease with which he could make a fool of himself.

When he entered the office, the CAG ops officer, Lieutenant Commander Seymore Jaye, waved him over to the table where Jaye sat with a bearded, khaki-clad figure without nametag or rank insignia. A civilian. "Grafton, this is Les Rucic, a reporter, and he wants to interview you."

The pilot leaned over and shook Rucic's outstretched hand. "Why me?" he asked Jaye.

The corners of Jaye's mouth turned down slightly. He had that habit. "I picked you, Cool Hand," he said, as if that were a sufficient answer and Grafton would be wise to leave the subject alone.

"You don't mind talking to me, do you?" Rucic asked with a smile.

"No problem." He gave his full name and hometown as Rucic carefully wrote it down in block letters.

"I asked the commander here if I could interview you. You were one of the pilots on this afternoon's strike? How'd it go?"

Jake was confused. What could he reveal that would be unclassified? Well, the gomers knew all about the mission, so why not tell the Americans? "No real problems," he said, and added, "Why'd you ask for me?"

Rucic gave him a frank and honest look. "I was recently talking to one of the fighter pilots, Fighting Joe Brett. He tells me you're one of the best pilots on this ship. I believe his phrase was more scatological. He said you were shit hot. 'Grafton is one shit-hot driver.' "

Jake colored slightly and shrugged. Joe Brett undoubtedly thought he was doing Jake a favor by giving his name to the reporter.

Rucic looked down at his notes. "Jacob Lee Grafton. From Virginia. Any relation to the Lee family?"

"No, I'm named after a grandfather who was named for Robert E. Lee. No relation. Personally, I always thought the original dude was a traitor but he had a big rep back in Virginia."

"Your father a military man?"

What did this have to do with dropping bombs on North Vietnam? "No, he's a farmer. He drove a tank for Patton in World War II, but he's been a farmer ever since."

"Is that the way you see yourself? Flying a plane for the admiral, or Richard Nixon?"

Jake glanced at Jaye, who was staring at the coffee pot in the corner as if it were the most interesting object he'd seen all day.

"I think of myself as flying a plane for Uncle Sam."

Rucic grinned, and Jake noticed three or four black hairs that protruded from each nostril. "How's it feel to be risking your life in combat when the war's about over?"

"Is it?"

"Kissinger says so."

"I wouldn't know. Diplomacy's a long way from my department."

"Tell me about your flight today."

"Well, there's not a whole lot to tell. We went, the weather was lousy, they shot a good bit, some of us managed to bomb in spite of the clouds, and we all came back to the ship in one piece."

The smallest trace of disappointment crossed Rucic's face. "But you hit the power plant?" So Jaye had briefed him.

"We dropped on it."

"But did you hit it?"

"I never looked back. Who knows?"

"But you must have some idea, lieutenant," the reporter persisted.

"Well, Les, it was like this. There was a lot of flak and missiles and I was pretty busy. After I pickled, I puckered my asshole and got the hell out of Dodge as fast as two engines and a prayer would take me."

Rucic paused, then scribbled in his notebook. "You know, Grafton, I flew F-86s in Korea. Air Force."

"Well, then, you have the background for your job."

"I know what it was like then. What's it like now over North Vietnam?"

"They shoot a lot."

"At night, too?"

"At night it's like the Fourth of July. Lots of tracers, and every now and then a SAM. Spectacular."

Rucic was writing on his pad. "Fourth of July. . . ."

Oh, Lord. Now he had done it. Rucic would write that Jake Grafton said flying over North Vietnam was just like the Fourth of July. "Uh, maybe you better not use that."

Rucic's pencil stopped, and he looked at the pilot.

"People might misunderstand. Know what I mean?"

Rucic smiled. "You still don't know if you got the power plant?"

Jake remained mute.

"What if the bombs hit a nonmilitary target?"

Jake knew the phrase "nonmilitary target" was loaded. It could mean anything from trees or dikes to schools or hospitals. "War is hell."

"They might've, from what you have told me."

"There's no such thing as a 'nonmilitary target,'" Jake replied. "Ask the V.C. what was off limits when they went into Hue. Anyway, my bombs hit the power plant or in the vicinity."

"How do you define 'vicinity'?"

"The 'vicinity' is anywhere the bombs hit when I'm aiming at the target."

"That could be a large area."

"How large depends on one's skill as a pilot. I'm good enough. 'Shit hot,' I believe you said."

"What—" But Grafton was up and leaving.

"Enjoy your cruise, Les." With a wave to Seymore, he went out the door. Rucic would probably crucify him in the press, paint him as an insensitive cliff ape who didn't care who he killed.

Well, I do care. I care about McPherson and the forty-seven shattered bodies and all the others, all those I don't know about and don't want to know about.

Fatigue pressed on him from all sides. He slapped the bulkhead with his hand. "Damn!"

FIFTEEN

After dinner that evening Jake went to the ship's library. Approaching the sailor at the desk, he said, "I'm interested in seeing what you have on North Vietnam."

"Oh, we get that request all the time."

"Well," the pilot said, "do you have any maps of the North?"

"As a matter of fact, *National Geographic* ran an article with a map a few years ago." The sailor opened a drawer and produced a well-thumbed copy of this waiting-room staple. "The map's in the back."

Jake signed for the magazine and tried not to look enthusiastic. "Any books or anything like that?"

"Well, you might try *Inside Asia,* by John Gunther. It's pretty old but a lot of people check it out." The librarian reached for the volume on a shelf beside him. "We get so many requests that we can only let you have it for a couple days."

Back in his stateroom, Jake examined the map first. It was colorful and showed the relief well, but it lacked the latitude and longitude grids necessary for measurement. The scale was also far too small. The map contained no city insets, not even of Saigon. Disappointed, he refolded it and laid it aside.

Inside Asia, published in 1939, divided Asia into four regions: Japan, China, India, and the Middle East. When the table of contents revealed no listing for Indochina, he flipped to the index. There it was, with two page numbers indicated. The author had devoted a page and a half to all of Indochina. Jake closed the book in disgust and read the Vietnam article in the *National Geographic.* Written in 1967, it quoted several military sources as stating that we were winning the war. Well, maybe they thought differently after Tet. Then again, maybe not.

He would need better data than this to plan a raid. He would need access to the charts and photos of Hanoi that Steiger had not brought forth last night. He had no doubt that Steiger had access to better stuff, and he would have to have the air intelligence officer's cooperation, as well as Cole's. But would Cole agree to help? He gathered up the library materials and returned them.

The pilot met Cole in the ready room to brief a night tanker hop. There the duty officer told them that the only available A-6B-qualified crew had been scrubbed from the night schedule because they had not had a day trap. Like most of the rules governing the aircrews' lives, the requirement that a pilot make a day landing before landing on the carrier at night after each in-port period was written in the blood of experience. "So," the duty officer said, "you two jaybirds get to fly the B."

"Hey," Jake protested, "I'm not B-qualified. I've never even sat in one of the damn things."

"Well, Cole has, and you two are all we have, so you fly. Cowboy says."

Cole reassured him with a slight movement at the corners of his mouth. "I used to be an instructor on the B. I'll tell you what to do."

The A-6B was an Intruder that had been converted to a launch platform for antiradiation missiles, or ARMs. In place of the navigation/attack computer, the A-6B had sensitive electronic equipment that identified an enemy radar so that the guidance system in the ARM could be slaved to the radar's frequency before the missile was launched. The squadron had two of these specialized machines.

The A-6B was capable of carrying two kinds of missiles, the Shrike and the Standard ARM, or STARM. The Shrike homed in on the target radar and could be defeated by the radar operator simply turning off the target radar while the missile was in flight. The North Vietnamese had quickly realized that. But the Shrike was useful anyway because it caused the enemy to shut down its radars. The STARM contained a computer and inertial navigation system that enabled the missile to memorize the location of the target radar antennae and to fly to that place even if the radar stopped operating. The Standard ARM was deadly effective and very expensive.

While Jake and Cole were knocking around in the A-6B, Sammy Lundeen and Harvey Wilson would be roaming the Red River Delta on bombing missions. Virgil Cole drew Jake over to the corner of the room and briefed him on the specialized equipment in the missile-shooter. As for tactics, the bombardier advised, "We'll just cruise along at altitude where everyone can see us and let it happen. Might be interesting."

Indeed it might, Jake thought. As he left the ready room, Sammy joined him for the short jaunt to the flight-gear lockers. "Notice ol' Rabbit Wilson has a night trap scheduled?"

"Yep. Must be a scorcher of a moon out there."
"Or a Silver Star."

They crossed the North Vietnamese coast at 18,000 feet with search radars beeping in their ears. The prevailing wind had pushed the low rain clouds of the afternoon westward against the mountains, and only the high cirrus layer was left to block off all starlight. The two bombers were not due to cross the coast for five more minutes. "Let's mosey in and get the gomers' attention before the other guys sneak in," Cole said, and Jake acquiesced because he knew so little of A-6B tactics.

Both the bombers were targeted against suspected truck parks on the eastern edges of Hanoi. Cole suggested an orbit about twenty miles to the east of the North Vietnamese capital so they could lob their missiles at the heavy concentration of enemy missile sites that guarded the approaches to the city.

They carried two Standard missiles on the inboard wing stations and two Shrikes on the outboard. On the flight deck Grafton had examined the white missiles carefully. The Standard missiles were huge, fourteen inches in diameter and about fifteen feet long, packed with solid propellant and carrying a warhead designed to destroy with shrapnel rather than by blast. The Shrikes were smaller, about eight inches in diameter and nine feet long, and were steered by canards—tiny wings—mounted in the middle of the tubular fuselage.

"You've fired rockets before?" Cole asked.

"Not at night."

"When these missiles light off at night, they'll blind you if you look outside. All the gomers will see the ignition, too, if the air is clear. Spectacular."

They were now set up to launch the Shrike on station five, which was outboard on the right wing. The pilot glanced back at the left wing stations, but the missiles were invisible in the gloom. They were there, though, and ready.

All the crew had to do was find a target. The first nibble came from a gun-control radar behind them, the type that NATO code-named "Firecan." It acquired them and stayed locked up. Jake began weaving at random to make it harder for the large-caliber artillery, which the Firecan usually directed, to find them. "Swing around and take a look," said Cole. Jake held the left turn and searched the darkness where the enemy radar had to be. He picked up flashes from the muzzles of the big guns. He also saw small-caliber weapons immediately beneath the plane shooting tracers in streams.

"All the backyard stuff just shoots at noise," said Cole. "Only the big stuff—the eighty-five and one hundred millimeter—is hooked into the radar net and can reach us up here."

Varying the altitude by up to 500 feet, Jake swung back toward the planned orbit. Off to his left he saw white flashes. Those would be shells from the big guns exploding at preset altitudes.

They heard the bombers give their coast-in calls. Jake checked the clock and saw that Sammy and Rabbit were running a few minutes late.

Ahead a glimmer caught his eye. "I think a SAM just lifted off," he told Cole and turned on the master arm switch. He knew the Soviet-built SA-2 surface-to-air missile that the North Vietnamese usually used was a two-stage missile that had to be guided from the ground because it lacked an active seeker-head. For its first seven seconds of flight, the missile was unguided as the first stage burned. When the second stage ignited, the first stage fell away and exposed a receiver on the rear of the second stage that could pick out the guidance commands embedded in the emissions from the Fansong missile-control radar. When the A-6's ECM equipment heard the Fansong radar, as NATO called this type of missile-control radar, it presented a steady missile-warning light and a continuous tone in Jake's ears. When the equipment detected guidance signals, the missile-warning light would flash and the tone in his ears would warble.

Jake turned right to increase the crossing angle as he watched the continuous light far below in the darkness, small but brilliant. The missile was flying but the Fansong was not yet guiding it. Then the missile light on his glare shield began to flash, and he heard the warble warning. The signal-detection indicator now told him there was a Fansong at eleven o'clock, which he already knew. He looked back at the SAM and saw a second missile ignite and lift off.

"Want to shoot?" he asked Cole.

"Naw, let them shoot up some of their expensive stuff before we show our cards."

Jake popped some chaff to confuse the Fansong. He watched the telltale fire from the missile exhausts and knew the missile was traveling at about two thousand miles per hour. He would have to let the missiles get close, but not too close, then maneuver to avoid them. The missiles were traveling too fast to turn with the Intruder. The wait was anything but easy.

When he could stand it no longer, he pumped the chaff button three times, then rolled the plane almost upside down.

"Not yet," Cole told him.

Jake pushed the stick forward and held the nose up. The fireballs were bigger and obviously closing. "Now!" Cole told him.

The pilot pulled until four Gs registered on the G meter. The nose came down and they were turning into and under the oncoming missiles. The missiles were now turning down toward them, but the lead missile would overshoot and fail to intercept the plane. Jake watched the missiles. The first streaked overhead at least a half mile away and exploded, probably detonated by the ground crew when they realized it would miss. The second one was correcting to intercept, so the pilot changed direction and dropped the nose further to increase the change in course required of the missile. The missile was just beginning to turn when it swept overhead. The missile light went out. Jake rolled the aircraft upright and used the excess airspeed to zoom back up to 18,000. The Firecan still had them.

"Hokey dokey," Cole said.

"You make it sound like this is more fun than watching your alma mater score at homecoming."

"More interesting, anyhow. Now if the gomers get about four missiles or so in the air at once, we'll give them the Shrike we've set up. If they shut down they'll lose all the missiles, and if they don't—"

Jake Grafton drew a ragged breath. One avoided SAMs by trading altitude and airspeed for angle-off, as they had just done, thereby placing the missile in a position where it could not make the turn required to intercept. If enough missiles were in the air, an aircraft could run out of altitude and airspeed before it had outmaneuvered all the missiles. Cole knew the facts of aerial life as well as he, probably better.

"Where'd you get all this confidence in my ability?" Jake asked.

"I had an uncle with a nose like yours."

The Firecan went off the air now, leaving only the pulse of search radars to break the silence. A Fansong painted them for several seconds, then it too fell silent.

Waiting is the toughest part, he thought. You wait for the brief, you wait for the cat shot, you wait to get shot at. It's an old complaint, as old as the first warrior, but knowing that doesn't make the waiting any easier.

The missile warning lit up again. Jake checked the strobe indicator on the detection gear, which told him the radar was at five o'clock. He swung hard, maintaining his altitude, and searched the blackness. Two missiles were in flight, and a third lifted off as he watched. The missile light flashed and the aural warning wailed. "Three SAMs up," Grafton said. A grunt was the only reply.

The pilot held the turn until the missiles were inbound at one o'clock, still low but climbing. On the ground a fourth missile ignited and raced skyward. "Four up," Jake said to Cole.

The bombardier straightened and looked around. "Point the plane at the radar and gimme fifteen degrees nose up," Cole said. As the pilot complied, the missiles disappeared from their view, hidden by the nose of the plane. "Hold it," said Cole.

Jake's gut was tying itself into a knot. Not being able to see the missiles terrified him. The falsetto screech of the missile warning made his heart beat wildly.

"Shoot!" Cole said, and the pilot squeezed the trigger with his finger and pushed the pickle button with his thumb. Cole had told him to hold both buttons for a second—the time delay was a safety feature to reduce the chances of inadvertent firing—and an age later the white fireball illuminated under the right wing with a "whoosh." Jake saw the bombardier limned in the brilliant light, which rocketed forward and faded to nothing in a fraction of a second.

"Split S," Cole ordered when the pilot didn't react with sufficient speed. Blinded by the unexpected radiance, Grafton instinctively jammed the stick to the left, spun the plane what he hoped was 180 degrees, then pulled hard toward the earth. He blinked rapidly because he had lost his night vision.

"Chaff," Cole reminded him. Jake pumped the button.

His vision was coming back. He could make out the panel and the VDI. Now he could read the VDI. The plane was seventy degrees nose down, inverted. The missile light still flashed.

Why hadn't the gomers shut down? He shoved the stick forward, rolled upright, and pulled the nose up while he searched the sky for the incoming missiles. He saw them strung out in trail, the first one way high and arching down, but it would overshoot.

"More behind us," Cole said. Jake dropped the left wing and clawed the plane around. He checked the indicator. The radar they had fired at had finally ceased transmitting, but another radar behind them was now guiding missiles. He found the oncoming pinpoints of light and continued his turn, dumping the nose slightly to keep his airspeed from bleeding off. He wanted to dive more steeply to pick up speed as he was moving at only 300 knots, but he was down to 12,000 feet and if they launched another SAM when he was below 10,000, he might be forced to descend almost to the surface.

The missiles were at two o'clock and at his altitude when Jake leveled the wings and shoved the stick forward until he and Cole floated weightless against the restraining straps at zero G. The nose fell slowly as he flew the parabola, but the engines' thrust was more effective without the induced drag from the wings—they weren't making lift at zero G—and the airspeed quickly increased to more than 400 knots. The lead missile appeared to be overshooting, but the trailer was correcting. The pilot squeezed chaff, rolled right, and yanked the stick hard. Now! The second missile was also overshooting. The missile warnings ceased as the second SA-2 detonated in a flash of white light about a thousand feet away.

Jake climbed and turned toward the northwest. His body trembled in the sudden hush. The aural warning was silent, the missile light was dark, but for how long?

To the south, fifteen or twenty miles away, antiaircraft guns cleft the night. "Looks like our bomber friends have arrived," said Jake over the ICS to Cole.

On the radio, Jake asked, "You up on this freq, Sammy?" With his gloved hand, he wiped the perspiration from his brow.

"Roger." Lundeen's voice.

"Five Oh Three?" he asked as he noticed another flak concentration a little farther north.

"We're up," Rabbit Wilson said.

Jake heard Cole key the mike. "Five Oh Six, how far from your target are you?"

"About forty miles out," Lundeen replied.

"Pop up to fifteen hundred feet and stay there a bit," Cole suggested. "We'll use you as bait." Lundeen clicked his mike.

Well, Jake thought, weren't they all bait?

"If they shoot at Lundeen out of Hanoi," Cole said to Jake, "we'll fire the Standard missile as soon as we see the first SAM. There's a site there that has been peeping once in a while and I've slaved the STARM to his signal." With luck, the STARM would be locked in on the Fansong even if it went off the air before the missile arrived. With luck.

Grafton reached 18,000 feet and reined in the power to ninety percent RPM. They had to save fuel somewhere. He pointed the nose toward Hanoi and let the airspeed decay as he climbed. Altitude could always be converted to airspeed simply by diving. "About five degrees nose-up, no more," Cole advised him.

Flak sparking in the darkness below marked Sammy's progress across the night sky. When would another SAM launch? Jake wiped his eyebrows again with a gloved finger. "Man, we're having fun now," he muttered. Cole looked at him. "Morgan liked to say that," Jake explained.

"There!" Cole pointed. The pilot saw the tiny pinpoint at one o'clock. This time he closed his eyes as he squeezed the buttons on the stick. He heard the whoosh as the missile ignited and felt the brightness of the STARM fireball behind his closed eyelids. Perhaps three seconds had passed since the first SAM was launched.

"You have a SAM in the air and a STARM," Cole told Lundeen. "Stay at fifteen hundred as long as you can." By the time he had finished speaking a second SA-2 had been launched and was following in the wake of the first. "They're guiding," Cole informed Grafton as he consulted the gear on his panel. Their own aural warning system remained silent because the Fansong radar was not pointed in their direction.

"Stay up, baby," Cole whispered over the ICS. Jake knew he was really whispering at the enemy radar operator who was sitting in a dark semitrailer van and watching the blip that was Devil 506. A few more seconds . . .

Jake's attention was riveted on the place in the darkness from which the two SAMs had been launched. He forced himself to ignore the exhaust plumes of the enemy missiles streaking along parallel to the invisible earth, streaking toward Sammy and Marty Greve.

"I've been up here long enough," Lundeen announced over the radio.

"It's off the air," Cole said.

The STARM was invisible because it had exhausted its fuel just before it began homing in on the emissions of the Fansong.

The pilot saw a faint flash. Grafton told Cole about it. The bombardier shrugged. "Maybe we got it." He manipulated the switches on the armament panel to put the second STARM in readiness.

The pilot turned and let the nose slide down. He stabilized at 18,000 feet. The search radars continued to paint them and a Firecan locked them up momentarily. Jake saw the rippling twinkles that were Lundeen's bombs, and a minute later, somewhat closer, a similar string of fireworks where the X.O.'s target must be. Tracer fire smeared the darkness near the bombers' tracks.

Jake and Cole continued to orbit as the bombers crossed the delta toward the coast. The missile-control radars were silent. Lundeen finally called "feet wet," and, a minute later, Rabbit Wilson as well.

They flew southeast toward the waiting ocean, steady at 400 knots at 18,000 feet. They heard a Fansong in the area of Haiphong, off to their left. It came on the air for several seconds, shut down, then repeated the cycle a half-minute later. Jake searched the darkness below for the moving points of light that betrayed the flight of SAMs. Nothing.

He was looking at the Fansong light on the indicator panel, now on again, when he noticed another light also lit: I-band. He examined the circular dial on the threat-direction indicator and, sure enough, a weak I-band strobe pointed behind them. When the Fansong fell silent he could even hear the other radar, a two-tone, high-frequency pulse. As he listened, he heard the audio separate into three distinct, clicking, rhythmic tones that repeated about once a second. Virgil Cole cocked his head at the direction indicator. He, too, seemed to be listening.

"Sounds like we have a MiG-21 on our tail," he announced. "Doesn't that sound like a conical scan to you?"

MiG! Even as Cole said it, Jake thought he could now hear the intermittent clicks. If it were a MiG, it was getting closer. Grafton jammed the throttles full forward and punched the chaff button three times as fast as he could, then slammed the stick full left and forward in one fluid motion. The nose tucked down and the plane flipped on its back, 180 degrees of roll in one second. In a continuation of the same motion he brought the stick aft and center, and the nose of the inverted warplane dropped through to the vertical where he stabilized in a straight-down dive. The altimeter spun insanely as Jake listened for the beat of the conical scan, mixed in with the wail of the Fansong now back on the air in the target-acquisition mode. If the MiG saw the false target the chaff created and went after it, he could escape out below. Near the ground the MiG couldn't acquire him. He hoped.

He rolled ninety degrees about the longitudinal axis and at 7000 feet began a hard, five-G pull in the direction of Haiphong, punching chaff all the way. The primary gyro tumbled, apparently, because the VDI still indicated a vertical descent. He ignored it and included the standby gyro in his scan. Virgil Cole said, "Pull up to twenty degrees nose up, ten degrees right, and we'll shoot the STARM."

"Are you crazy?" The radar altimeter dipped below 3000 feet, the nose still five degrees below the horizon. His right arm tightened slightly, six Gs, 540 knots indicated. The I-band warning was gone, the earphones silent. The MiG had lost them.

Cole's fist slammed into his right biceps. "Do like I told you!"

They bottomed out at 2000 feet and Jake kept the nose coming up. Stabilizing in a twenty-degree climb, he waited for Cole to ready the missile. The airspeed dropped below 480 knots, then 460.

"Come on, you crazy bastard," Jake shouted at Cole. "Let's shoot and get the fuck outta here before that MiG figures out which way we turned."

"Just a sec . . . almost. . . . Shoot!"

Jake heard the Fansong kick in his earphones as the last Standard missile ignited under the right wing and shot forward, trailing a dazzling sheet of fire. They were in trouble again unless that MiG pilot was blind. Grafton turned hard right to run for the coast.

"Black Eagle, Devil Five One One," Cole said over the radio. "We have a bandit on our tail. Get the BARCAP headed this way. Buster." "Buster" meant hurry, bust your ass.

Jake was at 5000 feet, 510 knots when he again heard the beat of the MiG's Spin Scan radar. It was out to his right, at four o'clock. He had to get *down,* near the ground. The MiG was coming in at an angle and he wouldn't have time to turn.

"Devil, this is Mustang. We're coming! State your posit."

"Thirty miles south of the lighthouse, fifteen miles inland," Cole said.

Jake selected the station for the remaining Shrike and held the buttons down. The missile shot forward toward the earth. Now to give the MiG a real false target, not just a chaff cloud. He depressed the emergency jettison button above the gear handle. The empty missile racks and belly tank were kicked away with a whump.

The MiG was closing fast from the side. Two thousand feet above the ground.

"Devil, don't let him get away!"

"Fuck you!" Grafton shouted and chopped the throttles to idle and deployed the speed brakes as he shoved the nose over.

A missile raced across the windscreen above and in front of him. He pulled up to avoid the ground. He pushed on the throttles but they wouldn't move! Then the cockpit went dark.

Mother of God! He had inadvertently pulled the throttles past the safety detents and had shut down the engines. The speed brakes were still out, but they should come into trail with the loss of electrical power. He desperately groped behind him for the handle to the ram-air turbine, the emergency generator. He had to have electrical power for a restart.

Where was it? Oh, God, no!

His fingers closed on the handle in the darkness. He pulled with the strength of the damned.

The lights came on. The left wing was down. He picked it up.

Two hundred fifty knots! He advanced the throttle on the left engine as he held the emergency ignition button on the throttle down with his thumb. Wings level, 400 feet.

Warning lights were erupting on the annunciator panel: both generators, fuel, oil pressure. It looked like a Christmas tree. Without the background noise of the engines the cockpit was quiet as a coffin.

"Light off!" he screamed at the recalcitrant engine as he checked the standby gyro. If the circuit breaker for the emergency igniters had popped, the engine would never light. The breaker was on a panel beside his left foot and he didn't have time to check it. He kept the ignition button firmly depressed. 210 knots. At this weight, without flaps or power, they would quit flying at maybe 180 knots.

The engine lit with an audible moan. The RPM came up toward the sixty percent idle range agonizingly slowly. Sweet Jesus! There! Sixty percent. He advanced the left throttle to the forward stop and reached for the right to repeat the procedure. One hundred ninety-five knots on the dial.

"Only a hundred feet," Cole advised. A glance again at the airspeed. Stable at 195. Left engine still winding up, passing eighty-five percent. He slipped in more back stick and trimmed. As the left engine reached full power, the right lit off.

When both throttles were full forward, he reset the generators. The radar-warning indicators were dark. Nothing in his earphones. The annunciator panel lights were all extinguished. Two hundred fifty knots and increasing.

"Black Eagle, Devil's feet wet," Cole said.

"Where were you? You didn't answer my call."

"Uh, we had a little mechanical problem back there, Black Eagle," Cole said. "Where's the bandit?"

"The Mustangs are after him."

"Glad I'm not driving that MiG with those Phantoms after me," Cole said over the ICS.

Jake climbed to 500 feet and stayed there, weaving erratically. They were thirty miles out to sea before Jake decided his heart might not after all beat itself out of his chest. Only then did he establish a climb and pull the throttles back off the stops.

As Cole talked on the radio, Jake took off his oxygen mask and wiped the sweat from his face. Lordy, lordy!

In Marshall, Jake Grafton told Cole he was a crazy fucker. "How come you wanted to shoot that last STARM?"

"That Fansong was providing altitude and position info to the interceptor pilot. They were vectoring him until he got close enough to lock us up. That's how the Red Baron knew just where to find us. How come you shot that last Shrike into the ground?"

"I figured if he was working on an infrared lock-up for a missile, the Shrike would give us a few seconds. And I was gonna jettison the racks and didn't want to give the gomers an unfired missile to play with."

"You know, Grafton, you're the only pilot I know who'd intentionally shut down the engines in combat. And that close to the ground."

"You know goddamn well that was a screw-up, an accident. I made a mistake. How come you didn't eject?"

"And have you pull your chestnuts out of the fire and go back to the ship without your bombardier? They'd laugh me out of the navy."

"We damn near bought the farm."

"Well, we didn't. That's what counts." The bombardier put his head back in the headrest and closed his eyes.

Jake Grafton climbed down the ladder from the cockpit, holding on carefully with both hands. His legs felt wobbly as he followed the tall figure of Virgil Cole. Too spent to remain standing, he asked Cole to do the intelligence debrief and went straight to the ready room where he collapsed into a chair. After a minute he decided he needed a cigarette, so he moved enough to retrieve the packet from his left sleeve pocket.

When Lundeen came in he fell into the chair next to Jake's. Grafton sketched out the MiG encounter. He was soon surrounded by half a dozen men who fired questions and laughed nervously at his answers.

"The Mustangs got that MiG," Marty Greve said.

" 'Don't let him get away!' " Lundeen shrieked. They all thought this was hilarious.

"Now I know how Jonah felt just before the whale swallowed him," Jake said.

"And how did Cole do?" Lundeen asked when the laughter faded.

"The fucking guy's a tiger," said Jake.

The nickname "Tiger" became firmly attached to the quiet bombardier. "It fits him," Jake would say to his friends with a smile.

SIXTEEN

When the movie started, Jake went down to his stateroom and undressed, then headed for the shower. The water felt good, and he was tempted to let it run while he soaped up but thought better of it.

Lathered from head to toe, he opened the taps again. The water squirted, slowed to a trickle, then to individual drops. Someone, somewhere on the ship had secured the water. Jake sagged against the side of the stall. The soap suds on his body made little popping noises.

Back in his stateroom, he sponged off the soap with water from the sink. After he used his towel to mop up the puddles around him, he put on clean underwear and sat down at his desk.

He held his hands under the light; they trembled like those of an old man. He had paperwork to do but couldn't summon up the energy or interest to do it. He looked into the shadows of the room and thought of Callie. What was she doing tonight? Dancing with some congressman? Their worlds were so different. Someday he would take her to the hills of Virginia, where the air was clean and smelled of pine.

Back in Virginia, winter would have closed in. The

trees would be bare, the leaves on the ground sodden after the late autumn rains. The cold would keep the squirrels in their nests until midday. The game birds would be lying in their secret places, the deer curled up in theirs. He remembered the deer, so graceful, so cautious. The does would jump from a bed beneath a laurel or pine bough, bound through the stark trees and perhaps pause at a safe distance and stare back at him, an intruder.

All would be still. The only sounds would be his breathing and his footfalls on wet leaves. He would find a stump or a log and sit with a cigarette or chew of tobacco. After a while the breeze would chill him. It would come out of the north or west, a gentle wind that would drift through the trees and flow up the hollows, seeking the gaps in the hills. Eventually the gathering clouds would thicken, and he would see a few lazily falling flakes, borne on the wind. He had sat through many snows in the forest, when the millions of airborne crystals would shrink the world to less than a hundred feet. In silence nature would transform a landscape. But soon the cold would seep through his clothing, layer by layer. He'd be forced to rise, to stamp his feet and swing his arms wide as his breath took form in vapor.

He relived the night's mission again. Waiting for the engine to light as the Intruder approached the stall—that was the longest moment of his life. Shutting the engines down had been a major mistake, the kind he had told Callie he didn't believe he would make. The more he thought about the course of his life, the more he felt he was losing control. Worse yet, he wondered if anyone was really in control. Somebody had to be planning the war! But the targets were shit. Lives were risked and lost, changing nothing. And the war went on.

He pounded the starch out of a clean uniform and

put it on. He took his leather flight jacket from a hook near the door and, locking the door behind him, set off down the passageway thinking about party headquarters in Hanoi. Would Cole go? Would Steiger help them find it? That Cole . . . he's a real piece of work. That was clear after the hop this evening. But what if he says no? But he'll say yes. Sure he will. But what if he doesn't?

He ran into Mad Jack in the passageway in front of the Sick Bay. "Why aren't you in the ready room watching the movie, Grafton?"

"I'm not interested."

"Rough hop tonight, huh? My prescription is a movie and a good night's sleep."

"Sure, Jack, sure. A few giggles and forty winks. Roger that." Jake kept walking and didn't slow until he had turned the corner.

Cole listened to Grafton, his face not revealing a clue to his reactions. They had just finished a night tanker hop. The two men were alone, drinking coffee in the dirty-shirt wardroom. When the pilot finished, Cole asked, "Why do you want to do this?"

"We need to hit something significant, something that'll convince them to talk seriously at the peace table."

"Is there any such target?"

"There might be. Party headquarters in Hanoi. Their leadership. There's a chance it might work. I think it's worth the risk."

"What do you want me to do?"

"We need Steiger's help with the planning materials. I lost my temper with him in the wardroom before we went into port last time. Things are a little tense between us. I think he'll help if we approach him the right way, but it'll be chancy."

"I'll talk to him," said Tiger Cole.

"If Steiger says no and tells somebody, your talking to him will be an affirmative act that could get you zapped the same as me." Jake shifted uncomfortably in his chair. "Anyway, you better think this through before you say a word to Abe. We could get court-martialed for even suggesting we're gonna bomb an unauthorized target."

"The same risk you ran a few minutes ago when you started this conversation?"

"Yeah," Jake said, flushing slightly.

Cole laughed, a sound like a gate creaking on rusty hinges. "The odds on the two of us dying in bed improve a lot if we're court-martialed."

An hour later there was a knock on Grafton's stateroom door. Jake opened the door to Cole and Steiger.

"Abe has some questions he wants to ask you," Cole said as the two men found seats.

"Did Cole tell me right? Do you really want to bomb Communist Party headquarters?"

"Yeah. That's right. We want to kick them in the nuts for a change."

Abe took off his glasses and cleaned them with a handkerchief. He took his time, inspecting them carefully to make sure they were spotless. Jake passed him a can of warm Coke. He opened it and took a long drink. "Why do you want to do this, Jake? Why take the chance someone will figure out it's you who bombed the reds in Hanoi?"

The pilot rubbed his face with his hands. He looked at Cole, then at Steiger. "We have to kick harder. That's all. We just have to kick them as hard as we can."

"Are you two planning on making a career in the navy?" Steiger asked. The pilot shrugged. "Cole?" The bombardier turned his thumb down. "Well, that's good, because you both seem to have an independent streak." He drummed his fingers on Jake's desk. "Y'know, for a while I thought I would—make the navy a career, I mean. But this last year, seeing you guys go out on missions, never risking anything myself, well, y'know, it's gotten to me." He looked at the two airmen. "Hell, I don't expect you to understand. You risk your butts out there, and in your eyes I'm just the little weenie who helps plan the missions."

"Don't forget," Cole said, "we're going right downtown. It won't be any piece of cake."

Jake caught the bombardier's eye and shook his head. He let the silence build for a moment before he spoke. "We know you carry your end of the log, Abe. We also realize we're asking a lot from you. It's true, as you say, that we put our chips up every night. Maybe it takes a few turns of the wheel to develop gambler's blood."

"You guys can't do this little deal without me, can you?" Abe said. "Suppose you should get bagged Then I'll be the pigeon denying any knowledge of what the hell you were doing over Hanoi. And I'm not a very good liar." He shook his head and his glasses slipped down his sweaty nose. He pushed them back with his middle finger.

"If we thought we couldn't get back, we wouldn't go," Cole said.

"We know you'd be running a big risk," said Jake.

"I do my job. I put the materials together, interpret the raw data, and help you guys plan the strikes." After a pause, Steiger added, "My job's nice and safe."

Jake lit a cigarette. The match shook in his hands. He glanced at Abe and saw that the air intelligence officer was staring at his own shoes. "Don't you see, Abe? Can't you see the blood and brains and pieces of smashed human beings? It's all murder! Just plain, ordinary, barroom murder dressed up so people won't puke. The people we kill with our bombs are never the right ones. We never get the guys who dug the holes at Hue and machine-gunned the civilians. We never get the guys who are cutting the schoolteachers' throats. We kill the kids and the old women and guys like you and me who just want to live through this thing. But this time we're going after the men who give the orders. This time we're going straight for the sons of bitches at the top."

"You can't stop it, Grafton. Not with just one plane. Not just two guys."

"Three guys," said Jake. He watched the smoke curl up from his cigarette. He looked at Steiger. "So we keep making craters in the runways at Kep. How many times have we done that? Or we bomb a 'suspected truck park' that turns out to be so many acres of forest, or mud flats along a river that somebody labeled a 'boat yard.' Just this once wouldn't you like to really hit 'em where it hurts? If we bomb their headquarters, maybe, just maybe, we'll take out their leadership."

"Or die trying."

"So Grafton and Cole get smoked! Won't be the end of the world. But if it happens, remember this: we didn't buy the farm killing dogfaces—we didn't die gutting little girls who live too close to a bombed-out power plant. We died going for the head motherfucker. You put that on our tombstones."

Steiger chewed on a fingernail. After a long pause, he said, "Maybe I've sat in this safe job long enough. Maybe it's time I hung out my ass for a change. Tomorrow, during the wardroom movie, why don't you come up to Mission Planning." Abe looked glum, then his face brightened. "Hell, maybe if you don't get the leaders, you might get Jane Fonda or Ramsey Clark."

Jake laughed. "Abe, if I had that kind of luck I'd have won the Irish Sweepstakes by now and be married to the Playmate of the Year." He stopped laughing and looked at Steiger. "By the way, Abe, I want to tell you that I'm sorry about shouting at you in the wardroom."

"Nah, it was my fault. I shouldn't have told you those things. I just thought you would want to know." He picked at a paint blister on the back of the door. "But thinking about it, if it were me, I wouldn't want to know. An infantryman has to know. He's so close. But if you don't have to know, then why would you want to?"

The chart lay open on the table. Two days had passed since Grafton and Cole had enlisted Steiger. In the interim Abe had been unable to find any information on Party Headquarters among the targeting materials aboard ship. "We could get the stuff," he had told Grafton and Cole, "but only if we send a message asking for it. That'd be like robbing a bank without a mask and making the getaway in your own car." They had agreed that the National Assembly building was the next best choice.

Things seemed to be breaking their way. The usual night strike carried a dozen 500-pounders, which would have merely scratched the well-built stone building. "We have a dozen thousand-pound Snakes for tonight's strike," Cole said to Jake and Abe. The Snakes, or Snake-eyes, were conventional general-purpose bombs fitted with clamshell fins that opened when the weapons were released and acted like parachutes to retard the weapons and let them fall almost straight down while the aircraft escaped the ensuing fragmentation. The Snake-eye fins would permit a delivery from as low as 500 feet.

"We'll dump four on the power plant and eight on the National Assembly," Cole said. "They won't be expecting us to turn for Hanoi, so we might be able to scoot across the city without too much opposition."

They all looked again at the chart and the route, which Abe had helped Tiger prepare. A thin black line marked the route they would fly. It stretched away from the ship in a northerly direction one hundred fifty miles to a point about ten miles east of the mouth of the Red River. The line then angled north-northwest across the coast, past the town of Hai Duong, to a fork in a stream a dozen miles short of Bac Giang, a town on the railroad that ran from Hanoi northeast into China. The river confluence was the Initial Point, the IP, and was so marked. Leaving the IP, the black line continued on to Bac Giang and the power station there. That was the target the navy had assigned for their night mission. What the navy didn't know was that after Bac Giang the black line went down the railroad track to Hanoi, across the city, then southeast, parallel to the Red River, past Nam Dinh to the sea. Jake Grafton and Tiger Cole studied the chart and tried to visualize the reality.

Cole laid a two-year-old photo of the power plant on the table. "We train off the four bombs, point oh six seconds apart." He then laid a six-year-old photo of the National Assembly on top of the picture of the power plant. "To hit this, we salvo the eight bombs we have left, four at a time, point oh six seconds between salvos."

"Maximizes the damage but minimizes the possibility of a hit," Jake observed.

Steiger pulled out a detailed overhead picture of Hanoi. He pointed a pencil at the North Vietnamese National Assembly building. "It's surrounded on three sides by other buildings. I haven't the foggiest idea what's in them. Probably government offices, but who can say?"

Jake gestured at the photograph of the stone building where the assembly met. "Maybe we ought to climb up high enough to drop the Snakes unretarded. If they're retarded they may not penetrate deep enough into this building to do a whole lot of damage."

Cole nodded. "Let's see how much flak there is and decide at the time."

Jake was dubious. He studied the photo. "If we drop them retarded they may bounce off this bastard. It looks damn solid to me." Each of the men evaluated the picture. Grafton was right. The bombs had to go in slick, which meant that the airplane would have to release them from at least 2500 feet above the ground to escape the fragments.

The pilot picked up the sectional chart that showed in detail the target area in Hanoi. This was the chart he had wanted the other night, but he didn't mention that to Steiger. He rotated the chart so the land and river lay as he would see them from the cockpit. He tried to memorize the turn of the river, the position of the boulevards, and the location of the target building. If the radar failed at the last moment there just might be enough light to drop visually.

Steiger's voice broke the silence. "The moon won't be up until about 2240. It's on the wane." But with the amount of flak the pilot suspected they would see, the target might nevertheless be visible. They would find it, one way or the other.

"How about fuel?" Jake asked Tiger.

"There'll be enough. We'll be late getting feet wet, but no one'll notice. If they do, we'll just say we had to make two runs."

"Where's the other strike going?" Jake inquired.

"Joe Wagner is gonna look for trucks on Route One," Abe replied.

"And the A-6B?"

"Not on this one," Abe said.

Good! No one in the squadron would ask any questions about all the flak around Hanoi. Some A-7 or F-4 drivers might see the fireworks, but they wouldn't know who was there nor would they care.

Jake looked closely again at the photo of the National Assembly building. Four buildings of similar size were nearby. "This thing'll be hard to break out of the clutter," he observed, referring to the radar picture that Cole would be looking at. The bombardier shrugged.

"Have you ever been downtown before?" Jake asked Cole as they packed the charts and radar predictions into the bombardier's flight bag.

"Yeah," Tiger Cole replied.

"How many times?" Abe asked.

"A few."

"How many is a few?"

"Four or five."

"How many times exactly?"

"Exactly eight. Back in '67, late summer and fall. Lyndon Johnson was going to teach them a lesson."

"How was it?" Abe absently tapped his pencil on the table.

"Bad."

"They shot a lot?"

"It was like sticking your dick into a hornet's nest. We lost a bunch of airplanes. I don't think we taught them much, except that we can be had."

As they left, Steiger momentarily put his arm around Jake's shoulders. "Watch your ass," he advised, his eyes wide and blinking behind his glasses.

In the passageway Jake said, "Well, you sure scared Abe."

"Then it's unanimous. We're all three scared."
"Why did you agree to do this?"
"Because you asked." As they went down a ladder, Cole first, the bombardier said over his shoulder, "And because you can't win a war unless you're willing to fight."

SEVENTEEN

The sea was a greasy mirror that reflected the grays of the evening sky. Not a breath of wind stirred. Even the swells had flattened under this heavy mass of dead air. In order to launch, the ship had to create a headwind; the deck vibrated as the four screws thrashed the still water into a river of foam that stretched aft into the thick haze that married the sea and sky.

From his cockpit Jake regarded the haze that at five hundred knots would impede visibility and threaten survival. He scoffed at his feeling of unease, but worry still clutched at him.

Jake was sitting behind the jet blast deflector for the number-three catapult on the waist when he saw Bosun Muldowski hold up a message board for the pilot of the Phantom on the cat. Although Grafton couldn't read the message, he could guess its contents. The cat officer was advising the pilot that he wouldn't get the usual fifteen-knots speed above the stall and was asking him to make do with less. The bosun turned away. Undoubtedly he had received a thumbs up from the pilot, who really had little choice but to accept whatever endspeed the cat could give him. The chief engineer in the boiler rooms was probably chewing his lip; the boilers couldn't provide the steam needed for the main turbines to drive the ship at flank speed and operate all four catapults at full power. Consequently he had to ration steam, and the first victims would be the giant catapult accumulators. Lower pressures in the accumulators meant the catapults would toss each plane off at a slower speed and the pilots would have to compensate. As usual, Jake thought, the solution to almost every problem ended up in the cockpit.

The Phantom on cat three wound up to full power as the catapult crewmen tumbled out from under the plane. The hurricane of exhaust gases over the top of the JBD shook the waiting Intruder. Now the afterburners lit and ten feet of fire shot from each tailpipe. The tailpipe nozzles opened to accommodate the white-hot flames. Muldowski returned the fighter pilot's salute and swung his arm toward the deck. The Phantom leaped forward toward the sky.

As the machine left the deck the nose quickly rose. It rose and rose and rose, until it was almost twenty-five degrees above the horizon.

"Jesus!" Cole exclaimed.

The Phantom pilot had pulled too vigorously on the stick and his plane had gotten away from him. Without the usual excess airspeed, the nose quickly passed the optimum climb attitude and the wings had begun to stall. This caused the center of lift to move forward and the nose to rise further into the stall despite the pilot's application of full forward stick.

With its nose unnaturally high, the plane hung spread-eagle against the sky. Then the Phantom sank from view below the edge of the deck.

The radio exploded to life. "Pickle your bombs!" "Jettison!" "Emergency jettison!" The transmissions continued, garbled, cutting in and out.

"There he is," Cole said, grabbing Jake's arm.

The fighter was out over the water, the nose of the plane reared back. With the burners almost in the water, the aircraft wallowed in the air, staggering from side to side as one wing fell, then the other. A giant splash obscured the plane.

"Did he go in?" Jake whispered.

"No, he's dropped his weapons and external fuel tank."

Almost a mile from the ship, the plane's nose dropped toward the water and the spray churned up by its engines lessened. The fighter began to rise from the deadly embrace of the sea. Now, he was flying!

The bosun approached the Intruder with his chalk board. "8+ knots" it read. Jake Grafton did as the fighter pilot before him: he signaled thumbs up. At least the A-6 has better low-speed aerodynamics than the supersonic F-4, he thought. The edge of the stall is not so razor thin.

Jake pushed the throttles to the stops and wrapped his fingers around the cat grip . . . cycled the controls . . . a murmur from Tiger Cole . . . the exhaust gas temperatures and RPMs had stabilized at full power when he snapped a salute to the bosun.

They rocketed forward toward the haze as the Gs mashed them back into the seat. Two and a half seconds later they were over the flat water, and Jake milked the stick, trading some of his precious altitude—he had only sixty feet—for airspeed. As the gear retracted, the needle on the vertical-speed indicator registered progress upward.

"I told Orville and I told Wilbur: that thing'll never fly," Cole announced as he turned on the radar and checked the computer.

They waited over the sea for the light to fade from the charcoal sky. With the autopilot engaged and the engines set at max conserve, the pilot listlessly scanned the instruments as Cole tuned the radar and monitored the computer and inertial. Jake wondered if this haze covered the land, and, although he hoped it didn't, he suspected that it did.

The sky was as placid as the sea, monotonously uniform, lacking definition. It seemed safe. The truth was, as Grafton knew, that moisture reduced visibility, which meant that the glowing artillery shells and the fireballs of the SAMs' exhaust would be hidden from his sight during the early parts of their flights. On such a night a man could die suddenly, without a chance.

He tugged at his harness strap, already as tight as he could stand it, and looked again at the chart Cole had prepared that depicted their planned route. The black line was so bold, so purposeful.

I should have written a will, he decided. Should have taken the time.

Well, Morgan, this one's for you. For you and all those guys who got zapped for nothing. This one isn't for nothing, Morgan. With a quart or two of luck some of the gomers who give the orders are going to see hell arrive right through the roof of their National Assembly tonight. Give me some luck, Morg.

Callie, I'm a little scared right now, God knows, a little scared—

"Let's do it," Cole said.

The plane flew in absolute darkness; the heavy moisture absorbed all light. With nothing to see outside, Jake concentrated on his instruments. The radar altimeter did not function over the smooth ocean so Jake used the pressure altimeter to hold them level at 500 feet as they approached the coast. He sneaked glances outside, searching for the beach, convinced that seeing it would be a good omen. He was still looking when Tiger called feet dry to Black Eagle and started the elapsed-time clock. Then Tiger rotated the safety collar around the master arm switch and turned it on.

After a minute the pilot noticed the muzzle flashes of small arms close to the plane. The stuttering blasts of a large weapon, perhaps fifty-seven millimeter, shot through the fog. Four rounds to a clip, white tracer; yes, it was a fifty-seven. He estimated visibility to be about a mile, sufficient to see the streaks of tracer in time—but not the SAMs. Doing some arithmetic in his head, he figured that a SAM at mach three would traverse the last mile in about two seconds.

The pilot checked the radar altimeter and wiped the sweat from his eyes. The radar altimeter came into play over land, and he descended to 400 feet.

Flak poured randomly into the sky, a poison spewed reflexively at the sound of approaching engines. A man coming in supersonic would have a quiet ride, Jake thought, because the gomers wouldn't hear him coming. But these gomers can't get us, even at only 420 knots. Nothing can get us, he told himself, and he waggled the stick. The sharp, agile movements of the plane provided reassurance.

The antiaircraft guns were usually in a line, from two or three to half a dozen, on roads on top of the paddy dikes. The reddish-orange tracers from the belt-fed lighter weapons—12.7, 14.5, and 23 millimeter—floated aloft in long ribbons. Tonight the fog pulsated with their glare. Within the cockpit, though, the defiant thunder was inaudible amid the background noise of the engines, the squawks and screeches of the ECM, and the static of the radio.

"Only two knots of wind," Cole told him. The bombardier was checking the computer readouts. To keep track of the aircraft's position and accurately solve the attack problem, the computer needed to know not only the aircraft's precise position, but the amount of wind affecting the aircraft's track over the ground as well. The wind would also affect the trajectory of the bombs after they were released. Any corrections that the bombardier made to velocity errors were understood by the computer to be extra wind. Tonight the minuscule wind readout meant the INS, the Doppler, and the computer were humming perfectly: they were "tight."

Cole identified the IP for the power plant without trouble. As they approached the initial point, Grafton went to full power.

"IP. New heading two eight seven."

Jake turned and let the machine climb to 500 feet as he retrimmed for the increasing airspeed. The sensor lights on the instrument panel blinked ominously and the beeps of radars seeking to acquire them sounded in his ears. But the plane was too low to be detected, still safely hidden in the ground cover of the earth. Jake concentrated on staying level at 500 feet and on course. Random muzzle flashes dotted the darkness on his left, like flashbulbs popping in a gigantic stadium.

"I'm on the target and in attack."

The computer-driven display on the VDI assumed a new complexity. The target symbol, a solid little black box, appeared just below the horizon in the center of the display. A highway, or pathway, led from the bottom of the display to a point on the horizon just above the target. On this apex rested the steering symbol, a hollow rectangle, that the computer skewed right or left to show the pilot the proper course to the calculated release point. Jake turned the aircraft to keep the hollow box centered in the display right above the target symbol. On the right side of the display a black line appeared, the release marker. It began to sink gradually toward the bottom of the display. The instant it dropped off the VDI the computer would release the weapons.

Without taking his eyes from the radar, the bombardier fingered the dozen switches on the armament panel. Jake noted this performance and was impressed: he still had to visually check armament switches.

Pulsating tracers loomed out of the fog. The fireballs were huge—traveling in slow motion and not changing their relative position—and Jake lifted the plane over the oncoming stream. As he did so a Firecan gun-control radar at ten o'clock locked them up. He punched chaff and descended once he had passed over the fiery flow. He punched off one more bundle of chaff, just to be sure, and was astonished at a bright flash under the aircraft.

"What was that?"

"IR flare in the chaff," Cole said.

Angry with himself for being startled, Jake divided his attention between the dancing steering symbol and the molten currents of flak.

"Thirty seconds or so," Cole said. "Ground lock." The pilot could see only darkness ahead. But the power plant was there. Cole said it was. "Gimme a discrete lock, baby," Cole muttered at the Intruder's track radar. If it would lock on the plant, the computer would read the range information. "No discrete tonight." Only the track's depression angle was going to the computer.

Jake dived 200 feet and let a flak stream pass overhead. After five seconds he pumped the stick to get back to altitude.

"Steady . . ." Cole whispered crossly, anxious not to jiggle the accelerometers of the INS with unnecessary movement.

The release marker fell relentlessly. As it dropped off the display Jake squashed the pickle with his thumb, backing up the computer's release signal with a manual one.

The four bombs were gone in a fifth of a second and he let the plane climb 200 feet as he turned hard left to ensure that he would not be caught by bomb fragments if a Snake-eye fin failed to open. Behind the speeding aircraft the bombs flashed. Jake looked back in time to see the explosions, then looked ahead.

Now for Hanoi.

The steering symbol lashed off to the right. "Ignore that. Cursors running. Your heading two oh five."

"What's wrong?"

"Ah, the fucking velocities went ape shit. It's either the INS or the computer." Cole studied the readouts. "It's the damn computer. We'll have to bomb without it."

Tiger administered a healthy kick to the pedestal between his legs. Actually, this was one of the unwritten procedures taught by experience for freeing the rotary-drum computer that represented state-of-the-art technology—in 1956. This time kicks and curses failed. Cole gave up on the computer and adjusted the radar cursor manually to the weapons-release range he had calculated on the ship. Without the computer, their chance of hitting the National Assembly decreased drastically.

Jake set the switches on the armament panel for the last eight bombs. He decided to leave the mode-selector switch in "train," which meant that instead of dropping the bombs in two sets of four—the "salvo" mode—they would release them one at a time. This increased the likelihood of getting at least one hit, though the damage a hit would cause would be less. Cole nodded his agreement. As they flew southwest at almost 500 knots, Tiger gave Jake small heading corrections.

They blasted across Bac Ninh at 400 feet, the guns below firing up and the big-caliber tracer shells so bright as they zoomed across the top of the plane that they lighted up the cockpit.

Jake swallowed hard. Hanoi would be heavily defended. When Cole called ten miles to the target, Jake continued to hold the plane low at 400 feet. The flak was getting thicker; there were just more guns. When Cole called eight miles, Jake decided to wait until six miles before climbing. In the glow of the enemy ordnance he could see the outline of the city.

"Six miles."

Jake pulled the stick aft, reaching 1500 feet before the threat indicator illuminated, warning of Firecans ahead and behind. He continued up and leveled at 2500 feet, where he was not sheltered by ground return. He noted that the visibility was better than he had expected.

A large battery of belt-fed guns exploded into action ahead. Ignoring Cole's heading calls, Jake turned the plane on knife-edge and sliced through a gap in the fire. *You gotta hand it to the little fuckers: they give it their best.* He then quickly leveled so that Cole could reidentify the target.

"I think I have it. Right five."

The pilot yanked the stick to get on course as fast as possible. He could see the city spread out before him. It looked unearthly in the flicker of the tracers, and more and more tracers darted up from every street corner.

"Left one . . . steady now." Without the computer Cole would have to provide the steering from studying the radar scope.

The Red River was a black snake slithering across the city.

"Hair left. Hold it."

The missile light began flashing and the aural warning sounded. The strobe on the ECM gear was long and brilliant, a powerful signal indicating that enemy radar was very near. The pilot searched the fog in the direction the strobe indicated, from two o'clock.

"Steadeee . . ."

They were much too high for the earth's shadow to

offer any cover. Grafton felt completely naked. He pumped chaff, hoping the blossoming false targets on the enemy's screen would fool the operator.

There! Two large fireballs . . . in the fog. . . . They mesmerized him, but he managed to ease the nose down and, without thinking, pumped more chaff. Going down, passing 1500 feet, descending. . . .

The first fireball came out of the fog, tracking the descending plane perfectly, coming down toward it. Jake hauled the stick hard aft and the missile flashed beneath their belly where it exploded, the concussion jolting the plane. Jake kept the Gs on and saw the glow of the second missile, which was correcting its trajectory. Like the plane, it was climbing.

He inverted the aircraft. Over the top at 3000 feet with the nose coming down . . . 2000 feet . . . four Gs. . . .

"Roll over. Pull out." Cole's voice was strained, urgent.

He waited another second, another lifetime, then slammed the stick sideways and righted the plane. At 1000 feet, fifteen degrees nose down, he pulled and pulled on the stick. The missile overshot them and exploded in a sickening crack that rocked the Intruder again and drove something through the plexiglas that stung Jake's legs.

They were at 400 feet. "Stay down," Cole urged. "Make a racetrack circle and give me some room to see the target."

The pilot complied. Cole held vigil over the radar. "Hill coming up. Climb a little." They soared to 1000 feet and the radar indicator illuminated again. More chaff. Another IR flare from the chaff dispenser, but this time the pilot merely flinched.

"You're clear," Cole told him. "Hold this heading." They were headed back northeast. Jake descended until he was level at 500 feet. The rear-view mirror reflected the streaking fury still rising from Hanoi. For the first time Jake became aware of his pounding heart.

"Now swing it around and we'll try it again," Cole said.

Though I walk through the valley . . .

"Seven miles. Let's get back up there and see if we can smack 'em good."

I shall fear no evil . . .

The pilot concentrated on climbing and leveling precisely at 2500 feet.

"I've got it. . . . Three degrees right. . . . Looking good."

The tracers rose from horizon to horizon.

"Get ready."

A Firecan gun-control radar locked them up and huge white tracers raced from the fog, four at a time. Jake desperately pumped the chaff button.

"One degree left. . . . Steadeee. . . ."

Jesus Christ!

The shells streaked behind and under the bomber.

"Now!"

The bombs kicked loose with a stuttering whump just as a SAM ignited to the right. The visibility was better over the city. The pilot held the heading and watched the missile gain altitude and level off with no change in bearing—it was on a collision course with the plane. Their bombs exploded below as the missile-warning light flashed.

He dumped the nose and turned to the right, away from the radar-controlled gun and across the missile's path as he released more chaff. But the missile continued tracking them very nicely. He cursed under his breath, fervently, and dropped to 100 feet. The needle on the radar altimeter jumped erratically as they swept across the rooftops. Jake, noticing that the strobe on the ECM gear was long and fat and bright, muttered, "We're almost on top of this radar."

"We're out of chaff," Cole reported.

"Man, we're having fun now."

The missile was at eleven o'clock now, now ten-thirty. He leveled the wings. The muzzle blasts of the flak guns formed an artificial horizon that was almost level with him. He was much too low.

The missile altered course and started down.

Wait a little longer, he told himself, just a little more, a little more. . . . Okay, pull! He began a steady 6-G ascent. The nose wrenched higher and higher. The large needle on the altimeter zipped around the dial.

The missile kept descending. Jake kept hitting the chaff button reflexively.

At nearly mach three the missile flashed beneath them trailing a white-hot exhaust and exploded. Jake heard the pitter-patter of shrapnel pelting the plane's skin.

"Another!" Cole cried. This one came in on the same bearing as the previous one but was lower and still climbing.

The altimeter registered 3000 feet. Jake kept the stick back and smoothly moved it left to begin a barrel roll. As they went inverted the ghostly city covered the canopy above their heads. The weaving fingers of fire were everywhere but Jake's eyes were on the missile.

"Nose on the horizon," Tiger said, advising him. "Five degrees down." Still upside down, four Gs on.

"Twenty-five hundred feet." The missile continued rising.

"Ten down, hundred and twenty degrees of bank, two thousand. . . ."

The missile was correcting, but too slowly. They would beat it!

"Fifteen down . . ." Cole's voice was rising and cracking.

The missile ceased tracking and began ballistic flight. Jake forced himself to concentrate on the instrument panel. Sweet Jesus, we're steep! He rolled faster and the Gs squeezed them and the radar altimeter needle sagged sickeningly as they went down, down to waiting death, still down. . . .

The needle on the radar altimeter stopped at 50 feet. Jake held the stick back. Something darker than the surrounding blackness zipped underneath, seemingly close enough to take off the belly tank.

Grafton stabilized at 200 feet and turned southeast, sweeping across Hanoi in a long arcing trajectory. As they banked, it appeared to Jake as though they were below the city, as though the flashes of the guns and shadows of buildings were above them. The optical illusion disoriented him and he wrestled the stick and rudder to avoid the ground. His only hope was to believe the red instruments before him and not his instincts. Don't lose it now, he thought. We've almost made it.

Then they were over the countryside at a safer 400 feet. One of the four hydraulic pumps showed zero pressure. In the rear-view mirror Jake saw the city still riddling the air with fire, trying to bring down the fleeing intruders. The flak thinned out and the intermittent flickers reflected on the rice paddies. They stole away, the throttles at the stops.

Jake's red anticollision light reflected on the helmet of the bombardier in the tanker. Big Augie looked across the empty space at the bomber.

"You look okay to us, Jake. You have a smear of hydraulic fluid coming out from between the exhaust pipes, but other than that you look okay. Maybe there're some little holes we can't see. . . ."

Jake blew the gear down and lowered the flaps electrically before they left the 20,000-foot tanker station. The tanker was dirty, too—had lowered its gear and flaps—and so stayed on his wing.

Jake's flying was erratic; he had lost all his smoothness.

"This landing's gonna be a piece of cake," Cole said.

"Yeah."

"Just a little burble from the ship's island. That's all. The sea's calm. That meatball will be as steady as a rock."

"Uh-huh."

Cole sat in silence as Jake jerked the plane to each new heading. Finally Cole unzipped his survival vest and opened a plastic baby bottle. "Take a swig of this. It'll help."

Jake reached for the bottle and put it to his lips. The liquid was fiery and he almost didn't get it down. "What the hell is that?"

"Brandy."

"Fuck! I didn't need that!"

"Well, you sure as hell need something. Now settle down or you're going to kill us both on the ramp."

Jake recognized he was 200 feet above the 5000-foot altitude assigned and corrected. "You motherfucker!"

"You can do this, Jake." Cole's voice was soft and soothing. "You can grease this plane onto a postage stamp if you have to. Be slow and smooth and keep your scan going. Watch your heading. That's it. Very nice. You've done this hundreds of times. Nothing to it." Cole pulled the handle to lower the tailhook. "Let's get on speed. We've plenty of gas and the tanker's right here."

"Okay, grandma. I'm okay now."

"Well, I feel like talking. We really smacked those little fuckers tonight. Now all we have to do is get aboard and we'll be done. You're going to fly the best goddamn pass those LSO weenies ever saw and catch the three wire. If you couldn't do it, I wouldn't be bombing Uncle Ho with you."

His voice was calm, so matter-of-fact that Jake's

nervousness dissipated. Cole chattered on, "I think I'm going to buy me a stereo the next time we hit Cubi. One of those reel-to-reel Jap jobs that has fifty-two buttons and six or eight of those little Vu needles that twitch to every beat. Never had one of those. Looks like fun though. Maybe I'll pick up one like Cowboy's." The controller interrupted with instructions.

He was still soliloquizing about stereos when the ship appeared at a mile on the glide path. His commentary switched to the business at hand. "Your wings are level . . . six hundred foot sink rate . . . little more power . . . you have 'er nailed . . . looking good. . . ."

The wheels hit the steel and the hook caught.

"Did you hit it?" Steiger asked Jake Grafton and Tiger Cole in the passageway after they had finished the mission debriefing. The airmen still wore their flight gear and reeked of stale sweat and cigarette smoke. Jake had his flight suit unzipped to mid-chest, revealing a sodden T-shirt.

Jake shrugged and stared at the bloodstains on his stinging thighs. The quack would have to pull out those metal slivers, which had penetrated the bladders in his G-suit. I guess I finally get a new G-suit, he thought.

Cole put his hand on Abe's shoulder. "You heard us tell you in there"—he nodded toward the debrief room—"that the computer had crapped out." He shifted his helmet bag to his left hand and rubbed his head, obviously uncomfortable. "The cursor on the radar screen is a thin line, yet it covers two hundred feet of the ground. We were trying to hit a target that was maybe a hundred fifty feet across. But a plane flying at five hundred knots covers that distance in less than a fifth of a second. We dropped the bombs in train to maximize our chances. The minimum interval between bombs is six-hundredths of a second, so at five hundred knots the bombs land fifty feet apart. Our string was only three hundred fifty feet long." He shook his head.

"The odds just aren't that good," Jake added. "If we were real lucky we didn't hit a hospital or apartment house a half-mile away."

Steiger bit his lip and examined each drawn face. It had all seemed so neat and easy in the Mission Planning spaces, with charts and lines and photographs. "You did the best you could. I understand," he said.

The pilot and bombardier trudged off down the passageway, their shoulders drooping.

Jake Grafton sat on the operating table in Sick Bay in his underwear with his legs dangling as Mad Jack worked on his thighs with tweezers, a needle, and disinfectant. Camparelli was astride a chair, his arms crossed on the backrest.

"Tell me about the missiles. Steiger says some of them came down at you."

"Yessir. A couple of them did. But I don't think they had heat-seekers. I think they were launching from one place and guiding from a radar that was a lot closer to us. We were just too close to the site that was guiding. And they put a missile in the air and waited for the first stage to drop off before they turned on the radar. They're getting smarter, or somebody who speaks Russian is helping them."

"Maybe." The Old Man ran his fingers through his short hair. "I didn't think that power plant would be so heavily defended. They hate to lose them, but they really don't need the juice. Damned rice farmers." He shook his head. "That airplane has a lot of holes in it. Nothing major, no structural damage and the wings weren't hit, thank God, but it's going to be a couple days before we can use it."

Jake said nothing.

"I better go tell Steiger to update the intelligence charts." He stood and addressed Mad Jack's rounded back. "Is he going to be able to fly?"

"Yes. Just some pinhole punctures that Band Aids will cover."

The skipper left the room.

They don't need the power plants, Jake thought. Why the hell even bomb them? In his mind's eye he saw the rising flak and the SAMs and once again felt the fear, and he imagined the stone capitol building gutted by explosion and fire.

"Relax a little," Mad Jack said without looking up, "or this is going to take all night."

[illegible]

[illegible]

[illegible]

[illegible]

[illegible]

EIGHTEEN

Three days after their Hanoi raid, Abe Steiger drew Jake aside in Mission Planning to show him an intelligence report. The North Vietnamese had complained to the international communist press that a bomb had fallen within ten feet of the National Assembly and had severely damaged the facade and had broken all the windows. Because the other seven bombs were not mentioned, Jake and Steiger assumed they had struck in the street in front of the building. The Vietnamese complained of a deliberate attempt by "Yankee air pirates" to destroy their seat of government and added, almost as an afterthought, that three bystanders had died in the blast. The intelligence summary discounted the complaint as pure propaganda or, if there had been any damage, suggested it had been caused by a SAM or antiaircraft artillery shell returning to earth.

"Do you think the gomers really believe the attack was intentional?" Steiger asked.

"Does God shave his upper lip? Was Adolf Hitler a fairy? Is there any sex in heaven? How the hell would I know, Abe?"

"Well, it's something to think about."

"I hope they're doing just that. I hope those mothers are racking their brains trying to figure it all out."

Jake told Tiger Cole about the report. "No cigar," was his comment.

One evening Grafton and Lundeen had a visit from New Guy.

"Want a warm Coke?" Sammy asked him.

"Sure," New said. "How come you guys never bought a refrigerator?"

"What brings you down to this den of sin and iniquity, anyway?" said Sammy. He tossed a can at New, knowing it would foam over when the flip top was pulled. It did. New wiped his sticky hand on his trousers.

"I'm turning in my wings," New announced. "I've been talking to the Skipper about it and he said I should talk it over with some of the guys, then come back and see him. He wanted me to be sure before I put in the paperwork."

Sammy and Jake exchanged glances. Most men do not willingly throw away almost two and a half years of extraordinarily hard work, which was the time it took for a pilot to get his first assignment to a fleet A-6 squadron: a year and a half in pilot training; a month in the instrument squadron earning a fleet instrument card; and eight months in an A-6 replacement squadron. Only then did the fledgling report to a fleet squadron. The attrition rate along the way was high; men dropped out or were washed out. Some were killed.

"You have an awful lot invested in that piece of metal." Jake gestured to the gold wings above the left pocket of New Guy's khaki shirt.

"Yeah, but I really think I could make a better contribution doing something else."

"You married?" Lundeen interjected.

New Guy nodded.

"What does your wife think?"

He became absorbed with his shoes. "She thinks the war is wrong and we ought to get out of Vietnam."

"She's got plenty of company. What do you think?"

"I don't know."

"If you keep flying, will that end your marriage?" Jake asked.

"It might," New Guy admitted.

"She threatened a divorce?" continued Sammy.

New Guy shrugged.

"Well," said Grafton. "This is your career, not hers."

"It's my decision," New Guy insisted.

Jake gazed thoughtfully at that smooth, ingenuous face. "If you're scared of bullets and SAMs, you're in pretty goddamn good company. Everybody's scared over the beach. That's no reason to be ashamed or to quit."

The new pilot shook his head. "It's not that."

"Then what the hell is it?" Lundeen demanded.

"I just feel that, everything considered, I would have more to offer the navy as a maintenance or surface officer."

"Let's cut the bullshit, shall we?" said Lundeen. "Go ahead and turn those wings in and leave the fighting to others. If somebody gets killed on a mission you should've flown, that'll be just fine with you. Let the other guys do the bleeding and the dying." New Guy shriveled under Lundeen's wrath. "You yellow little coward. The States are full of assholes like you, fucking draft-dodgers who don't want to hang their precious asses on the line. No, they want other people to do the bleeding and dying while they sit at home and enjoy their freedom and salve their consciences by assuring each other the war is immoral."

"That's enough, Sam," Jake said, aware that he had

said much the same thing to Callie not many days ago. If Lundeen kept on he might shame New Guy into staying in the cockpit. Then what bombardier would you sentence to fly with him? Without self-confidence a pilot would never get aboard at night, never wait long enough before he outmaneuvered the SAMs, never try hard enough to get the bombs on target. Without faith in his own ability to conquer whatever might come, a pilot would be overwhelmed by the terror. No, if New didn't have it, he didn't have it. "You can tell the Skipper you talked to us. It's your decision and your life. Maybe you've made the right choice."

New Guy stood up slowly. He tried to smile but Jake's cold eyes stopped him. Jake said, "This flying game takes a lot out of a man. You have to crawl up that boarding ladder into that ejection seat again and again. There's nobody around to tell you you're doing the right thing." Jake lowered his gaze to his outstretched, palsied hands. He raised his head and stared at New Guy. "I don't know what you believe in, but I don't think you believe in yourself."

"You had better leave," Lundeen told New Guy.

The skipper sent New Guy's request for a change of designator to the Bureau of Naval Personnel, recommending approval. New became the permanent squadron duty officer in the ready room every day from noon to midnight. As lieutenants and below rotated this twelve-hour watch, New Guy's assignment, which gave him half these watches, meant that the others would have to stand the duty only half as often. This they liked. Those who resented New's decision made it known by not speaking to him except when they had to. Those who did this were few. Most did not shun New but treated him as if he were a somewhat impaired younger brother.

* * *

Jake Grafton and Tiger Cole trotted up to the dirty-shirt wardroom for a late dinner. They had been on a strike at noon and were ravenous. When each man had an aluminum tray full of creamed chipped beef on toast, also known as SOS—shit on a shingle—they looked for two seats in the wardroom. Cowboy Parker waved them over to his table. He was seated next to an officer wearing a green two-piece air force flight suit.

"This is Major Frank Allen. Frank and I went to school together at UT."

"In Knoxville?" Cole inquired.

Jake grinned as Parker rose to the occasion and haughtily informed the bombardier that his alma mater was in Austin. Frank Allen smiled.

Cowboy told them his former classmate was visiting the *Shiloh* under an unofficial "liaison" program that brought together navy airmen and the air force types stationed at Nakhon Phanom in Thailand, a place referred to by the military as NKP, or "naked fanny." Two months earlier a captain stationed there who flew F-105 Wild Weasels, the air force's equivalent of the A-6B, had visited the ship. Big Augie had then wangled a trip to Thailand to visit these brothers-in-arms and when he returned had regaled his squadron-mates with such stories of bars and whorehouses that they almost believed he had spent his entire three days there in a sexual and alcoholic orgy of epic intensity. Big's stories had the effect he had hoped for on the Boxman, who had written three official requests to go to Nakhon Phanom and had been turned down each time.

"Do you fly F-105s?" Jake asked Frank Allen.

"Nope. A-1s. Skyraiders. You navy boys call them Spads. I do a bit of search and rescue work when we're not bombing with a FAC."

"We're taking him on a tanker hop tomorrow," said Parker. "Gonna get him a cat shot and a trap so he can join the Tailhook Association and go to the next convention in Las Vegas." Almost all the navy airmen belonged, and they considered the Las Vegas weekend one whale of a blowout.

After dinner the four of them retreated to Cowboy's stateroom. In the course of a game of penny-ante poker, Jake mentioned the trip Big had taken to Thailand and his stories of goodtime houses and their effect on Box. After some discussion the Boxman was invited down. When he had won fifty cents or so in the game, the conversation turned to the city near the air force base where Allen was stationed.

Frank Allen shook his head. "They have the biggest whorehouse east of Port Said," he confided. "It's really something. Over a hundred women, just girls really, little brown fucking machines, and for five bucks American you can spend the night. You can have as many girls as you want, no extra charge." Box tossed his hand on the table and stared at Allen.

"The thing I like the best," Allen continued, leaning forward, "is when you strip stark naked and lay down on this table. These girls lick you all over until you have a hard on, then they lower a girl in a stirrup device right onto your crank. You are in her but the only contact is the sexual one." Allen shuddered as he appeared to recall the ecstasy. Grafton casually picked up Box's discarded hand; Box had thrown away a pair of kings.

"Are these girls clean?" Box wanted to know, gulping down the last of his drink and holding his glass out for a refill. Jake couldn't imagine why he asked, since he was now being treated for his third dose on this cruise.

"Oh, yeah," Allen assured him. "They all wear white socks. That's how you can tell." The other men laughed. Box grinned ruefully.

Early the next morning Box wrote out yet another request to visit the sin capital of the Orient. The skipper denied the request by burning it in the ready room with Box looking on.

Frank Allen flew his tanker flight, got his trap, then gave a presentation on search-and-rescue techniques and equipment at a specially called all-officers meeting. He was invited by the CAG to repeat it for the other ready rooms. When Allen was ready to leave the ship, Cowboy and the others arranged for Boxman to escort him to the cargo plane and wish him bon voyage.

At three o'clock one morning Jake Grafton was in his flight suit alone in the dirty-shirt wardroom. He held the coffee cup with both hands to prevent the liquid from slopping onto the tablecloth. He was staring at the crumbs and stains on the cloth.

"Ah, Mister Grafton. May I join you?" Les Rucic sat down on the other side of the table. He sipped his coffee and lit a cigarette. "Been flying?"

"Hmmm."

"A strike?"

"Uh-huh."

"Too bad a man can't get a drink around here," Rucic commented.

Jake kept his eyes on his coffee cup. Does he know about the Hanoi raid? Is that why he's here? The pilot felt his muscles tense.

"Looks like I'll be leaving tomorrow."

Jake let his gaze wander over the reporter's features. The man hadn't trimmed his nose hairs since the pilot had last seen him.

"I'll probably spend a week or so in Saigon, get the feel of the place if you know what I mean, then go on back to the States. Is there anybody back home I can call for you?"

Yes, Mrs. Grafton, I met your son on the *Shiloh*. He's doing just fine and asked me to call to wish you a Merry Christmas. How do you feel about what he's doing in Vietnam? Do you think America should be over there? Grafton wondered if his disgust for Rucic showed on his face.

"Are we winning or losing?" Rucic pressed.

"What?"

"Winning or losing the war?"

"Damned if I know."

"Come on. Give a little. I've interviewed some of the other pilots and naval flight officers, and they've given me some pretty good stuff." He waved his notebook.

Jake felt the tension leaving his muscles. Surely if Rucic knew about the National Assembly he would be after it by now. Feeling relieved, Jake asked, "What'd they say?"

Rucic thumbed through several pages of his notebook. "We're buying time for the South Vietnamese," he read. "Whether the time is worth the cost will depend on what they—the South Vietnamese—do with it. . . . Freedom is the most expensive commodity on earth. . . ."

"Putting that in the paper would be a waste, Rucic," Grafton sneered. "Why don't you save it for a Fourth of July speech?"

Rucic sipped his coffee. "I wonder if you could tell me anything about the flight on which your bombardier was killed?" He looked at the notebook again. "Morgan McPherson."

So the sonuvabitch had been looking for him.

"Can you tell me anything about it? I wasn't aware you had lost your bombardier when I interviewed you the other day."

Jake just stared.

"Listen, Grafton. I have a right to be here and to ask these questions. If you don't cooperate I'll have to say as much to your superiors." Rucic's eyes reminded Jake of the eyes in dead fish he had seen in Hong Kong alleys.

The pilot stood up. He put his fists on the table and leaned toward the reporter. "I don't have to talk to you, motherfucker. If you use my name in your stories, I'll sue your rag—and you—for invasion of privacy." The pitch of his voice rose but he couldn't help it. "Your papers sell better when you mix a little blood with the ink, don't they?"

Realizing he was losing control, Jake walked awav.

NINETEEN

Jake Grafton was strapping himself into the cockpit one cloudless morning when Cowboy Parker ran across the flight deck toward the aircraft. Grafton and Tiger Cole had briefed a strike on a suspected fuel dump with Little Augie and Big Augie, who were manning the machine next to Grafton's. They planned to set this target afire with the sixteen Rockeyes each plane carried. Boxman and his pilot, Corey Ford, were manning the spare, armed with sixteen Mark 82 500-pounders, which would go only if one of the other bombers had a mechanical problem before launch. Grafton watched Parker with a sinking feeling. Not a hurry-up target!

Cowboy climbed the boarding ladder. "You got a new target, Jake. Forget the fuel dump." Holding up a piece of a chart, he pointed to a crude triangle drawn in pencil. Jake saw it was a North Vietnamese airfield.

"What's there?"

"MiGs," Parker said. "One or two, maybe three. They landed less than two hours ago and the decision's been made to try to bag them before they sortie again. You have the lead. We're going to launch the spare so there'll be three of you. Brief on squadron tactical after you rendezvous." Cowboy handed him the strip of chart and several aerial recon photos of the airfield. He took one step down the ladder, paused, and looked back at Grafton "This'll be a tough one. It's heavily defended."

"Tell the other guys to meet me at ten grand overhead."

Cowboy nodded and disappeared down the ladder.

Jake examined the chart with Tiger. "Shit," Cole muttered. "The son-of-a-bitch is in Laos." The target airfield lay five or six miles across the Laotian border on the far side of Barthelemy Pass, which the chart showed at 3937 feet above sea level. Jake remembered from the weather brief that low clouds covered the mountains.

How should they approach? If they flew all the way to Hue, then west to Laos and north to the airfield—what was the name?—Nong Het, the trip would be long and the bad guys would have a lot of warning. Fuel would run low only if they elected to return by the same route. If they flew straight in, across North Vietnam, they'd attract flak en route, but there would be less time for the North Vietnamese to prepare a reception at the airfield. If the MiGs were bait to lure the lion, the less warning the better.

Jake Grafton rubbed his chin and stared at the swells on the sea. He thought about the flak and the airfield in the bottom of a valley. Maybe they should go straight in. "What do you think, Tiger? Straight in?"

"Yep."

The plane captain signaled for a start. Jake gave the chart and pictures to the bombardier and busied himself with the starting procedure. He was too preoccupied to enjoy the cat shot when it came.

They rendezvoused over the ship at 10,000 feet. When all three planes had joined, Jake took the lead, and Corey Ford flanked him on the left with Little Augie on the right. Jake then used his hand to signal the switch to the squadron tactical frequency and began a gentle climb to altitude.

"Two's up." Little's voice.

"Three's up." That was Corey.

"Let's go covered voice." All three turned on their scramblers, which encrypted the voice transmissions. To a listener without a scrambler with the daily code properly set, the conversation would be merely an incomprehensible buzz. "Okay, guys. We're going straight at it. Coast in north of Vinh, find the right valley, get under the clouds, go through the pass, and drop down on that airfield like the angel of doom. Any gripes?"

When all he heard was silence, Jake continued, "This field will no doubt be oriented east and west, up and down the valley." Cole was looking at the photos and concurred with a thumbs up. "Little, you take the right side of the field, and Corey and I'll take the left. Put the ordnance just inside the tree lines. They'll park those MiGs under cover. I'm willing to bet they'll be in the trees. But if you see them out on the airfield, you'll know what to do. Okay so far?"

Mikes clicked in response. "As I read this chart, the target will be in a valley that curves around to the left. High mountains on both sides. The mountains on the right peak at more than sixty-two hundred feet. After we drop, Little, you're on your own. Just to be safe, I want you to make a right turn off target and get out the best way you can. Corey, you stick with me and we'll turn left off target. They may try to put a SAM up somebody's ass as we leave. Everybody's to avoid flying into one of those granite clouds. Any questions?"

There were none. The flight switched back to the Strike frequency.

"Think we'll surprise them?" Jake asked Tiger.

The bombardier shook his head.

"Me neither," Jake grunted. "I have a sneaking

suspicion we're trying to steal the cheese out of a mousetrap."

They had only two practical choices on the method of attack: go in high above the mountains and the cloud tops, or go in low on the deck below the clouds. If Rockeyes were released too high, the clamshell opened too soon and the bomblets would disperse so widely that the pattern density was unacceptably low. So they really had no choice at all. Jake thought about these matters as he followed the computer steering for the coast-in point Cole had chosen twenty miles north of Vinh. They would approach the coast from the southeast. He leveled at 20,000 feet and scanned the distant horizon. He could see the land obliquely on his left and the clouds on the mountains that rose beyond the coastal plain.

Jake instructed the other crews to reengage the scramblers. "Devil Three, since you have GP bombs, you may have to pop up high enough for the fuses to arm." Corey Ford clicked his mike. "Just don't get so wrapped up in the attack that you hit a ridge."

"Roger that."

"After you drop your load, climb over the ridges and beat feet. No rendezvous."

"I gotcha."

"Boxman, how's your radar?" Since Grafton was the leader, he let his concerns show.

"It's fine, Jake. A sweet system."

"You may have to S-turn or slow down a little to let me move ahead a bit before you drop." Corey clicked his mike. Jake wanted to make sure that Corey would delay his release so that Jake, down low, would not be struck by his bombs or caught in their blast. A second or two delay would be enough.

Jake thought of one more point. "This hole's probably heavily defended. So if anyone takes a hit and goes down, he's on his own. Don't stay and watch for chutes or any of that crap. Everybody else haul ass out of there." Mike clicks were his reply.

They flew on in silence. Jake's mouth was so dry he took a swig from his water bottle. He offered the bottle to Cole, who took his mask off, tilted the bottle, then passed it back.

Jake eased the nose over and trimmed for a descent Each crew worked through the combat checklist. Passing 10,000 feet, fifteen miles from the coast, Jake reported to the airborne controller that he was strangling the parrot and secured the IFF. They were on their own. He checked his wingmen and told them to spread out some more. When each plane was about one hundred feet away he turned his attention to the land ahead. Rice paddies reflected the afternoon sun.

Frank Camparelli and Cowboy Parker huddled over a chart in Mission Planning. The skipper had three aircraft on their way to a well-defended target, in daytime, without adequate planning, and the possibilities for disaster ate at him.

"How do you think Grafton will go in?"

"Jake'll go straight at 'em, Skipper. He thinks feints and deceptions in a theatre this small just give the enemy more time to alert their defenses."

"That's true." Camparelli went to the flak chart on the wall. Pins bristled around the airfield. "I think they're waiting for us in that valley."

"Maybe so, but they've baited the trap with real MiGs." Parker joined Camparelli at the wall chart. "The MiGs are there," he said, thinking of the electronic intelligence report that described MiG-19 radar signals as emanating from the Nong Het airfield for the last two hours. "The hard fact is we can afford to trade plane for plane."

Camparelli turned slowly and looked over Cowboy from head to toe. "You'll make a good admiral someday, Parker."

Cowboy reddened. "Skipper, I didn't mean—"

"I know, I know." Camparelli cut him off with a gesture and scanned the charts and tables as he ran his hand over his hair. Six men, three airplanes. Six lives and eighteen million dollars worth of hardware at risk for one or two fifteen-year-old single-seat day fighters that in the air would be mincemeat for Phantoms. "Why don't you go to Combat and listen in on the Strike frequency."

"Aye, aye, sir." Parker left immediately.

The skipper wandered from chart to chart. He stopped at the SAM-threat display and examined it with interest. From the Nong Het airfield his gaze meandered north toward Hanoi. Because Grafton was on his mind he looked at the area around the power plant at Bac Giang.

"Steiger!" The commander strode to the door of the photorecon space. "Steiger! Where's Steiger?"

Thirty seconds later a flushed Abe Steiger stood before the SAM-threat chart staring through his glasses at Camparelli's finger, which tapped imperiously on the black dot on the railroad labeled Bac Giang. "Why aren't there SAM sites here? Where are those sites that shot at Grafton the other night?"

The air intelligence officer opened and closed his mouth several times.

"I told you I wanted those sites that shot at Grafton spotted on these charts. I told you specifically to make sure they were in the intelligence report." The finger pointed. "Get me that report, Mister Steiger. Now. I want to see it."

"The sites aren't in the reports, sir." Abe couldn't lift his eyes. The hand on the table was absolutely still.

"I think you had better come down to my stateroom, Mister Steiger, and we'll have a little chat."

The Intruders crossed the coast at 480 knots at 6000 feet, still descending. "Devil flight, feet dry," Jake told the Hawkeye circling somewhere in the Gulf of Tonkin.

He received the usual reply. "Good hunting."

The cloud base seemed to be at about 2500 feet, but Jake kept descending. If they were going in low in the daytime, they had better skim the trees to give the gunners the toughest shots. And the lower they were, the fewer the people who could see them.

They passed directly over a crossroads village at 1000 feet descending. Flashes in the air revealed flak, so all three planes jinked slightly while holding their formation. When they leveled at 50 feet, just above the trees, there was no room left for jinking. All they had was speed. Jake advanced the throttles to the stops, expecting to be told if someone could not keep up. In less than a minute, Corey's voice came over the radio: "Gimme a couple, Jake."

Grafton pulled two percent RPM off the engines and tightened the friction lock that would prevent him from inadvertently advancing the throttles. He concentrated on the task of threading the machine over the occasional tree lines. The warplanes rushed over acres of rice paddies, a road, shacks, more rice paddies, another road, a tree line, and more paddies. The sensation of speed was sublime.

"We're in the valley," Cole told him.

He saw the powerline almost as he crossed over it, missing by inches.

A flock of birds burst from a tree right under his nose. Jake saw them flash beneath and knew the birds would be slammed back into the trees by the downwash from his machine.

Guns on the road ahead. Muzzle flashes. A row of them, like flash bulbs popping. The Intruders rocketed toward the road and in an instant it lay behind.

The valley floor was rising. There were more trees now. The sensation of speed was lessening. Unconsciously he pushed the throttles, then remembered the friction lock and checked that he still had the proper power setting. I'll die of old age before we get there, he thought.

Within half a minute the walls began closing in and the planes picked their way up the valley. Thick tropical foilage covered the flanks of the hills, whose ridges reached higher and higher until they touched the clouds. Jake checked the altimeter. They were 1700 feet above sea level.

Back in the States, Jake Grafton had taken great pleasure in flights like this along training routes over stretches of wilderness where the legal altitude was a minimum of 500 feet above the ground. Being young and full of himself, he often flew as low as his nerves allowed just for the sheer hell of it. In those days, when military planes were still permitted to fly under visual flight rules, he would occasionally return to NAS Whidbey Island over the Cascade Range at 200 or 300 feet above the floor of the craggy valleys, shoot through the passes at full throttle and snake his way down between the cliffs, following the streams until they emptied into rivers that flowed into Puget Sound. He had wondered what the hikers had thought of the man-made eagle that split the solitude with a roar, then disappeared as quickly as it had come. Higher authority had finally stopped the illegal flights. Now he was glad he had had the experience.

The valley became serpentine. The altimeter revealed they were climbing rapidly. Not much farther now. "Master arm," he said over the radio. Cole flipped the switch with his left hand, then fingered the other armament switches to satisfy himself that they were in the correct positions.

Jake saw the end of the valley ahead, a gentle upslope to a ridge not quite touching the clouds. The green forest seemed to caress the undersides of the planes as they shot up the slope.

Through the bombsight glass, Grafton saw the ridge and the flashing guns that lined the treeless summit. Streaks of white-hot artillery shells veined the air.

They can't miss. They can't. We're too close. Jake sensed the white bolts racing straight for the cockpit, then, at the last possible instant, veer away and flash to the right or left or over.

They can't miss. They can't. We're too close.

He looked down as he crossed the naked summit. Impressed on his brain for as long as he had yet to live was the confused image of flashing guns, men in black loading and firing the weapons, and rising dust clouds.

He glanced across at Corey Ford and the Boxman and saw that their plane was almost abreast about a hundred feet away. A streak of fire ripped aft from its belly. Then the machine exploded.

The fireball was yellow with a white core. It slowed as it expanded and disappeared behind.

Jake and Little Augie swept down into the valley.

"They got Ford," Little said over the radio.

"There's the runway," Cole told him. The narrow valley was filled with the rising streaks from automatic weapons. The dust devils created by the hammering guns lined the sides of the runway like sentries from a netherworld. Knowing that Little would take the right, Jake aimed his plane down the trees on the left side of the runway. He held the plane level and let the ground fall away.

Whump!

The Intruder took a sledgehammer blow. The pilot's eyes flicked to the instrument panel—right RPM unwinding, right exhaust gas temperature climbing. He chopped the throttle on the dying engine to cutoff and began a hard turn to the left to climb the ridge.

Panic and revulsion welled up in him and he thought, Got to get the hell out of here before they get the other engine!

Then from the middle of the tree line halfway down the runway a glint of light on silver caught his eye. A MiG!

What the hell! We're dead anyway!

Jake flung the plane toward the MiG. As the target reached the bottom of the sight glass, he brought his thumb down on the bomb-release pickle. He felt the small, slow thumps as the Rockeyes kicked off the racks, a pair each third of a second.

A stream of white streaks licked across the top of the canopy and smashed into the Intruder's tail. The needle on the airspeed indicator flipped to zero.

On the west end of the airfield only two lone artillery pieces blasted into the sky.

With the last of the bombs gone, he pulled the plane left and up. He would climb the ridge. One last look over his shoulder at the airfield. A fireball was rising from the trees. "Got one," he whispered.

The clouds enveloped them. "We should have come in from the west," he told Cole.

Back over the ocean Jake reported on covered Strike frequency the loss of his wingman to the ship. He told them that if they sent another strike it should come in from the west and get up into the clouds off target. Then he called Little to arrange a rendezvous.

The other A-6 appeared as a white seed floating in a sunbleached sky. The seed sprouted wings and a tail. Soon Jake could distinguish the men in the cockpit. Little Augie brought his plane in alongside until Jake could see each rivet, each streak of oil, each smudge of dirt.

"You have four or five nice holes in the tail, Jake." Augie slid under and lingered there, then surfaced on the right side. "No holes around the right intake. Can't see anything. Maybe something went down the intake?" Something sure as hell had, something launched from a gun barrel. "You have two small holes in the right flap, Jake. And some bad dings in the armor plate over the right engine. Other than that. . . ."

Jake and Cole examined the other A-6 inch by inch and found only a small hole in the left horizontal stabilizer.

When Jake had the lead again, he dropped his hook, then raised it. He tested the gear and flaps. The plane tended to slew right or left as he added or subtracted power, but this was normal for single-engine flight and easily corrected with rudder. "You look pretty good to me," Little informed him. Jake raised the gear and dropped the nose to get enough airspeed to raise the flaps. The extent of the damage was reported to the ship, and in a few moments the Strike controller ordered Jake to land aboard rather than divert to Da Nang.

The damaged Intruder was the last jet aboard the ship. Jake flew a straight-in approach without speed brakes. He knew that the most common error of single-engine approaches was a pilot's reluctance to reduce power on the good engine for fear of entering a descent that the one engine could not break, so he concentrated on reducing power when necessary and on doubling his power additions. He caught the three wire, and Cole said, "Not bad for a single-engine approach."

The wings folded slowly because only one hydraulic pump supplied the pressure. He was directed to the number-two elevator and was immediately lowered to the hangar deck. After taxiing off the elevator into the cavernous bay and waiting for the blue-shirted men of the tie-down crew to install chocks and chains, he opened the canopy and chopped the engine.

A crowd of somber men waited at the foot of the boarding ladder. Grafton took refuge in the familiar tasks—lifting the safety latches on the ejection seat handles, securing the proper switches, and unfastening the lapbelt and parachute riser fittings. When he could put the moment off no longer, he climbed from the cockpit and lowered himself down the ladder.

Cowboy met him. "I'm sorry, shipmate."

Jake Grafton began to weep. He had not cried since his grandmother had died when he was sixteen. Cowboy and Sammy Lundeen led him to a stairwell off the hangar deck where he sat on the ladder.

Cowboy closed the hatch leading to the hangar bay and lit a cigarette that he passed to Jake. "Have his hands been like that very long?" Jake heard Cowboy ask Sammy.

The raw smoke after two hours on oxygen scoured his lungs. The cigarette burned out when the fire reached the filter. Carefully he put the butt in his left sleeve pocket. "I'm all right now," Jake said. He stood up and looked his roommate in the eye. "I made the wrong choice. I should've come in from the west."

"You couldn't have known that." Sammy put his hand on Jake's shoulder. "Hang in there, Jake. Hang in."

Jake nodded. He would try. But it was becoming more and more difficult, and he was getting so damned tired.

TWENTY

He woke up and looked at his watch: eight o'clock, but A.M. or P.M.? He heard Sammy snoring in the bunk overhead, so he decided that it must be eight at night or Sammy would be on duty. He lay there awhile, trying to brush aside the shrouds hanging over his memory. He recalled a large red capsule held out to him in the white palm of Mad Jack. He had downed the sedative without waiting for water. Why had he been so willing? The sounds of the ship echoed in his ears, and the sight of the plane exploding in a fireball replayed in his mind. Corey Ford and the Boxman, that was why.

The sedative had left him with a headache. He inched one leg out of bed and lowered his foot to the floor. The other leg followed. He rested. Finally, slowly, he raised his body until he was sitting. He lurched over to the sink and wet a facecloth. Collapsing back on the bunk, he put the cold cloth on his forehead. He had done this so many times before—for hangovers.

Lying there in the darkness, he tried to draw the maximum benefit from the cool cloth over his eyes even while scenes from the previous morning's flight kept flashing into his returning consciousness. After fifteen minutes he was fully awake. He threw the washcloth toward the sink. He changed his underwear and dressed in a khaki uniform, grabbed his flight jacket and shut the door behind him.

He found Devil 502, the plane he had flown the previous day, in a corner of the hangar where machines were stored that were badly damaged or awaiting spare parts. Devil 502 had become a hangar queen. Well, the goddamn computer had never worked properly, anyway. Still, the old girl had held together and had brought back Cole and him.

He climbed up a work stand placed against the rear of the fuselage and stepped across to the horizontal stabilizer. The holes in the tail were about three-quarters of an inch in diameter and went clear through. Five of them. Peering through one jagged hole, he saw that the internal structure had been damaged, one metal stringer being completely severed.

Lieutenant Commander Joe Wagner, the squadron maintenance officer, stood near the nose of the plane and Jake climbed down to join him. "Really a mess, huh?" Wagner called.

Jake nodded.

"You're a lucky man, Grafton, a lucky man. I just came up here to look at this wreck again and marvel at your luck and see if some'll rub off on me."

Jake snorted. "You wouldn't want my luck."

"Don't be so sure. See those holes? My guess is fourteen point five millimeter. One, maybe two, of those shells had explosive heads. But they didn't explode. That's where you were extremely fortunate, because if they had you might have lost half the vertical fin. I don't know if this thing will fly with half a tail. Those shells penetrated the only spot on this plane that has so little resistance that the contact fuses in the shells weren't crushed. Come here, I'll show you something else." He led Jake over to the right intake and stood back so Jake could see.

Most of the axial fairing inside the intake was gone, and the compressor blades were badly twisted and bent. "I suspect that shell was a thirty-seven-millimeter, a big momma. It hit dead center on that fairing and smashed it, and the pieces of the fairing were sucked into the compressor. Luckily you shut this engine down right quick, or the compressor blades would've been flung off through the fuselage, cutting this aluminum skin like a knife through butter. On the inside, the blades probably would have cut into the main fuel cell, and fuel would have shot back onto that hot engine, and this plane would have blown up about one-thousandth of a second later. Even if the blades didn't cut into the fuel cell, if you'd kept the engine turning at power, it would have torn itself off its mounts since the first two bearings were destroyed by the shell."

Jake Grafton nodded. "A thousandth of a second. That is just about how long Ford and Box had. They were there, then they were gone in a fireball."

Joe Wagner looked away. "Maybe an explosive shell in the main fuel cell. Maybe a shell hit one of the bombs and detonated it. We'll never know."

They talked awhile, then Jake left Joe and climbed to the flight deck. He picked his way aft until he reached the island, then he descended to the catwalk. An ammunition ship lay alongside the enormous *Shiloh*. Jake could see down onto the bridge of the supply ship, which rose and fell with the swells much more than the carrier. Deadly weapons flowed from the smaller vessel to the larger. Wires spanned the space between the two ships, and the bombs swung across, occasionally dipping into the swells. Jake watched the operation—the forklifts darting here and there, the men struggling with the heavy crates of unfused bombs—and felt it had no connection with his deliveries of the same bombs.

He turned up the collar of his flight jacket and walked away.

The flight schedule told him he had two watches in Pri-Fly after the sun came up. It was now only midnight. Restless, unable to sleep, he made his way down to the dirty-shirt wardroom where he ate a hamburger as the space reverberated under the pile-driver strokes of the bow catapults launching the first flights of the new day. When the catapult shuttles smashed to a stop in the water brakes, making a stupendous crash, the room shook and the crockery rattled. Jake lingered over his coffee and smoked a cigarette as he thought about the men riding the catapults into the night sky. When the launch was over he doused his butt in the coffee cup and left for the ready room to check his mail, hoping for a letter from Callie. Tonight, though, his mailbox contained only official paperwork. Taking a seat, he began to plow through it.

After a few moments he sensed that New Guy was surreptitiously watching him from his chair at the duty officer's desk. Except for the two of them, the room was empty. Jake kept his eyes locked on the paperwork. What was New thinking? Was he angry at Grafton, or perhaps at Ford and Box for having the ill grace to get killed? Or was he angry at himself, comparing himself with the pilots who passed through the ready room? New Guy had once been one of them, had once sat in the padded chairs and had listened to the briefs. Like them, he had opened his locker and reached in for his survival vest, G-suit, and torso harness, and smelled the stale sweat and remembered the past terrors even as he prepared to go aloft again. Was he ashamed of himself for quitting? If so, he wouldn't blame himself long. He'd blame others: the skipper, the system, the other pilots, or his wife.

The phone on the duty officer's desk rang, and New

Guy seized it as if it were a rope thrown to a drowning man. When he hung up he kept his hand on the telephone and said, "Jake, the Skipper wants to see you in his stateroom."

Moving slowly, Jake returned his papers to the mailbox. He glanced back at New Guy on his way out and saw that he was slumped over the flight schedule, rereading yet again the names of those men among whom he had once counted himself.

Jake's knock was answered with a grunt. He entered and found the Old Man at his desk and Cowboy Parker on the bunk, looking grim. Commander Camparelli looked Jake over from head to toe, then waved in the direction of the couch.

Camparelli lit a cigarette and ran his fingertips through his crewcut. Jake waited while he scanned a document. The skipper edged around in his chair and eyed Grafton. "A dead bombardier, a plane blown out of the sky, and now this." He shook the paper in his hand and scrutinized Grafton as if he were a scientific curiosity. "Do you know what this is?"

"No, sir."

"This is a secret message from me to Seventh Fleet, with copies to everyone in the chain of command. Your name's smeared all over it. Care to guess what tidbits about you this little missive contains?"

Jake shook his head.

"Yesterday I was up in Mission Planning looking at the order-of-battle SAM charts and for the life of me I couldn't find all those SAM sites that fired at you when you were going after the Bac Giang power plant. So I looked up the daily intelligence reports and asked a couple questions here and there. Then I sat down and had a friendly chat with your pal Steiger. What do you think he might have said?"

"I don't know, sir." Jake's breathing quickened.

"Too bad. I would bet a thousand dollars you could've guessed." His face was contorted and the veins in his neck stood out. "Mister Steiger had a confession to make. This happened after he tried to explain why all those missiles you dodged around Bac Giang were not in the intelligence report or on the maps, even though I'd given him a direct order to include them. Seems he knew the sites weren't exactly where you said they were in your after-action report." His voice rose to a parade-ground bellow. "In short, he said you and Cole weren't around Bac Giang when those SAMs were trying to asshole you. He allowed as how you were down over Hanoi on a little private party."

Jake dropped his eyes.

"So it's true, huh? Do you have any idea just what the hell you've done? Before I get through with you, you're going to wish to God it had been you instead of McPherson that stopped that fucking bullet. Stand at attention, Mister Grafton." The "mister" curled off his lips contemptuously.

Jake snapped to attention, eyes fastened on the bulkhead. Camparelli moved to within inches of him. "I've been in the navy for twenty years and worked my ass off to get this command. Now, behind my back, you've abused the trust, my trust, and the trust of every officer in this squadron. My God, don't you understand that the military runs on trust? No one except your bombardier can ride in that plane with you. If you can't, or won't, follow orders, you're not worth a tinker's damn. Even that chicken half-wit New is worth ten of you. I can trust him to be a yellow coward. But I can trust him. Do you understand me?" He shouted the last question.

Jake's gaze rested on the Old Man's accusing eyes.

"You took an oath, Grafton, when you got your commission. 'I will support and defend the Constitution of the United States against all enemies, foreign and domestic, and *obey the orders of the officers appointed over me.'* That's the same oath every officer in the navy has sworn for damn-near two hundred years. And you violated that oath. You disobeyed." The skipper sat down. "Keep your eyes on that bulkhead, mister."

When Camparelli spoke again, his voice was more controlled but still bitter. "People are spitting on soldiers and sailors in airports and bus stations all over America. ROTC cadets refuse to wear their uniforms because they're cursed at and ridiculed. Can you believe that? Americans spitting on the men who have sworn to defend them, on the men who've sworn to obey the orders of the elected, civilian government." He pounded his fist on his desk. "For two hundred years the military has obeyed the civilians who were the elected government. Those civilians were not always wise, not always right, sometimes not even very smart. In fact, many presidents of this country have been hack politicians with no qualification for the job other than the fact that they fooled a majority of the people. But even the worst hacks are obeyed. Do you know why? Can you guess?"

Jake stood silent.

"Answer me, Mister Grafton!"

"No, sir."

"Then I'll explain it so even you can understand. If the officers at the top ever get it into their heads that they have the right to follow their consciences, to do what they think is right instead of what they are told, then the United States is in for a military dictatorship. We'll be just another chaotic banana republic."

Jake heard the click of a cigarette lighter. The commander stood again and confronted Jake eyeball to eyeball. His voice was a dry whisper. "You have no right whatsoever to disobey orders. None. You will do as you are told even if it kills you. You will obey even if it costs you your life and your immortal soul, if you have one. I don't give a flying fuck if your father is the Pope and you have a direct line to God Almighty. This is our country and our navy we're talking about, you fool." Camparelli paced the room. "There are enough weapons in the magazines of this ship to wipe Vietnam or China clean off the face of the earth. What if the captain decided he had the power and foresight to act on his own?"

He paused in front of the still-rigid Grafton. "The backbone of the navy is obedience. America will always need the navy." He turned and took two steps toward the desk. "And she will need the navy to obey. What you've done is wrong. Basic, rock-bottom wrong."

Frank Camparelli sat down heavily. "So you think this piss-ant war in this shit-hole country is worth compromising the U.S. Navy, huh? You think you can personally whip these commie bastards with an airplane and a few bombs and make good Democrats and Republicans out of them?" The Old Man took a drag on his cigarette. He sighed. "You're a damned fool, a fool because you haven't grasped that we have to obey whether or not we all lose our lives or even the goddamned war.

"What's your problem, Grafton? We're not aggressive enough in your opinion? Shit! Too bad we can't arrange it so you can ask Ford and Box if we're aggressive enough to suit them."

The silence hung in the air like the smell of a dead animal.

Jake felt his eyes smarting. Cowboy cleared his throat to catch the skipper's attention and glanced at Jake's trembling hands. The skipper looked, then averted his gaze.

"When you walk out that door you will go to Sick Bay and inform Mad Jack I want a complete physical done on you. If he approves, I'm sending you to the beach on the morning cargo plane. You're to take all your flight gear with you. Two new planes are coming in from the States on a Trans-Pac, and I can't spare any fighting crews to go get them. Take that psychopath Cole with you. An investigation will begin in your absence, and you'll be questioned when you return. When the new planes reach Cubi, you'll send a message notifying us of their arrival and we'll send you an overhead time. Then you'll fly one of those planes out to the ship and we'll send a crew in for the other. I want you to report to the duty officer at Cubi when you arrive and each and every morning you are there. Are these orders explicit enough for you?"

Jake nodded.

"Answer me!" The roar was savage.

"Yessir. The orders are explicit enough."

"Then see that you obey, Grafton. See that you obey." Camparelli paused, then continued. "Steiger's confined to quarters without visitors. He's been ordered not to answer the phone. You will make no attempt to see or speak with him. Now get the hell out of my sight before I personally try to find out what you've been using for brains."

Jake left.

The second class petty officer in Sick Bay told him that he should come back during the 0700 Sick Call. Grafton wasn't in the mood. "I want to see the Jungle Quack right fucking now, sailor. Find him." It turned out that the doctor was in his office after all. Apparently he had been on the phone with Camparelli.

Stripped to his skivvies, Jake ignored the proddings and indignities of the routine physical examination. His mind was elsewhere. He saw Morgan and the faces of the men he had known who were now dead. Two had been killed in automobile accidents, but a half dozen or so had died in plane crashes. One had ejected from an F-9 in the training command when it caught fire and had made the long, long fall when his parachute failed to open. He had known Morgan best, but he had also been good friends with a boy from California who had flown his A-6 into the Nevada desert on a night training mission.

Mad Jack looked at Jake's hands. "Are you fit to fly?" the doctor asked.

"I'm not a doctor," Jake said. "I just fly the planes. For Uncle Sam. . . ." he added, his voice trailing off. The skipper would have a comment or two about that. Well, Frank Camparelli was right. But so was he. There was a limit to just how much stupidity in high places men ought to endure. If those elected civilians didn't intend to put on enough pressure to win, then they had no right to waste lives just screwing around. Camparelli makes no apologies for stupidity; he merely accepts it. Maybe the problem is that the admirals and generals never tell the elected officials what fools they are.

"Are you fit to fly?" the doctor asked again.

"What do you think? You flew with me a few weeks ago. Was I dangerous? Was all that medical education your parents paid for in jeopardy?"

"You can put your clothes on." Mad Jack began scrawling in the medical record.

"What's your professional opinion, Quack? Are you going to let me drive these flying pigs or aren't you?"

"What do you want?" the doctor asked. "Do you want to keep flying?"

Jake pulled on his shoes. "I don't know, Doc." He spoke slowly, trying to concentrate. "I've been flying since I was fifteen. Flying's all I know. If this war goes on I expect I'll die in an airplane." He picked up his wallet and keys from the desk. "The truth of it is, I really don't give a damn."

The doctor looked intently at the pilot. "When we

flew to the beach a few weeks ago, you asked me a question that I thought you knew the answer to. You asked, 'Is life worth the final smashup?' Well, what's your answer? Is it?"

"I don't remember saying that." The pilot sat with his elbows on his knees. "I always thought flying was worth the sacrifices," he said at last.

"Life is a hell of a lot more mundane than flying, isn't it? It's a lot more complex. Not much glory. It doesn't have many of those right or wrong, black or white decisions that flying's so full of." Mad Jack droned on, something about good pilots making rotten choices in life, but Jake's attention had wandered to the framed prints that hung on the bulkheads. The prints were of famous moments in naval history: Dewey in Manila Bay; Farragut steaming past the forts at Mobile; the *Monitor* and the *Merrimack* at Hampton Roads.

Mad Jack had another picture. It showed a squad of marines pinned on the beach at Iwo Jima, their faces contorted by the strain of combat. There had been no glory there.

TWENTY-ONE

Jake left Tiger Cole at the bar in the Cubi Point O Club. Without a carrier in port, the place was dead. Carrying a fresh scotch, he headed for the pay telephone, his pockets weighted down with thirty dollars in quarters. He and Cole had arrived the day before, signed in at the BOQ, and reported to the duty officer—as Camparelli had instructed them to do. At the bar Cole had said, "You should call."

"It's a lot to ask of her," said Jake.

Cole shook the dice cup and rolled. "Call her." He selected a pair of threes and returned the other dice to the cup. "Wish I had your problem." He rolled again. A third three. "Go on."

Jake felt as though he were feeding quarters into a slot machine. Less than half his scotch remained when he heard Callie's voice amid a hum and intermittent static.

"It's me. Jake."

There was a pause. "Jake! Great to hear your voice! I thought you were at sea. Where are you?"

"Cubi Point in the Philippines. I flew here yesterday afternoon in a cargo plane with another guy, my bombardier."

There was another pause. "Are you on leave?"

"Sort of."

"Jake! You've been hurt!"

"No, no. I'm fine. Really, I'm okay. I'm calling from the O Club, and I've got a scotch in my hand."

"If you're drinking scotch, I suppose you must be all right."

"Well, actually, everything's not all right. I got into some trouble."

"Trouble? What kind of trouble?"

He began searching his pockets for cigarettes. "I got into trouble with the navy. I did something wrong, didn't follow orders exactly."

"How serious is it? This trouble you're in."

"Oh, it could be worse. They're not going to shoot me or anything. I'll survive. I'm going back to the ship in maybe three days to deliver a new plane. But I'd sure like to see you before I go."

"I'd like to see you, too. I really would."

"Could you come?"

"Huh? You mean fly out to the Philippines? Now?"

"Yeah. I know it's a lot—"

"It'd be very difficult to leave just now. My job . It's such short notice. Maybe—"

"Callie, I need to see you." Waiting for her reply, he cradled the receiver between his head and shoulder, and lit a cigarette.

"How would I get there?"

"You fly to Manila. I can meet you there and bring you back to Cubi."

"Why not stay in Manila?"

"Can't. I've got to report to the duty officer here every morning."

"It's really serious, isn't it?"

Jake took a breath before answering. "Yes. It's pretty serious."

"Hold on. I'll see if there's anything I can work out right now. You can hold, can't you?"

"Sure."

After a few minutes he was told to add more quarters. He fed the slot as quickly as he could. One coin slipped from his hand, hit the counter, and fell to the floor. He didn't bother to pick it up. Finally she came back on.

"Jake?"

"Right here."

"I can't come until the day after tomorrow."

"That's okay."

"I can catch a flight arriving in Manila at one-fifteen Saturday. That doesn't give us much time together. Do you still want me to come?"

"You bet. I really want to see you."

"Okay. I'll be on Cathay Pacific flight 923."

"Got it. Hey, I can't wait to see you—and thanks."

After promising Callie that he'd relax and take good care of himself, Jake made another phone call, then returned to the bar and came up behind Cole. "She's coming, shipmate!" Cole acknowledged this with a hint of a smile. Jake went on, "This guy I know in the flying club here will fly me to Manila to meet her."

Jake picked up the dice and put them in the cup. After a shake he turned it over on the counter.

Five aces.

They looked at each other, then stared at the sign behind the bar: "Five naturals buys the party, five aces buys the bar."

Cole made a show of surveying the empty room. "Barkeep," Tiger called. "Give me a double of the most expensive stuff you have back there. And pour yourself one, too." His blue eyes met Jake's and the corners of his mouth twitched. "Without a doubt, Grafton, you're the luckiest man I've ever met."

* * *

Jake stood with his arm around Callie while Harold made a thorough preflight inspection of the four-seat Cessna 172. Harold's caution impressed Jake. Most pilots who had completed the first half of a flight would check nothing more than the fuel and oil before taking off again the same day. Even so, Jake knew that he would not be at ease with Harold at the controls. He was not comfortable in an airplane unless he was flying it.

"I hope this flight is better than my last one," said Callie. She had complained about the turbulence on her flight from Hong Kong soon after Jake had kissed her at the customs exit and given her a long hug.

"It was pretty smooth at four thousand feet coming over here," Jake said.

Callie squeezed Jake's hand and said, "I don't want to hassle you, but when we're on the plane maybe you could tell me about the trouble you're in."

Jake smiled. "These prop planes are pretty noisy. You have to shout to be heard. I thought that when we land at Cubi, we'd check into a hotel and then, if you'd like, we could go to the beach. I know one that's sugar white and very quiet. I found it one day when I was flying. It'd be a good place to talk."

Callie grinned. "Sounds like a good plan to me."

The air was bumpy in the climb, but when the plane passed through 3700 feet, the ride suddenly became smooth. Harold's seat was higher than those in the rear, where Jake and Callie sat, and the angle of the climb made it appear even higher. To Jake it seemed as though Harold sat on a throne. His bald pate shone in the afternoon sun. It saddened Jake to think that after one more flight in the Intruder, he would never again have control of his destiny in the air.

When they were flying downwind to the runway at Cubi Point, Jake estimated from the direction and shape of the windsock that Harold would be fighting about a fifteen-knot crosswind from the left on final approach—tough for a Cessna to handle. As soon as Harold turned from left base to final he pushed on the right rudder to align the nose of the plane with the runway. Jake watched Harold put the Cessna in a slip by holding right rudder and dipping the left wing. Now the airplane could track straight down the final approach course in spite of the stiff crosswind. Jake heard a chirp as the Cessna touched down on the left wheel, and then a softer chirp as the right wheel eased down and the plane settled on the runway. Jake said loudly. "Good job! You caught the three wire!"

He and Callie took a cab to the Subic main gate They walked across the bridge to the nearby hotel Earlier, he had paid the clerk a premium price for the best room available.

Callie surveyed the room. The dark green paint was peeling. Water stains blotched the ceiling and wall. The faucet dripped in the chipped porcelain sink. "I feel like I'm in the Hide-A-Wee Hotel for a sordid affair."

Saying nothing, Jake went over to try to stop the leak. His hand froze on the faucet handle—a waterlogged black roach, about an inch long, lay upside down on the drain, with one bent antenna stuck to the bottom of the rust-stained sink. Jake stepped quickly into the bathroom and tore off a bundle of toilet paper. When he came out, Callie was staring at a picture of a black and white cow that stared back at her with a lugubrious expression. It stood in a field of very green grass. "This print looks like it was cut from a dairy ad."

"American export art."

He stood in front of the sink, half-hiding it from Callie. Reaching into the bowl, he scooped up the roach in the toilet paper, taking care not to squeeze too tightly. Callie's voice came from behind.

"What's that in your hand?"

"It's, uh, nothing much—"

"What is it? A bug of some sort? Is that what it is?"

"Yeah."

"What kind?"

"It's a black bug."

"It's a what?"

Jake sighed. "It's a cockroach."

Callie sat gingerly on the side of one of the two single beds, causing its springs to make boinging noises.

Jake reached for the closed toilet lid and hesitated; he decided to flush the toilet first.

"How big was that roach, anyway?" Callie called from the other room.

The toilet groaned and rattled as it filled up. "I didn't measure it."

"It's a big one. I know it."

He lifted the lid, plopped in the wad of tissue paper, and flushed again.

"My God, it's bigger than I thought. Hasn't it gone down yet?"

"Callie. Relax. I didn't try flushing it down the first time."

"Then why did you flush the toilet?"

"Just checking it out, that's all. It really seems to be working great."

The toilet gave out a screech just before it stopped filling up. Jake watched it long enough to know it wouldn't overflow, then he went and sat down next to Callie. She was on the edge of her bed with her head in her hands. Jake was relieved to see that she was tearless. "I know this place is the pits." He put his arm around her shoulders. "I'm sorry."

She looked at him. "Does the bathroom have a shower or a bath?"

"No. But there's a shower down the hall."

"I have a brilliant idea. Why don't we go to the

Hilton instead? Or the Holiday Inn? That'd be fine, too."

"I think we're stuck. There aren't any decent places around here."

"Well, check the beds for crawling things. I want to be sure I'm not the next meal for something. If the beds pass inspection, I guess I'll survive. Will you?"

"Sure. As long as I have you."

The jeepney was orange and white, and frilly tassels jiggled from its canvas top. With Callie and Jake in back, it left Po City behind and headed out on a macadam road that was mined with potholes. The young Filipino driver seemed to delight in hitting the holes at full speed and ignored Jake's pleas to slow down. His passengers were knocked about and, at times, propelled straight up into the air.

Callie asked, "How much longer?"

"Twenty or thirty minutes."

"I don't think I can last that long."

"Hang tough."

"If I were pregnant, I'd lose the baby after this ride." The driver honked his tinny horn at some chickens in the road.

They got out of the jeepney on the outskirts of a small fishing village. Jake persuaded the driver to wait for them by tearing a twenty-dollar bill and giving him half. Then they trudged more than two hundred yards to the beach.

Holding hands, Callie and Jake strolled barefoot on the clean white sand where it was soft and damp from dissipating waves. Jake liked it when the fizzing water of a wave swirled around his ankles and, as it receded, washed between his toes and sucked at the sand beneath his soles. Jake and Callie were alone on the beach.

Callie said, "That sunset is gorgeous."

"You should see one at thirty thousand feet."

"I'd like to. It must be spectacular."

"It is. I hope I see another one from the air."

Callie was wearing Jake's Jersey City Athletic Club T-shirt; on her it looked like a nightie. Jake was bare-chested and he had rolled up his jeans. They had walked a distance on the damp sand and now they headed back toward the blanket they had taken from the hotel closet, the dark blue blanket that Jake suspected was navy-issue.

Callie asked, "What can happen to you?"

"They could court-martial me. They could send me to prison."

"Surely they wouldn't send you to prison."

"It's a possibility. They're conducting an investigation on the ship now. When it's over, they'll probably decide to court-martial us."

"But a court-martial is like a trial, isn't it?"

"Yes. It's the military's version of it."

"Then it could be decided in your favor."

"Not likely."

"But it could be."

"Listen, what I did was damned serious. A few weeks ago one of my sailors lied to me. I wanted the skipper to hammer him good, but the Old Man decided not to. I wanted this guy disciplined because he lied, because he broke my trust. What I did is a lot worse than what that sailor did. They'll come down hard on me, you can count on that. They won't let me get away with disobeying orders, not something this big. The State Department will have to be told, maybe even the president."

"I understand. I'm not trying to minimize the seriousness of what you did. But I don't think you should assume there's no hope. Now what else could the navy do to you, short of sending you to prison?"

"They could boot me out with a dishonorable discharge. I'd have one helluva tough time getting a job in the civilian world with a dishonorable on my record. Or they could ask me to resign my commission, and give me an honorable. That way, I could at least get a flying job."

"Anything else they could do?"

"Well, at the very least I guess they could give me a letter of reprimand or censure, which would be put in my personnel file. If that happened, I could stay in the navy for a while. But there wouldn't be much point in it. I'd never be promoted. I'd be a lieutenant for the rest of my career."

"Couldn't they just bawl you out and leave it at that?"

"Slap my wrist and send me on my way? Fat chance. Any way you cut it, my career in the navy is over."

Callie didn't respond.

The sun had been replaced by a bright three-quarter moon. The air was cooler and they sat shoulder to shoulder on the blanket. Callie's arms encircled her drawn-up legs, which were almost hidden by the T-shirt. "How will you handle it if it turns out you can't fly any more?"

"I don't know. I guess I'll just have to adjust somehow. But I sure as hell won't miss the war. The bombing. The killing. I'm sure tired of all that."

"You've done your part."

"I wouldn't say that. I don't like the idea of leaving the fighting to others. It'd be like . . . running out on the other guys. Sure, the war sucks. But I'll quit fighting only because the navy *makes* me quit." Then he added, "You think we should *all* quit. Now. Right?"

"Yes," she said. "That's my opinion. But we don't want to get into that again, do we?"

Jake thought about it. "Nah. Who wants to talk

about the war, anyway? The hell with it. Let's go for a swim."

Jake moved about thirty feet to the left of the blanket to undress. While removing his jeans and underpants he stole some glances at Callie, who undressed sitting down, taking off her shorts and panties beneath the T-shirt, which she kept on. When she giggled it startled him. He'd never heard her giggle before.

"What's so funny?" he asked.

Now she laughed. "You present such an interesting silhouette."

Jake looked down and understood what she meant.

Callie said, "I wish I'd thought to bring my sketchbook with me. You cut such a heroic figure."

Jake turned away from her and said, over his shoulder, "You're not going swimming with my T-shirt on, are you?"

"I might."

"That's my good shirt, you know."

"Jake, do you really think it's swimming that you're *up* for?"

Jake laughed. He sidled back to the blanket in a half crouch. She held up her arms and he helped her take off the shirt. They stretched out on their sides and held each other. Callie loosened her embrace and lay back on the blanket while Jake, still on his side, propped himself up on one elbow. With his fingers he gently rimmed her nipples and felt them become erect under his touch. He leaned over and kissed her breasts, then softly kissed her belly and ran his tongue around her navel. "That tickles," Callie said with a chuckle. "Are you sure that cab driver doesn't have binoculars?"

"They'd have to be infrared for him to see anything. Anyway, he can't see over this dune."

Callie suddenly sucked in her breath and sighed as Jake's hand, having traveled lightly up her thigh, stopped where he found moistness.

"You're a beautiful person, Callie."

Later they stood holding each other in the swirling shallows, watching the dark waves glistening in the moonlight. The only sound was the rhythmic rushing of the sea.

The room reeked of insecticide. Jake concluded that the motel clerk he had bellowed at earlier had taken him seriously. The bathroom didn't look much cleaner, but Jake conceded that not much could be done with it. They dressed hurriedly for dinner, having decided that it would be wise to leave the windows closed to allow the insecticide to do its job well.

The dining room in the Subic Bay O Club was nearly empty. The picture window reflected the flickering candle on their table. Callie said, "I have a present for you."

"What is it?"

She handed him something flat wrapped in tissue paper. He opened it up. Callie said, "It's a sand dollar. I found it on the beach today. A perfect specimen."

"Thanks a lot."

"It's for good luck."

"Then I'll take good care of it. I need all the good luck I can get." He swallowed some beer before going on. "What do you think about what I did—bombing an unauthorized target?"

Callie finished chewing a cracker, then took a sip of her gin and tonic. "I guess I feel as you do. You shouldn't have done it. But I can understand what drove you to it. And I know that I don't think any less of you because of what you've done. You know how I feel about the war, but I have to admire you for risking your life—and your career—to do what you believe in."

"I appreciate that. I'm sure glad you're here."

"I'm glad I'm here, too. But I regret that I didn't bring my sketch pad with me."

Although the windows in the room were wide open, the smell lingered. Callie asked, "Where're your pajamas?"

"I don't own any. I always sleep in my underwear."

"The modern gentleman," she said, carefully turning back the bed covers and looking between the sheets before she climbed in.

Jake turned off the overhead light and felt his way to her bed. The springs groaned loudly as he sat on it, and she laughed.

"What's so funny?" he asked.

"My friends think I've dashed away for a wildly romantic weekend. And here we are. In a dreadful hotel. And you in your underwear."

"Next time, I promise—champagne, roses, and violins." He shifted his weight deliberately to provide creaking accompaniment. He said softly, "Callie, it's been a great day."

Her hand found his. "Yes, it has."

He bent down to her lips. They were moist and firm and parted willingly. Her breath was warm on his cheek. She still smelled of the sea. "I hope we have more days like this."

"Kiss me again."

His bed was more comfortable than he had expected, and he went to sleep quickly. When Callie left her bed and moved in with him sometime during the night, he turned on his side; she did the same and nestled against him. He fell asleep again luxuriating in her warmth and closeness.

Shortly after seven they checked out of the hotel and took a taxi to the BOQ. While they were having breakfast Jake kept looking for Cole. Finally he excused himself and called Tiger's room.

"What's up?" Cole asked groggily.

"You forgetting we have to fly today?"

"No."

"Don't you think you ought to haul your ass out of bed?"

"No. I checked in at ops yesterday."

"When are the planes due in?"

"About ten-thirty. They called me a while ago with an in-bound report. Just show up at the field with your flight gear. I'll take care of everything else."

"Sounds good."

"No need for you to check in with the duty officer, either. I've got it covered."

"Hey, thanks."

"Anytime."

After breakfast they took a cab to the aircraft parking mat beside the carrier pier. Jake put his gear and Callie's overnighter in front of the line shack and paid the driver.

He and Callie sat on a bench in the sun in front of the small one-story tin building. It was warm, and the sharp kerosene smell of jet fuel wafted through the air. Jake heard a distant murmur. Then he saw the two Intruders, glinting in the sun, far away over the mouth of Subic Bay. He said to Callie, "See them?"

"Not yet." A half minute later she said, "Now I do."

The jets dropped their landing gear and flew the final approach in formation. Jake ducked into the line shack. "Here they come," he told the crew chief. "Got any beer?"

"Plenty."

Jake took a six-pack from the refrigerator and gave the chief a five-dollar bill. Then he went and sat with Callie as the bombers taxied in, trailing shimmering exhaust gas, their whining engines growing louder. They stopped not more than fifty yards away and Callie plugged her ears. When the pilots shut down the engines, she said, "They're so loud." Jake walked out quickly to the planes and threw cans of beer to the men in the cockpits.

Jake brought the airmen over and introduced each man to her. She stood and chatted with them about their trip across the Pacific while Jake went back to the aircraft to supervise the fueling and servicing. When the crews had departed in a gray navy van, she returned to the bench and watched Jake hover around the sailors working on the planes, making a comment here, lending a hand there.

When he came back he asked Callie, "Want to see an A-6 up close?"

"I'd love to."

As they neared the planes, Jake said, "Not exactly beautiful, with that blunt nose. Flies great, though."

"The wings look huge."

"Fifty-three-foot wing span. The top of the tail is sixteen feet off the ground. The plane's fifty-five feet long."

"It's big."

"It has to be, to carry all the fuel and ordnance." He put his hand on the nose of the plane. "It's a great plane. Built by Grumman. They built it to fly."

Jake led her around the aircraft, identifying major components and explaining their functions. Then he climbed up the boarding ladder and stepped on the air intake of the left engine. He stooped and held out his hand. "Come on up. You can sit in the cockpit." She climbed up awkwardly and started to step on the pilot's seat cushion. Jake said, "Not there."

"Then where do I put my feet?" Jake showed her how to swing herself into the cockpit. Once she was seated she looked around. "There must be some mistake," she said. "This plane is too complicated for anybody to fly." Jake laughed and discussed the functions of the altimeter, airspeed indicator, vertical speed indicator, and other primary flight instruments. He skipped over the more complicated navigational instruments, the ECM gear, and other electronic equipment that would be difficult to explain in a short time. He showed her the stick and throttles and told her how they worked. She said, "All these buttons on the stick look like warts."

"They're there so the pilot doesn't have to take his hand from the stick to operate them."

"Which one releases the bombs?"

"This one." He pointed to a red button on the side of the stick grip.

"I want to see you in the pilot's seat."

"Okay. Can you move over and be my bombardier?" She pulled her skirt up to her thighs and Jake helped her step over the center console and into the right seat. He asked, "What do you think?"

Callie had to look up at him because the bombardier's seat was several inches below and behind the pilot's. "I'm awed. All these dials, buttons, switches, knobs. I can see why it takes two people to fly this plane."

"All it takes is training. You could learn to fly it."

"I couldn't imagine it."

They fell silent. The airfield was quiet and Jake could hear the tinkle of the engine compressor blades rotating slowly in the breeze. "It's almost time for my last flight as a navy pilot."

Callie sighed. "I wish I could make everything right for you."

"I wanted to fly because I love the freedom of it, but now I've ended up in a war. And I've learned how high the price is. I was stupid. I should've known that the navy didn't pay for my flying so I could have a good time."

"I think you're being too hard on yourself. How many pilots do you know who joined the navy wanting to fight in a war? They just wanted to fly too, didn't they?"

"Sure, they all just wanted to fly. But I think most of them knew the chances were good they'd end up in Vietnam." Jake paused. "Yeah, I knew it too. Maybe I even wanted to fly in combat. I thought it would be like in the books—knights-in-the-sky stuff. What I'm trying to say is that I never expected it to be this *kind* of war. The kind of absolutely nutty war we're fighting in Vietnam."

"Who would've?"

Jake looked away from Callie and saw Tiger Cole standing in front of the line shack. He was wearing his flight suit and his arms were crossed. Jake said, "Time to go." Then he turned to Callie, smiled, and shook his head slowly. "You know, I think I love you." When he leaned down to kiss her, she reached up and put her hands around his neck.

"What a lovely thing to say to your bombardier. Jake, I want you to fly forever."

"Why do they call you Tiger?" asked Callie.

Cole's eyebrows lifted a fraction. Jake said, "Because he's a fighter. He's a tiger."

Callie said to Jake, "Do you have a nickname?" Jake shrugged and grinned. She looked at Cole. "Does he?"

"Cool Hand," said Cole. "Cool Hand Jake."

"Cool Hand? Why's he called that?"

"Because he's cool when the shooting starts. Real cool."

"I can believe that," said Callie. "What about Sammy? Does he have a nickname, too?"

"He has one," said Jake. "But not too many people know about it." Jake caught Cole's eye. "Actually, it's very private."

Callie began to speak when Cole said, "Ops sent a message to the ship. We have to be wheels-in-the-well in forty minutes."

"How's the weather?"

"Good," said Cole, "but we'll have a stiff head-wind."

"Any problems?"

"No sweat."

Jake said to Callie, "I'll see if one of the guys in the line shack can run you over to the flying club. Be right back."

Callie and the bombardier stood facing the airplanes. "So this may be your last flight in a navy airplane, too?"

"Yeah," Cole replied, "but I won't miss it like Jake will. He doesn't fly an airplane—he puts it on and wears it."

Cole inspected the Intruder they would fly as Jake loaded Callie's overnighter into a gray sedan beside the line shack.

"Please let me know what happens," she said.

"I will."

"As soon as you can."

"I'll write just as soon as I know something."

"Got the sand dollar?"

"Right here," said Jake, patting his left sleeve pock-et. "Thanks for coming. That was beyond the call of duty."

"I'm very glad I came."

As she was getting into the car, Callie said, "Keep the faith, Jake."

TWENTY-TWO

Sammy was seated at the duty desk when Jake and Tiger entered the ready room and laid their baggage across two chairs near the door. Four other officers in the room ignored the two men. Tiger bent over a table and began filling out the maintenance sheets as Jake walked over to the duty desk and drew up a chair. Facing his roommate, he lit a cigarette and said, "Hey, shipmate."

Sammy's face was drawn. "How was the beach, Jake?"

"Empty. No carrier in. Nobody there."

"Did you call Callie?"

"She came down from Hong Kong."

Sammy looked at his notes. "There's some kind of hearing tomorrow at 1400 in the lounge forward of the dirty-shirt wardroom. A captain and two staff types from Washington. They must've jumped a plane within hours of the Skipper's bomb. They got here yesterday and have been talking to everyone, me included." He paused and eyed his friend. "This is hot, Jake. Sizzling. Somebody's going to fry."

"Yeah. Me. What'd you tell them?"

Sammy's voice was barely audible. "I lied. Told them

you never said a word to me that indicated you thought the targets were lousy and were looking to free lance. The Skipper didn't buy it and reamed me good, but I stuck to it. Don't sell me out."

"You know I won't."

Sammy continued, "You and Tiger aren't on the flight schedule. The Skipper wanted to see you as soon as you land. I'm supposed to call him. That bird you flew—what's its condition?"

Jake shook his head. "A few minor problems. Nothing they can't fix during the acceptance inspection." He told Sammy exactly what the gripes were.

Sammy dialed Maintenance Control and passed on the gripes. He then dialed the skipper's extension and told whoever answered that Grafton and Cole were back. He listened a few seconds, aye aye'd, and hung up.

"The Old Man wants to see you, Jake. In ten minutes. He'll send for Cole after he's done with you."

Jake stubbed his cigarette out in the ashtray and stood up. Going back to where Tiger was hunched over the maintenance forms, he said, "Looks like it's time to pay the man. I'm going to see Camparelli now. You're next."

"Fine."

Tiger's cool got on Jake's nerves. "For once it'd be nice if you were just a wee bit uptight."

"I'm scared shitless," Cole replied calmly.

Jake looked at him and managed a laugh. "Try to hide it. Don't always wear your emotions on your sleeve."

Jake hung his flight gear in the locker room and descended the ladder to his stateroom, where he dumped his suit bag in the middle of the floor and lit another cigarette. He smoked it down quickly and then left for Camparelli's stateroom.

At his knock, Cowboy opened the door. Jake entered and stood until the skipper, seated at his desk, waved him over to the bunk. A khaki shirt with wings hung on a hook on the back of the door. The Old Man looked tired, as if he hadn't slept much recently. Jake thought that was probably the case.

"Truth or consequences, Grafton." Commander Camparelli's eyes bored into Jake. "What do you have to say for yourself?"

Jake swallowed. "What do you want to know, sir?"

"I want you to tell me just exactly what you and that maniac Cole did. I want to be the first to hear what you're gonna tell that Pentagon headhunter tomorrow at your hearing. Speak, boy."

"Sir, Cole and I tried to take out the National Assembly building in Hanoi with eight Mark Eight-Three slick snakes after we hit the power plant at Bac Giang the other night. Apparently we missed."

"Now tell me about the other unauthorized, unfragged targets you and Cole in your combined wisdom—which wouldn't fill the head of an ant—decided to take out."

"That was it, sir! There was only the one raid. But I wish that we'd blasted that National Assembly into a pile of bricks. We'd have tried harder if we'd known it'd come to this." He knew he was exaggerating. They couldn't have tried harder if the target had been Ho Chi Minh himself.

"What does Lundeen know about this?"

"Not a thing." He could lie for his friends but not for himself.

"Bullshit, Grafton!" Camparelli stood up and put his nose inches from Jake's face. "You're lying."

"Hanging me and Cole'll have to do, Commander."

"How about Cowboy?"

Jake was startled and glanced at Parker, who betrayed no emotion. Jake shook his head. "No, sir. Emphatically no. I talked Cole into the National Assembly job and we enlisted Steiger. Cowboy didn't know a damn thing about it—and neither did anyone else."

"'Job.' You talk about a 'job.' Just who the hell did you think you were—a couple of safecrackers or Mafia hit men? Come to think of it, those'll be just about the only careers open to you after this, if you're lucky enough to avoid Leavenworth." Camparelli sat on the edge of his desk. He was silent for a moment. "Why? Why'd you do it?"

Jake examined the skipper's lined face. "You hit it on the head the other night, Skipper. Stupidity. I just wanted to hit them harder than the frag list allowed. I figured if I was going to risk my ass and my bombardier's, I wanted them to know we'd been there."

"Well, you sure fucked up." Camparelli shook his head. "If my career survives this, it'll be a miracle—like a dog laying an egg. I've got too much invested in the navy to want to kiss it all off."

"I'm sorry, Skipper. I know we've blown your trust."

The skipper rubbed the side of his head with the heel of his hand. "Yes, you sure as hell did, Jake." He turned to Parker. "Cowboy, you and I better get some sleep. Grafton isn't flying and neither is New, so somebody has to. First brief at 2200." He looked at his watch. "Six hours from now."

Cowboy stood up. "Jake," the skipper said, "when we're in that hearing tomorrow, I want you to make damn sure you tell the truth. Tell the God's truth and let the chips fall where they will and maybe somehow we'll all be able to live with this."

In the passageway Jake apologized to Cowboy, who momentarily put his arm around the smaller man's shoulders. "Nothing to apologize for. I just wish you'd wasted that building and the entire goddamn National Assembly."

Jake went to his room and locked the door. He thought about pouring a drink but decided against it. A warm can of Coke would do instead.

The untidy room and the pale green walls and the sounds of the ship weighed on him. He wanted Callie McKenzie with him and not just for a night or a weekend. He didn't even have a photograph of her. He dug through the stuff on his desk until he came up with a writing tablet with white, lined paper. Halfway through the first page, he suddenly wanted to buy an engagement ring for her the next time he was in port. If he could get off the ship. Then he remembered he'd seen some rings in the window of the ship's store. Maybe it was still open. Checkbook in hand, he slammed the door behind him.

They sat in the empty wardroom next to the lounge where the hearing was being held. Jake and Tiger were there, as well as Sammy, Cowboy Parker, and Abe Steiger. Commander Camparelli and Rabbit Wilson were already inside. Everyone was wearing freshly starched khakis. Most of the men were smoking cigarettes; no one had anything to say. A marine corporal in dress uniform stood at parade rest near the door.

At last the door opened and a lieutenant in whites stuck his head out. "They're ready for you, Grafton."

Jake levered himself upright and turned toward the door. Sammy caught his eye. "Keep the faith, Jake." The pilot nodded and passed through the door, which the orderly closed behind him.

"What faith?" Abe Steiger asked. Sammy just looked at him.

The presiding officer's long-sleeved khaki shirt, unbuttoned at the throat, barely contained his bulging torso. Silver eagles shone on each collar and a set of gold wings gleamed on his chest. His sleeves were rolled up, exposing forearms bristling with black hair. The stubble on his head was less luxuriant.

"Mister Grafton." He spoke from behind a long table. "Please take a seat. I'm Captain Fairleigh Copeland. I invited you in to hear Doctor Catton testify about the results of the physical examination he recently gave you. Physicals are supposed to be held in confidence. Since this is an official inquiry I can hear it and enter it into the record without your consent. But I wanted to ask you if these other gentlemen can hear what the doctor has to say."

Jake had never before heard Mad Jack the Jungle Quack referred to by his surname. His eyes swept the room. The commanding officer of the *Shiloh,* Captain Boma, was there, dressed in his customary white uniform even though every other officer on the ship wore wash khakis. The task force commander's chief of staff, a captain, sat beside him. The other chairs contained the CAG, the air operations officer, Commander Camparelli, Rabbit Wilson, and a couple of younger officers Jake didn't know. He assumed the lightweights had come from Washington to help Captain Copeland slay the infidels. "That's fine with me, sir," he told Copeland.

"Okay, Doctor. What did you find when you examined Lieutenant Grafton?"

"I examined Lieutenant Grafton in the early morning hours of 7 December." Mad Jack consulted his notes. "He's a physically sound Caucasian male, age twenty-seven, with 20-15 vision in both eyes and excellent hearing. His heart rate and blood pressure are at the low end of normal limits. The only physical abnormality is an incipient case of hemorrhoids. As you gentlemen are well aware, this is an occupational disease in jet pilots and is aggravated by extreme

G-loadings. Other than that, he's in perfect physical health."

Mad Jack folded his notes and laid them on his lap. "I should mention one other thing. Lieutenant Grafton had palsied hands when I examined him. This is usually associated with the aged or those with nervous disorders. In his case, I believe the palsy can be attributed to the constant, heavy stress this officer has been under for an extended period. I've seen the same disorder in marines after lengthy patrols in hostile territory when the tension was unrelenting. Palsy may be one of the ways the body reacts to continuous adrenal stimulation. But in view of his otherwise healthy state, Lieutenant Grafton's hand tremors have no medical significance other than demonstrating that he needs a break from the stress."

Jake cast a quick look at his hands, which trembled only a little. "Anything else?" Copeland prompted.

"No, sir."

"How about his mental state?"

"I'm not a psychiatrist, Captain, but I'd say that on the morning I examined him his emotional state was about what one would expect in an individual under high stress. For what it's worth, I suspect that Lieutenant Grafton is not the only aviator or naval flight officer on this ship who exhibits symptoms of stress."

"What about his judgment?"

"I'm not trained to assess that. You gentlemen are as qualified to form an opinion about that as I am."

"Thank you, Doctor. I would appreciate it if you would put your evaluation in writing and give it to one of my assistants."

Captain Copeland glanced at the others in the room, then instructed an aide to admit the men waiting outside. Copeland doodled on a legal pad while they all found seats.

"Gentlemen, this is an informal investigation ordered by the commander-in-chief of the Pacific Fleet. It's to be conducted in accordance with the Manual of the Judge Advocate General. I'm Captain Copeland and I've had conversations with almost everyone in this room during the last forty-eight hours. Some people I've visited with several times. I'll make a report of my findings to CINCPAC, who will act on them as he sees fit. One of his options, I'd like to point out, is to convene general courts-martial." His eyes traveled from face to face.

"My assistant here"—he gestured with his left thumb—"has in his briefcase blank permanent change-of-station orders already signed by the chief of naval personnel. All I have to do is fill in the names. These orders are to places like Adak, Alaska, Diego Garcia in the Indian Ocean, the Canal Zone, and several other garden spots. If anyone here fails to cooperate fully with my investigation, he'll be gone from this ship this afternoon and can count on rotting in one of those vacation spas while awaiting his court-martial or the processing of his resignation. I can tell you for a fact that it'll take three or four years to process a resignation. I hope I'm making myself understood."

He drew a breath. "I assume you all wish to talk to me, so I'm going to skip the legal mumbo-jumbo about your right to consult a lawyer and remain silent. You should all consider yourselves under oath. By God, each of you will tell the truth, the whole truth and nothing but the truth. Is that clear?"

Dead silence. Copeland then asked, "Clear, Mister Grafton?"

"Perfectly clear, sir."

"Are you ready to answer my questions?"

"Yes, sir."

"Have you ever attacked an unfragged target?"

Jake said, "Yessir, I have."

"When and what was it?"

"About a week ago Lieutenant Cole and I hit the fragged target, saved eight bombs, and then took a shot at the National Assembly building in Hanoi. That's it."

"Just one mission?"

"Yessir. Just that one."

"You're damn sure about that?" Copeland's mouth puckered into an O, then relaxed.

"Yessir."

"Lieutenant, I certainly hope that you realize that now is the time to come to Jesus. You're in a helluva lot of trouble, and if you don't come clean you're going to have every captain in the U.S. Navy fighting to be the president of your court-martial. When this hearing's over, there'd better be no surprises, no revelations that crop up—something that slipped your mind." He leaned forward and slammed his fist down. "I want the whole damned story here and now—teeth, hair, asshole, and all." The senior officers at the other table sat flagpole straight.

"You are getting the whole story, sir. There was only one mission."

"Is that right, Mister Cole?"

"He said there was only one mission," Cole answered.

Copeland's arm shot out and he leveled his finger at Tiger. "Mister Cole, you're just one answer away from becoming the naval attaché in Nepal. Now I'm going to ask you one more time. Is Lieutenant Grafton's testimony correct?"

"Yes, sir, it is."

"You and he bombed *one* unauthorized target?"

"Yes, sir."

The captain's attention returned to Jake. "Did you report this strike at the intelligence debriefings?"

"No, sir."

"Did you report it on your after-action report?"

"No, sir."

"Did you tell anyone you were going to bomb an unauthorized target?"

"Mister Steiger, sir."

"No one else knew what the hell you were doing?"

"Just Cole, Steiger, and me."

"How about you, Cole? Have you shared the tale of your adventures with anyone?"

"No, sir. I haven't. I'm naturally blabby, but I sat on this one." That sally drew a frigid stare from Copeland as Cowboy Parker had a coughing fit and Camparelli turned red. Jake Grafton worried his lower lip and glanced at Sammy, who remained expressionless. Copeland finally subjected Cole to closer scrutiny as if to goad the lieutenant into trifling with him further, but Cole, impassive, said nothing else.

Copeland sipped a glass of water, then turned his attention to his legal pad and wrote some notes. Like most interrogators, he had apparently learned long ago that silence was a very effective weapon. Jake imagined, as he felt the tension grow in the silent room, that Copeland used it often on thieves, dope peddlers, embezzlers, fraudulent defense contractors—and the professionally doomed. At last Copeland broke the silence, asking Grafton, "And just how did you identify and target this blow for freedom?"

The pilot knew that the ice was thin and cracking. "We used charts. And photos we borrowed from the Intelligence Center."

"Classified aerial reconnaissance photographs?"

"Yes, sir."

"You removed them from the Intelligence Center in violation of the security regulations?"

"Yes, sir." Pilots often took them on daylight missions to help identify the target, but there was no sense bearding the lion.

"With Mister Steiger's help?"

"Yes, sir. We needed his assistance. What we really

wanted to attack in Hanoi was Communist Party Headquarters, but we couldn't identify it. Even with his help."

"Is that right, Mister Steiger?"

Behind his thick glasses Abe looked even more wide-eyed than usual.

"I didn't hear your answer, Mister Steiger."

"I helped Grafton and Cole plan their raid on Hanoi."

"Thank you, Mister Steiger. I understand this matter came to light when Commander Camparelli examined the order-of-battle charts and the intelligence reports and found, much to his surprise, that they didn't show the SAM sites that shot at Grafton. You helped plan this raid, so why didn't you fake those reports?"

Abe blinked behind his glasses. "I couldn't do that. I knew where the missile sites were that had fired on Lieutenant Grafton. They were already in the system as known sites. I couldn't bring myself to put fake sites into the system."

"Did you tell Grafton that you weren't going to falsify the data?"

"No, sir. I didn't discuss it with him. I didn't have to. Lieutenant Grafton is a damn fine officer, regardless of what he's done wrong, and I knew he'd rather risk being discovered than report false data."

"What would be the danger in listing nonexistent SAM sites?"

"Bombardiers plan their routes to avoid the worst of the ground defenses. I couldn't take the chance that someone might fly near a real site in order to avoid a fake one."

Copeland grunted. "That's the only time you used good judgment in this escapade." He sifted through some notes. To Jake's ears the rustling of papers in the otherwise silent room sounded as loud as rifle shots.

"Well, Mister Grafton. You have an attentive audience here. Perhaps you could take this opportunity to explain why you felt a one-plane war was the way to go."

"Was that really a question, sir?"

"Uh-huh." Copeland gazed at the far bulkhead.

"It seemed like a good idea at the time."

Copeland fixed his eyes on the pilot. "Come, come, Mister Grafton. We're all sitting here with bated breath anxiously awaiting your explanation. Why would a seemingly sane pilot and bombardier get wild hairs up their asses and violate every goddamned targeting regulation the navy has? Not to mention several dozen security breaches and false official statements. C'mon. Shed some light on this mystery."

Jake took a deep breath. "I can only speak for myself. I got tired of risking my ass and my bombardier's, plus a valuable airplane, night after night, bombing targets that were absolutely worthless: suspected truck stops, suspected troop bivouacs, sampan repair yards that had been bombed ten times before, road intersections—you get the idea." He took another deep breath. "I don't know who picks the targets, but I'll bet a year's pay that they don't fly through the flak and risk their precious asses bombing them."

He looked around at the other faces in the room. "My first bombardier, Morgan McPherson, and about fifty thousand other Americans are dead. Not all these men died actually fighting. Some died on flight decks, launching planes. But they were all engaged in one effort. So, what did they all die for? Does anybody know? I don't, but I do know this: McPherson didn't get killed hitting a worthwhile target. He died bombing a bunch of trees. I only wish he and I had been swinging with our best punch against a target that made sense when he caught that bullet."

He leaned forward. "I guess this sane pilot questioned the sanity of those officers and politicians who think that the way to fight a war is to tie one hand behind the fighter's back. Commander Camparelli pointed out to me the other night that America's armed forces are her sole defense against enemies much more powerful than that bunch of communist crackpots in Hanoi will ever be. And America needs her military to obey. America also needs warriors. Yet our military leadership doesn't insist on military objectives that make sense. The lives of our fighting men are being wasted every day. Either we end this war or we fight like we mean it. If we pussy-foot around much longer, America may not have an army or navy to defend her—we won't be able to recruit good people to serve, and we won't be able to get Congress to buy us the weapons to fight with.

"So, Captain, you can tell all those admirals in Washington that Lieutenant Nobody is perfectly willing to obey orders," he nodded at Camparelli. "But I for one hope those gentlemen with stars remember that a naval officer's job is to sail in harm's way, not to work the cocktail-party circuit. Or we won't have a navy worthy of the name for them to lead."

Jake lowered his voice. "Captain, you asked. My opinion is mine alone. I don't speak for anyone but myself. I disobeyed orders and I regret it. Nothing I've said excuses my conduct. I'm ready to accept whatever punishment the navy feels appropriate."

"Is there anything more you want to say?" Copeland asked.

Jake thought a moment. "No, sir."

"All right, lieutenant. You're dismissed."

Jake was sitting on his bunk when Sammy came in. "He kicked us junior folk out soon after you left," Sammy told him and plopped into his desk chair. "You know, I don't think I've ever been as scared in my life as I was at that hearing."

"Yeah," Grafton agreed. "Man, I really screwed up. But I said what I've wanted to say for a long time. Now all I have to do is plead guilty at the court-martial." He reached into his pocket. "Look at this," he said, holding out the ring.

Sammy looked at it as if he had never seen an engagement ring before in his life. "What's this? A fucking engagement ring? At a time like this you're buying a fucking engagement ring?"

"Yep," Grafton said. "I finally figured out what's important. What do you think of it?"

Sammy looked with incredulous eyes from the ring to his roommate and back to the ring. "Did you get this in the ship's store?"

"Yep." Jake smiled happily.

"You've flipped out, man. They're going to hang you from the yardarm and you're buying rocks in the ship's store. I don't believe this." He put his fingertips on his forehead. "How much did you pay?"

"Three hundred bucks."

"Well, it looks like a good one to me, but I don't know a goddamn thing about diamond rings. I don't want to learn, either."

"I haven't asked her yet, but I think she'll say yes. I'm going to ask her the next time I see her." He held the ring under the light.

Sammy watched his friend out of the corner of his eye. He lit a cigarette and smoked it slowly. Finally he said, "Let me see that ring again." He was making appreciative comments when there was a knock on the door.

Camparelli entered. "Take a hike, Sammy, will ya? I want to talk to Jake." The Old Man stood at the end of the bunks. He drew a deep breath. "There probably won't be a court-martial, but there's no guarantee on that." He looked around the stateroom. "You guys keep any booze in this slum?"

Jake spirited a bottle out of the desk safe and poured several fingers in a glass for Camparelli.

"Have a drink yourself. You're one lucky sonuvabitch."

"What happened? I thought keelhauling was gonna be too good for me."

Camparelli took a swallow. "Needs ice. It seems," he said, "that your explanation for doing what you did hit pretty close to home. The feeling in the White House is that we haven't been aggressive enough. In about twenty-four hours the President of the United States will announce a general air offensive against North Vietnam. Nixon's authorizing the use of B-52s against targets in the North. We're going to use every aerial asset we have, except nuclear weapons, to pound the living shit out of North Vietnam. No civilian targets, of course, but we're going to hit everything we can find of any military significance." He shook his head. "The powers that be have decided that we'd look like real idiots having a public court-martial of a twenty-seven-year-old pilot for doing what the President of the United States has just told us all to do."

Jake shook his head. So Copeland had merely been taking names and making everyone in sight sweat to make sure the heresy was rooted out. The leviathan had felt the pinprick, had lashed with annoyance, but had not crushed him.

Camparelli continued. "You understand that what you did was wrong. Dead wrong. The only reason you're being given a second chance is that right now the military has a public relations problem that makes the Mafia's press look good. The left thinks we're criminals and the right thinks we're pansies. There's no point in kicking over a hornet's nest, which is what a public court-martial would be." Camparelli shifted uncomfortably in his chair and seemed to grope for words. "War is our profession. I, for one, am fed up with naval theorists and systems analysts who couldn't fight their way out of a whorehouse."

"May I quote you on that, sir?" Jake said with a nervous laugh.

"You sure as hell may not." The Old Man took another swallow. "We're professional military men. From the CNO right on down, we do as we're told. It can't be any other way and I wouldn't want it any other way. But do we have a duty to disobey under some circumstances? Perhaps we do. But where? And when? You, Grafton, are not equipped to decide."

"I understand."

"You are, however, fit to fly. Cowboy's putting you and Cole on tonight's flight schedule. You can have the tanker I was scheduled for. And I'll have me a night in bed." He raised his voice. "Lundeen, you can come in now."

Sammy, slightly abashed, entered.

Camparelli spoke. "Grafton's flying tonight." Sammy nodded and the skipper motioned for him to sit down. He passed him a glass from the sink and splashed some whiskey in it, then remarked conversationally, "Someone shit up in the forecastle last night."

"Wasn't me, Skipper," Sammy hastily assured him.

Frank Camparelli sipped his drink. "I figured as much. If I thought it was you, Sam, you'd be on your way to the States this very minute wearing your testicles on your collar. But I do think it'd be a good idea if you kept Jake company aboard ship next time we're in port. Make that the next two times in port."

"But I didn't do it," Sammy protested, pouring another liberal shot into the skipper's glass.

"No, but it was your idea. So you're in hack. If anyone asks why, I suggest you tell them that I found liquor in your room. You're supposed to be a naval officer, Sam, not some screwball frat rat." He took another drink. "This is pretty good stuff."

They sat in silence. After a moment Camparelli saw the ring in Jake's hand and reached out for it. He held the diamond to the light, twisting it slowly so he could see it sparkle. Finally he returned it without comment.

The Old Man finished his drink about the same time as his cigarette. He stubbed out the butt and rinsed the glass in the sink. He paused before opening the door. "Watch your ass out there, Jake. That girl will want you in one piece." The door closed with a soft click.

TWENTY-THREE

The press in the States called it the Christmas Offensive. Massive B-52 formations thundered over North Vietnam, aiming to bomb the negotiators back to the Paris peace talks. At home in America there were widespread protests and, on some college campuses, riots. In the waning days of '72, Jake Grafton read about the bombing and the protests in newsmagazines and the Chicago *Tribune,* which, as a serviceman in the war zone, he received free. When the bundled papers arrived each week Jake would open them, arrange them in order, and read each one closely.

To Jake it seemed that America would tear itself apart before the North became reasonable at the bargaining table. While he had no doubt that the communist regime could not endure an all-out, extended aerial assault, he did wonder how long the U.S. government would assert its will in the face of mounting protests. The question of whose will would break first was unanswerable. To escape futile speculation, Jake turned to the advertisements celebrating the bounty of an American Christmas. The *Tribune*'s editorials might denounce the commercialism of the holiday, but the pilot on the other side of the world reveled in the images of happy people fulfilling their hearts' desires by buying clothes, cars, perfume, and expensive liquor. Somewhere in the world, as the photographs of beautiful women and men of distinction in front of holiday fireplaces seemed to say, there was warmth and stability.

The night missions of the squadron had changed. Rockeyes that cost over five thousand dollars each were loaded sixteen to a plane and dropped on SAM sites minutes before the B-52s came within range. For Jake the change in American policy was a stroke of luck. It had meant that he could continue to fly. Most of the time he flew bombers, but occasionally he and Tiger flew the A-6B to protect the B-52s from enemy missiles. Despite the efforts to foil the enemy missile defenses, Jake and Tiger witnessed the deaths of some of the great planes in the night skies over North Vietnam. The bombers, trailing fire, would veer out of the formation, yellow specks against the black night. The B-52 pilots would calmly report their disaster on the radio, and then the six-man crew, or those men still alive after the missile strike, would jump and fall the miles through the intense cold of inner space while their plane made its fiery plunge.

Jake had received several letters from Callie since their time together in Cubi, but he was impatient for a reply to his letter telling her of the hearing and its outcome. The evening after Christmas he found a pale yellow envelope in his mailbox. He smiled as he waved the letter under his nose and caught the scent of lilacs. To savor the pleasure of reading her letter, he decided to open it back in his stateroom. He turned to leave the ready room when New Guy called to him.

"Expecting good news, Jake? You look like the cat that swallowed the canary."

Grafton let his grin widen. "How's your life going, New?"

"Oh, pretty good. How about relieving me for a half hour or so while I get a hamburger?"

"Well, okay." Jake took the chair at the duty officer's desk that New vacated. "What's happening?" he asked, wondering if he'd have time to catch some glimpses at Callie's letter.

"We just launched two bombers on the last cycle of the day, which went at 2230. The go tanker went down on the cat and they shot the spare."

Jake examined the flight schedule. Rabbit Wilson and Fred Mogollon had downed the tanker on the catapult.

"Maintenance Control will call you in just a minute with the side-number of the roundup tanker for the last recovery," New continued. "The brief should start in ten minutes or so. Skipper's in his stateroom." The roundup tanker would sit on deck manned and ready during the last recovery in case extra fuel was needed aloft.

"Okay. Go eat. I gotcha covered."

Ferdinand Magellan entered the ready room, picked up the maintenance forms, and came over to the duty officer's desk. Pulling up a chair, he reached into a box of Christmas candy New's wife had sent him and pushed the box toward Jake.

"What happened to your plane?" Jake asked, his mouth full. He checked the flight schedule. "Five twenty-two?"

"X.O. downed it right on the cat. Said something was wrong with the port engine. He ran it up to full power about four times while the cat officer went bananas, then he refused to go. So they taxied us off and shot Snake Jones and Dick Clark instead."

"Where did they have it spotted when you manned up?"

"On cat two. We sat there and stared at the black hole."

"Dark out there?"

"Blacker than a black cat in a coal bin at midnight on a moonless night. Blacker than Hitler's heart. Blacker than—"

"So how do you like the fleet, Ferd?" Grafton interrupted as Wilson walked in.

"I'm eating this shit with a spoon," the BN said and completed his paperwork in silence while Jake pored over the flight schedule.

The commander sat in his chair just behind the duty officer's. "We gotta do better keeping these tankers up," Wilson remarked. "What other gripes you writing up, Mogollon?" Ferd mentioned two minor problems and Rabbit told him, "Well, take them over to Maintenance Control and give them to the Chief. I just motivated him in detail about that engine. So there's no excuse if they can't fix it."

"Yessir." The bombardier left, taking the forms with him.

The telephone rang. The chief in Maintenance Control told Jake, "We're still working on the roundup tanker. Call you back in a bit."

"Okay, Chief." Jake annotated the flight schedule as the video tape of the last recovery began playing on the television.

"So how's every little thing with you, Grafton, after the miracle of the hearing?" Wilson asked Jake's back.

"Fine, sir," Jake said over his shoulder.

"You must have an uncle who's a senator. It's a damn good thing for you that the decision wasn't up to me. I know a hot dog when I see one."

Jake swiveled the chair and looked the commander in the face. "That's the second time you've called me that. I don't like it."

"Oh, you don't, eh? You're all balls, Grafton, but you don't have enough brains to load a fly up to max gross weight. That's a hot dog in my book. What would you call it?"

"At least I've got some balls."

"Just what do you mean by that?" Wilson's eyes narrowed and he flushed slightly.

Jake pursed his lips as he considered just how far he could go. "I've heard that some of the men call you Rabbit. Behind your back, of course. I don't think they're referring to your breeding habits, Rabbit."

"You sonuvabitch! I'm a commander! No weenie in railroad tracks makes a crack like that to me." Wilson's face was very red as he sprang to his feet. "No goddamn body talks to me like that." He jutted out his chin. "You think you're so shit hot. I'm sick to death of all-balls assholes like you."

The telephone rang. Jake reached for it without taking his eyes off the man standing over him with his fists clenched. "Lieutenant Grafton." He was having trouble with his voice.

"This is Joe Wagner. Where's the Skipper?"

"In his stateroom."

"I just completed a full power turn-up of Five Two Two. There's nothing wrong with that airplane's engines. Put it on the schedule as the roundup tanker."

"Aye aye, sir." Jake hung up and looked at the commander. "By the way, twenty-two is up again."

"What?" Wilson said in disbelief. "Shit! I just downed that plane. Who was that on the phone?"

"Joe Wagner," said Jake calmly. "He says it's okay."

"We'll see about that. I'll take care of *you* later." As Wilson strode quickly out of the room, he mumbled, "Goddamned hot dog."

Jake sat at the desk and breathed deeply. Overhead, on the television monitor, landing after landing flickered silently across the screen. The recently landed air crews began filtering into the ready room. New returned from the wardroom just as the phone rang again. "Ready four, Lieutenant Grafton, sir."

"Is the X.O. there?" It was Camparelli.

"No, sir. I think he may be over in Maintenance Control looking for Joe Wagner."

"Joe's down here in my room. Send someone to find Commander Wilson and ask him to come down. I want to see him." The skipper hung up.

"New, go find the X.O. He's probably over in Maintenance Control raising hell." Jake tried in vain to keep the satisfaction out of his voice. "Tell him the Skipper wants to see him in his stateroom."

When New Guy returned, Jake left for his room. Now, at last, he could read Callie's letter. He no sooner had settled down at his desk with her letter in his hand than the phone rang.

"Wanna hear a hot one?" Sammy chortled. "Rabbit Wilson's not flying anymore. He's off flight status."

"How off is 'off'?"

"Off like in no more. Like in cut off, chopped off, whacked off. We're talking amputation."

"You don't say?"

"The word is he got cold feet once too often."

Jake cleared his throat. "Pretty tough for him," he managed.

"Breaks my fucking heart," Sammy snorted and hung up.

The pilot put the telephone back on its cradle and laughed aloud. He laughed until tears came to his eyes.

Finally, he unfolded the pages of Callie's letter. She had enclosed a photograph, which he held under the light. She stood on Victoria Peak, with the mountains of the New Territories forming a blurry backdrop. It was just a photo of an attractive woman in a simple summer dress the color of wheat—an unremarkable picture really—but to Jake every detail of it held deep interest. He looked at her lips, which were curved up in a smile, and remembered how she looked just before he had last kissed her.

He shook his head. He slipped the photo behind the pages and began reading. "Dear Jake," she wrote, "I'm very happy to hear that everything has turned out so well. That sand dollar I gave you in Cubi for luck must be pretty potent magic!" She congratulated him on his return to flight status, and he was pleased she understood. A few sentences later, he read, "I know how important flying is to you and I was afraid that if you were unable to fly again, you would feel as though a large part of you, perhaps the vital part, had died."

He thought about that there in the sanctuary of his stateroom, about flying being vital to him. As a boy, he had found in flying a freedom and heady excitement that life had otherwise lacked. But how did he feel about it now, when flying meant waiting to outmaneuver SAMs or turning on knife-edge to slice through a curtain of tracers? He realized that only when the SAMs and tracers were reaching for him, only when he was naked and running flat out, did he feel fully alive. He had become addicted to the adrenaline high of taunting death.

He examined Callie's picture again, then read on. "I have looked all my life for a man who doesn't wear a mask, for a man who truly is what he appears to be, for someone who knows what he is about and engages in no pretenses. I think I've found him."

He finished the letter and folded it into the envelope. He propped up the photo on his desk. He remembered the sand dollar in the left sleeve pocket of his flight suit and found it still intact, which was fortunate as it was so delicate. After wrapping it in toilet paper, he placed it in the envelope with the letter. Then he put the envelope in his desk safe.

Removing the ring from its blue box, he held the

diamond under the lamp. Points of colored light played against the wall. Maybe it's not so crazy after all, he thought. He put the engagement ring in the flight suit pocket where the sand dollar had been and zipped it closed.

On December 28 Jake and Tiger learned they were scheduled for their fifth SAM-suppression mission; this time the target was on the northern edge of Hanoi.

"Maybe our best route is to go all the way around the city," Tiger suggested.

Jake examined the wall chart. Concentrations of flak and SAMs were shown by color-coded pinheads. Hanoi was a pin cushion. Well, he and Cole had been there before. He came back to the table where Tiger had laid out his charts. "Uh-huh," he said. Then he asked, "When will the big mothers be along?"

"The B-52s roll in about ten minutes after our drop time of 1933."

Jake inspected the aerial photos of the SAM site, which Steiger had collected. They revealed the classic tactical deployment of the SA-2 surface-to-air missile system: six missiles on their trailer launchers were arranged in a circle around a semitrailer with a radar antenna. The launchers sat in indentations gouged in the earth, so that if a missile was destroyed or blew up on the launcher, the blast would be deflected away from the other missiles and the semitrailer with the electronic control equipment. Off to one side Jake could make out two parked tractors. He had seen photos of hundreds of sites that looked just like this. He checked the date; the photos were more than eighteen months old.

There was a blur in the upper-right corner. He knew it was a gun shooting at the Vigilante that had taken the picture.

He tossed the photos back on the table and examined

the route Tiger had marked out. The bombardier planned to coast-in just south of the lighthouse at the entrance of Haiphong harbor, proceed straight to an island in the river on the northern edge of Hanoi, and turn to the attack heading. After bombing, they would move left in a sweeping turn that would let them circumnavigate the city and would spit them out on the southeast side, headed for the ocean and safety. The pilot studied a sectional chart that showed in detail the terrain around the island, tonight's Initial Point, and around the target. Maybe there would be enough light to see the rivers. Like hell!

"Another good navy deal," he said and patted his bombardier on the shoulder. He paused again at the flak chart, then went off to the wardroom for a cup of coffee before the brief.

The Augies had a tanker hop and were in the locker room when Jake and Tiger entered. Little Augie had not exchanged a word with Jake since he had returned from Cubi. Now he spoke. "Where're you headed tonight?"

Grafton told him but didn't bother to look at the diminutive pilot. Little Augie lingered, watching Jake inspect the cartridges for his .357 Magnum and then carefully load it. Jake had returned his issue .38 to supply long ago so he could carry this more powerful weapon.

"If you get bagged tonight, can I have your stereo?"

Jake grinned. Apparently whatever sins Little Augie thought him guilty of were forgiven. "If you can find it," Jake told him. Unlike almost everyone else, he had not bought an expensive Japanese sound system at the Cubi Point Exchange. Little punched him on the shoulder and walked out of the locker room.

Jake put the contents of his pockets, including his wallet, onto the top shelf of the locker. He placed a folded cardcase, which contained a green navy ID card, a Geneva convention card, and a twenty-dollar bill, in one of the big chest pockets of his flight suit. Like most airmen, he carried several thousand dollars worth of small, navy-issue gold wafers in his survival vest in case he had to barter with or bribe local people, but he brought nothing else of monetary or personal value. Except the ring. This he had in the left sleeve pocket of the flight suit where he had kept the sand dollar.

Dressed, with helmet bag in hand, he paused before closing his locker. He examined its contents, as he had done on every mission before. Morbidly, he knew that if he were shot down or killed, Sammy Lundeen would have the job of clearing out these little pieces of his life. Well, he had logged the same number of landings as takeoffs, so far. He felt for the ring, assured himself the pocket was completely zipped, then slammed the locker door and spun the combination lock.

They launched at twilight. Jake took the Intruder to 20,000 feet and cruised leisurely up the Gulf. Spectacular reds and oranges and yellows, afterglow of the setting sun, filtered through the clouds that lay over the mountains in Laos. Deep blues and purples began to vanquish the lingering gold. He had witnessed many sunsets and sunrises from the sky, but the pageant never failed to move him. Someday he would share a sunset aloft with Callie.

"The system looks real good," Tiger announced. Jake engaged the autopilot. The steady beep of a search radar was clearly audible now. "Commie sonsuvbitches have found us," Tiger muttered.

A falling star caught Jake's eye. What could he wish for? To survive? To get back to Callie safely? He also wished for more stars, and as the minutes passed his wish was granted.

"I've got an update on the lighthouse." The lighthouse on the Do Son peninsula, which jutted out into the mouth of Haiphong harbor, had not been illuminated for years. "We have six minutes to kill. How about a six-minute turn to the right?"

Jake nudged the stick over, then released it. The autopilot held the warplane at the selected angle-of-bank. "You're pretty talkative tonight," he told the bombardier.

"Checklist," Tiger prompted. Together they set the switches on the armament panel, double-checked the ECM panels, and watched the compass and clock hands rotate. As they completed their turn, Tiger checked their position again. The steering on the VDI in front of the pilot swung to the coast-in point. Jake caught Tiger's eye for a second, then turned the autopilot off. When they had descended a thousand feet, Jake turned off the exterior lights, IFF, and TACAN. "Devil Five Oh Oh, strangling parrot."

"Black Eagle copies, Five Double-nuts."

The plane descended toward the sea. The beeps of the enemy radar sounded closer together now. The operator was in a sector search, painting them repeatedly, measuring their course and speed. Jake leveled off at 500 feet and allowed the speed to bleed off to 420 knots. "Three miles to coast-in," Tiger informed him. The enemy radar was back on area sweep. Perhaps their plane had faded in radar return from the sea.

Jake blinked the perspiration from his eyes and looked ahead for the silver ribbon of sand that divided the land and sea. A mile out, he saw it and the thin, wavering lines of breakers washing ashore. He thought of Callie on the beach.

"Black Eagle, Devil Five Oh Oh is feet dry."

"Roger Five Oh Oh. Feet dry at 1919." Fourteen minutes to the target.

The starlight reflected off the paddies and wide creeks flowing to meet the sea. No flak came up at them yet. The search radar still beeped, about once every twelve seconds, but at 400 feet over the table-flat delta they were invisible in ground return.

From the left the first flak of the night shot out in their direction. Jake concentrated on maintaining altitude and heading.

Tiger called the IP; Jake flipped on the master arm switch and advanced the throttles to the stops as he laid the plane into the turn. Halfway through the heading change a row of guns erupted ahead. The pilot saw the streams of tracer rise and reacted instinctively, rolling the plane almost ninety degrees to squeeze it through an empty space between the tracers. They were almost on the outskirts of Hanoi.

As he entered the gap another gun opened up.

Horrified, Jake momentarily froze as the molten finger of death reached for him. The Intruder shuddered from the blows; then, suddenly, it was through the flak into the dark void beyond. It was all over in less than a heartbeat.

As Jake rolled the wings level, the brilliant red of the left engine fire-warning light filled the cockpit. A look in the rear-view mirror showed no visible fire yet. But the exhaust gas temperature on the sick engine had risen to more than 700 degrees centigrade, and the RPM had dropped by more than ten percent. Jake felt the warplane shimmy through his seat, the floor, the throttles, and the stick. The bird was badly hurt. Quickly he shut off the flow of fuel to the left engine.

The bombardier leaned away from the scope hood and peered at the engine instruments in front of Jake's left knee. "How bad is it?" The fire-warning light reflected off his helmet visor.

"Left engine's gone. Do you have the target?"

Tiger put his face back to the scope hood. "Come left ten degrees."

Jake centered the steering. He glanced at the mileage readout between his knees. Eight more miles to go. The attack light lit up on the VDI, and Jake squeezed the commit trigger. As the plane slowed to only 350 knots the left generator dropped off the line. With only one generator they would have the radar and computer but not the ECM. Jake's earphones were silent, and it wasn't because the gomers had shut down for the night. All the console lights on the bombardier's panels were now dark.

Those lucky fuckers! Smacked us with a cheap shot!

The hydraulic gauges captured Jake's eyes. One of the two hydraulic systems showed zero pressure. And only one of the pumps in the other system was still working. Damn. From four pumps to one, just like that.

He looked at the computer steering symbol. Almost centered. The fire-warning light was so brilliant that he reached to cover it with his hand, but then it went out. The cockpit was dark again.

"Three more miles," Tiger called.

More flak ripped the night. Jake tried to ignore it, to concentrate on flying a perfect run. Something ahead caught his eye.

A blazing streak of pure white fire hurtled toward them. Quicker than thought Jake pulled back the stick, and the enemy missile tore by. God, too close! Jake tweaked the nose of the Intruder, pointing it straight at the offending missile launcher.

"I've got the radar van," Cole advised.

Jake watched the release marker descend the VDI. He savagely mashed the pickle to back up the computer-derived release signal.

The bombs did not release.

Jake pressed the pickle button again and again. No release.

He cycled the master armament switch, selected a manual release, and punched the pickle button. Nothing.

Heavy flak ahead. "Can you find it again?" he demanded of Cole.

"Yeah."

Jake lowered the left wing and turned south. This time he planned on jettisoning the bomb racks with the emergency release. The Rockeyes would not spread out but would remain in their cases, attached to the racks. There'd be hell to pay when they exploded all together. "We're not whipped yet," he said to Cole. "Better tell 'em we're in trouble."

The bombardier got on the radio as they turned.

More fire from heavy weapons rippled through the air, but not too close. Jake nursed the plane through the turn, frequently checking the pressure gauge for the lone hydraulic pump. Because the plane's controls were actuated by hydraulic pressure, a violent jerk on the stick could overload the pump and leave the pilot dependent on the electrically driven backup pump, which had a very limited output. The backup pump was working—the BACKUP HYD light was lit on the annunciator panel—but it would only give him enough pressure to operate the stabilator and rudder at reduced effectiveness. The tightrope was fraying.

"What type weapon do you want selected?" Dropping the racks was Jake's only choice. Of the more than fifty preprogrammed options available to tell the computer about the ballistic trajectory of the weapons, none of the options fit the dropping of the entire bomb rack. So Cole had asked the crucial question.

"What do you think?" asked Jake.

"The racks will go down about like a retarded Snake, maybe a little flatter," said Cole. "We'll use that, and I'll type in a correction."

The pilot checked the airspeed indicator. Steady at

325 knots. Very slow, but they would pick up thirty knots or so when they dropped the weapons.

Fireballs tore around them. Something smashed into a wing and the stick wiggled hard in Jake's fist. He shot a glance at the left wing. All okay. But on the right wing fuel was erupting through two holes and being blasted back into the slipstream.

Oh, Jesus! Sweet Jesus, help us get out of this alive.

"I've got the target and we're in attack," Tiger said. The last spurts of the right-wing fuel siphoned away. There was still a ton in the left wing but both wings drained through a common pump, which needed fuel from both wings to be effective. Jake had no choice. He opened the wing dumps and let the unusable fuel pour into the slipstream. They still had nine thousand pounds internal, and if they could make it to the tanker in the Gulf they'd have a chance.

"Two miles." The pilot readied his finger over the emergency jettison button. The release marker was marching down.

"Gimme one second's warning," he reminded Tiger. The circuit had a safety feature that required the button be held at least a second to prevent inadvertent jettisoning.

"Now!"

Jake depressed the button and held it. Whump! He slammed the stick over and turned left hard. The hydraulic pressure and the airspeed sagged, but he had to escape the impact area or they would be caught in the blast. The bombs exploded. A blinding light flashed in the mirrors, and the concussion buffeted, but did not harm, the plane. The Intruder was headed south over the city.

Tiger keyed his radio mike and spoke to the Black Eagle controller, safe and snug in his E-2 over the Gulf. "Five Double-nuts is off target and coming out."

"Roger that. Are you declaring an emergency?"

"Affirmative. We're going to need a tanker as soon as we're feet wet."

Jake selected the main internal tank on the fuel gauge and dodged flak while he waited for the needle to register the correct amount.

My God! Only five thousand pounds left. The tank must be spewing the stuff out. There won't be enough fuel to make it even to the tanker. We're going to have to eject! But where? Just to make it out of North Vietnam would be tricky.

Tracers rose ahead in shimmering curtains of fire. Now they were over Hanoi, and the flak was in front and on all sides. The black shapes of rooftops and trees stood out clearly in the starlight and the eerie glow of the tracers. Jake descended until he was skimming the rooftops. Hell, just to make it out of Hanoi would be a trick and a half.

At this height, in this light, they were visible to every man, woman, and child with a weapon. He felt the thumps of small-arms bullets penetrating the side of the aircraft. The hounds had the fox nearly at bay.

As he pointed out the fuel indicator to Cole a stream of fire came from the right and headed straight for the windshield. Jake porpoised up and over the stream and both men flinched, a useless reflex. They were lucky. Thumps in the tail only.

"What's your position?" someone asked on the radio.

"Right over Hanoi," Grafton shouted. Illuminated by tracers, the city looked like an open door into hell. Every building seemed to have a coven of antiaircraft guns mounted on it.

"The radio is dead," Tiger said.

More thumps from something hitting the plane. The annunciator panel, normally dark, glowed with yellow lights. Left generator gone, left speed drive out, hydraulic pumps, fuel filter. . . . Why the fuel filter? Jake didn't have time to think about it. Yellow fireballs wound out at them and something smashed against the wings.

The bird was dying. Jake glanced at Tiger. "You can jump ship now if you want—"

"Keep rolling the dice," Tiger said.

Jake swung into a hard right turn and spoke into the dead radio. "Devil Five Oh Oh's turning west. We're going to Laos."

He concentrated on keeping the nose up and flying just above the buildings. The gunners could see the plane in this light, so he needed to be as low as possible to make their aiming more difficult. On the chance that the transmissions might be heard, the bombardier continued to report their intentions over the radio.

Ahead, to the left, a gunner opened up with a long continuous burst. The tracers came in a flat arc. Jake pulled up slightly and the shells streaked underneath. But the gunner corrected. The pilot retarded the single throttle momentarily and the plane decelerated, causing the stream of tracers to pass ahead of them. Jake shoved the throttle back to the stops and dived as low as he dared. The tracers seemed to correct in slow motion. "You'll burn the fucking barrel up," he screamed at the enemy gunner. Ahead loomed a building taller than its neighbors. The plane banked around the right side and the shells slammed into the building.

Flashes. White flashes off to the right. Jake narrowed his eyes in that direction. Trip-hammer flashes, a dozen a second, marched across the city.

"B-52 raid," Tiger whispered in awe.

The city lay naked in the pulsating light of the bombs. The Intruder, rocked by concussion waves, hung suspended in the popping-light universe of flashing bombs and white-hot fireballs. For almost a minute the unseen B-52s scourged the city. The A-6 shot into the darkness over the rice paddies. In the rear-view mirror, Jake saw fires burning and the streaks of flak still rising.

"Sweet Jesus," Tiger Cole said.

"We're gonna make it, man," Jake said, his voice cracking.

The fuel gauge showed four thousand pounds. Occasional flashes of burp guns lit the night—pinpricks after what they'd been through. Grafton floated the plane up to almost 500 feet on the radar altimeter. The barometric altimeter was frozen.

"Come right five degrees," Tiger said. "The computer quit a while back but the radar still works. We're coming into the mouth of a valley, and I'll steer us up it."

The land was rising. Jake nudged the plane up to hold at 500 feet above the ground. The darkness outside the plane was complete. They flew on, Tiger ordering minor heading changes.

The left fire-warning light came on again. It was distractingly bright, so Jake smashed it with his flashlight. He watched the fuel indicator. Thirty-two hundred pounds. They topped the crest of the valley and continued to climb. In a moment they went beyond the maximum altitude of the radar altimeter, and it stopped working, as it was designed to do.

"Swing left ten and hold that course."

Tiger turned the radio transmitter to Guard, an emergency frequency that was always monitored. These calls went out over a separate transmitter, so maybe they were being heard by someone even though the crew's earphones remained silent. Jake's eyes were itching. He loosened his oxygen mask and sniffed the cockpit air. Something burning. He turned off the air-conditioning switch. The smell hung in the cockpit. He replaced his mask and cinched it tight.

Jake could actually see the needle on the fuel indicator dropping. Where was that fuel going? It had to be spraying into the left engine bay through the holes smashed by the flak shells. If it ignites, we'll be strumming harps with Corey Ford and the Boxman. Those engine burner cans and the tailpipe have to be still hot enough to ignite that fuel. He rechecked the engine/fuel master switch to ensure that no electrical power was reaching the burner-can igniters. The switch was off, but he didn't remember toggling it, although if he hadn't they probably would be dead by now.

Twenty-three hundred pounds on the dial. Almost three hundred pounds a minute was disappearing, partly into the right engine and partly into the air. Jake calculated that was eighteen thousand pounds an hour. They had eight more minutes, maybe another fifty miles.

Every mile they traveled increased their chances of being rescued instead of captured. The Air Force SAR teams could pick them up in Laos, but North Vietnam was too heavily defended for a helicopter to survive.

Come on, baby! Don't fail us now.

Eighteen hundred pounds left. His gut was tied in a knot and he had trouble thinking about their dilemma. "Have you ever jumped before?" he asked Tiger Cole.

"Yep, and I broke my leg."

The terror of every combat pilot had finally become real for them. They would have to eject into enemy territory and survive on their wits and what little equipment they carried in their survival vests. Failure to be rescued meant death or imprisonment in a tiny cell. Capture itself was a living death.

Twelve hundred pounds. The low-fuel warning light was lit.

A faint glow in the clouds caught his attention. He adjusted the mirror. A yellow tongue of flame flickered under the left wing.

"We're on fire," he shouted. They would have to eject *now*.

"Not yet," Cole said and put his left arm across the pilot's chest. "Maybe a few more miles."

"Burning jets have a nasty habit of exploding, you know," said Jake. In his mind he could see the line in the operating manual for the A-6 Intruder: "At the first sign of visible fire, eject."

The nose of the airplane dipped. He tugged the stick aft, but the nose continued down. There was no pressure at all on the hydraulic gauges. The fire had melted the hydraulic lines.

Tiger stopped talking on the radio and looked at Jake.

Slowly, slowly, the nose started back up, but the plane rolled left. Jake waggled the stick and rudder. No response. Devil 500 was finished.

The two men looked into each other's eyes.

Tiger Cole reached up with both hands, grasped the primary ejection handle, and pulled it down over his head in a swift, clean motion. Instantly he was gone in a thunderclap of noise, wind, and plexiglas.

One last time, out of habit, Jake's eyes swept the instrument panel, then he pulled the alternate firing handle between his legs. In the fraction of a second before the ejection seat smashed its way upward through the plexiglas, the image of the panel and the yellow fire reflected in the mirror indelibly seared his memory.

Something was hammering at his body, pounding every inch of his chest, arms, legs, and neck. Even as he realized it had to be drops of rain, a tremendous jolt tore at his crotch as his parachute opened.

After the deafening rush of wind on ejection there was silence. He could not see a thing. In a near panic, he groped above him for the parachute risers. The straps rising from his shoulders were firm as steel cables. Reassured, he tried to think.

Why was he blind? He wasn't; there simply wasn't enough light to see by. Firmly grasping the nylon straps on each side of his neck, he let the seconds tick by. His ears momentarily picked up the faint whine of a jet engine.

The oxygen mask! If he were knocked out on landing and still had it on, he would suffocate when the oxygen in the seat pan ran out. He had to get rid of it. With his right hand he fumbled for the catches that held the mask to his helmet. He had no dexterity, and terror threatened to overwhelm him. He fought down the killing panic and fingered the place where the catches had to be. He found them and disconnected the mask and threw it out into the darkness. Through it all, he kept a death grip on the left riser.

Again using his right hand, he felt for the quick-release fittings on the lap belt. He would have no need for the seat pan, which was for landing in water. He unlatched the right-hand fitting and was aware of the weight shifting on the back of his thighs. Carefully changing hands on the risers, he struggled with the left fitting. Finally the weight on his legs vanished as the seat pan fell away. His right hand automatically seized the right riser again.

He heard the dull boom of a distant explosion. His airplane, probably. The end of Devil 500.

A faint breeze fanned his face. Somewhere below, the jungle waited. When will it come up? The darkness was total. He thought of his flashlight in the survival vest, but he didn't want to risk losing it on landing.

The pounding of his heart and the gentle kiss of the wind and rain and the reassuring tautness of the riser straps were the only sensory stimuli in the dark silence.

He began to think. Would he land in trees or a paddy or a rock-strewn creek? Would he be dashed against a cliff? He hooked his legs together to protect his crotch and placed his left hand on his right shoulder and his right hand on his left, then lowered his face into the crook of his elbows. Now to wait.

His body was tense, awaiting the impact. Relax, he told himself. No, stay tense. Keep those legs together and protect the family jewels.

Something tore at his legs, then smashed into his body. He was pummeled by a series of rapid, rock-hard blows, and he felt his legs become separated and a fire of agony ripped up his left side. He was tumbling and his arms were flailing, searching for the risers that were no longer there. He took bullwhip lashes across the lower part of his face. Then he lost consciousness.

TWENTY-FOUR

Major Frank Allen sat in the cockpit of an A-1 Skyraider over Laos. An airborne flight controller was working with the FACs to find Allen a target worthy of his ordnance. He and his wingman, a thousand feet below, had been holding for nearly an hour when the controller advised them of a downed aircraft, a navy A-6 Intruder, call sign Devil Five Oh Oh. Allen, after acknowledging the information, checked his fuel and noted the time on his kneeboard pad.

"Nomad One Seven, we're going to send you up that way to see if you can make radio contact. Standby," the controller said.

"Roger, Nomad One Seven."

The controller reported the suspected area of the crash, and Allen scanned his chart. When the aircraft had proceeded around its holding circle and was headed in the proper direction, Allen leveled the wings and adjusted the throttle and the fuel-mixture knob. The big piston engine of the A-1 responded smoothly and the needle on the airspeed indicator slid up to 140 knots. His wingman swung into trail. Allen plotted the coordinates he had been given for the crash and measured the distance—about an hour's flying time. He refined his heading and flipped the second radio to the Guard channel and, turning up the volume and toning down the squelch, he transmitted: "Devil Five Oh Oh, Devil Five Oh Oh, this is Nomad One Seven on Guard, over."

Silence. A number of transmissions failed to bring any response, and he quit trying. The stars illuminated the top of the overcast several thousand feet below him. He thought about the two American airmen on the ground, who were fighting for their survival. He hoped that one of them was not his old University of Texas classmate, Cowboy Parker.

The Pathet Lao guerrillas often killed their prisoners at capture rather than bother to transport and feed them. But if these two men were caught by North Vietnamese Army regulars, who patrolled the Ho Chi Minh Trail, they might be taken to Hanoi to be imprisoned with the other POWs. Or they might just as easily be tied to a tree and skinned alive. As he considered the prospects of a flier in the jungle below, Frank Allen scanned his gauges and listened carefully to the beat of his engine, just as he had on more than two hundred missions.

The engine sounded healthy. His thoughts soon turned to his planned rotation date in three weeks. Should he go back to the States or extend for another tour? He was still undecided. He often mulled over the question these days at odd moments.

The clouds would cause trouble in the morning when it came time to pull the navy fliers out of the jungle. If only the clouds would break up, or lift enough for planes and choppers to work.

He turned up the volume on the secondary radio and flew on.

* * *

Jake Grafton stood alone in a large room, the walls of which were veiled in mist. Two wooden coffins yawned on the unvarnished floor. He walked toward them, his steps echoing, until he could see down into them. Tiger Cole lay in one but the other was empty. Instead of red silk and satin, the empty coffin was lined with earth and decomposing leaves. He turned away in revulsion only to find a crowd advancing toward him, shoulder to shoulder. Businessmen in suits and college students with long hair and little yellow men in black pajamas—all closing in on him. He felt hands lifting him, and he felt himself spiraling down into the darkness.

Rain striking his face awakened him. He was disoriented and unable to move. Nausea came over him in waves. He closed his mouth and tried to breath, but his nose was clogged. He opened his mouth again and gulped the air and rain. His head, he realized, was *below* his legs. For what seemed like a long time, he hung in the darkness, gathering his strength.

He pawed around and his right hand brushed something. Something soft but firm. Dirt and leaves. He discovered that he was hanging only a foot or so from the ground, and the panic subsided. Gritting his teeth against a pain in his side, he fumbled in the darkness for the harness-release fittings. They were always on his chest, just below the collarbones. But he could not find them and, infuriated and sick with fear and pain, he tore off his gloves, frantically feeling everywhere, trying to find the familiar metal shapes. Frustration bred panic and he stopped squirming just before it overwhelmed him.

Maybe the fittings had moved as he had twisted around inside the harness. He explored slowly. He found the left catch over his shoulder. It opened readily, freeing his head and left shoulder. Now that he knew where to feel, he located the right one easily, and his body slumped down until he was partly on the ground. His legs, though, were still entangled above his head.

He needed his flashlight. He forced himself to remember where he had stowed his pencil flash, then he worked methodically to retrieve it. The beam pierced the darkness. His eyes took several seconds to focus, and he saw that his legs were caught in shroud lines that extended upward into the trees.

Something wet was running into his mouth. It tasted coppery. Blood? He patted his face with his hand, then shone the beam on his hand. It was bright red. He picked pieces of his helmet's plexiglas visor out of his face. When he touched his nose pain shot through him. Broken.

A minute passed before he worked up enough nerve to move again. He dug out the parachute shroud cutter from a vest pocket and slashed at the nylon lines around his legs. There were many lines. He paused to rest and swung the light around. Dark foliage in every direction.

Cursing silently, he resumed slashing at the tangled white cords that trapped him like a fly in a spider's web. Pain in his left side restricted his movements. More blood flowed into his mouth, and he spat it out. He was wet with a mixture of rain, sweat, vomit, and bloody spittle. His right leg finally came free. His body slipped again, and now he lay on the ground with one leg still caught.

The closeness of freedom galvanized him. He tore at the remaining cords with the cutter. At last, his left leg also came free with a jolt of pain that seared him.

He groaned, the first sound that had escaped from him. When the pain lessened, he pushed himself into a sitting position and examined his left leg carefully with the penlight. At his knee, which his G-suit didn't cover, his flight suit was ripped, and blood covered his knee and the ragged edges of the cloth. The joint was swollen, but he could still bend it.

He cleaned the dirt and leaves from the neck of his flight suit, then took off his helmet. The visor was shattered. He ran his fingers through his hair, which was sticky and stiff.

The radios! He reached into the front pocket of his survival vest and pulled out one of the two radios he carried. With the penlight, he inspected it. It looked undamaged. He turned on the emergency beacon, which would allow someone searching for him to home in on him. Then he silenced the beacon, put the device to transmit/receive, and adjusted the volume.

"Tiger, this is Jake." No answer. He tried several more times at minute intervals and finally received a response.

"Hey, Jake." The voice, though weak, filled the pilot with elation.

"Where are you?"

"How the hell would I know?"

"I'm okay. You okay?"

The answering voice was tired and faint. "Not really. I can't get out of my chute."

Shit!

"I'm out of mine. I'll find you. Just hang tough until I get there."

"I ain't going anyplace."

Jake lowered the radio and flashed the penlight around: trees and underbrush in every direction. Still sitting, he found one of his plastic baby bottles and drained it, pausing only once for air. The water was warm, but it cleaned out the salty, coppery taste in his mouth. He was still thirsty, but he would hold the other bottle until later when he would be thirstier still. Capping the empty bottle, he slipped it back in his vest.

"Devil Five Oh Oh, Devil Five Oh Oh, how do you read, over?"

Jake's heart leapt and he struggled with the radio. "Devil Five Oh Oh Alpha reads you loud and clear, over."

"Devil, this is Nomad One Seven. Give me thirty seconds of beeper, over."

"Roger beeper." Jake turned the beacon feature of the radio on and held the radio so that the little antenna pointed straight up. Now the Nomad pilot could home in on the beacon with his automatic-direction-finding, or ADF, equipment. After thirty seconds, Jake switched back to voice. "Nomad, Devil Five Oh Oh Alpha, did you copy, over?"

"Roger, we got your beeper. Identify yourself, over."

"Jacob Lee Grafton, lieutenant, seven three five niner niner four."

"Copy. Wait."

Jake sat in the darkness and let hope and elation run through him. We've been found already! We'll be rescued!

"Devil, Nomad. Have you two joined up and are you hurt?"

"Negative join-up and pilot has minor injuries. Tiger, are you hurt, over?"

Silence, which the rescue pilot eventually broke. "Copy negative join-up and pilot minor injuries."

"My bombardier is hung up," Jake explained.

"Okay, Devil Alpha. Keep the faith. I'll call you again in several minutes. Wait."

Depression replaced elation. As he huddled in the darkness, Jake reviewed the flight and catalogued every error. They should not have run that target a second time. He should have pushed the emergency jettison button and hauled ass out to sea. Right now he and

Tiger could be sitting in their rafts waiting for the Angel. Yeah, with sharks circling in the dark water—

"Devil Alpha, this is Nomad. Give me another thirty seconds of beeper."

Jake complied.

"Okay, Devil," the Nomad pilot told him, "we have a couple good cuts on your posit. We'll come to get you at first light. You guys find a hole and crawl in it. Still have your watch?"

Jake looked at his wrist; the luminous hands of the watch glowed in the darkness. "Yes. It's 2057."

"Okay. Somebody will call you at 2200 and every hour on the hour after that. Got it?"

Jake rogered and the conversation ended. He laid the radio beside him and tried to think. The first priority was to find Cole and free him of his chute. Could he be found in this jungle?

They had been heading 250 degrees when they ejected. How much time had there been between ejections? He could recall the exact reading on the airspeed indicator: 245 knots. He had jumped maybe a second or two behind the bombardier. He tried to work the arithmetic of converting their airspeed to feet per second but gave up and decided it couldn't be more than a thousand feet. No more than the length of the *Shiloh*'s flight deck, and probably less. Cole was somewhere in this jungle within a thousand feet of where he sat.

He drew out his compass and unwound the parachute shroud line he had wrapped around it many months ago. He placed the loop around his neck, and the compass dangled.

He checked himself over one more time before setting out. He was bloody both at his knee and on his side, but the blood seemed to have coagulated. His survival vest contained a bandage, which he wrapped around his knee—G-suit, flight suit, and all. There was nothing he could do about the tear in his side, but he wasn't hurting too badly—yet.

He gathered up the penlight and radio and, leaning against a tree trunk, he maneuvered himself upright. He had been wrong; the pain in his side was very bad. He put some weight on the torn leg, and it buckled. He had to repeat the whole effort. The adrenaline was wearing off. His face throbbed, and his side and knee screamed with pain. Every muscle ached from the blows he had received as he fell through the trees. He found, though, that if he kept the injured knee rigid he could limp along. He checked the compass and started out.

After some painful hobbling, Jake paused. What if he passed Cole in the darkness?

"Tiger?" Jake whispered into the radio. It had occurred to him that they were probably not alone in this jungle.

A soft-voiced reply: "Yes?"

"If you hear me thrashing around, you tell me. Okay? I'm going to get you out of this mess."

"Yes." That was all he said. Jake listened, holding the radio against his ear, hoping for more. That one word was the entire message. He left the radio set to receive, stowed it in his pocket, and zipped the pocket shut. A glance at the compass and he began to move again.

The going was slow and hard. He tripped over roots and vines, and limbs and branches stung his face. He fell repeatedly, but each time forced himself to rise. After a while he looked at his watch. Only fifteen minutes had passed. How far had he traveled? Two hundred yards? He knew hunters and hikers tended to overestimate the distance they had traveled. He was in agony from the pain in his side; he must have broken several ribs. He cast around his small beam of light, and a wilderness of dripping vegetation met his eyes.

He estimated another fifteen minutes had passed, and he spoke into the radio: "Tiger?"

No answer. He waited almost a minute, then tried again. He held the small speaker against his ear.

"Yes." A weak whisper.

"Heard anything? I've really been thrashing around."

"No."

Why hadn't Cole answered when he was asked about his injuries? "How badly are you hurt?" Jake waited. Perhaps Tiger had not heard the question. But of course he had. Why didn't he answer?

"I think my back is broken."

Frank Allen pounded his fist on his thigh. A broken back! A badly injured man could not evade the enemy or hook himself to the rescue hoist. The chopper would have to lower a crewman, maybe two, to pack the man in a litter. A lot of lives would be at risk as the chopper hovered.

Allen spoke to the airborne controller about the bombardier's injuries over his primary radio on a discrete tactical frequency. The controller, for his part, gave Allen the names of the downed men. The nickname "Tiger" had sounded familiar, but now Allen remembered who the men were and was able to connect faces with names. How long had it been since he was on the *Shiloh?* Three or four weeks? After several more conversations, the controller directed Allen and his wingman to return to Nakhon Phanom, their base. Allen was scheduled to lead the next search and rescue mission, or SAR. His call sign would be Sandy One.

Frank Allen had much to do before the sun rose. He

jotted down some notes to himself on his kneeboard. At least two Jolly Green helicopters should be on the scene. They would actually lift the men out. But Allen and his flight of Skyraiders would have to locate the downed crewmen and do whatever was necessary to make the area safe for helicopters. If need be, jets could be diverted from all over Southeast Asia to attack enemy positions.

Consulting the chart again, he rechecked the lines he had drawn from the ADF readings, and his TACAN bearing and range plots from Nakhon Phanom. The two ADF cuts intersected at a position only four miles from Devil 500's last known position, as reported by the airborne controller. But given the distances involved and the sensitivity of the equipment, he decided the agreement was merely coincidence. The two crewmen might be anywhere within ten miles of the two locations. He drew a ten-mile circle around both points and studied the chart under his red flashlight. Peaks up to 5800 feet and the villages of Sam Neua and Ban Na Yeung lay within the circle. He hoped the airmen had not gone down near the villages, for if the villagers had heard the crash they would be out in force at daylight, looking for parachutes and beating every bush.

The chart showed a road running west through Sam Neua toward the upper reaches of the Mekong and the Plain of Jars. One of the northern feeders to Ho's Trail, the dirt track wound through a valley that Frank Allen knew would be covered with dense vegetation and flanked with limestone karst ridges. A road meant men. Men and trucks and guns. He wrote the word "napalm" and underlined it.

Jake made the 2300 check-in call, but Tiger did not. Although the airborne controller had tried to encourage Grafton, when they had each signed off, Jake remained alone with his despair. Not only did he feel the danger of his and Cole's position, but he was completely exhausted from the exertions of the last hour.

The desire for water and a cigarette roused him. The water would have to wait, he decided, but he would have a smoke. He wiped his dirty hands on his thighs and felt his pockets for cigarettes. The half-full pack in his sleeve pocket was soggy and crushed. He discarded it, then thought it might dry out later and retrieved the pack. He found a new pack and a lighter in the lower left pocket of his G-suit. With trembling hands, he tore off the cellophane.

The smoke felt good filling his lungs, but when he exhaled, it sent needle-sharp pains through his nose. He blew the smoke out through his mouth, then greedily dragged in another lungful.

The smoke! What if the gooks smelled it? He almost stubbed out the cigarette before he decided his fears were exaggerated. He did, though, take out his revolver and hold it with his finger on the trigger, the muzzle pointing off into the total darkness that surrounded him. The only light came from the glow of his cigarette tip.

The heft and shape of the weapon helped to settle his nerves. The cool steel of the barrel, the gentle curve of the butt, the roughness of the wooden grips, the serrations on the hammer—all spoke of power and security. But against a squad armed with assault rifles, this was merely a popgun. It was nevertheless reassuring to hold.

He remembered the ring he had bought for Callie. He patted his left sleeve pocket and felt it there, thin and hard. He brought it out and fingered it to ensure that the stone was still in its setting. Returning the ring to his pocket, he pulled the zipper completely shut.

He smoked the cigarette and held the revolver and listened to the night sounds of the jungle. He tried to think. He had to hook up with Tiger and make him as comfortable as possible. At dawn when the Sandys came, he could direct them in. After the Sandys had pinpointed their position, they would wait for the Jolly Greens to arrive and pull them up to safety. Tiger would go up first in a litter while he waited on the ground. Then the chopper crew would lower a jungle penetrator for him, a bright-orange, projectile-shaped weight designed to pass through thick foliage. Okay, that is what has to be done. Now to make it happen.

With his penlight, he searched about him for a walking stick. He saw a likely looking sapling and hacked it off near the ground with his knife. Then he cut a length about six feet long. He heaved himself upright, supporting himself with the stick. After checking the compass under the penlight, he tottered off to the east.

He fell often. Lifting his foot for the next step was a labor. He held on to the stick with both hands, bracing the penlight between the stick and his right hand. He pulled himself over uneven ground, picking his way through thick, resistant jungle. He forgot about the compass and concentrated on placing one foot in front of the other. Leaden with fatigue, he took longer and longer to rise after each stumble. The penlight slipped to the jungle floor, but he didn't notice. He had only one thought in a mind encased in fatigue and pain: Find Tiger Cole.

After an eternity of wandering, Jake tripped and fell into a small brook, striking his broken nose on a stone. The pain cut through the fatigue, and the cold rushing water revived him. He drank—short gulps, taking deep breaths in between. When he was satiated, he rolled over on his back, still in the stream.

He had to go on. Find Tiger Cole. That was the only reason for his existence. He groped for the stick but could not put his hand on it. Summoning all his strength, he rolled over onto his stomach and began crawling. His nose seemed to bump up against every low-lying branch, and his knee found every rock.

Finally he could go no further. Exhaustion and pain overtook him, and he fell into a deep sleep.

The rain ceased two hours before dawn as the storm drifted across the mountains and down the valley of the Red River toward the sea. The saturated air continued to give up moisture. Drops of water condensed on leaves and branches and formed rivulets that channeled through the layers of vegetation, eventually descending to the jungle floor where the moisture soaked further into the rotting carpet. Of this Jake Grafton knew nothing. He lay where his body had failed him.

TWENTY-FIVE

At the SAR Command Post at NKP, Frank Allen learned at 0015 that neither A-6 crewman had responded to the airborne controller's midnight call. It didn't look good, and Allen paused in his efforts to organize and brief the rescue mission to weigh the difficulties.

The weather forecasters seemed optimistic about the possibility of the cloud cover breaking up in the SAR area at dawn, but that was the only bright spot in a bad situation. In this area of steep limestone karst ridges and deep valleys, it would be relatively easy to pick up the downed airmen if they were high on a ridge. If they were low in the valley, though, the SAR forces might be exposed to heavy antiaircraft fire from guns sited on the high terrain.

The bombardier was seriously injured and the pilot no longer answered his radio. Allen wondered if he had been captured. He had told him to stay put, but of course the guy was probably wandering all over hell's half acre looking for his buddy. He might have walked into an NVA camp or truck refueling dump near the highway. Maybe he had lost the radio or walked over a cliff.

Allen gave up imagining possible scenarios and dedicated his attention to the details that might help, details of ordnance and call signs and fuel and navigation checkpoints, details that would give him options as events developed. The one certainty in his mind was that he would need options to win the battle that was coming.

By five in the morning Allen was airborne. The ten Skyraiders—piston-engined holdovers in the age of jets—flew north above the clouds; dark rifts had begun to appear in them. Each plane had four twenty-millimeter guns in the wings. In addition, each carried two external fuel tanks, one under each wing, and a variety of ordnance that included 2.75-inch rockets, white phosphorus smoke rockets, and four 250-pound bombs equipped with thirty-six-inch extender-fuses, or daisy-cutters.

When they reached the holding fix, a point Allen had chosen and named "Alpha," eight of the Skyraiders began to orbit at maximum endurance airspeed—the most fuel-efficient airspeed—while Allen and his wingman flew on toward the SAR area. Allen had decided to hold the bulk of his forces in reserve until he knew where the downed crewmen were and the extent of the enemy opposition.

The pink fingers of dawn edged over the eastern horizon. Frank Allen flipped on his master arm switch and checked the sighting dot on his gunsight glass. It was there, just as it should be. The stars retreated as the sky brightened. He checked the authentication questions he would ask the survivors if he could make contact. These personal questions, made up by each man and kept on file at SAR headquarters, helped determine that the respondents were who they said they were. NVA English-speakers had been known to try to lure in rescue aircraft. Or the survivors could be captured and be forced to talk on the radio. Only the correct response, as known by the man who wrote the question, would bring the helicopters in.

"Devil Five Oh Oh, Sandy One on Guard. Are you with us?" The question went out over the emergency frequency four or five times, as it had each hour of the night. There was no answer.

The waiting was harder now. The cloud tops were shot with red fire. Allen glanced down through the gaps in the clouds, wondering what would greet them on their descent.

How had the two airmen on the ground fared during the night? Would there be flak? He drummed his fingers on the canopy rail and whistled a nameless tune.

The thunder of a Skyraider engine just above the trees woke Jake Grafton. He lay awake and listened to the receding throb. The darkness of the night had given way to a gray half-light. He fumbled for his radio and found the on-off switch. His first hasty transmission elicited only silence. After a second try, a voice boomed at him, "Devil Five Oh Oh, this is Sandy One. Give me thirty seconds of beeper if able, over."

"Roger that." Jake manipulated the controls with numb fingers.

"Copy your beeper. Come up on two eight two point oh, over."

"Wilco." Jake switched to the secondary emergency frequency. He heard, ". . . and that parachute is about fifty yards north of the road."

Jake pressed the transmit button, his words tumbling out. "Sandy, this is Devil Five Oh Oh Alpha. A Spad just went over me a moment ago. Right over me. God, I'm sure glad you guys are here."

A cheerful, confident voice answered. "Good morning, Devil Alpha. We're glad to be here. Time for authentication questions. What is the finest automobile ever made?"

"A '57 Chevy."

"And what color is the finest automobile ever made?"

"Blue."

"Wait." Jake was breathing so quickly he had to force himself to slow down. "Devil Alpha, we have a parachute in sight about fifty yards north of a road. Are you near it?"

Jake looked about him. Nothing but jungle. Miserable, he replied, "I don't know."

"Well, give me another fifteen seconds of beeper, then sit tight and tell me when the next plane comes back near you."

"Roger."

Jake listened above the pounding of his heart. The air was filled with the deep rumbles of the big piston engines, throaty and promising of freedom and safety. The sounds seemed to come from all directions.

Mounting excitement made him want to get up and run. He waited, his ears straining to pick out the one engine that was louder than the rest. He grew more tense as the engine sound increased. Jake craned his head, trying to see through the forest, which rose almost two hundred feet above him. Impossible. He would see no blue sky through that leafy canopy.

"You're getting closer," he shouted into the mike.

The machine was almost upon him. The engine noise swelled, crested, and washed over him. "Now," he screamed. "You just went over my head." He had not seen the plane.

The engine noise retreated rapidly. "Okay. You seem to be about forty yards or so west of a parachute. Make that forty yards northwest. The chute is about fifty yards north of a road running east and west and the chute may be visible from the road. Is it your chute?"

Jake's mind leaped. "Christ! It could be my BN's—

Devil Bravo. Maybe." He added the "maybe" as memory of the night's aimless wandering came back. "Have you heard from Devil Bravo?"

"Negative."

Jake was on his feet and checking his compass, which still hung from the cord around his neck.

"Sandy, that may be my bombardier's chute. I'm going over there and check it out. My chute should be west of here someplace."

He started hobbling southeast. Dear God, let Tiger be under that chute.

"Jake? Can you think of the name of our mutual friend from Texas?"

Texas? "Cowboy!" Who the hell is this? Could it be Frank Allen?

"That's the man! Now listen, Jake. You're right beside a road and from the looks of it the gomers have been driving up and down it a good bit. No one's shot at us yet, but they're down there and they're undoubtedly looking for you."

Thoroughly frightened, Jake put the radio in his left hand and turned down the volume. He drew his revolver with his right.

"Watch your ass, Jake."

"Okay," he whispered.

He walked on. Finally he saw it, a sliver of white amid the foliage. Thank God it wasn't in the tops of the trees or the gomers would have homed in on it by now. And Tiger would be hanging a hundred feet in the air. Jake stood motionless and listened. His heart was pounding and he was gasping for breath in the humid air. He heard leaves rustling but, it seemed, in response to a breeze in the treetops. His knee throbbed. He bent and touched it with the back of his hand, and fresh pain shot through him. Damn! He started to take a step, then paused and checked the gun. He had unconsciously thumbed back the hammer. If he tripped, it could go off accidentally. He tucked the radio under his arm and used both thumbs to let the hammer down.

Even with the radio muffled under his arm, Jake could hear the pilots talking to each other. Apparently they had found the other chute. To him, the radio sounded as loud as a brass band. He knew the gomers were somewhere in the jungle around him, stalking him, and before a voice could come over the air like the crashing of cymbals, he turned off the set.

With the radio off and the drone of aircraft engines far away, the forest around Jake seemed ominously still. Spasms of shivering racked his body. He flexed his fingers around the butt of the revolver. As in an animal at bay, every sense was alert. He waited, and then finally took a step forward, toward the slash of white silk clashing against the green of the jungle. Look, listen, step . . . look . . . listen . . . step . . . look . . .

Tiger Cole lay on a boulder, about knee-high, on his back with his arms outstretched downward. His head was bare; his helmet was beside the rock. Tangles of shroud line lay around and over him. He had landed near a stream in an area strewn with boulders and stones.

Cole's eyes were closed and his lips parted. His face was mottled and swollen, apparently from insect bites. Jake touched his cheek. It was warm. The chest was moving.

Dear God! He was alive!

He remembered the planes overhead and turned the radio back on. "I've found him and he's alive but unconscious. We're right here under this chute."

"Roger."

Jake gently moved Cole's head back and forth and massaged the cheeks. "Hey, Tiger! Hey, Tiger! Wake up! It's me, Jake."

The eyelids flickered, then opened. Tiger gazed into

the distance before bringing his eyes to rest on Jake's face. Finally his eyes focused.

"Jake?"

"Yeah. I'm here, shipmate. The good guys have found us and the bad guys haven't. You're going to be okay." Jake unzipped Cole's vest and took out one of his bottles, unscrewed the cap, and elevated the bombardier's head.

The back of Cole's head felt pulpy. Grafton looked. It was covered with blood. He looked again at the helmet at the base of the rock. It was broken almost in two, the helmet that had probably saved Cole's life.

Jake trickled some of the water between the parted lips. Cole's adam's apple bobbed as he swallowed. Jake poured more water into Cole's mouth.

"Enough," Cole spluttered.

"Where're you hurt?"

"Back's broken. Can't move. Can't see too good, either. And I think I pass out once in a while."

"Maybe it isn't broken. Can you feel this?" Jake grasped the near hand.

"Yeah."

Jake grasped Cole's thigh. "This?"

"A little, but I can't move."

He put his hand on the bombardier's forehead, partly to wipe away the perspiration and partly just to touch him. A tear or two dropped down Jake's cheeks. Through his own watery eyes, he saw that one of Cole's pupils was dilated.

"Get me off this fucking rock."

"Moving you might kill you."

"We all have to go sometime. Now get me off this fucking rock and lay me out in the leaves."

Jake unsnapped Cole's parachute-release fittings and pulled away the tangles of shroud line. No, Cole's spinal cord was still intact, and moving him might kill him or paralyze him for life. "You're going to have to stay on that rock until the chopper crewman can help me get you into the litter."

Cole cursed Jake, who ignored him and picked up the shroud lines and tried to pull the chute down. He tugged from several angles, even hanging on the lines with his feet off the ground in spite of the pain in his side. The chute was in the treetops to stay. The sky was visible through several open places in the forest canopy because, in this rocky terrain, the jungle foliage was thinner.

"I got us into a helluva fix this time, Tiger. We're really in deep . . ." but Jake saw that Cole had passed out. Jake unzipped a pocket of his survival vest and found the only bandage he had left. He tore off the wrapper and placed the bandage under Cole's head. At least it was softer and cleaner than the rock. He picked up Cole's radio from the ground—Cole had apparently dropped it during the night—and turned it off to save the batteries. Then Jake checked in again with the Sandys.

That done, he turned his attention to Cole. "Wake up, Tiger, wake up! Come on, Virgil." He sprinkled water on Cole's face. Cole opened his eyes.

"Jake, what the hell? Are you baptizing me or is this the last sacrament?"

"You stay awake. It's gonna take both of us to get our asses out of this one. Stay awake now. You're not gonna die on me, you sonuvabitch."

"No way. Hey, you have something on your neck. Looks like a leech."

Something cold and slimy met his touch. Trying not to tear the creature in half, Jake pulled and felt a stab of pain as a piece of skin came with it He trembled with revulsion. If there was one, there were others. He quickly unzipped his survival vest and torso harness and felt himself frantically. He found another on his back, just above the shoulder blade, and ripped at it, tearing it apart. Two more were on his left arm. Three were attached to his legs just above his boot tops. They were fat, swollen with blood. When he had plucked them all off, he wiped his bloody hand on his thigh.

He inspected Cole and ran his hand down inside Cole's clothing. He could find nothing. He began to unzip Cole's gear.

"Don't. I got enough blood to spare a little. Just let me lie here."

Jake put on his torso harness and survival vest and made certain the pockets were zipped closed. He sat down near Cole's head and put the revolver in his lap.

"I heard voices last night," Cole whispered. "The gomers are around."

Frank Allen had a problem. He had not yet seen any sign of the North Vietnamese, yet they must use this road frequently. If there were guns positioned on the steep karst ridges that ran east and west and towered several thousand feet up to the base of the clouds, nothing that flew would be safe in this valley. No doubt the NVA were waiting for the helicopters to arrive before they showed themselves.

Allen banked the plane and thundered down the road again, hoping to draw fire or to spot a camouflaged flak site. No luck.

In a few minutes the sun would be high enough to shine down this east-west valley and muzzle flashes and tracers would not be so easy to see. Acutely aware of how dangerous this was, he trolled across the rising ground for a mile on either side of the downed crew's position. His wingman flew above and off to one side behind him, in position to attack enemy fire. But there was nothing.

"It's too quiet," he told his wingman, Captain Bobby "Pear" Bartlett, an excellent pilot on his first tour.

"Let's strafe the south side of the road and see what happens."

"Okay."

Frank flew toward the east. The sky was bright there, and the two Skyraiders, framed low against the bright sky, would make a tempting target. Allen repeated to Grafton, who could hear their radio transmissions, their intentions, then lifted a wing and turned to go back down the road.

The red dot in his gunsight walked across the trees. When he reached an altitude of 1000 feet, he squeezed the trigger on the stick. The Skyraider shuddered from the recoil of its twenty-millimeters as tracers floated down toward the jungle. He waggled the rudder as he kept the trigger down. After a one-second burst, he released the trigger and Pear fired a burst. On they went up the valley, firing alternately.

A squirt of tracer reached for them from the north side of the road. Both pilots saw it at the same time and jinked violently.

"Looks like a twenty-three mike-mike under some kind of camouflage netting," Pear Bartlett opined.

They made a turn just under the broken clouds at 4000 feet above the jungle and started back down, Allen in the lead and Bartlett behind him and off to one side. Allen concentrated on the spot where the invisible gunner should be. Again the red dot in his gunsight paced across the jungle.

Now! He squeezed the trigger and his shells ripped into the forest.

From both sides of the road gunfire erupted, reaching for the lead plane. "Pull up, Frank," Bartlett shouted.

The instrument panel in front of Frank Allen exploded and a tremendous force smashed his left leg. But he kept his grip on the stick and tried to lift the nose of the plane. The canopy glass was disintegrating and pieces of the engine cowling were going by the cockpit as the machine shuddered under the impact of heavy shells. Oil poured back onto the windscreen, and he could no longer see forward.

Then he was out of the flak and floating across the top of the forest. Only a few of the eighteen cylinders were still firing. Airspeed was bleeding off rapidly, and he was settling toward the trees. He slapped the emergency jettison button and his ordnance fell away. Automatically he glanced at the airspeed indicator, but where the instrument had been there was now a gaping hole where pieces of naked wire dangled.

He had no feeling at all in his left leg. When he tried to push on the rudder the plane did not respond.

It was time to go. He jerked the handle on the extraction system. Nothing happened.

Sweet Jesus! He was too low to jump. No more than 300 feet over the trees now.

The road! Maybe he could put the old gal down on the road. She seemed to be mushing, running out of airspeed. He scanned the terrain on the left, trying to find the ribbon of bare earth.

There, parallel but too far. Oh, too far, too far.

He slapped the flap handle down and milked every ounce of lift as the flaps came creeping out.

He wasn't going to make it. As the tops of the trees reached for the shattered plane, Frank Allen cut the switch and the engine died completely. The trees caressed the ship; she bounced once, then settled in.

Frank Allen was slammed violently forward in his seat, and his world went black.

When Jake Grafton first heard the word "strafe" over his radio, he lay down beside the bombardier, relying on the boulder and nearby trees for protection. His knee hurt like hell.

Now, in the better light of day, he checked his

revolver to see that it had ball cartridges—not flares—in each of the cylinder chambers. Then he examined Tiger's weapon, a Colt .45 automatic. He jacked the slide back all the way and chambered a round. He left the hammer back and thumbed the safety on.

When the rolling thunder of the Skyraider guns reached him, Jake buried his head in his arms. The big bullets could tear through trees and brush and ricochet off earth and rocks. The thumb-size slugs could split a man in half.

He heard the rippling cracks of the gomer's twenty-three millimeter, and over his radio, the Sandy drivers talking about the gun. He lifted his head and tried to figure out where the gun was located, but the sounds bounced off the walls of the valley. He heard the throb of the piston engines, and a burst of fire that swelled in intensity as more guns joined. Abruptly the fury subsided, and Jake's ears picked up the muffled, irregular beat of a ruined engine.

Jake could feel his heart hammering, feel every throb of blood coursing through his temples and injured nose.

He heard the crash: a sickening smack, then the tortured, drawn-out agony of metal twisting and bending and tearing. The final silence, when it came, was eerie.

The pilot looked around wildly. Where was the crash? Who had it been? Did the pilot get out?

The radio told him it had been Frank Allen, and Frank Allen rode it in. Jake thought he should go and help him. Allen might be alive, trapped in the wreckage. But he was afraid to leave Cole. What if the North Vietnamese came while he was gone?

Goddamnit! He pounded his fists on the ground and swore at his impotence. They were trapped here, the NVA using them as bait for the Sandys and choppers. And it was all his fault. He should never have made that second bombing attempt. He should have run for the sea instead. He cursed himself and damned his own stupidity. He pulled his good leg up and hugged it, moaning softly.

Somewhere in Frank Allen's world there was a light—a bright familiar light. He searched through his memory, but his mind seemed like an empty room. He could hear a sound like a faucet dripping.

Oh, the light must be the sun. Yes, the sun. There must be a break in the clouds and the sun must be up.

With great effort he made his eyes move. He was sitting in the cockpit but the instruments were not in their proper places. The gaping holes in the panel troubled him vaguely and he tried to sort things out. Little by little, he arranged the jumbled images in his mind. His eyes moved again. The plane was sitting in red mud, an ugly slash through the jungle. He tried to move his hands. No good. He could not feel them. He could not feel anything. So he had made it through the trees to the road. Maybe that was why he was still alive.

Why couldn't he move?

He managed to tilt his head forward and look down. The bottom of the instrument panel almost touched the front of the seat. The control stick was jammed against the panel and badly twisted. His legs were trapped under the panel and blood oozed from his flight suit. The panel was where his legs should have been.

His left arm was not in sight. It seemed to come down out of his shoulder all right, but then it made an abrupt turn behind the seat. The seat itself had been torn from its mountings. Well, at least his right hand and arm appeared to be in one piece. That was something.

The effort to move his right arm required more will and energy than he had. His head sank back.

Something was dripping. What was it? Fuel leaking from a torn tank? Then he saw the red smear against the glare shield on the top of the instrument panel. The metal was dented. By his head? His face did feel wet. The dripping continued. Curious, he rocked his head forward again. Now he saw it, a stain of blood on the front of his vest and drops coming from his chin. Oh yes, his helmet visor was gone, shattered probably.

His curiosity satisfied, his head sagged back and his mind wandered, thinking of this and that and nothing in particular. His eyes found the trees along the road and saw the yellow shafts where the sun illuminated the faint mist. The sunlight came across the top of the instrument panel through the hole where the windscreen had been and was warm on his face. Hadn't he been flying with the sun at his back when he was hit? In the violence of the crash the machine must have spun around. He noted the fact and dismissed it, sleep seeming much more important.

No, he could not sleep. The gooks would be along here soon. But what could he do? He couldn't think of any practical course, and his mind strayed off the problem. He watched an insect walk along the top of the instrument panel.

The gooks would be coming along this road. The problem was back and he worked on it. They would never try to get him out of this crumpled wreck, and under no circumstances could he do it himself. Perhaps the helicopter rescue crewmen could cut him out. Even as he contemplated it, he knew such an attempt would be fatal for anyone who tried it.

He made a supreme effort, using all the strength he could muster, and forced his right hand to move from its resting place on his lap down to the holster strapped to his thigh. He felt the butt of the pistol, hard and cold.

The work was very taxing so he rested again, eyes half closed against the glare of the sun. Too bad it had come to this. What would she say when she heard? It had been so good. Why had she left him?

The pain started now. It felt as if he had a knife between his shoulder blades. The pain would probably get worse.

Gritting his teeth, he forced his right hand to pull the pistol from its holster and rest it in his lap. He could do no more. Moving his shoulder increased the agony in his back and left arm. Perspiration trickled into his eyes and mouth. He tasted the salt.

Oh, he could really feel it now—searing jolts of pain knifing their way through his consciousness.

With each passing minute he hurt a little more. He blinked the perspiration from his eyes and tried to call up memories, tried to think of the things that he had loved. But it was difficult to keep the images in view.

Something was moving on the edge of the road, deep in the shadows where the rising sun had not penetrated. His eyes perceived the motion but could not focus on the hidden figure. Slowly and stealthily, a slight figure in dark clothing stepped into the sun. The figure carried a rifle, pointed at Frank Allen.

The pilot followed the man with his eyes. The Oriental seemed tall, far too tall. The perspective was wrong. Oh yes, the aircraft fuselage was lying on the ground instead of sitting on its landing gear.

Engine noise broke the silence. The soldier checked the sky, ready to run, then apparently changed his mind and resumed his slow pace toward the cockpit. Now Frank could see his eyes. Finally he stepped onto the stump of the left wing and gazed through the shattered canopy at the trapped man. A grin exposed yellow, broken teeth.

The pistol in Frank's lap exploded and the man fell backward with a look of wide-eyed astonishment.

The pistol was gone. The weapon's recoil had been

too much for his weak grasp. He waited for the soldier to rise. Every breath hurt now.

Maybe the soldier was dead.

Frank tilted his head forward and looked for the pistol. It must have gone down through the narrow gap between the seat and the right-side panel. There was less than a half-inch clearance between the front of the seat and the forward panel.

You silly shit, Frank. You should have shot yourself!

He heard several Skyraiders sweep over with their engines at full throttle and the distant roar of twenty-three millimeters. In a moment he heard the muffled whoosh of napalm lighting off.

The radio! His emergency radio was in his vest. He got his good hand up to his vest and tugged at the zipper. He was so weak he could not move it. Unable to keep his hand elevated he sat back and listened to the thudding of his heart. Finally he tried again. This time he managed to open the zipper and reach the radio.

Tears were flowing into his eyes from the pain. He ground his teeth together and tried to blink away the tears.

God! It hurt so much!

His breathing was shallow and rapid and every heave of his chest seemed to grind something down inside him.

Unable to lift the radio to his lips, he squeezed the mike and tried to speak. "Sandy One." It came out a hoarse whisper, and the effort sent another flaming spear through him.

"Sandy One, are you okay? Are you out of the cockpit?"

Steeling himself, he squeezed the transmit button and lifted the radio a few inches toward his lips. "No." He breathed again. "I'm trapped, and I'm finished."

"Hang tough, Frank. The Jolly Greens will be here in

about half an hour. We're going to hose the area, then we'll get you out. Keep the faith."

Tears coursed down Frank Allen's cheeks. Bartlett is a terrible liar. He can't call in the Jollys until this valley is worked over good. It could take hours.

"I can't make it, Bob. . . . Help me now."

"You've got to hang in there, Frank. We'll keep them off you until the Jollys arrive."

"I'd do it myself, Bob . . . but I can't. Christ, Bob . . . I'd do the same for you. . . ."

The exertion cost him too much. His hand fell back into his lap. He was biting his lip now and blood from that wound mixed with the blood still trickling down from his forehead.

A low moan tore itself loose from deep inside him and escaped his lips. Oh God! *Jesus I have sinned. Hail Mary Mother of God Oh Jesus I am torn apart and you died for me and I confess my sins and beg your forgiveness and Hail Mary Mother of God stop the pain . . .*

He heard the roar of a big radial engine over his screams, and he saw the Skyraider just above the sun. He saw the sun shimmer on the prop arc, and he saw the twinkles of the muzzle flashes on the front of the wings. Then the darkness came.

about half an hour. We're going to [illegible] then
we'll get you out. Hang on, Leah.
Leah [illegible] down [illegible] Allen's [illegible]
a terrible [illegible] until the [illegible]
is [illegible] it could take hours.
"I can't make it, [illegible]. Help me now."
"You're going to make it, [illegible]. We'll keep [illegible]
[illegible] until the [illegible]."
"[illegible] but I [illegible]
[illegible] I'll do the same for you."
[illegible] too much. His hand fell back
onto his lap. He was taking his [illegible]
[illegible] with the [illegible] down
[illegible] his forehead.
A low moan [illegible] deep inside him
[illegible] Oh God [illegible]
Mary, Mother of God. [illegible]
[illegible]
[illegible] Hail Mary, Mother of God, pray for
us.
He heard the [illegible] of a big [illegible] engine over the
[illegible] and he saw [illegible] about the [illegible]
[illegible] saw the [illegible]
the [illegible] of the [illegible] on the front of the
[illegible]. The [illegible] came.

TWENTY-SIX

Jake Grafton lay on the ground, curled up around the radio. He had heard it all: the pleading and the moaning, the long rolling thunder of the twenties, and the stark, terminal silence. A man had died for him.

The distant whine of jet engines penetrated his consciousness. On they came, louder and louder. The jets flayed the jungle with a steel whip. Cannon shells lashed and tore, and bombs exploded and rockets swooshed, and the crack of twenty-three-millimeter antiaircraft guns pulsated through the trees. Occasionally the crackling of napalm reached him. Jake lost track of time as the concussions pounded around him. In his soul he continued to hear the last words of the Skyraider pilot. The pitiful pleading branded him in a way that nothing else had yet in his life.

He waited there in the dirt with the stench of the jungle humus seeping through his shattered nose. The antiaircraft guns fell silent as, Jake imagined, their crews died under the storm of fire and steel. Eventually even the ripsaw roar of the twenties faded as the airborne marksmen discovered they had run out of targets.

Jake turned his head and looked at Tiger Cole, who lay exactly in the same position in which Jake had found him, but that big chest still rose and fell. There was a fighting heart.

"Jake?" Tiger's voice was a croak. The pilot got up on his good knee so the bombardier could see him. "There was nothing you could have done for that guy, Jake, except what his friend did for him."

"You heard?"

"Yeah."

"I was scared," Jake confessed and buried his face in his hands. He looked at Cole again. "I wish I could've gone. No man should have to die alone." Jake clutched Tiger's arm.

Tiger spoke softly. "I know what scared is." He paused and breathed awhile. "I could never be a pilot because I'm scared of the boat. I wouldn't be able to pull the power back or drop the nose." He blinked rapidly. "I'm scared now."

"We'll get out," Grafton said with no conviction.

"Damn you, Grafton. God damn you! He *died* trying to help us." Exhausted, he closed his eyes. When he opened them he said, "Look at that blue sky up there. You can see little pieces of it through the leaves." Cole's eyes came back to Jake. "You'll get out. I've come far enough. I don't want to live in a wheelchair for forty years. I want to die here. I want you to—"

"Devil," the radio interrupted, "we have three or four bad guys heading your way. They just ran across the road and apparently they've seen the chute. They'll be there before we can make a pass. Better take cover if you can."

"Roger," Jake said softly into the mike. He coiled, dropped the radio, and searched the brush in all directions.

"Get out of here," Tiger Cole insisted. "I'm done for. Go! Get moving!"

The revolver seemed to leap into Jake's hand of its own volition. He scanned the trees in the direction of the road. The bombardier's urgings resounded in his ears. He straightened up and backed away from Cole, then turned and ran. He had not gone very far before he fell.

Facedown in the undergrowth, he was overwhelmed with panic. He scrambled to his feet and lunged forward. Forty yards later he fell again. This time he stayed down.

What are you doing? How will you ever live with this? The Spad driver was finished but Cole isn't. You're all he has to get him onto that chopper and out of here. He wants you to make it, even if it costs him his life. He's kept the faith.

The panic left him and he felt in its place a calmness. He was certain of one thing: he would rather die than leave Tiger Cole.

He got to his feet and took out both weapons. He pulled back the slide on the automatic just enough to see the gleam of brass in the chamber, then he clicked the safety on. He placed it in his right hand with his thumb on the safety lever. He reviewed the times he had fired an automatic, remembering how quickly it could be brought into action if you slipped the safety off with your thumb as you squeezed the trigger. He held the .357 Magnum revolver in his left hand with the hammer down. Not yet.

He crept back the way he had come. When he glimpsed Tiger lying there, he moved behind a broad tree trunk and listened. He heard the wind rustling through the foliage overhead and, in the distance, the sounds of piston and jet engines.

Once more he was waiting for a deer in the Appalachian mountains, expectant, without fear.

If he died here, he would lie near Frank Allen and Tiger Cole. If he survived, there would be Callie. He moved his right hand to the sleeve pocket and felt the hardness and promise of the ring.

You'll have to get closer if you're going to have a chance. You'll have to be close enough to kill them before they get their assault rifles into action. He waited with a calm fatalism, but his breathing was shallow. He held the automatic in his right hand and the magnum in his left. It would be very chancy. They were seasoned jungle fighters who would be alert for the unexpected; he was a warrior from the sky.

He was distracted by the deep thunder of a Skyraider approaching low over the treetops. He glanced up and when he looked at Cole again, a man stood near him. Jake moved forward as the engine noise increased. The standing man, clad in black, his back toward Grafton, tilted his head toward the sky. Jake made out another figure, bending over Tiger. As the sound intensified, an assault rifle ripped a burst. The pilot flinched, then slowly relaxed. There was much to do before a bullet found him.

With infinite patience he took another step.

Through the foliage he discerned a third man lowering an AK-47 from his shoulder as the noise of the Skyraider faded. Then he scanned the jungle. None of the soldiers detected the pilot in a green flight suit in a world of green.

All three of the soldiers crowded around the supine figure and talked excitedly in low tones. One of them leaned over and slapped Cole's face, and the others laughed, sure of sanctuary now from the steel wrath of the warplanes.

Three soldiers with automatic rifles. Are there any more? Careful, Grafton. If there's a man you don't see, you won't get off a shot.

He waited. He was still more than fifty feet away, too far to be sure of getting them all. One or two would not be enough. He would have to shoot if they tried to kill

Tiger, but for now he waited. He examined their black cotton clothes and the dark bush hats they wore. Their only provisions were carried in belts around their waists.

Very faintly he heard the radio. The three men scrambled around in the ankle-high detritus of the jungle floor. One of them picked up the radio triumphantly and held it out for the others to see.

Jake moved forward one step, then another. The men were clustered around the box and were still partially obscured by the jungle. Grafton advanced two more steps.

If they would only keep looking at the radio!

He took another step. They were just forty feet away.

He extended the automatic to arm's length as he shifted his weight for another step. The man in the middle, facing him, saw him at that instant. A look of surprise registered on the brown face as a slug from the .45 hit him square in the chest. His head snapped forward and the rimmed hat came off as he fell.

The man on the right twisted and turned while trying to position his weapon. The pilot fired. Thinking he had scored a hit, he swung the .45 toward the falling figure on his left and jerked off three fast shots as the man hit the ground and rolled away amid flying debris kicked up by the bullets. Wait! Aim!

The man kept rolling in the brush as Jake took careful aim with the pistol and fired again. The body jerked under the impact of the bullet and came to a stop, quivering.

Jake swung back toward the man on his right, who was rising from the ground and struggling with his rifle. Jake fired quickly and missed. The rifle barrel was coming level. He fired again and the rifle fell as the soldier collapsed.

The man on the left, partly hidden by brush, was still

moving, so Jake took several steps toward him, forcing himself to concentrate on the front sight as he steadied the automatic. He squeezed the trigger. Nothing happened. It was empty. He dropped the automatic, grasped the .357 with both hands, and eared back the hammer.

The man was on his back now, in the leaves. He was screaming. Jake moved sideways to get a better shot. The man's rifle flashed repeatedly as Jake tried to aim at the squirming figure. He squeezed the trigger just as something hammered into his head.

His head was splitting with pain. His vision was blurred. He tried to move but the effort made the pain in his head unbearable.

"Jake?"

The sound was distorted and far away.

"Jake?"

The voice seemed closer. He reached out with his arm.

"I'm behind you, Jake."

With great care, Jake turned over until he was looking up. The world was spinning and he felt as if he were falling, but gradually the spinning slowed. After a rest he tried to sit up. He fell back moaning.

"Looks like a bullet clipped you on the temple, Jake. But you got the bastard."

The pilot rolled onto his left side. He gazed at the bombardier, eight feet or so away, his head turned toward Jake. Jake's vision slowly came into focus, although Cole shimmered with every heartbeat.

"I knew you'd be back, Grafton."

Slowly, slowly, Jake curled up and eased into a sitting position. He put both hands like a vise on the sides of his head.

"You probably have a concussion from that bullet."

He let his gaze wander. The North Vietnamese

sprawled around him, their bodies slack, the life smashed out.

So this is what it looks like.

He crawled with glacial slowness toward the nearest body. The dead eyes were focused on a point far, far away, beyond the ken of living men. This was the first man he had shot. He moved closer. The soldier had traveled many roads, come many miles, seen many things, probably killed many people, and died here in the jungle with his friends. The smell of feces registered in spite of his clogged nostrils. The dead man's sphincter had relaxed. So, the smell of death is the smell of shit. Appropriate.

He sat up straighter and waited for the spinning sensation to pass. The throbbing in his head and the whirling nauseated him and he retched. The world settled down. He looked again at the dead men. Already the bodies seemed to be returning to the earth; they were partly covered by leaves from the forest floor.

Near him lay a rifle. They would need it if more North Vietnamese came. He picked up the weapon and saw that it was on full automatic. Inside the action he could see cartridges waiting to be stripped into the barrel by the closing bolt. He turned the weapon upside down and leaves and dirt fell out of the open action. The pain in his head was subsiding to one hell of a headache. He braced the butt of the rifle on the ground and slowly climbed erect.

"I thought you were dead. You going to make it?" Tiger asked.

"Yeah."

"Then why don't you find that damn radio and ask those flyboys when they're going to get us the fuck outta here. If they dick around much longer, you're going to have to kill a whole regiment."

Jake found the radio. Bending over very carefully, he

retrieved it. He picked up the .357 with the same care and scanned the leaves for the Colt .45.

"If you're looking for the automatic, I think maybe you dropped it over there. Jesus, Jake, you looked like Wyatt Earp when you gunned those guys. Remind me to always call you 'Sir.' "

Jake picked up the .45 and keyed the mike. "I got the gomers. They're dead. When does the chopper get here?"

"What's your service number?"

He stared at the radio, trying to think. "I can't fucking remember. Oh, Jesus! Come get us, you fucking bastards!"

"What's the finest automobile in the world?"

"A '57 Chevy."

"So you got those guys, huh? Way to go! The chopper'll be here in five minutes. Now listen up. They're going to lower a litter with a crewman and take your bombardier up first. You stay on the ground. Keep your head down until the jungle penetrator comes down, then hook on and we'll jerk you and the crewman out, over."

"Okay. But no screwing around."

"There's going to be a lot of fire and smoke, Devil Alpha. We think we got the big guns but there're lots of folks down there with small arms. If there's too much lead flying, the chopper might have to pull off for a while and leave you and the crewman on the ground. Don't panic."

"Got it." He lowered the radio and wiped blood from his left eye.

"Now just sit tight and let me know when the chopper's right over you."

"Yeah."

He sat beside the bombardier and replaced the spent cartridge in the revolver with one from his survival vest, then put the gun in its holster. He got a full clip for the .45 from Cole's vest and tossed the empty one away. Then he tucked the automatic into the top of his survival vest.

With the rifle across his lap, he sat with his back against the rock Cole lay on and scanned the jungle around them and the canopy above. The pain in his head localized in his left temple, and it throbbed with every pulse beat.

"Maybe you oughta search the bodies. Maybe they got documents."

"Fuck it."

"If we don't get picked up soon, there'll be more of 'em along. This place must be crawling with 'em. If the gomers catch us near these bodies, we'll be a long time dying."

"They ain't gonna get us." The rifle felt heavy on his thighs. "We'll get out of here—Frank Allen died to get us out."

"Is that why you came back?"

Jake remembered what Callie had said after he told her about Morgan—it seemed so long ago—*you did what you could do, you can't do more than that. You kept the faith.* He tried to find the words to answer Cole. "I had to. Frank Allen didn't run out on us. Morgan didn't. You and I did a lousy job of trying to win the war by ourselves. But you stood by me."

"I'm glad we flew together," Cole said. "Listen!" The background buzz of piston engines was swelling in volume. Jake lay flat.

The fires of hell erupted along the road. Napalm lit with a roar as the air rushed in to feed the jellied gasoline. Black, noxious smoke drifted through the trees.

After several minutes the Skyraiders made another run. The pale gray smoke of white phosphorus—Willy Pete—wafted between the tall tree trunks, dark columns forever hidden from the light.

Then Jake heard the sound he had been waiting for. Above the throb of piston engines at full throttle came the wail of jet engines pulsated by beating rotors. He searched the foliage above for signs of rotor wash. A calm voice said over the radio, "Okay, I have the parachute in sight."

"They're right under that chute."

The beat of the rotors and the scream of the engines intensified. Salvation was arriving with a roar.

Jake glimpsed the swaying mass of green metal floating above wildly agitated foliage. A hurricane of wind engulfed him, and leaves and twigs flew through the air. He shouted into the radio, "We're here! We're here! You're right overhead. Stop!"

The helicopter hung suspended above him. Jake was on his feet, moving excitedly, unable to contain his elation.

A helmeted man, part of his face obscured by his visor, rode the litter down. The air was thick with leaves and dirt, and it was hard to see. In the charged air, Jake had to push to breathe. He kept his eyes half shut, looking out through his lashes, screening the grit in the air. When the litter touched the ground, Grafton, who had crouched down against the wind storm, moved forward and helped the crewman unhook it and carry it across to Cole. Jake screamed into his ear, "His back is broken."

"I know." The crewman's head swiveled left and right, taking in the three bodies. "What the hell? . . ."

They reached Cole and the crewman bent over him and checked his eyes. He motioned for Jake to take Cole's legs. Together the two lifted the helpless man just enough to swing him into the litter. Jake was still trying to fasten the lower restraint straps when the crewman finished his and came to help.

The crewman pointed at the hook on the end of the cable. Jake brought it over and they snapped all four of the suspension eyes to it. They moved away and the crewman spoke into his hand-held radio.

Jake saw Tiger Cole looking at him. Tears ran down the man's cheeks. Jake squeezed his hand fleetingly as the slack went out of the cable. The litter came off the ground, swung slightly, then moved upward and disappeared into the churning foliage above.

Unable to contain his euphoria any longer, Jake threw his arms around the crewman and hugged him with all his strength. The crewman hugged back vigorously. "We're gonna make it," he yelled into Jake's ear.

Jake Grafton nodded joyfully and squeezed the man again. Now the crewman led him to the jungle penetrator and clipped the snap-link on Jake's torso harness to the cable at the top of the device and then hooked himself on. He spoke into his radio, and both men were swept off the ground.

As they went upward through the branches, the noise and fury increased. Then, incredibly, all sound seemed to soften, leaving a dull ache and a distant roaring in Jake's ears. Without his helmet to protect his ears, he was going deaf.

As they cleared the treetops, the helicopter began to move forward, dragging Jake and the crewman with it. He could glimpse heavy black smoke and fire in the slashes where the napalm had struck. As the smoke thinned Jake saw the jungle stretching up the hillsides, giving up its moisture in wisps of rising mist that looked ethereal in the horizontal rays of the morning sun. Souls wending their way to heaven, Jake thought.

The moving air fanned and cooled his face.

Jake saw that the crewman was watching him and laughing. When the hoist operator pulled them into the helicopter, their hands were locked together.